ALSO BY E.E. HOLMES

THE WORLD OF THE GATEWAY

The Gateway Trilogy (Series 1)
Spirit Legacy
Spirit Prophecy
Spirit Ascendancy
The Gateway Trackers (Series 2)
Whispers of the Walker
Plague of the Shattered
Awakening of the Seer
Portraits of the Forsaken
Heart of the Rebellion
Soul of the Sentinel
Gift of the Darkness
Rise of the Coven
Tales from the Gateway

THE RIFTMAGIC SAGA
What the Lady's Maid Knew
The Rebel Beneath the Stairs
The Girl at the Heart of the Storm

GIFT OF THE DARKNESS

GIFT OF THE DARKNESS

The Gateway Trackers Book 7

E.E. HOLMES

Lily Faire Publishing

Lily Faire Publishing
Townsend, MA

www.lilyfairepublishing.com
www.eeholmes.com

ISBN 978-1-7339352-3-4 (Print edition)
ISBN 978-1-7339352-2-7 (Digital edition)

Publisher's note: This is a work of fiction. Names, characters, places and incidents are either the product of the author's imagination or are used fictitiously.

Cover design by James T. Egan of Bookfly Design LLC
Author photography by Cydney Scott Photography

*To you, Reader, who has traversed every page of this journey
with me, thank you for the adventure.*

To die, to sleep;

To sleep: perchance to dream: ay, there's the rub;

For in that sleep of death what dreams may come

When we have shuffled off this mortal coil,

Must give us pause: there's the respect

That makes calamity of so long life;

For who would bear the whips and scorns of time,

The oppressor's wrong, the proud man's contumely,

The pangs of despised love, the law's delay,

The insolence of office and the spurns

That patient merit of the unworthy takes,

When he himself might his quietus make

With a bare bodkin? who would fardels bear,

To grunt and sweat under a weary life,

But that the dread of something after death,

The undiscover'd country from whose bourn

No traveller returns, puzzles the will

And makes us rather bear those ills we have

Than fly to others that we know not of?

-Hamlet, Act III scene i

PROLOGUE

———

"WHY DID NO ONE come to fetch me?" Finn's voice was sharp with fear.

"I didn't want to leave her," Flavia replied, tearful.

Finn turned on Kiernan with an accusatory stare. "And you?"

"Don't blame him, Finn, you're the one who told him to keep watch over them and make sure they weren't discovered," Hannah cut in, taking a step closer to Kiernan.

"We all agreed not to draw attention to what Jess was doing," Milo said. "We could hardly have come bursting into a Caomhnóir meeting without setting off all kinds of alarm bells. Everyone is freaking out as it is."

Finn began pacing, running a frantic hand through his hair. "How long has it been?"

"Seven hours and thirty-two minutes," Flavia said at once.

"Have you ever known a Traveler to Rift that long?" Finn asked.

Flavia shook her head. "The Casting is temporary. The effects of the herbs wear off naturally, and once they do, the Rifter should awaken involuntarily if they haven't already chosen to do so."

"What do you mean, chosen to do so? How do you choose to wake up?" Milo asked.

"While you are Rifting, in the vision, there is always a door you can choose to walk through. The decision to walk through that door will end the Rifting no matter how quickly you choose to take it," Flavia explained.

"So, then, what if Jess couldn't find the door?" Hannah asked. "What if there just wasn't one?"

Flavia shook her head. "That's not how it works. There's always a door."

"This isn't how it works either!" Finn cried. "You said that she should be awake by now."

Flavia blinked tears out of her eyes and swiped them furiously off her flushed cheeks. "I know. I'm sorry, Finn, I wish I had the answer."

Everyone in the room stared down at Jess. She lay precisely where she had settled herself, one hand resting peacefully on her stomach, the other wrapped around the teacup full of herbs, from which the last of the smoke had long since risen, leaving nothing but a heap of cold fragrant ashes. Her face was utterly impassive, betraying not a twitch of an eyelid nor a murmured word. If it weren't for the steady rising and falling of her chest, there would be not a single indication that she was even present inside her body.

Finn knelt beside her and tenderly brushed a stray hair from her cheek with his finger. "Last time, when she had trouble coming out of it, she was thrashing about, clearly agitated."

"Yes, I remember," Flavia said.

"This is altogether different," Finn said, continuing to stroke Jess' forehead. "She's so calm, so peaceful."

"I know that ought to make me feel better somehow, but it doesn't," Flavia said. "Not at all."

Hannah gave a dry sob. Kiernan hesitated a moment, and then put his arm around her shoulder. Hannah leaned into him gratefully, clutching at his shirt.

"So, what do we do?" Milo asked, trying to sound robustly logical, but failing as his voice cracked with fear. "What is Rifting protocol here? What does the 'Pocket Handbook for Rifting with Friends' have to say about this?"

Flavia gave him a sad smile. "Traveler traditions are largely oral—even our language. It has been one of the most challenging aspects of being a Traveler Scribe—the lack of comprehensive written documents. There is no handbook for this. But my experiences with Rifting have been extensive. I have studied it and I have participated in it. I have experimented with it, and observed others experiment. I do not have a precedent for this."

"It's as though she's reached a deeper level of sleep—a deeper trance. Is that possible?" Finn asked.

"Anything is possible, I suppose," Flavia replied. "The artwork provided by Agnes Isherwood was unique. It may have allowed for Jess to have a unique Rifting experience. We won't know until she comes out of it and is able to express to us what happened to her."

"But what if she doesn't wake up?" Hannah cried.

"Hannah, don't—" Milo began, but Hannah silenced him with a hand.

"Don't what? Don't say out loud what everyone in this room is thinking? Don't look a very real possibility in the face? I'm scared, Milo. We never should have let her do this. We don't know anything about that Tansy Hag thing, and we just did exactly what she said, even though she's been locked up for centuries in a place reserved for the most dangerous spirits in the world! What the hell were we all thinking, taking the word of that... that *thing* and letting Jess stake her life on it?!"

"That *thing* is just a Traveler woman's spirit, and nothing more," Flavia said, and her voice, though quiet, had an edge to it that cut through the room. "Do not let your fear cloud your knowledge. You know that every spirit is just a human being."

"Human beings can be evil," Hannah countered.

"I don't deny it," Flavia said. "We both know that, firsthand. But Jess had faith that this was what she was meant to do. She believed that the path of clues had been laid out for her, and for her alone. To have ignored them, after finding this, would have been madness," Flavia said, holding up Agnes Isherwood's portrait of Jess.

"Flavia is right," Finn said, and Hannah looked at him as though his words were a betrayal. "I'm scared, too, Hannah, but we are letting our fear control us. We didn't know what would happen before Jess Rifted, and we don't understand it now, but Jess was unflinching in her belief that this was the right thing to do. We have to cling to that belief for her until she comes back to us, however long that takes."

Hannah sobbed again, unable to reply.

"We must keep her safe from discovery until she returns," Finn continued, addressing everyone now. "The events in the courtyard have the entire castle on edge. I shudder to think what might happen if we add another log to this inferno. No one must know, do you hear me? We watch over her until the Rifting is done."

Milo nodded once, his expression fierce. Kiernan too, inclined his head. Flavia gave Finn an encouraging smile. Hannah alone could find no strength to reply, instead burying her face in Kiernan's shoulder and succumbing to a storm of tears.

Finn bent down and kissed Jess lightly on the forehead. "Come back to me, love," he whispered to her, so quietly that none of the others could hear. "Find what you were meant to find and come back to me."

THE PLACE BEYOND THE DOOR

"Y OU'RE... YOU'RE AGNES Isherwood, aren't you?" I asked, although the answer was already ringing in my bones. That feeling I'd had before, when I'd first seen the rolling hills of the English countryside, or the first time that Hannah and I had grasped our hands together, ran through my body once again, singing in my veins—that sense of belonging and connection, that sense that I was coming home to something.

"Yes," Agnes replied, taking a step closer. "And you're Jessica. I recognize your face. I have seen it in my dreams. I was afraid you may never come."

Agnes turned and started walking away from me, her candle illuminating a narrow slice of the darkness, but revealing nothing. I took a step to follow her, across a floor that seemed to have no substance, through a place that had no defining features.

"Come along," she said over her shoulder, smiling encouragingly at me.

"Where are we going?" I asked.

"That's not exactly the right question," Agnes replied.

I rolled this cryptic answer around in my head for a moment as the darkness around me began to resolve itself. The blackness gathered into some places and receded from others, creating shadows and shapes that grew more and more distinctive. A stone floor gradually appeared beneath my feet, and a stone ceiling above my head. My legs began to strain as the floor beneath me rose in a steady incline and formed into stairs.

"So... what is the right question?" I asked.

"There isn't really a 'where,' here," Agnes said, rising up the endless stairs as though floating. "Nor is there a 'when.'"

"I'm... I'm afraid I don't understand."

"I don't expect you to. Not yet. Perhaps not ever. Do not let it trouble you."

"Easy for you to say," I muttered under my breath.

Agnes pushed through a door that materialized from nothing the moment she placed her hand upon it. I gasped. We stood inside a round castle tower that I knew very well.

"We're at Fairhaven," I said wonderingly to myself. "This is Fiona's tower."

Agnes set her candle down upon a desk under the window. Outside the tower, I could see neither sun, nor cloud, nor stars—only a strange and empty blackness. "This is Fairhaven, yes, but it is not Fiona's tower. It is mine."

"Yours?" I whispered.

"Yes, indeed," Agnes said, and turned to gaze at me again.

It was remarkable how strong the resemblance was—I could see Karen and my mother and Hannah, all staring back out at me as one from that singular, lovely face. And a remarkable face it was—wide, shining eyes, ivory complexion, rose-tinted mouth. I wondered if her flawless skin and lustrous hair were a result of Leeching, like so many Durupinen, or simply a manifestation of the Rift. I decided I didn't have the courage to ask her.

"You said that you've been waiting for me," I prompted.

"Oh, yes."

"For... for how long?"

"As I told you before, there is no 'when' here."

"Okay," I said slowly, trying to wrap my brain around what she meant but failing miserably. "I know you said there's no 'where' here, but... this *is* the Rift, right? It's different than when I've been here before. It feels so... *real*."

It was true. It had only just occurred to me, but the dreamlike quality of the Rift had seeped away, revealing something altogether more... solid. The wonderland surreality of it all had faded. Now the stone beneath my feet felt hard and rough. The night air raised goosebumps on the skin of my forearms, and the room in which we stood had none of the strange, nonsensical elements I'd come to expect in the Rift. The details had resolved now—a fur rug on the floor before the fireplace; herbs hanging in bunches, drying from the rafters; piles of scrolls and books upon shelves; a desk scattered over with parchment and quills. It looked and felt, in every respect, like a perfectly ordinary room.

"Let me see your arms," Agnes said, holding her hands out to me.

"Huh...?" But she had already grasped my hands in hers. They were warm and familiar, and I felt, not for the first time, a rush of energy, the electricity of blood that recognized itself coursing through another person's veins. But if Agnes felt the same thing, she did not remark upon it. Instead, she turned my hands over in hers, revealing the intricate artwork I had copied from her sketch.

"You've done well," she said with an approving nod, pushing up the sleeves of her dress to reveal the very same artwork, slightly faded, upon her own forearms. "I must say, I was worried it may not work. I had the Traveler Scribe to help me, but I feared you may not put all the pieces together without help, too."

"I... I *did* have help," I muttered. "Sorry, but... when you say a Traveler helped you... did you mean the Tansy Hag?"

Agnes' face scrunched into a frown. "The who?"

"I... nevermind." My head swam as Agnes' touch continued to make my blood race.

"We mustn't waste time," Agnes said, her hands slipping from mine. Her face was creased with concentration as she took up her candle again and used it to light the other candles that had been placed around the room. "I do not know how long the door will last."

My heart sped up. "You don't know—what?"

"The door, the door," Agnes said. "The door I created so that I could find you. The second door. I do not know how long we have. We are stretching the boundaries of known magic."

My head was beginning to spin. I felt sick. "Please explain. Now."

Agnes clearly read something alarming in my face, because she composed herself at once. She put her candle down in a carved wooden bracket upon the wall and turned back to me. "Allow me to explain as best I can, although, I must warn you that even I do not fully understand it." She took a deep breath and when she spoke again, seemed to be choosing her words very deliberately. "Time is not the straight and narrow road that so many of us believe it to be. Our lives are not destined to march along its strict path, never wavering, never veering. The threads of our lives are intertwined. They are woven in and out of each other, twisted and tangled and knotted together, broken and snipped and retied again, resolving at last into the tapestries that we recognize as ourselves. The feelings and memories and connections that intrude upon us at unlikely moments are simply those threads, looping back upon themselves, connecting our past, our present, and our future into a single, living, pulsing thing. Do you understand?"

"I... I'm not sure," I admitted. "I guess so. So what you're saying is that I... I haven't gone back in time, but time sort of... overlaps with itself here?"

Agnes nodded her head encouragingly. "More or less," she said. "And as I don't know how long we have until our threads part ways again, I will be brief. First, I need for you to answer a question for me. When you awaken, in the time and place you inhabit, is there something unusual happening there? Something to do with the Geatgrimas?"

My breath caught in my throat. "Yes. Yes, that's why I'm here. That's why I went Rifting. I've been trying to understand what's going on, and I thought I might get some clarity here. Do... do you know what's happening with the Geatgrima?"

Agnes' eyes were closed, a pained expression on her face. "I knew it. I knew the time would come when we would pay for what we've done."

"What are you talking about?" I asked, a shred of desperation in my voice now. "What have we done?"

Agnes sank down onto the fur rug before the fire, and I lowered myself beside her. When she opened her eyes again, her expression was almost unfathomably sad. "Before I tell you, you must understand that we had little choice. The Necromancers had stormed every stronghold. We were outnumbered and desperate. The spirit world was in danger of falling into their hands, of being exploited and torn apart in the Necromancer quest for immortality."

"I understand," I said, hoping the lie would wipe just a tiny portion of the guilt and horror from her face.

"We had to find a way to preserve the Gateways. We could not let them fall, could not risk that they might close or be reversed. The results would have been devastating. Spirits, trapped forever upon the earth, unable ever to answer the call of the Aether. Spirits from the Aether, dragged back and tortured into revealing the world beyond. We could not let it happen. We could not betray the spirits we had sworn to protect."

"Of course you couldn't," I said softly, reaching out a tentative hand to brush away the tears that were now spilling down her face.

Agnes looked up at me, solemn now. "I advised against it. I pled before the Council, but I was only a Scribe at the time, and they were all too scared, too panicked to listen to me. I cannot say that I blame them. Who can worry about the shadowy possibility of a repercussion hundreds of years in the future in the face of imminent danger?"

I did not answer. I did not want to interrupt her. We were getting to it now, the secret at the heart of everything.

"You only know the Geatgrimas as symbolic representations of the Gateways—constructed at our seats of power as monuments to our gifts as the vessels of the Gateways themselves. Is that what you have been taught?"

"Yes," I said, feeling my heart begin to race. "Our teachers told us that the Durupinen have opened the Gateways so frequently at Fairhaven that the fabric between the living world and the Aether is very thin there, and the Geatgrima marks the place."

Agnes gave a bitter laugh. "The tale has been well-told, it seems. And no one doubts that the Geatgrima's purpose is simply symbolic. Have you never wondered why its pull is so strong? Why its lure is so powerful?"

"I... I've noticed it," I said. "But what reason would I have to doubt what the Durupinen at Fairhaven have told me?"

"Why, indeed," Agnes said softly. "Follow me."

Agnes stood up and walked over to her window. I followed her, and the two of us gazed down into the moon-bathed courtyard below. The familiar shape of the courtyard was marred by differences that jarred my senses. There were no flagstones, no benches, no flower beds around the outer edges, none of the details to which I had grown accustomed. There was only the Geatgrima, standing alone within a circle of grass, the castle walls around it charred and battered, as though Fairhaven had recently withstood a fierce battle.

"You see it there? If it looks like nothing more than an empty stone archway, that's because it is one. But that was not true just a few years ago. The Geatgrimas are not monuments to our power. They are not symbolic markers of our strongholds. They are the Gateways themselves, stripped of their power and forced shut, in a desperate bid to protect the spirit world."

I tore my eyes from the Geatgrima to stare at Agnes. "Stripped?

By whom?" But I already knew the answer. It was filling my lungs, sour and choking and horrid.

"By the Durupinen," Agnes said. "We have always been as one with the spirit world. We have always been able to connect with spirits, to see and to hear them. We have been Guardians of the Geatgrimas, protecting their locations, and guiding spirits to them, so that they might Cross of their own free will. But we were not meant to be the vessels of the Gateways. That was never our true purpose."

"But… but our gift… the Gateway is in our blood," I whispered.

"It is now," Agnes murmured. "Because we put it there."

My legs turned to water beneath me. Agnes caught me before I hit the floor, and we sank to the stones together. "I… I still don't…"

"There are Geatgrimas all over the world. The Durupinen sisterhood has acted as protectors of each of those sites since the dawn of time. We kept them secret and guarded them with our very lives. But there came a time when the Necromancers rose to power. They were not content to allow the Gateways to remain under our protection. They sought to oust us, and to use the Gateways to unlock the secrets of life after death, and by so doing, achieve immortality for themselves. Their armies were powerful. They planned their siege for decades. When they finally carried it out, it became clear that our forces could not contend. They were poised to destroy the Gateways, unless we did something drastic to protect them. And so we did."

"How?" I asked in a strangled whisper.

"We brought together the greatest minds of the Durupinen world and devised a Casting that would lock the Gateways and hide the means to open them with the Durupinen themselves. As long as the access to the Gateways remained hidden in our bloodlines, the Geatgrimas could no longer be targets. The spirit world would be safe."

"But then… wouldn't the Durupinen become the targets instead?" I asked. "How is that any safer?"

"Ah, but people can be hidden. They can be disguised. We formed the Caomhnóir Brotherhood to protect them. But the locations of the Geatgrimas were finite. They were fixed. Once they were known, there was no more protecting them," Agnes said.

"Okay, that makes sense," I said slowly. "It sounds like the Durupinen did the right thing, then. Right?"

Agnes shook her head. "The immediacy of a solution can sometimes blind us to the longevity of a solution. I was one of the Scribes tasked with helping us to understand how we might succeed in internalizing the Gateways. I am sorry to say that I succeeded."

"Sorry? Why are you sorry?"

"I went to the International High Council with my findings. I told them that, while I thought it was possible to do as they wished, I had serious misgivings about going through with it. To remove power from its source was dangerous, I argued. It would make the Geatgrimas unstable. I could not predict how long they would hold up, but I was sure that, one day, they would collapse. My warnings were not heeded. The Council dismissed me, took what they needed from my findings, and created the Casting that would make us all the keepers of the Gateways."

My mouth opened and closed uselessly; all ability to form coherent sentences had slipped away from me on the tide of this news. For the second time in my life, I was trying desperately not to drown in the thought that my entire life—everything I'd believed to be true about myself—was a lie.

"Jessica?"

"Huh?"

"Do you understand what I've just told you?"

"I... uh... yeah," I stammered.

"Do you understand why I've brought you here?"

"I..."

"That moment I feared, when the Geatgrimas would fail at last—it has come, hasn't it? In your time?"

"I don't know," I said, shaking my head and hoping that the whirring thoughts would settle. "I... my friend... she's a Durupinen, but something's happened to her. She was visiting the Geatgrima every night, like she was drawn to it, and now the Geatgrima seems to have her in some kind of trance. They're... connected."

Agnes nodded her head, her lips trembling. "Yes. It has begun."

A strange feeling struck me, like the whole room in which we sat had suddenly tilted at an odd angle. Agnes felt it too. Her eyes grew wide.

"I fear our time is running short," she said, speaking quickly now. "Listen carefully. There are only three who know the truth, and you must bring them together to reverse this madness, or it will be too late, for your friend and for all of us. They are the three keys."

"Who are they?" I asked.

"The High Priestess of the Traveler Clans. The Keeper of the Elementals. The High Priestess of the International High Council."

My brain whirled as I committed this to memory. "But what do I tell them?"

"Tell them the Sentinels have begun their watch. They will understand," Agnes said.

"The Sentinels have begun their watch," I repeated. "But what does that mean?"

"They will know what it means."

"But how do I explain to them that I know this? How am I supposed to convince them to listen to me?" I asked.

"That will be up to you, Jessica. The words will come to you. Have faith."

"Faith?!" I half-laughed. "What have I got left to have faith in?"

"Yourself," Agnes said, placing a hand upon my cheek. "It's all we ever have, in the end."

The room lurched again. The door through which we had entered swung open. Agnes and I both stared at it. She turned back to me.

"One last question, Jessica," she said, her voice urgent. "This is very important. How did you find the drawings?"

"What?"

"My sketches. The one of you and the artwork for your Rifting Casting?"

I frowned. "The call number that you left for me."

"Call number?"

"Yeah, you know. The call number that led me to the..." My voice trailed away as I registered the blank look on her face. "You don't know what I'm talking about, do you?"

Agnes shook her head.

I stood up and staggered over to Agnes' desk as the room gave another lurch. I plucked the quill from its inkwell and scrawled the call number on one of the scraps of parchment that littered the desk. "This number. You left it for me in your tapestry. That's how I knew to look for the drawing in the catacomb archives at Skye."

Agnes took the number from my hand, staring at it with wonder. "In a tapestry, you say?"

"Yes, in the tapestry they made of you when you became High Priestess," I replied. "How can you not know what I'm... oh my God." All the air went out of my lungs, and the next words came out in a gasp. "It hasn't happened yet. You aren't even High Priestess yet, are you? You... there is no tapestry."

Agnes let loose a half-frightened, half-awed burst of laughter. "It is as I said. Our threads are woven in incomprehensible ways."

The room pitched and lurched again, and this time I slid across the floor back toward the desk, which I had to cling to in order to keep myself upright. "What's happening?"

"The door is closing," Agnes said, and she staggered across the room to me. "We are out of time, my dear. You must go."

Our eyes met, and I felt a strange sense of loss at the thought of leaving this woman who was both a part of me and yet distant enough to be little more than a dream. Even as I looked at her, she seemed to become less substantial, shimmering and fading at the edges.

"I don't know if I can do this," I confided to her, this figment of family who had my eyes.

"That has never stopped a woman of our line from trying, and it will not stop you," Agnes called, her voice already so far, so far away. "Godspeed, Jessica."

I had no idea what to say. Goodbye felt wrong. Good luck felt trite and empty. What came out of my mouth instead was, "I can't believe I'm talking to the woman whose prophecy set my entire life in motion."

Agnes' forehead wrinkled, her expression blank. "What prophecy?"

As I opened my mouth to answer, the room gave a final, jarring lurch. With a gasp, I tumbled away from Agnes, falling head over heels through the door into a whirling jumble of color and sound and sensation and then landing with a jolt at last in black silence.

THE WAKING

I SPRANG SUDDENLY BACK into consciousness, as if the Rift had actually hurled me back into my body with the speed of a freight train. I felt my brain connect with my senses with a painful snap, as my whole body was flung up off the floor, so that I was instantaneously kneeling on all fours, gasping for breath like I'd surfaced from deep-sea diving.

A cacophony of voices assaulted my ears.

"Jess!"

"Holy SHIT!"

"Oh my God, thank God, thank GOD!"

"Stay back, give her room!"

Flooded with sensory information, it took several seconds of processing the onslaught of light and colors and sounds before I could bring the real world back into focus. When I did, the first thing I saw was Finn's face, stark white and shadowed with stubble and deep purple rings under his eyes, but lit with a euphoric smile.

"How are you feeling, love?" he whispered.

I assessed myself, and replied in a dry husk of a voice, "Thirsty."

He let out a relieved bark of laughter, and as if by magic, a mug of cold water was thrust into my hand. I gulped it down greedily, feeling it spill down over my chin in icy rivulets.

"Take it easy," another voice said, and Flavia's face appeared beside Finn's. "You must be very dehydrated. We were just deciding whether or not to steal an IV and fluids from the hospital ward."

"An IV?" I croaked, gesturing for her to fill the cup again. "How long was I out?"

"Almost forty-eight hours," Finn said, his voice cracking. "The longest forty-eight hours of my life, if truth be told."

"Two days?" I gasped. "I've been Rifting for *two days*? But that's impossible. It felt so quick—I barely had time to..." I tried to wrap my brain around what had happened in the Rift, but it was all jumbled, like confetti thrown into the air. The thoughts and memories were still floating and fluttering around, still settling.

"Jess, sweetness, do me a favor and test the connection out, would you?" Milo floated into view looking as frazzled and relieved as the others. "Hannah's been losing her mind. She had to go to a Council meeting to maintain the appearance that nothing strange is going on, but I promised I'd let her know if there was any change. She'd be so relieved to hear your voice."

"So, does… no one knows I've been unconscious for two days?" I asked.

"Nope," Milo said. "We told people you and Flavia both came down with something at Skye. So, right now the official story is that you're both in self-imposed quarantine puking your guts out."

"Gross," I said between sips of a fresh cup of water. "Couldn't you come up with a slightly less disgusting cover story?"

"Not if we wanted to keep people far away from this room," Milo insisted. "Anyway, stop complaining. It worked, didn't it? Now please contact your sister before her head explodes."

It took several attempts to feel my way into the connection—the falling confetti thoughts kept distracting me. As exhausted as I was, I felt jumpy, like there was something I was supposed to be doing at that exact moment that was very, very important.

"Hannah?"

"JESS?! IS THAT REALLY YOU? OH MY GOD THANK GOD THANK GOD THANK GOD!"

The intensity of her emotions actually made me cry out and clutch at my head in pain.

"Jess? Are you all right?" Finn cried out from beside me, gripping my arm.

"I will be as soon as my sister stops screeching like a banshee inside my skull," I told him through gritted teeth. I turned my focus back to Hannah, who was now unleashing an unintelligible mixture of sobbing and yelling. "Hannah! It's okay! Just calm down, I'm fine! Everything's fine!"

"Don't… you… ever… tell… me… to… calm… down… ever… again!" she gasped between sobs. "I thought you were gone! I thought you'd never wake up! I thought I lost my sister! Don't you dare tell me to calm down!"

"I know, I know, I'm sorry, okay? But you have to calm down or I have to close the connection. Seriously, Hannah, my head!"

"Close it then, I'm coming up! I hate you for—well, no I love you,

I'm sorry, I'm just... I can't..." the rest of her thought was such a tangle of emotion that it sounded like radio static and then, abruptly, she cut out.

"Whoa," I said aloud as my headspace became my own again. "Milo, you'd better go meet her. She is a hot mess right now. I'm not sure how she's going to get up here without drawing attention to herself."

"Shall... shall I do it?" Kiernan asked hesitantly. "I don't mind going, honestly."

"It's okay, lover boy, I've got this one. I can be quicker," Milo said, giving the mortified Kiernan a salacious wink and popping out of existence at once.

"So, what happened in there, Jess?" Flavia asked. "The Casting ought to have worn off ages ago. Did something go wrong?"

"I... I'm not sure... it wasn't wrong, exactly, there was just... I'm trying to remember..."

"After all of that, you don't even remember what happened?" Finn asked, flabbergasted. "Are you saying we've all gone through this ordeal for nothing?"

"No, that's not what I... it's just all jumbled in my... in my head," I said.

"It's normal to feel disoriented and confused in the aftermath of Rifting, even when the Casting proceeds as expected. Just give it a little time, and it will start to come back to you," Flavia assured me in a soothing voice. "How about I brew you a cuppa and we scrounge up something for you to eat? You'll feel better when you've eaten something."

"I... yeah, okay," I said, though the thought of food was not appealing in the least. My stomach was roiling as though in anticipation of something I couldn't remember.

As my eyes followed Flavia over to the bedside table, where she retrieved an electric kettle, I began to take in the rest of the room, which looked like more of a makeshift emergency shelter than my bedroom. Several air mattresses were set up on the floor. Blankets, pillows, and clothing were strewn everywhere. A stack of dirty dishes and glasses covered the desk. A fire crackled in the fireplace, from which several bunches of dried herbs hung ready for Castings.

Huh. Dried bunches of herbs. That stirred a shadow of a recollection, but I still couldn't remember the details.

"When you didn't wake up, Flavia began using some other Castings to try to rouse you," Finn explained, gesturing toward the hearth, which was littered with books, a mortar and pestle, and the stripped stems and leaves of used plants. "There's no Casting designed to rouse a person from Rifting, so she had to… experiment."

"I was not inclined to do so," Flavia said, and her voice had a sense of forced calm about it. "Until I saw this." She reached out as she walked by me, took my hand, and flipped my arm over so that my forearm was visible. I gasped.

The artwork I had so painstakingly copied and transferred to my skin was gone. Not just faded or smudged, but gone. As though it had never existed at all. As though it had been nothing but a dream.

"How did… when did that happen?" I asked.

"About twenty-four hours into your Rifting," Finn said. He was still holding my other hand, stroking my palm with his thumb. "We thought it might mean that something had gone wrong, and so we tried to bring you back."

"I… I think I remember that," I said slowly.

Flavia looked up in surprise. "You do?"

"Yes," I said, nodding as this element of my journey settled itself in my mind. "There was a point where the Rift sort of started rocking and lurching around. I remember I was talking to someone, and I kept losing my balance and having to grab onto things. Eventually, I just fell right back through the door."

"You were talking to someone?" Finn asked eagerly. "Who?"

"I… I'm trying to remember. It's still hazy. A… a woman, I think," I said, trying to sift through the scattered thoughts still fluttering down in my brain.

"Don't force it, let it come," Flavia advised me. She disappeared into the bathroom to fill the kettle at the sink.

"So you really had no idea how long you were gone?" Finn asked me quietly.

I shook my head. "Not a clue. The details are hazy, but it felt like I was there for hardly any time at all."

"How opposite our experiences have been, then," Finn said with a wan smile, "for these have been two of the longest days of my life."

"I'm sorry, Finn," I said. "I had no idea it would be so—"

Hannah came bursting into the room, Milo on her heels, looking flustered.

"Good luck explaining *that* dramatic exit to the Council," I heard him mutter before Hannah descended upon me like a wailing, leaking, hugging tornado. It took a solid ten minutes to calm her down enough to even begin to have a conversation, by which time Flavia had successfully brewed me a cup of tea. It felt as good as a hot bath after a long day running down my throat, and seemed to clear my head a little.

"Well?" Hannah finally said when she had blown her nose one last enthusiastic time.

"Well, what?" I asked.

Her left eye gave a spastic twitch as she glared at me. "What do you mean, 'well, what?' What did we put ourselves through all of this for? Savvy? The Tansy Hag? The secret code that Agnes Isherwood left for you? Haven't you found anything out, or did we all just torture ourselves for two days for nothing?"

Thunk. The rest of my confettied thoughts hit the ground like lead. And now that they lay still, I could finally see them clearly.

Oh, God.

"Oh, God," I whispered.

"What? What is it? Did you remember something?" Finn asked.

"I... I remembered everything," I choked.

"Well, what? What is it, tell us!" Hannah cried.

"Start from the beginning," Flavia cut in. "The order of events matters."

I took a shaky breath. "I woke up in a tansy patch."

Milo frowned. "What's a tansy—"

"Flowers," I snapped. "A little patch of flowers. Don't interrupt me, okay? Just... just let me get through it."

"Right, sorry, shutting up now," Milo muttered.

"It was like that picture we found, Flavia," I told her. "The one in the archives, in that old children's book, remember? I was one of the little girls in the meadow, wearing a white dress, and Eleanora Larkin was there with me, making flower crowns."

"Eleanora?" Hannah asked, wonder in her voice. "What... how was she?"

The question baffled me for a moment until Flavia jumped in to answer it. "It's not like that. The Rift is just a heightened mental state, not an actual place. Jess saw Eleanora because Eleanora was in her subconscious. The spirit uses what's available in the brain as a sort of tool kit to explore within the space."

"I was less confused before you tried to explain it," Milo said, shaking his head.

"Anyway," I broke in before Flavia could go down a scholarly rabbit hole. "She made me a crown, and while she was doing it, I could see the Tansy Hag waiting for us in the woods. Oh, yeah, there were woods. They just kind of appeared behind us. So, then Eleanora put the sun in her crown and we walked through the woods…"

"She put the *sun* in her crown? Holy shit, so this is like… *heavy* hallucinogenic stuff, huh?" Milo asked, leaning his chin on his hand and gazing at me, fascinated. "What's in those herbs, huh, Flavia?"

Flavia smirked but did not reply. I went on, each image becoming clear in my brain as I spoke them aloud.

"Then Eleanora told me it was time for bed, but the bed was actually a tomb and I had to jump down into it, and I landed in the spirit ward of Skye Príosún. Savvy was there, waiting for me, and…" I stopped suddenly. "Savvy! Oh my God, what the hell is wrong with me, I didn't even ask… how's Savvy?"

"The same," said Finn solemnly. "There's been no change—no change at all. But we'll get to all that, Jess. This is important. Tell us what happened in the Rift."

"I… okay, right. Sorry," I said, trying to pick up the thread of my memory. "So, yeah. Savvy was there. She didn't speak to me—just pointed me into the Tansy Hag's cell. But when I got into the cell, it wasn't a cell at all—it led right into the central courtyard of Fairhaven, right to the Geatgrima."

Everyone was rapt and silent. No one moved. Hannah seemed to have stopped breathing.

"But the Geatgrima was gone. Well, not gone, exactly, but damaged. Most of it had crumbled away, and Irina was there, trying to rebuild it from a pile of stone."

Flavia looked shocked, too. "Irina? Really?"

"Yup. She was just as cryptic as ever. Then I looked up and she had turned into the Tansy Hag." ___

Hannah gasped. "You're not telling me... you don't think she really *was* the—"

"No," I said firmly, shaking my head. "The Tansy Hag lived centuries ago. Her spirit's been trapped in the *príosún* ever since. There's no way she and Irina are the same person in real life. But for some reason my brain connected them—probably because they were both Travelers. Anyway, the Tansy Hag pointed me toward the Geatgrima again, and it had disappeared and turned into a door."

"See?" Flavia clapped her hands together in triumph that this detail, at least, was how she had predicted it would be. "What did I tell you! There is always a door. That's how it works. You can always choose to come back by simply walking through it."

I shook my head. "Not that door."

"What do you mean?" Flavia asked, her smile fading.

"The door was there, the one you're talking about. I could always see it and it was always open just a crack, just to let me know how easy it would be to walk through it. But that's not the door I'm talking about. The door that appeared on the dais was tightly closed. I tried over and over again to force it open, but it wouldn't budge."

"But what was this second door?" Flavia asked, her face a blank slate of shock. "Why did you try to open it instead of just going back through the first one—the door you knew would lead out of the trance?"

"Because I didn't have any answers yet!" I said. "Nothing was any clearer, and the Tansy Hag told me that this new door would... would lead me to..."

"To what?" Hannah and Milo cried out at the same time.

"*Vortimo*," I whispered. "Truth."

"So, what happened, then?" Finn asked. "When you couldn't open the door?"

"My artwork was the key," I said, looking down at the bare white flesh of my forearms, imagining that I could still see the delicate vines and leaves and runes unfurling across it. "I pressed first my hands, then my arms against the wood of the door, and it sort of... lit up, revealing the same hidden artwork carved into the surface. And then the door opened and... and she was there."

"Who was there?" Finn asked.

"Agnes. Agnes Isherwood."

And even as I said her name the entire conversation came flooding back to me, and it hit me with the force of a tidal wave. I gasped with the force of it, startling everyone around me.

"Our gift… our gift is stolen!" I said it out loud to get the awful truth out of my head, but hearing it out loud only made it worse—more real.

"Huh?"

"Jess, what are you on about?"

But I was on my feet now, panic infecting my veins like poison. "I have to see Celeste! I have to warn her!"

I stumbled toward the door, but Kiernan, looking alarmed, stepped in front of it. Finn intercepted me, grasping me by my upper arms both to steady me and to prevent me from leaving. "Jess, calm down! You can't go see anyone until we know what's going on!"

"Please, it's the Geatgrima! It's taking the Gateways back! It's going to happen all over! We're running out of time!" I implored him, my voice cracking with fear.

"Kiernan, help me!" Finn said, and I realized as he looked at me that he was as scared as I was, though for a different reason. He was looking warily into my eyes, searching for a spark of reason.

Kiernan hurried over to help Finn drag me over to the chair by the fire, kicking aside the mess of mattresses and clothes and food debris as they went. I struggled against them as they worked together to muscle me into the chair.

"Let go of me!" I cried. "I have to…"

"Blast it, Jess, you're not going anywhere until we understand what the bloody hell you're talking about, so you might as well stop fighting us and just explain!" Finn grunted.

"Focus, Jess," Flavia said, her voice a lullaby as she came over to sit beside me. "Tell us exactly what happened, everything you can remember, just like the rest of the vision."

I tried to master my ragged breathing, but my heart felt like a wild animal caught in my chest. "I… Agnes Isherwood was there—on the other side of the door. She said she'd been waiting for me for a very long time."

"Good, good," Flavia said, nodding encouragingly. "Go on."

I felt Finn and Kiernan release their grips on me ever so slightly.

I took another uneven breath. "She led me to her tower. Well, it's Fiona's tower now, but it was her tower then. And she told me… told me that there was no 'where' and no 'when' in the Rift, and that she had created the door so that she could meet me and give me a warning."

"Go on," Flavia repeated, though her voice had a distinct tremor in it.

"She… she told me that I had done well. She had the same artwork on her arms, she showed me. She told me a Traveler woman had helped her with it, but when I asked her if it was the Tansy Hag, she didn't know what I was talking about. Then she… she asked me if something strange was happening in my time with the Geatgrimas."

Everyone looked at each other, clearly stunned.

"I told her about Savvy, and it was almost like she was expecting it. Then she told me… she told me about the Gateways." I took a deep breath, afraid that the words wouldn't come, that they would cling to my insides, refusing to be spoken aloud, refusing to let the terrible truth be brought to light. "Hundreds of years ago, in Agnes' time, the Gateways did not reside in our blood. They lived in the Geatgrimas themselves. The Durupinen were only meant to lead spirits to the Geatgrimas so that they could Cross on their own, when they were ready. But then the Necromancers grew powerful, and they launched attacks against the Durupinen fortresses. The Durupinen couldn't hold them off, they knew the Gateways were in danger—and so they created a Casting that would strip the Gateways from the Geatgrimas and hide them in the Durupinen bloodlines."

No one spoke. No one even seemed to be breathing. Every horrified pair of eyes was fixed on me, waiting for what devastation would next cross my lips.

"They had no choice, she said. It was either that or let the Gateways fall into Necromancer hands. Agnes was a Scribe at the time, and she was the one who figured out how to do it. But she warned them that it could not last forever—that one day the Geatgrimas would collapse or something like that—and now it's happening. Whatever it is she feared—it's happening right now, right out in the courtyard."

Hannah found her voice first. "What is it? What's happening?"

"The Sentinels have begun their watch," I whispered.

"What does it mean?" Hannah asked.

"I don't know," I said. "She couldn't explain it to me. Or wouldn't. I'm not sure. Anyway, we ran out of time. But she told me who would know, so we've got to go, now!"

I stood up and stumbled toward the door again, but stopped with my hand on the doorknob. I turned around. No one had tried to stop me. No one had followed me. Everyone was just sitting there, staring at me.

"What are we waiting for? We have to go! There's not a lot of time!"

"Jess…" The tone of Finn's voice was so hesitant, almost frightened. "Jess, you need to slow down. Just… just stop and think for a moment."

"I'd love to, Finn, but Agnes made it pretty clear there's no time for that," I said, throwing up my hands in exasperation.

"Finn's right, Jess," Flavia said, and she too, sounded strange, like she was trying to convince me to put down a dangerous weapon or something. "You just came out of the longest Rifting I've ever seen. You're exhausted and confused and famished, I'd imagine. You need to gather yourself and get some rest so that we can start interpreting what you experienced."

I glared at her. "What do you mean, interpret it? I've just told you what it means. Agnes told me everything we need to know."

Flavia's eyes flicked toward Hannah, who met her gaze warily. "Jess, you… you didn't really speak to Agnes Isherwood. Or Eleanora Larkin, or Irina Faa, or anyone else for that matter. You've just been dreaming, in a sense—allowing your brain to explore and interpret information that has come about as a result of your spirit connection."

"What do you mean I didn't talk to her? Haven't you been listening? I…" I stopped short, the realization hitting me. "Oh, my God. You don't believe me. None of you believe me, do you?"

"Of course we believe you, love," Finn said at once. "It's just…"

"Just WHAT?" I cried.

Finn looked lost and turned to Hannah, who cleared her throat. "We're just trying to help you, Jess. If we all put our heads together, we can probably make sense of the vision."

"I don't need you to make sense of it!" I snapped. "Agnes

explained everything to me. She went into the Rift and put that door there so that we would find each other. That's why it took me so long to come out of the trance. It wasn't a normal Rifting trance at all. I went somewhere else, somewhere deeper, and Agnes Isherwood is the one who created that place, so that she could find me."

"But... she's been dead for centuries, Jess," Milo said, in a voice that almost begged me to make sense.

"Don't you think I know that?" I cried. "And anyway, she explained that part to me. She told me our... our lives are threads, or... something... but anyway, it means that time doesn't work the way we think it does, okay? It made sense when she said it."

"She didn't say it, Jess, your subconscious did," Flavia said gently.

"NO, IT FUCKING DIDN'T!" I shouted, making them all jump. "Look, I've been in the Rift before, okay? It was like a weird acid trip, like a dream. It started out that way again just now, but then it changed, do you understand? I went through that second door and the place it took me wasn't really the Rift at all. It was... more *real*, more solid. And Agnes wasn't some strange hallucination who was there one minute and gone the next. I could see every unchanging detail of her. I could feel the warmth of her hands when she took mine. I could see Hannah and mom in the color of her eyes. I could smell herbs and smoke when she turned her head."

"Okay, Jess, let's just say all of that is true," Hannah began.

"It *is* true, Hannah, for the love of—"

"Okay, okay! But, Jess, if she really did make that door, and somehow waited there for you in... like... another dimension or something—how did she know to wait for you? How did she know you would be coming? And how did she leave the clues for you so that you would know how to find her?"

"She had a vision of me!" I said. "You know she was a famous Seer—she just... Saw me! And as for the clues... well, I told her to leave them for me."

"You... what?" Milo asked weakly.

"The last thing she asked me before I woke up was how I knew what to do—how I found her sketches and everything. And so I told her about the call number. She had no idea what I was talking about—the tapestry hadn't been _made_ yet. Hell, she wasn't even

High Priestess yet. But I told her how and where I found the number so... so I think I actually left the clues for myself."

"But that's... I can't... does that even make sense?" Milo asked in a whisper.

"I don't know!" I shouted. "And honestly, I don't fucking care at this point. It's like she said, time doesn't work the way we think it does! You want to hear something else insane? She hadn't even made the Prophecy yet. You know, the one that literally created the law that Hannah is trying so hard to overturn, the one that destroyed our parents and separated us for our entire childhoods and set us on a collision course with destruction? That little Prophecy? Yeah, she had no idea what I was talking about. I was the first one to mention it to her. So, I'm not sure if I'm supposed to apologize for that, or if I'm somehow responsible for it now, but there it is."

No one interrupted me now, and I couldn't tell if it was because they were starting to believe what I was saying, or because they were more scared than ever that I'd lost my damn mind, but I didn't care. I just plowed forward, telling them the things they needed to hear, the things I couldn't bear to be the only one to know.

"Look, she didn't just bring me there to warn me. She had specific instructions for me. I am supposed to find the three people here and now who will understand her warning and know what to do about it. The first is the High Priestess of the International High Council. The second is the High Priestess of the Traveler Clans. And the third is the Keeper of the Elementals, whatever that means. I have to get her message to them, because... well, because she told me to."

A loaded silence met this pronouncement. It stretched on for so long that I became afraid to dare to break it. Finally, Hannah cleared her throat.

"You're serious. You... you really spoke to her."

"That's what I've been trying to tell you."

"This is madness," Flavia whispered. "This is utter madness."

"I'm not disagreeing with you in the least," I said with a sigh.

"You do realize what you're saying, don't you?" Milo asked. "That you've somehow gone back in time and that your own ancestor told you that the Durupinen aren't actually supposed to *be* the Durupinen at all?"

"Yes. I promise you, I do know exactly what I'm saying, and also how ludicrous it sounds."

"Okay," Finn said, and he ran his hands over his face and through his hair, his eyes closed, his eyebrows pulled into a deep, contemplative "v" below his creased forehead. "Okay. Okay, let's all just slow down for a minute here."

"Finn, there's no *time* to slow—"

"Jess, I believe you, love, truly I do, but you've got to appreciate that we need a moment to process all of this. It's a lot of information to be hit with after forty-eight hours of worrying and waiting."

I swallowed back my impatience, trying hard to imagine how I would feel hearing this information again for the first time, but my overwrought brain couldn't quite manage it. Even as Agnes had told it to me, even as the truth invaded my ears and burrowed its way into my heart like a scared animal, I hadn't doubted it even for a moment. How could they hear that same truth from me now and not understand instantly that it was both very real and very urgent?

Finn took one last deep breath and seemed to master himself. He turned to Flavia. "You're the Scribe. Have you ever come across anything at all that might have hinted at what Jess has told us?"

Flavia shook her head. "No. The origins of our lore begin with our gift. Before that, there is nothing."

"Our gift," Hannah whispered, her eyes wide. "Is it possible it isn't a gift at all? Is it possible we really... took it?"

"I don't dare consider it," Flavia murmured. "It's almost too awful to fathom."

"Isn't it possible," I interjected, attempting to stay calm, "that the reason there is no record of us internalizing the Gateways is that we wanted to cover it up? I mean, we wouldn't want people to know what we had done, right? We messed with the natural order of things. People would have protested. They would have spoken out. They wouldn't have allowed it to continue."

"So, you think we buried it? On purpose?" Hannah asked.

"It makes sense. History is written by the victors. We wrote it out of our history to protect the Gateways... and probably ourselves," I said.

Flavia looked deeply uncomfortable with this notion, and of course I knew why. History and documentation were the foundations of her life's work. The idea that she might not be able to trust the written history of Durupinen lore meant those foundations were nothing more than dust.

"If, as Agnes said, the Durupinen knew there might come a time when the Gateways would become endangered, it makes sense that they would have a system in place to fix it—a kind of failsafe," Finn said, rising from the floor and pacing over to the window and gazing out of it thoughtfully. "It also makes sense that they would impart the truth not just to a single person, but to several people. It keeps the truth from becoming lost, as it could if a single person was the sole depository of such knowledge. It's like keeping spare keys to your home and making sure others you trust have a copy."

"That's an appropriate comparison because 'keys' is exactly the word that Agnes used. It also protects the knowledge from being misused," I added. "What if, say, only the High Priestess of the International High Council knew, and she didn't want to reveal the truth for some reason? This way, there are two others to keep her in check and ensure that the truth comes out so that the crisis can be addressed."

"But what *is* the crisis?" Hannah asked, throwing her hands up in exasperation. "What are we actually facing here? I'm still not sure what's going on, and Agnes didn't explain it very well, did she?"

"We know enough to know that something really dangerous is happening," I said, feeling my frustration rise again. Why was no one else grasping the urgency of the situation? "Agnes said that one day, removing the power from the Geatgrimas would cause them to collapse. That must be what's happening now."

"But what does it mean for the Gateways if the Geatgrima collapses? They don't contain the Gateways anymore, so why does it matter?" asked Milo.

"I don't know. But it must be a bad thing, or Agnes wouldn't have gone through all the trouble to warn me about it," I said.

"And what was the thing she said about Sentinels?" Milo jumped in. "Because that sounded fairly ominous."

"The Sentinels have begun their watch," Finn replied before I could answer.

They all began to talk over each other.

"Who are the Sentinels?"

"Do you think she's talking about Savvy?"

"If she is, then there must be others, right? Sentinels, plural."

"And what happens if—?"

"I DON'T KNOW!" I shrieked, and everyone fell silent again, looking shocked. "I don't have the answers to any of these questions! I'm working in the dark here! I've only got the instructions she gave me, and nothing else. And maybe it sounds insane to run with this on the word of a woman who's been dead for hundreds of years and who I may have only dreamed a conversation with, but I know what I have to do. And if I have to do it myself, I will; but it would be a hell of a lot easier if you stopped asking me questions I have no way of answering, and started helping me figure out how in the world we're going to do this!"

Finn was across the room before I'd even finished speaking. He wrapped his arms around me, holding me together at the exact moment I was sure I would come flying apart. "You're absolutely right, love. I'm sorry. Take a deep breath. Please understand we are just trying to catch up—just trying to process it all. We're going to help you, of course we are."

"I'm sorry, too." Milo said. "We're here, Jess, just like always. Whatever you need."

"Of course," Flavia added swiftly.

"At your disposal," Kiernan said with a respectful nod.

Hannah gave a little whimper but nodded as well.

"But you believe me? You believe that Agnes told me the truth?" I asked.

"Yes, we believe you," Finn said at once, staring down each of the others until they nodded. "And I know you're eager to get started. I agree, there is little time to be wasted. But our first steps must be carefully planned, or you do Agnes a great disservice. She waited in the Rift for you for centuries. You can manage a few hours of rest and preparation to carry out her instructions, starting with a decent meal."

I felt all the fight drain out of me. "I... yeah, okay," I said with a sigh. The moment I allowed myself to think of food, I realized how ravenously hungry I was. And still quite thirsty.

"Let's all have something to eat," Flavia said, glancing at her watch. "I don't think they will have quite cleaned up from dinner yet. And then, after we've all gotten a little sleep, let's set to work, figuring out what to do next."

No one dared to answer her, all looking to me for permission to agree to this plan. I nodded wearily, and it was with a collective sigh of relief that everyone stood up, stretched, and began hunting around the room for shoes and other personal belongings so they could go downstairs. I realized they were all in the same clothes they'd been in when I'd first entered the Rift.

"Thank you, guys," I said. My voice was quiet, but everyone froze in what they were doing to look at me. "Thanks for staying with me and for keeping me safe while I was… down there, or whatever. I'm sorry you were all so stressed out. I didn't mean to freak out on you. I'm just… that experience was intense, and I woke up feeling really anxious. It's all a lot to process. I'm glad you're here to help me do it."

Finn gave my hand a squeeze. Kiernan and Flavia smiled and nodded. Milo shrugged and muttered, "Obviously." Only Hannah said nothing, staring down at her own hands in her lap.

"I… think I'm going to stay here and go to sleep," she said. "I don't think I can eat anything."

"Are you sure?" Milo asked, frowning at her.

"Yeah," Hannah said. "I'm fine. Just… overwhelmed."

"We're all feeling that," Flavia said.

"We'll bring you back a sandwich, shall we, in case you change your mind?" Kiernan asked, looking at her with concern.

Hannah gave a bewildered sort of shrug and disappeared into the bathroom. For a moment, I considered going after her, but my stomach gave a rumbling growl, and I decided I couldn't ignore it any longer.

"See you in a bit," I called and, when she didn't reply, closed the door between us.

PROMISES

"JESSICA!"

I'd barely taken ten steps down the hallway when the voice rang out behind me. I turned to see Karen hurrying toward us, her face twisted in concern, with a paper bag tucked under her arm.

"Karen! Hi!" I cried out, my voice a bit shrill in my surprise. I threw a panicked glance at Finn, but all he could do was return it. What did Karen know? Had Hannah filled her in on what was happening while I was unconscious for two days? How much should I tell her? Luckily, though, her next words took the edge off my anxiety.

"How are you feeling, honey? Hannah filled me in, about the stomach bug. Here, I picked up some stuff for you in London."

She thrust the bag toward me. I took it and peered into the top. I spotted some Gatorade, a box of saltine crackers, and a take-out container of chicken broth. I expelled a breath and tried to muster a smile for Karen. "That's great, thanks, Karen. I'm... starting to feel a bit better. In fact, I was headed down to the dining room for some dinner."

Karen reached out and laid the back of her hand first against my cheek, then against my forehead. "Don't push yourself, Jess. You still look flushed. You haven't been running a fever, have you?"

"No, no fever," I said quickly. "I'll uh... I'll try some of these crackers and soup before I move on to anything heavier."

Karen gave a nod, apparently satisfied that I wasn't on my way downstairs to gorge myself on a five-course meal. "Where's Hannah? She hasn't caught it, has she? Those viruses are terribly contagious."

"No, she's just... uh... catching up on some work for the Council," I said. "I'm sure she'll be down to eat in a bit. So, um... thanks, and I'll see you later, okay?"

I turned to go, but Karen reached out and caught my sleeve. "Jess, hang on. That's not the only reason I came to find you." She pulled me away from the rest of the group, the rest of whom hung back awkwardly.

For the first time since she appeared in the hallway, I really looked at Karen. Her usually flawless makeup was not enough to mask how truly awful she looked. She was pale and drawn, with deep shadows under her red-rimmed eyes.

"Karen, is everything okay?" I asked her, wondering if it was even possible for me to process any more bad news.

Karen's face gave a strange, spastic twitch before she was able to compose it and answer. "Yes… don't worry… it's just… well, it's your grandfather, honey. He's passed away."

I blinked. For an embarrassingly long moment, I felt absolutely nothing at all. The words were empty, meaningless. And then…

"He… he finally went back," I whispered.

I'd spent time with my grandfather several times over the last five years, but I'd never met him—not really. Many years before, he had interrupted Karen and my mother during a Crossing with devastating results. Unable to resist the lure of the Gateway, his soul was partially pulled from his body, and he was never right again. Desperate to return to the glimpse of the Aether his soul had managed to get before it returned to his body, he had lived the rest of his life lost in a dream of anticipation, wanting nothing more than to Cross.

I had once asked Karen, as we drove away from the nursing home, "Did you ever consider just… letting him go?"

I thought she might think I was some kind of monster for even suggesting it, but she didn't. She nodded very seriously before replying, "Yes. Many times. But the thought of ending a life… I could never face it. I suppose he managed to get that much of his religion into me."

She gave me the same sad smile now that she had given me then. "Yes. He's finally gone back."

"What happened?"

"Old age, it seems. The nurses said that he went in his sleep, peacefully."

I nodded. Surely it was the first peace he'd felt since the moment his soul had touched the Aether all those years ago. "I'm so sorry, Karen."

"Me, too," Karen said. "He was the only family I had left, the last link to that part of my life. It wasn't a happy childhood, or a simple one; but it was mine, and I was grateful for a lot of what he was able to give to me. I've felt so terribly guilty over the past few months, choosing to move here. It felt like I was abandoning him. I was trying to sort out the legalities of bringing him over to be with me, but that's all over now, of course."

"Don't feel guilty, Karen. He's been gone for a long time. He would have wanted you to make the decisions that were right for you and your life. I don't believe for a second that he would have begrudged you the chance to be closer to Hannah and me." I reached out and squeezed her hand. "Because he wasn't the only family you had left, remember?"

Karen smiled, her eyes brimming over with tears. I pulled her in for a long hug, stroking her hair, hoping she could pull a little comfort from knowing that she still had Hannah and me. She hugged me back, her shoulders shaking as she wept silently. Flavia, Finn, Milo, and Kiernan stood quietly by, each keeping their eyes down, trying to make themselves as unobtrusive as possible so as not to intrude on the family moment.

At last, Karen pulled back, laying a hand on my cheek and patting it tenderly. "You really are just like your mother sometimes, Jess. She always knew exactly what I needed to hear when I was upset. You have that gift, too."

I shrugged off the compliment awkwardly before asking, "So does this mean you need to go back to the States?"

Karen gave a sniff and nodded. "Yes, I'll need to make all of the necessary arrangements—funeral and burial and estate, all of that will need to be sorted."

I felt a faint flutter of panic in my stomach. "Karen, I... do you need help? Only I'm not sure that I can leave right now with—"

But Karen was already shaking her head. "No, honey. I appreciate the thought, but I know Fiona needs you here right now."

"Right," I said quickly. "Right, Fiona. Yeah, I can't really leave her alone right now."

"And I'm sure you want to be close by for Savannah as well," Karen said, her expression clouding over again. "Hannah's told me what happened. Has the Council had any luck at all figuring out what's going on?"

"No, not that I know of," I answered. "We're all just waiting."

Karen frowned. "I hope Celeste will come to her senses and call in the International High Council. I understand why she's hesitant, but it's all just too strange not to report it." She reached out and squeezed my shoulder. "I'm sorry to heap this news about your grandfather on top of your concern for your friend. Are you sure you'll be all right while I'm gone?"

I mustered a smile. "Don't worry about me, Karen. I've got Finn and Hannah and Milo here with me. Whatever is going on with Savvy, I'm sure the Council will figure it out soon. It will be okay. It has to be."

"Yes," Karen agreed, though the smile she gave me seemed forced. "Yes, I'm sure you're right. Well, I've got some packing to do, so I'm going to head to my room. I'll be there if you need me. Maybe stop by later for a cup of tea, if you're up for it?"

"Yeah," I said. "Yeah, if I'm up for it."

Karen gave me one last hug and, with a friendly nod to the others, walked away in the direction of her room.

"Jess, love, I'm so sorry," Finn said, stepping forward and slipping his hand into mine. Milo, Flavia, and Kiernan added their murmured condolences.

"It's okay," I told them. "Really it is. I'm fine. It's much better that he's at peace now." It was also much better that Karen was going to be distracted and away from Fairhaven over the next couple of weeks, I added silently. I felt like an asshole even thinking it, but I wasn't ready to tell Karen what Agnes had revealed to me, and it would be much easier figuring out how to carry out her orders without Karen hovering like an overprotective hummingbird, questioning my every move. I was breaking my recent promise to be more open and honest with her, but I preferred the guilt to the responsibility of having yet another person in on this devastating secret I was now tasked with carrying.

No one spoke much as we ate dinner in the dining room that night. Our mouths were very busy being crammed with food, of course, and anyway, we couldn't discuss the events of the Rifting for fear of being overheard. A few people came over to greet both Flavia and me, asking how we were feeling and expressing their happiness at seeing us up and about again. We smiled and made small talk, eager to confirm the cover story Hannah had concocted for us. Then we all headed off in our separate directions, Finn and Kiernan to the barracks, Flavia to her own room, and Milo to the central courtyard, where he promised to continue his vigil for Savvy.

When I got back to our room, Hannah was already curled in a ball under her blankets. As much as I wanted to talk, I decided not to disturb her. After all, my Rifting had probably been more traumatic for her than it had been for me, and adding the news of our grandfather just felt cruel. I texted Karen that I'd see her in the morning, pulled on a clean pair of pajamas, and practically fell into bed.

I ought to have been asleep before my head hit the pillow, so achingly exhausted was my body, but my brain would not shut down. It was not racing with images of Agnes or the Tansy Hag or giant flower patches or dead girls climbing into tombs, nor was it dwelling on thoughts of my grandfather and his long-awaited Crossing. No matter how much I tried to reign them in, my thoughts just kept wandering out to the courtyard, where Savvy and the Geatgrima were locked in their standoff. At dinner, I had agreed to wait until the morning to visit her, but as the sleepless hours stretched on, I knew I couldn't wait. Finally, I picked up my phone and texted Finn.

Are you awake?

I am now. Is everything all right?

I need to see Savvy.

I know. We'll arrange it in the morning.

Can't wait. I need to see her now. Please.

There was a long pause. Finally, he replied.

Meet me by the east entrance to the courtyard in fifteen minutes.

I expelled a sigh of relief and slipped silently out of bed, determined not to wake Hannah. I pulled a sweatshirt on over my pajamas and slid my feet into my slippers. I was halfway to the door when I backtracked to the desk and scribbled a quick note for Hannah explaining where I'd gone. The last thing she needed was to wake up and have another scare that something dreadful had happened to me.

Went to the courtyard to visit Savvy. Please don't worry, Finn is with me. Be back soon. Love you.

I didn't pass a single soul, living or dead, until I reached the front doors. The Caomhnóir there narrowed his eyes at me but allowed me to pass without giving me the third degree, for which

I was grateful. The grounds were eerily silent as well, giving the impression that the natural world was holding its breath, rapt with the same anticipation as the rest of us for what would come to pass in the courtyard.

Finn was already waiting for me when I rounded the east corner of the castle. I wouldn't have blamed him if he had been thoroughly annoyed, or even angry with me for pulling him out of bed for a totally unnecessary midnight excursion; but his face betrayed no such reactions. Indeed, the smile with which he greeted me was so luminous, so pure and full of love, that I stopped in my tracks and basked in it for a moment, wondering, as I did so, how the hell I ever got lucky enough to find someone who looked at me like that. Somewhere a karmic accountant had royally fucked up, but I was so grateful.

"Hello, love," he said, reaching out his hand for mine and pulling me in to close the rest of the distance between us. I pushed up onto my tiptoes and kissed him in reply.

"Well, that was quite the greeting," he said a bit breathlessly when I pulled away.

"It wasn't a greeting, it was an apology," I told him. "I'm sorry for dragging you out of bed like this. I know it's ridiculous, but…"

He caught my chin with the crook of his finger and tilted it upward so that I was looking at him. "It's not ridiculous. It's natural. You don't need to apologize to me." With that, he took my hand and began walking along the eastern wall of the courtyard toward the entrance.

"How many Caomhnóir are on duty in here?" I asked.

"Just one," Finn said. "And Milo, of course. He came to me right away when the shifts were being sorted out. He made the argument that it was important to have a spirit guard as well as a living one. Spirits can notify leadership or alert for help much more quickly and efficiently than Caomhnóir can, and of course, there's no chance a spirit will doze off on the watch."

My heart surged with affection for Milo. "But he's not taking all the shifts by himself, is he?" I asked.

Finn shook his head. "No, he recruited several other trustworthy spirits from the grounds who agreed to devote their time to the task. The spirits are just as concerned as the living about what's happening with the Geatgrima. There's been a shift in the energy from the Aether that they find troubling. Hannah told us that several of them came before the Council yesterday to testify as much."

"A shift in the energy?" I asked, a new cause for alarm blossoming in my chest. "What does that mean?"

"They've described it as a sort of shift of focus. The Geatgrima used to exert a kind of pull on all of those around it, Durupinen and spirit alike. But now, that pull seems to have concentrated itself on Savvy alone, so that others can come and go in the Geatgrima's presence and feel... well, nothing."

My eyes widened. "That's... bad, isn't it?"

Finn shrugged his shoulders but his expression was very serious. "I cannot say. But I certainly don't think it's cause for celebration."

I felt the urgency I'd experienced in the immediate aftermath of the Rifting surge again in my chest. The fact that Savvy had neither moved nor spoken in the last few days had perhaps given everyone a false sense of security that the situation, however strange, was at least at some kind of standstill. But these observations by the spirits on the grounds dispelled this comfortable notion. We may not be able to see what was happening to Savvy, but something was indeed changing—shifting—and every minute lost was precious. We could not afford, for her sake, to wait and see. We needed to act swiftly.

Finn came to a sudden stop just a few steps short of the archway that would reveal the courtyard interior. He turned to me, leaning in close so that I could hear his whispered instructions over the breeze that had picked up over the trees. "Wait here while I speak to the Caomhnóir on duty. Those who have stood guard within the courtyard walls have reported strange symptoms—fatigue, headaches, confusion, disorientation. One of the older Caomhnóir even blacked out. As a result, it is not unusual to check in with them and put them on break if they need it. I'll send this bloke on his way, and then flag you down when the coast is clear to enter."

"Why do I need to wait for the other Caomhnóir to leave?" I asked. "Is the courtyard off limits?"

"No, but we don't want to draw any attention to you at present," Finn said. "Savvy is your friend, of course, but if the Caomhnóir reports that you are sneaking out to visit her in the middle of the night, it's going to cause suspicion. Better to have him safely out of the way and sidestep the whole mess."

"Won't he report the fact that you relieved him of duty?" I pointed out.

Finn grinned. "He reports to me."

I grinned back. He winked at me and disappeared through the entrance into the courtyard. I tiptoed along the wall until I came to a carved niche that revealed a view of the far corner of the courtyard. Although I could not see Savvy, the Caomhnóir was stationed within my line of sight. He was a tall, thin, gangly kid, barely out of his teen years, with a shock of straw-blonde hair and a heavily freckled face. He did not seem to see or hear Finn approach until he was right in front of him; he kept his eyes trained on Savvy, his mouth slightly open.

"MacDonald!" Finn barked, and the boy leapt back in shock, shaking his head to clear it and staring around wildly before he managed to focus on Finn, who was barely a yard away.

"S-sir!" MacDonald stammered, snapping quickly back to attention.

"I'm relieving you of duty. Take a break, clear your head, come back in an hour," Finn said with a dismissive wave of his hand.

"That's all right, sir, I don't need to be relieved," MacDonald said, throwing out his chest.

"I'll be the judge of your fitness, MacDonald," Finn barked. "I was so close before you noticed me, I could have beat you round the head. That's no proper frame of mind to stand guard. Now get your head cleared properly and I'll see you in one hour. Not a minute before, understood?"

"Yes, sir. Thank you, sir," MacDonald said, dropping his eyes to his feet and heaving a sigh. "My head is pounding fit to burst."

"Evans is on duty in the medic's office. He'll get you sorted with a paracetamol or the like," Finn said, and his voice was a bit kinder. "Go on, now."

MacDonald turned and marched out of the courtyard, the tops of his ears bright red on either side of his head. Finn took MacDonald's post and, after seeing him safely out of earshot, waved for me to join him.

The sight that greeted me as I entered the courtyard was essentially unchanged from the last time I'd seen it. There was Savvy, frozen at attention. There was the Geatgrima, ancient, crumbling, and mysterious. And there was the strange, glowing current of energy now connecting them. I'd seen it all before, and yet it looked new to me, because my understanding of it had changed.

I walked forward slowly, pausing only to give a wave to Milo, who was hovering above the scene like a guardian angel. He blew me a kiss and gave me a sad little smile before turning his watchful eye back on Savvy. As I drew nearer, I thought I could understand what the spirits who had testified before the Council were talking about. The lure of the Geatgrima was there, of course—I could feel the nearness to the Aether, just like always. But that lure seemed very focused now, like a bright light that had been narrowed to a thin beam, and was no longer bathing all the surrounding souls in its light—it was trained very specifically on Savvy. The current of energy itself—the glowing threads of connectivity linking them together—drew my attention as I approached closer and closer. It became clear, as I watched it, that it was not a one way current, where the Geatgrima was sucking or leeching something from her, as I had originally feared. Instead, it seemed as though Savvy had completed some kind of circuit, and the energy (or power or whatever that glowing substance was) was flowing back and forth in both directions, so that it seemed, in a way, that Savvy was attracting the Geatgrima as much as it was attracting her. I didn't know if this made the whole situation more or less terrifying, but it tightened my grasp on the reality of it, and that was something.

I approached as near as I dared—or rather, as near as I could get before Finn started forward in a panic and I had to hold up a hand to let him know I wouldn't get any closer. Even I wasn't foolish enough to reach out and touch Savvy, though I wanted nothing more than to tear her away from the Geatgrima's grip and wrap her in the fiercest of hugs. So instead, I spoke to her.

"Hey, Sav," I said, but the words barely made it out of my mouth. I cleared my throat and tried again. "Hi, Savvy. Boy, I leave for two days, and you get into an existential tug of war with the source of all Durupinen power. I just can't take my eyes off you for a second, can I?"

She didn't reply, of course, though the Savvy in my head gave a raucous chuckle at that.

"I know you're still in there, so I'm going to assume that you can hear me," I said. "Everyone thinks I'm mad for trying to talk to you, but if there's one person at Fairhaven who deserves to know what's going on, it's you."

Somewhere over my head, Milo was sniffling. I tried to ignore it, but my own eyes were getting blurry as I lost some ground in the battle with my tears.

"I promised you I would try to find out what was going on, and I did. Or at least, I'm on the right track. Everything I tell you is going to sound crazy, but no crazier than what's happening to you right now, so I trust you to roll with it."

And I told her everything—about the tapestry, and the Tansy Hag, and my wild ride into the deepest depths of the Rifting, and everything that Agnes had waited hundreds of years to tell me.

"I haven't quite made sense of it all yet, but it seems to me that you might be the Sentinel she's talking about," I explained, speaking the theory aloud for the first time, as though checking to see if it sounded any more plausible in reality than it did in my head. "I think the Geatgrima might be trying to get its power back. I'm not sure if it's trying to steal it from you, or if you're keeping it from collapsing, but either way, we've reached a point where there's no going back."

This was the darkest heart of it, I thought. This unknown leap we had to take, and knowing that Savvy, at least, hung in the balance. It was almost unbearable to think about.

"I don't know what's going to happen next," I whispered, "but I know what I have to do. I have to follow Agnes' instructions. I have to find a way to get her message to all three of the people she told me. I have to trust that those three people will do the right thing before it's too late."

Even as I said it, I wanted to scream, because I didn't trust them, and I didn't trust myself, and I didn't want this fucking job. It was too much on my shoulders, too many ways it could spiral into disaster, too much, too much, too much… but I swallowed that scream because I couldn't bear to add it to Savvy's burden which, though I did not understand it entirely, I knew to be far more cumbersome than mine. I mean, how the hell could I complain as she stood here, locked in some kind of silent, epic struggle for the integrity of the Gateways?

I waited until I could be sure that my voice would remain steady before I went on. "I can't promise you that you'll come out of this okay. I can't promise that, Savvy, even though I want to. But I can promise that I'm going to fight for you as hard as you are fighting for all of us right now. I can promise you that."

I gasped. For the tiniest fraction of a second, I could have sworn that Savvy's right eyelid flickered. The movement was so tiny, so fleeting, that I swallowed my shout to tell Finn and Milo what I'd seen. Instead, I kept it for myself, choosing to believe that she had heard me, and that, even while locked in the deepest of spiritual trances, she had found a way to tell me she was all right, that she understood, and that she wasn't gone at all, but was right in front of me, whole and complete.

A laugh bubbled up from some deep place inside me, and I was never so grateful in my life to receive even the merest suggestion of a trademark Savannah Todd wink.

"Jess, are you okay? Are you... laughing?" Finn asked, in a whisper that nonetheless carried clearly across the courtyard.

"Yeah," I said, wiping away the tears that had finally spilled out of my eyes. "Yeah, I'm fine. I think I might be able to go to sleep now."

A SECOND SENTINEL

B Y THE TIME I MADE IT back up to my bed from the courtyard, I could barely keep my eyes open. I half-expected Agnes and the Tansy Hag to be waiting for me behind my eyelids, but my sleep was dreamless and deep, and when I woke the next day, the sun high in the sky, it was with a clarity I hardly dared to hope for. The frenzied hysteria of the night before had evaporated, leaving in its place a galvanized certainty that I was doing the right thing. I would not question whether I should carry out Agnes' instructions. I would only question how. I wasn't exactly calm—there was still an undercurrent of anxiety—but I felt ready to plan my next move. I rolled over, hoping to talk to Hannah about it all, but found a note on my nightstand instead, scribbled on the back of the note I'd left for her when I'd gone to see Savvy:

Had to do damage control with the Council after last night. Will catch up with you when I'm done. Flavia wants to see you in the library once you're up. I saw Karen this morning, and she told me about Grandfather. I'm okay. I hope you are, too. xo Hannah

I texted Finn, who was organizing morning rounds with the Caomhnóir, and then swung through the dining room to grab a coffee and a muffin on my way to the library. I'd barely made it out of the dining room, however, before a voice called out.

"Oi, Jessica!"

I turned to see Catriona marching toward me, her face a thundercloud.

"Aw, shit," I muttered to myself, before foisting a smile on my face and raising my hand. "Hi, Cat."

"Don't 'hi, Cat' me," she snapped, grabbing me by the elbow and steering me into a darkened corner of the entrance hall under the second-floor gallery. "Where have you been, then? I agree to send you off to the *príosún,* completely against Tracker protocol, for some reason you refuse to divulge to me; and then when you arrive back, you vanish for two days solid amidst all of this madness." She gestured toward the front doors, which I could only assume was a reference to Savvy and the Geatgrima.

"I, um, got sick," I said, wondering if it was too late to try to look pale or exhausted or... mildly nauseous. "Stomach thing."

"Oh, come off it, Jessica, what kind of fool do you take me for?" Catriona hissed at me. "I did you the courtesy of trusting you when you asked to go to the *príosún*. Do me the same courtesy now."

I froze. I was not prepared for this. I had not anticipated telling anyone else about what Agnes had told me, and there was no way in hell I was going to just blurt it out in the middle of the hallway to a Council member, no matter how much I might trust her; and it was true that, unlikely as it would have seemed even a year ago, I trusted Catriona more than nearly anyone else in the castle. But with this?

Catriona interpreted my hesitation as weakness and plowed on. "I'm not completely clueless, you know. I talked to Lucida night before last," she said.

I could see the coffee sloshing around in my trembling cup and fought to steady my hand. "Oh, did you?" I asked, trying and failing to sound casual. "How's she doing?"

"She's a bloody disaster," Catriona said. "Are you aware she hasn't called me once in all the years she's been incarcerated? Not a single phone call. But last night, wouldn't you know it, my mobile rang and it was Lucida. And do you know who she wanted to ask me about?"

"No, who?" I asked in a small voice.

"You," Catriona said, throwing the word at me like a dart. "All concerned she was, wondering if you'd gotten back and if I'd talked to you at all, and if you'd perhaps come to me or the Council with any sort of information."

I said nothing. It was no use playing dumb at this point. I was absolute shit at lying anyway.

"Now, why is it that Lucida knew you were at the *príosún* in the first place, and why would she think that you'd have information that I needed to know?" Catriona asked, glaring at me with narrowed eyes.

"Why didn't you ask her?" I countered.

"Oh, you can be sure I *did* ask her. Repeatedly. She refused to explain what she was talking about and asked me to get in touch when I'd spoken to you. And then, when I attempted to track you down, your sister told me that you were locked away in your room with a terrible illness, not to be disturbed."

"Yeah, I... wasn't well," I hedged. It wasn't entirely a lie.

"How convenient," Catriona sneered. "Well, now that you seem to have recovered yourself, perhaps you could take a moment to explain to me what the bloody hell is going on?"

I took a deep breath and blew it out again. "I can't."

"Come again?" The words barely managed to escape the prison of Catriona's tightly clenched teeth.

"I can't tell you. Not right now."

Catriona closed her eyes and pinched the top of her nose, trying to regain her composure. "Jessica, may I please remind you that I am your superior and that your autonomy within the ranks of the Trackers only extends so far."

"Fine, then. I quit," I replied.

Catriona's eyes flew open. "You *what*?!"

"I quit," I repeated, quite calmly. "I don't necessarily *want* to, but if your intention is to use my job to bully something out of me, you leave me no choice."

"I'm not giving you an ultimatum here, Jessica. I'm just tired of being kept in the dark," Catriona said. And beneath the edge of anger in her voice, something else was detectable—something fragile and afraid. The call from Lucida had clearly left her shaken.

"I'm not trying to keep you or anyone else in the dark," I said. "I'm just... I'm trying to figure something out, and I can't share it until I understand exactly what it is I'm dealing with."

"Does this... has this got anything to do with what's happening in the central courtyard right now?" Catriona asked, all anger vanished, eyes wide and vulnerable.

"Yes."

"Do you know what's happening to Savannah?"

"Not exactly. But I might have found a way to find out."

"And why haven't you brought this information to the Council? Why not let them share the burden of this... this knowledge, or whatever it is? We've been in near-constant session since it started, trying to figure out what's going on."

"Because the information wasn't given to them. It was given to me."

"By whom?"

"Even if I could tell you that, you would never believe me."

Catriona pressed her lips together. I could see her frustration building again. "Give me one good reason why I shouldn't march you into the Grand Council Room right now and demand you explain yourself to the High Priestess."

"I haven't got one," I said. "Except that if I'm thrown in a cell for contempt of the Council, this crisis will never get solved, and that's a promise." I sighed. "Cat, I'm sorry. It's not that I don't trust you, but there's a method to all of this madness, and I'm trying to follow it. If I can get this right... if I manage not to royally fuck up just this one thing, then everything that's been happening lately—with the *príosún*, with the Necromancers, with Savvy and the Geatgrima—it just might finally make sense. But it's a... a very *delicate* thing, and I need you to trust me just this one last time. I know you don't owe it to me, but I'm asking you to anyway."

Catriona stared blankly at me. It was hard to tell if she had processed a single word I'd just said. Then, without warning, it was as though someone had flicked a switch and she was right back into Tracker mode.

"What do you need from the Trackers? Anything? Resources? Transportation? Protection?"

I stammered for a moment at the sudden about-face but recovered myself. "I... no, nothing right now. Just... just time. And your patience."

"I'm rather limited on both, I'm afraid," Catriona said, crossing her arms and looking truculent.

"I understand that," I said. "Just give me what you can."

Catriona nodded once, brusquely, and then her expression faltered, shivered with a repressed sob. "What the hell has Lucida gotten herself tangled up with this time?"

"Believe it or not, Cat, this one isn't Lucida's fault at all. She was just in the wrong place at the wrong time. But I wouldn't be on the right track if she hadn't helped me, so we should be thanking her this time, not cursing her."

The corner of Catriona's mouth twitched before falling back into a thin line of misery. "First time for everything isn't there?" she muttered, shaking her head. She pointed a stern finger in my face. "The next time I come to you for answers I won't be leaving without them. Count on that." Then she turned and walked away, golden hair swinging behind her like the pendulum of a clock.

I felt a squirm of guilt in the pit of my stomach as I made my way to the library. I was glad that I hadn't lied to Catriona, but I still felt ashamed that I hadn't been able to confide the full truth to her. But it just wasn't an option. Fairhaven was full of Durupinen who defined themselves by the gift of the Gateway in their blood. It was the aspect of themselves that they revered and protected above everything else. It was the only answer they would ever consider giving to the question, "Who are you?" I couldn't imagine any of them willingly helping me to destroy that identity, even if they could bring themselves to believe what Agnes had told me. For many on the Council, I was still one half of the troublemaking pair who brought the Durupinen world to the brink of destruction.

Now that I thought about it, this was all pretty on-brand for me. At least I was consistent.

I found Flavia just where I expected her to be, in her tiny office off the main reading room in the library. She was half buried, as was her custom, in a teetering pile of scrolls and books, but she looked up and smiled when she heard me come in.

"Jess, there you are! How are you feeling? Did you sleep all right?" she asked, standing up and pulling a giant musty book off the only other chair so that I could sit down.

"Not well at first. But after I visited Savvy, I slept like a rock. I thought I'd be a restless mess, but I woke up feeling really clear-headed, for a change."

"You visited Savvy?" Flavia asked, raising her eyebrows. "I didn't think they were allowing anyone in the courtyard?"

I winked. "I've got friends in high places. Well, one friend, really, but he's kind of a big deal."

Flavia's expression cleared. "Ah, I see. And how... how was she?"

I sighed. "The same. I just needed to see her—to tell her that I hadn't forgotten her, and that everything would be okay."

"Of course you did. I'm sure she would have done the same for you."

I took a large swallow of my coffee to help choke down the lump in my throat. "How about you? Did you sleep at all?" I asked, my voice hoarse.

"Hardly more than ten minutes at a stretch," Flavia said with a wan smile. Her eyes were deeply shadowed behind her thick glasses. "I tossed and turned all night. The stress of the day was part of it, of course, but something else kept nagging at me—something that was tugging on the edges of my memory that I just couldn't quite get a hold of. Finally, around four o'clock, it came to me, and there was no hope for sleep after that. I got dressed and I've been here since."

"Well, what was it?" I asked eagerly.

"There was a moment when you were telling us about what Agnes said about the Geatgrimas, when I had the feeling of déjà vu, but I couldn't quite put my finger on it. For several years before I met you, I had worked on a research project with the other Traveler Scribes. We were trying to gather documentation of anomalous events surrounding the Geatgrimas. Like most of our research back then, it all had to do with the Prophecy; in this case, we were hoping to get a better understanding of what might happen if the Necromancers succeeded in reversing the Gateways. We thought that by studying the behavior of the Geatgrimas themselves, we might glean enough information to make some predictions of what we might face, should the Prophecy come to pass. The Geatgrimas, despite their symbolic importance to our culture, have always been rather shrouded in mystery—now I fear we may know why. Anyway, I remembered reading about something to do with a Geatgrima and a Durupinen who was drawn to it, but I couldn't remember the details. When it finally came to me early this morning, I came down to see if your library here had documentation of it, and I found it."

She extracted a book from the stack, laid it open on the desktop between us, and flipped through the delicate pages to the place she had marked with a length of silk ribbon. We bent over it from opposite sides of the desk, so that our heads nearly came together.

"Just over a hundred years ago over in America, a young Durupinen girl disappeared from her family's home in the middle of the night. She was a Key, highly sensitive to spirits since birth, and from a powerful and prominent family. So naturally, the leadership was alerted. Amidst fears that the Necromancers might somehow be involved, additional Caomhnóir and even some Trackers were brought in to aid in the search. The girl was found just before dawn trying to break into the cellar of the manor house on a nearby plantation. She seemed to be in some kind of trance, and it was not until the sun rose that she was able to be roused from it. When she came to, she had no memory of leaving her bed or how she had arrived at the plantation. A thorough investigation of the property revealed the remains of a Geatgrima deep in the basement."

I gasped. "That sounds an awful lot like what happened to Savvy, doesn't it?"

"Too right, it does," Flavia agreed with a solemn nod of her head. "And it doesn't end there. The next night, the girl attempted to escape again. And again the next night. Every night for a week she went to bed, rose with the moon as though sleepwalking, and tried desperately to return to the site of the Geatgrima until the sun rose. No sense could be made of her behavior. No Castings had been placed upon her, and no spirit could be found to be exacting any undue influence over her. The Geatgrima itself was examined, and nothing at all remarkable could be discovered about it. It was, by all accounts, simply an unremarkable pile of rubble, though marking, as all Geatgrimas did, a certain proximity to the Aether. At a complete loss, the girl's parents decided to put as much distance between the girl and the Geatgrima as they could. They packed their bags and the Trackers relocated them to a clan property in New England, hundreds of miles away. It did no good at all."

"You mean she still tried to return to it?" I whispered. "Even from so far away?"

Flavia nodded. "The very first night in their new home, the girl escaped again. It was the dead of winter, and there was a fierce snowstorm. By the time they found her, several miles south, she had frozen to death."

"She *died*?" I murmured, horrified. "She died trying to get back to that Geatgrima?"

"She did," Flavia said, closing the book with a terrible finality. "But with her, it seemed, the mysterious influence of that Geatgrima also died. No other Durupinen was ever drawn to the place, and so the incident was soon forgotten. The Tracker report on the events seemed to cast aspersions on the girl's mental well-being, indicating that her own sanity—or lack thereof—was to blame."

But I was barely listening, for a realization had just hit me with all the subtlety of a sledgehammer. "Flavia," I interrupted, jumping up from my chair and causing her to push back from her desk in alarm.

"This Geatgrima, the one the little girl kept trying to visit—where was it located?"

"Oh! Um... well, there's a map in the file," Flavia said, digging around in her mounds of papers until she found a scroll, which she hastily unrolled and smoothed open on top of the book. "Yes, here it is, just a few miles outside of New Orleans, Louisiana."

A feeling not unlike fireworks erupted in the pit of my stomach. "I knew it," I whispered, then looked up into Flavia's bewildered face. "Flavia, I've been there. That plantation is the one Jeremiah Campbell bought and turned into his spiritual retreat, The Whispering Seraph. And you remember who his "angel" was, don't you, who was guiding his hand?"

Flavia clapped a hand over her mouth, and it was several seconds before she managed to squeak, "Irina!"

"Bingo," I replied. "She was drawn there as well, remember? From hundreds of miles away, she wound up there, of all places. She used Campbell to secure the location and then to start rebuilding the Geatgrima itself. She told me she wanted to take it back for the spirits to Cross freely whenever they chose, without the Durupinen in control." Irina's words echoed distantly in the back of my head, and I repeated them aloud for perhaps the first time, somehow recalling them perfectly, even after all this time. "She spoke of the other spirits at the plantation. 'What of the others?' she had demanded. 'All of the others forced to wait their turn! All of the spirits left to the mercy of the Durupinen! The Durupinen, who dictate when the spirits are allowed to Cross! Why should they have this power over us? I will create a Gate free of the tyranny of Gatekeepers! Have you ever heard of anything so beautiful?'"

Flavia's eyes were bright with welling tears. "My God," she whispered.

"And I thought she was mad, just like everyone else," I said, shaking my head in disgust. "I chalked her plan up to Walker-induced insanity. No Geatgrima could work without the Durupinen to open it, I told her, and when she scoffed, I was sure it was her madness talking. And then again, during the Rifting, there she was, toiling to rebuild the shattered remains of a Geatgrima, demanding I help her before it was too late." I gave a bitter laugh.

"So that's two instances in which a Durupinen in close proximity to that Geatgrima was drawn to it in an unnatural way," Flavia said, her eyes gazing off into the middle distance, lost in thought. "Each time, the Geatgrima exerted some kind of pull over them. Who's to say, if that little girl hadn't died, that she wouldn't have found a way down into that basement and begun rebuilding the thing stone by stone as well. We'll never know."

"But this just proves that there's a precedent for this," I said, and it was hard to keep the excitement out of my voice. "It's further proof that Geatgrimas aren't just monuments to Durupinen strongholds. They have a power all their own, power that Durupinen are helpless to overcome. Savvy isn't the first Durupinen to be targeted, and if Agnes' warning is right, she won't be the last. Sentinels, she said. Plural."

Flavia pulled off her glasses, gave her eyes a vigorous rub, and stood up, a renewed fire in her voice. "Right. Well, if we're going to convince anyone this is true, we're going to need more than two examples. I'm going to keep digging into every account of the Geatgrimas I can find. With any luck, I can build a case that will back up everything that Agnes told you so that when you meet resistance, which you undoubtedly will, we can combat it with facts. And of course, I intend to dive as far back into our written history as possible. If there's any written reference to the Geatgrimas' true purpose, however obscure, I intend to find it."

I smiled at her. "You're, like... a research superhero."

Flavia gave a little bow. "At your service. If I manage to find anything today, I'll bring it along when we all meet after Finn's shift. What are you going to do until then?"

"Well, I need to go see Fiona," I told her. "I promised to be here to help her adjust to her new situation with her eyesight, and then I abandoned her for almost a week."

Flavia gave me a sympathetic smile. "You might need another coffee before you do that."

"Undoubtedly," I replied, and downed the rest of my cup in a single swallow.

CONTROL

I KNOCKED ON Fiona's tower door and pushed it open before she could tell me to go away.

"Fiona? Are you here? It's Jess!" I called into the darkness. Fiona hadn't bothered to draw the drapes or turn on any lights, so the place was as dark as a tomb which, I supposed, would really only bother you if you could see.

"Well, well. So, you're still alive, are you?" came the snappish reply out of the gloom.

I took the greeting in stride. I probably deserved it, after all. "That depends," I said. "How well can you aim a paint can with that bandage thing on your face?"

Fiona cackled. Also, no paint can flew through the air at my head. Two good signs.

"Where've you been, then?" Fiona asked.

"At the *príosún*, remember? I told you before I left," I said, keeping my tone light.

"What kind of prat do you take me for, lass?" Fiona barked. "I mean since you've been back. Your sister said you were ill."

"I guess you have your answer, then," I said.

"Your sister's a worse liar than you are," Fiona countered.

"All right then, I wasn't ill. I was... working on something."

Fiona stepped into a dim patch of light that had snuck in around the edges of a curtain. Her hair was a bit disheveled, but otherwise, it seemed that she had managed to take care of herself. She was dressed, and the remains of her lunch sat on a plate by the sink. The room, as far as I could tell, was nearly as I had left it a few days before. The tapestry of Agnes Isherwood still dominated the west wall, and all the tools we had been using to restore her image were still laid out neatly on a small rolling cart. The only major difference was the corner where Fiona kept her potter's wheel. She had evidently been spending a good deal of time at it; the surrounding walls were spattered with fresh clay, and several partially formed sculptures stood nearby, alongside half a dozen pots she had thrown.

"And you're not going to tell me what that 'something' is, I suppose?" Fiona asked, hand on her hip.

"Not at the moment, no," I said. "But I promise it was important, or I wouldn't have left you on your own for so long. I'm really sorry about that."

Fiona raised her chin like she was trying to sniff the answer out. "You need my help?" she asked shortly.

"No. Thanks, Fiona, I'm okay. And I'm not trying to be cryptic or bullshit you or anything. I'm just... not ready to tell you yet, okay?"

Fiona shrugged. "Fair enough. Far be it from me not to know when to mind my own damn business."

I heaved a sigh. That was far less painful than I'd imagined. I hated lying to Fiona even more than I hated lying to Catriona or even Karen, but at least Fiona didn't make me feel like shit about it. Besides, I told myself, I would tell her everything when the moment was right—whenever the hell that was.

"How've you been coping while I've been away?" I asked her.

She shrugged. "Haven't had much time to worry about myself, not since the business in the courtyard started up. I suppose you've seen that since you got back? After all, she's one of your best mates, isn't she?"

"Yeah," I said.

"And I suppose you noticed that the whole scene looks an awful lot like my sculpture."

"Yes, I couldn't miss it," I said.

"So, you can see, then, why I had to take it to the Council," Fiona groused.

I gasped. "You what?! You took it to the Council? But I thought—"

"Be sensible, girl, what choice did I have?" Fiona cried, and I could hear the defensiveness in her voice. "I don't like involving the rest of the Council any more than you do, but hiding that sculpture once I realized what it was would have been tantamount to treason!"

"But you've been helping me hide my Seer abilities for months!" I cried. "You did it to protect me, and I'm grateful. Why won't you protect yourself?"

"It's not the same thing," Fiona grumbled, turning away from me and feeling her way back to her desk.

"It is the same thing! You're the one who warned me against what they do to Seers! You're the one who told me they would exploit my abilities and demand prophecies! And now they're going to do the same to you!"

"Yeah, well, I can handle it," Fiona said. "You're just a kid."

I stared at her for a full minute, the way her shoulders slumped, the way she hung her head. For the first time since I met her, Fiona looked... small.

"You are not expendable," I said quietly.

"I never said I was—"

"You didn't have to. Now, listen to me again. You. Are. Not. Expendable. I know what you are going through right now is tough, but you don't have to become the Council's psychic bloody pincushion to suddenly matter again, do you understand? You are still an artist. You are still the most knowledgeable art historian I've ever met. None of that has changed."

Fiona did not reply, but screwed her face up in a pout like a child who'd been caught doing something she knew was forbidden.

"What did the Council say? When you brought them the sculpture?" I asked.

"They had a lot of questions," Fiona mumbled, still brooding. "Very few of which I could answer. I don't think they are much concerned with me at the moment, if I'm honest. After all, it's not a prophecy anymore, is it? It's already happening."

"And you're not worried they're going to try to force more information out of you like they did with your mother?"

"Nothing I can do about it now if they do," Fiona said. "What's told can't be untold."

"Shit," I muttered, beginning to pace. "Shit, shit, shit."

"Look, I don't know what you're fussing over me for," Fiona said. "The one you ought to be worried about is your friend down in the courtyard there."

"Her name is Savannah, and I *am* worried about her," I snapped back. I pressed my hands to my forehead, as though this pressure could somehow stop the whirling dervish inside my skull. "Oh my God, this is a nightmare."

"Jess, if there's something you need to tell me, now would be a good time to—"

A sharp pounding on the door interrupted Fiona's words, causing us both to whip around in alarm. I jogged over to the door and opened it. A square-jawed Caomhnóir stood on the other side of it.

"The Council requests your presence at an urgent session to commence immediately in the Grand Council Room," he announced to the tower at large.

"Who?" I asked.

"Both of you," the Caomhnóir replied, still staring straight ahead as though determined not to make direct eye contact.

"Why does the Council want me there?" I asked, barely able to keep the anxiety out of my voice.

"They want everyone in the castle to attend," the Caomhnóir replied. "It is a briefing on the situation in the courtyard. The High Priestess commands it."

My heart pounding, I turned back to Fiona. She did not offer her usual grumbling resistance to being summoned somewhere, but was groping around for her cardigan. I hurried over to her, snatched the cardigan off the back of a nearby chair, and helped her into it. Then, gripping her arm, we followed the Caomhnóir out of the tower and down the stairs.

Fiona and I spoke not a word to each other the entire way down to the Grand Council Room. My heart was pounding so fiercely, I was sure passersby would be able to hear it thundering like a bass drum. What was Celeste going to say? Had there been some kind of development? Had something changed since I'd seen Savvy the previous night? Or had she somehow found out that I was hiding something from the Council? Fiona certainly sensed my panic. Her thumb was rubbing small, soothing circles into the palm of my hand as I guided her through the open Grand Council Room doors and up to the platform to take her place on the Council benches.

As I settled her into her seat, I scanned the milling crowd for Hannah and found her slipping in the door behind a knot of middle-aged Durupinen who were whispering anxiously together. Her face, when she found mine, was full of the same fear and unanswered questions that were crippling me. She made a movement that was half-shrug, half-head shake, and scurried to her seat in the benches.

Her meaning was clear; she had no idea why the meeting had been called.

Within seconds, Milo and Finn had entered the room as well. Finn gave me a fleeting, cryptic look before taking his place along the back wall, where he was charged with guarding the doors. Milo soared straight to Hannah, engaged in a brief, whispered conversation, and then sailed back over the crowd to drift down into the seat beside me.

"Do you have any idea what—" he began.

"Not a clue," I replied. "And neither did Fiona. I was in her tower when we were summoned down."

Milo just nodded. His form was vibrating so hard with nervous energy that his entire outline was blurred. Whatever else he might want to say, he swallowed it back as Karen hurried down the aisle and dropped into the seat on my other side.

"Do you have any idea why—?" she began, but I was already shaking my head.

Catriona was now sliding her way between the upper benches to her seat. The moment she was settled into it, she fixed the full intensity of her stare directly on me in a silent interrogation. Again, I was forced to shrug and shake my head, but her eyes continued to bore into me, as though she thought she might be able to worm her way into my connection by sheer ocular force and soak up my thoughts like a dry sponge. I was very grateful she could not.

All around us, Durupinen were filling the benches and falling into a silence heavy with anticipation. It seemed like every pair of eyes was now fixed on the doors to the adjoining chamber, from which Celeste would at any moment enter the room. And indeed, there was a collective gasp when the door swung open a few minutes later revealing Celeste, Siobhán, and Patricia Lightfoot, who all moved swiftly to their seats. I'd never heard the room so silent as Celeste took her place at the podium and cleared her throat. She spoke in a voice of determined calm.

"I thank you for answering the summons to be here on such short notice. As you all know by now, Fairhaven finds itself in a mystifying and unprecedented situation. One of our own Durupinen, Savannah Todd of the Clan Lunnainn has entered into some kind of connection between herself and the Fairhaven Geatgrima. You have all shown great patience as we have worked to determine the nature of that connection."

"Patience, indeed. As if we had any choice in the matter," said a voice to my right, not bothering to whisper. Others were murmuring as well. Personally, I could barely restrain myself from having a hysterical reaction to the ludicrous neutrality of a term like "connection."

"And have you? Have you determined the nature of this 'connection?'" a second voice rang out, slightly shrill. It felt as though the entire room was walking on a tiny ledge, narrowly avoiding toppling into a roiling sea of panic. Even now the spray was licking at our feet. The Caomhnóir could certainly feel it. They were shifting uncomfortably, hands drifting to their weaponry, eyes darting over the crowd. Celeste, on the other hand, took the interruption in stride. She seemed to expect the unrest—had, in fact, steeled herself for it. Her voice, as she continued, was brimming with both authority and patience.

"Our Scribes have been working night and day, consulting the most ancient and obscure texts," she said.

"That's a 'no,' then," Milo murmured in my ear. I gave a tiny nod to indicate that I agreed with him.

"I am going to invite our Chief Scribe to the lectern at this point to update you all on what they have found thus far," Celeste said, and stepped aside as a tall, willowy woman took her place at the podium, unrolling a scroll in front of her. I had seen her many times before, during my time spent in the Fairhaven library. Her name was Morgan MacEnney, and the library was her undisputed domain. She was at least six feet tall, with pointed features, and pale, watery blue eyes which I'd only ever seen over the tops of a pair of wire-framed spectacles that hung on a fine gold chain around her abnormally long neck. Today these glasses were perched on her nose and yet another pair was glinting in the frazzled nest of her graying blonde hair. She cleared her throat and began to speak in a quavering voice.

"Thank you, High Priestess. I wish that I had more definitive answers for you all, but the situation we face appears to be unprecedented in our history. I can find no account, written or otherwise, in official records or even in lore, that describes what is currently happening in the central courtyard."

I threw an anxious glance at Flavia, who was standing by in

the knot of other Scribes, and who managed to keep a completely impassive expression, though her hands were clenched into fists at her sides. I knew she had taken a great risk, keeping what she knew from the other Scribes. I could only hope she did not come to regret it.

Scribe MacEnney cleared her throat again, then brushed several wisps of hair away from her face before continuing. "Despite the fact that we have not been able to determine a precedent for the situation at hand, we have managed to establish several facts that clarify what is happening. First, the nature of the connection between Ms. Todd and the Fairhaven Gateway, while unique, is not unidentifiable. Our tests and research show that what flows at this moment between them, visible as a glowing current of energy, is, in fact, the Gateway itself."

This piece of information caused an uproar that took several minutes to settle down, during which Scribe MacEnney glared at us over the rims of her glasses, the classic school marm refusing to continue with the lesson until her unruly pupils got a grip on themselves.

A shrill voice rang out, "But where is it coming from? From Savannah Todd or from the Geatgrima?"

"We do not know," Scribe MacEnney replied patiently. "The energy is moving through and between them in a kind of cycle. It is, in fact, very similar to the way that the Gateway flows through the joined bodies of the Key and the Passage once they have linked hands and begun a Crossing."

This statement caused a heightened buzzing in the room. Several people actually got up from their seats and moved to other places, eager to confer with relatives or friends.

"So, are you saying that the Gateway is actually open right now? Can spirits Cross through it?" Siobhán asked, raising a hand in the air as she spoke like an eager student.

Scribe MacEnney shook her head, flapping her hands to quiet a renewed volley of cries and shouts that had risen at Siobhán's words like a flock of frightened birds. "No. The energy is contained between them. The spirits who are aiding in our investigation have reported that the pull of the Aether is not directed at them, though it is still present. We have used Casting after Casting in an attempt to detect any changes in the ebb, flow, intensity or direction of the energy. So far it has stayed at a steady state."

"And what of Savannah Todd?" a familiar voice cried out. Mackie had jumped to her feet. I didn't even know she was in the castle; other than a brief return to Fairhaven to assist with the Airechtas, she'd been living and teaching near Oxford. I would have been thrilled to see her if the situation hadn't been so dire. Her face was stricken with concern, for Savvy was one of her good friends. "Why can't she communicate? What is being done to free her from this situation?"

Scribe MacEnney looked over at Celeste for help at this point, and Celeste stepped up beside her, so that they were side by side at the podium. "At the moment, nothing is being done. We are not at all sure that attempting to remove her from the situation is the wise course of action," Celeste said.

It was Keira who spoke up now. She looked pale and drawn, as though she hadn't slept in days. "And why not? She cannot simply be left to languish there. Surely, she cannot continue in this state. No living person can."

"I can speak to that," Scribe MacEnney said, relieved, it seemed, to be able to greet a question with an actual answer. "We have examined Ms. Todd as thoroughly as we can without actually making contact with her. She has entered into what can only be described as a state of suspended animation."

She seemed to think this statement to be self-explanatory and so jumped in surprise when Fiona's voice barked out from behind her on the Council benches, "And what the bloody hell does that mean, for the rest of us who aren't fluent in absolute codswallop?"

Celeste narrowed her eyes at Fiona but refrained from reprimanding her on her foul language. Scribe MacEnney, however, was quick to reply—"It means her body has, in essence, hit the pause button. She does not require what living people require. She does not need to eat or drink or sleep. She simply exists. It is not unlike what happens to the body of a Walker when they choose to Walk."

Predictably, every head in the room turned toward me. I felt my cheeks flushing, but kept my chin turned defiantly upward. I tried to ignore the attention and focus instead on what Scribe MacEnney was now explaining in more detail, but which I already understood. The truth was that this explanation provided me with a modicum of relief. I had been concerned for Savvy's physical well-being, wondering how long she could possibly sustain herself in such a state, unable to take sustenance or even to sit down. But now I grasped a tiny piece of what she was experiencing, and it helped me breathe just a little bit easier.

When I met Irina for the first time, confined to a dilapidated Traveler wagon like a dangerous animal, I was stunned to learn that she was more than seventy years old. Her body was young and supple, her skin unwrinkled and her eyes bright. She looked no more than twenty-five, and Anca had explained to me the reason behind this phenomenon. Irina's body did not age when she was Walking, and so the many years she spent refusing to be reunited with her physical form meant that, though decades had passed, they had passed right by her. My own body, I realized, had done the same, but only for a matter of hours, not years; for Walking did not hold the same, irresistible lure for me that it had held for her. My body would always feel like my home, not my prison—one of the many reasons why I was meant to be a Walker, and Irina ought to have stopped. If she had never been captured and returned to her body, her physical form would have lain agelessly for eternity, like a fairytale princess awaiting a wayward prince with a penchant for necrophilia to break the spell.

"It is the opinion of the Scribes that Ms. Todd is in no immediate physical danger," Scribe MacEnney's voice sliced through my reverie like a knife.

"And what of other dangers?" a woman directly behind me shouted, making me jump. "What of dangers to the rest of us? To the spirits we serve? What if the Geatgrima reaches out to claim another of us? Or all of us?"

"It's because we broke the traditions!" another woman cried. "We let that upstart young woman into the ranks of the Caomhnóir. We've flown in the face of our God-given roles, and now we are reaping the wrath of the spirit world!"

This was too much for me. I stood up and rounded on the woman, entirely surprised that I did not shoot literal lightning bolts out of my eyeballs. "Oh, for fuck's sake, get a *grip* on yourself!" I snapped at her. "God didn't invent the asinine rules like Sanctity Lines that govern our existence, *we* did! The spirit world doesn't care if Savvy took part in a few training exercises. This kind of bullshit superstition is the reason we're all panicking instead of listening to the facts. Now, sit down and let Scribe MacEnney finish her report. You're embarrassing yourself."

The woman huffed and puffed in indignation, as though she was going to blow my proverbial house down, but then seemed to deflate, sinking into her chair.

Celeste held both hands up in the air, shaking her head. "While I do not approve of this kind of language amongst our company, I agree with the spirit of what Jessica has to say. This kind of speculation has no value. It stirs up fears and prevents us from responding rationally."

"No value?" the woman persisted with an incredulous splutter. "No value?! Would you have us sit and do nothing?

"Of course not," Celeste said, still betraying not a crack in her veneer of calm. "But we'll never fully understand what's happening if we continue to give in to fear and superstition. Now, Scribe MacEnney, can you tell us anything else?"

"The effects of this phenomenon, whatever they might be, seem so far to be concentrated on Ms. Todd exclusively, at least since we have made the decision not to interfere with it. Initially, one of the Caomhnóir who discovered Ms. Todd in the courtyard chose to grab hold of her and try to pull her away, and has been in the hospital ward ever since. Mrs. Mistlemoore, do we have any update on his condition?"

Mrs. Mistlemoore, who had been sitting in the front row of seats, rose and turned to address the assembly. "He was thrown quite forcefully across the courtyard when he made contact with Ms. Todd. Although we have been able to detect no physical injury that would cause prolonged unconsciousness, he still has not awakened. Vitals are steady and all major systems are functioning normally."

Seamus stepped forward from his post at the base of the platform. "High Priestess? If I may?"

"Yes, Seamus, thank you," Celeste said.

"Our men report a number of physical symptoms that have manifested if left on duty too long in the courtyard. Headaches, dizziness, disorientation, even fainting. We have adapted our shift schedule to minimize the effects."

"And have they observed any changes at all in the state of the situation during their watch?" Celeste asked.

"No, High Priestess. None at all. It is as though the courtyard has frozen in time."

"And there were no warning signs at all that this was coming?" A woman who had been sitting next to Mrs. Mistlemoore rose to her feet as she asked the question, her hand raised politely in the air. She looked so like Mrs. Mistlemoore that I felt sure she must be her sister, if not her twin.

Celeste cast a quick look over at Fiona, who had grown tense in her seat. "Fiona came to us with a sculpture she created shortly before Savannah was discovered locked into connection with the Geatgrima. The image is identical to what is happening out in the Courtyard now."

"A prophetic sculpture?" someone cried out, and a wave of frightened voices rose behind it.

"We cannot be sure it was not spirit-induced," Celeste said, clearly trying to deflect away.

"But if it *was* prophetic…"

"*Another* prophecy?"

I stood up, my hand shooting into the air like a teacher's pet.

I felt stirrings within the connection, Milo and Hannah's panicked questions, wondering what the hell I was doing, what I was going to say…

"Yes, Jessica Ballard of Clan Sassanaigh?" Celeste said, gesturing to me to speak but also fixing me with a warning look, which I knew to mean that I should watch my language.

"I don't think it was prophetic at all," I said. "I believe Savvy was visiting the Geatgrima for days before she entered into this trance."

I patiently waited through the predictable flurry of response to this pronouncement. Celeste shushed the assembly and said, "What do you mean?"

"Savvy told me that she was waking up every morning sore and exhausted, like she hadn't slept at all. At first, she thought it was just the rigorous nature of her Caomhnóir training, but her boots were muddy, too, like they'd been worn outside during the night. She had no memory of it—thought maybe she might be sleepwalking. I think she must have been visiting the Geatgrima at night, and it was already happening when Fiona made her sculpture."

Celeste turned to Scribe MacEnney, who immediately began adding this information. Then she fixed me again with a piercing look. "Why didn't you come forward with this information before?"

"I couldn't, High Priestess," I said, trying to sound surprised at the question, which of course, I knew was coming. "I was away on Tracker business at Skye Príosún when this all started, and when I got back, I was so sick that I couldn't even leave my room. I went straight to Fiona this afternoon to tell her about it, and that's when we got summoned to this meeting."

Celeste narrowed her eyes at me, but if she thought any part of my answer was bullshit, she didn't call me out on it. Instead, she sighed, gestured for Scribe MacEnney to take her seat again, and resumed her solitary place at the podium.

"As you can all see, we have made some progress in understanding what is happening in the courtyard, but there are still many unanswered questions. I am not yet confident we know enough to take this matter to the International High Council," she said.

Behind her, Siobhán and Keira exchanged an exasperated look. Renewed muttering through the hall made it clear that this decision was not popular. Patricia Lightfoot, I noticed, was barely repressing a smirk, which struck me as odd. Karen seemed to have noticed it, too. She was glaring at Patricia with narrowed eyes.

"High Priestess, if you please, couldn't the International High Council help with this matter?" A young Durupinen rose to her feet now, looking positively terrified to speak in front of such a large group of people. It was Frankie York, a Durupinen Apprentice and first-generation Gateway whom Savvy had helped mentor through the rocky transition to accepting her gifts. "Surely if our own resources have been exhausted in understanding what's happening to Savvy, then the International High Council is the next step."

Celeste's voice as she spoke to Frankie was firm, but not unkind. "Thank you for that input, Miss York. I know that Savannah is very important to you, as your mentor and friend. I promise you, she is important to me, too. But the International High Council is a law unto itself. If we involve them in this private Northern Clan matter, all control of the situation will be removed from our Council. We will have no say, no autonomy to handle the situation as we choose. We relinquish all hope of making what we feel are the best decisions for Savannah."

"But if we're out of answers..."

"The International High Council will not give us answers. They will leave us in the dark. We have worked so hard over the centuries to remove ourselves from the reach of that body, and I will not see us back at its mercy simply because we let fear cloud reason."

Milo leaned in. "Sounds like she's the one letting fear cloud reason," he murmured to me.

Milo was right. If the real goal was to understand what was happening, and to protect Savvy, then why weren't we asking for help from everywhere, using every possible resource? Who cared if the International High Council took over? What did it matter who was in charge? Unless the actual first goal was to maintain power, at the expense of truth and safety? What if Celeste, new to her role as High Priestess, was more concerned with asserting her authority than with doing the right thing for Savvy? For all of us?

I didn't want to believe it, but as I gazed at the stern, almost truculent look on Celeste's face, I couldn't help but think it might be true. Finvarra had made the same mistake in the run-up to the Prophecy, refusing to acknowledge the possibility that the Necromancers might be a threat. I wouldn't have thought Celeste vulnerable to that same weakness—I guess I was wrong.

Many on the Council were nodding along, eager, it seemed, to keep this matter off the radar of the International High Council, but I could spot dissent as well. Fiona, for one, was shaking her head, her expression grim. Catriona was gnawing anxiously on one fingernail, looking generally disgusted with the proceedings. Keira merely looked tired and bewildered, as though she really didn't know what would be the best thing to do, and just wanted someone to reassure her that everything was going to be all right. Hannah caught my eye, and I read the same disappointment in her expression that I felt inside myself.

The one tiny glimmer of good news I could find in this mess was the fact that it might buy me some time. One of the three people I had to deliver Agnes' words to was the International High Priestess herself. Celeste's hesitation to involve them might mean that I had the chance to get there first, to head off the confusion, to control the narrative.

"I am not interested," Celeste began again, raising her voice so that it echoed around the hall and silenced the chatter, "in discussing the matter further. It is my decision when and how to involve the International High Council. We shall do so when I deem it appropriate, and not before. Now, moving forward, I am asking everyone to continue acting with discretion. This must continue to remain a matter for the Northern Clans alone. Some of our Scribes, including Scribe MacEnney, will be leaving tomorrow morning for Skye Príosún. They will take full advantage of the resources at the Catacomb Archives to further research the situation in the courtyard, and I have the greatest faith that they will soon uncover the nature of the Geatgrima's connection with Savannah; and therefore, how to intervene appropriately. In the meantime, we must remain vigilant of—"

A loud and prolonged squeak interrupted Celeste's words as one of the massive doors to the entrance hall opened inward. Every head turned in time to see a woman enter, flanked on either side by a Caomhnóir, and wearing a smart blue suit and an insufferably smug smile upon her face.

Marion Clark.

The place went into an immediate uproar. The Caomhnóir were shifting around looking for instructions as the leadership hastily ran around to find each other and confer. Members of the Council were standing and shouting, pointing accusatory fingers at her. Members of the assembly were all craning their heads and standing up to get a better look at her, some whispering to each other, others shouting words of welcome or derision.

Marion, being Marion, soaked it all in like a welcome breath of fresh air. The woman thrived on self-induced drama the way the rest of the population thrived on oxygen.

"Well, well, well," she said when the room had fallen into a quiet muttering. "What a greeting. I really ought to get myself banished a little more often. It makes a girl feel so special."

She strode down the aisle with all the confidence of royalty, pausing to shake several hands before stopping about halfway to the Council platform. "Please do excuse the interruption. I had rather farther to travel to answer the summons, and the traffic was just hideous."

Celeste finally seemed to recover herself from the shock of seeing Marion within the castle walls. She drew herself up and replied in her most commanding of tones. "I'm afraid what you need to excuse is not your interruption, but your very presence. You have been banished from this castle for insubordination and treason. What are you doing here? Explain yourself please, so that we can fully understand the meaning of this visit before I have you promptly escorted back out."

Marion clicked her tongue. "Tsk, tsk, Celeste. Your rise to the High Priestesshood has rendered you a bit touchy, it seems." She took several more steps toward the benches, but a line of Caomhnóir fell into ranks before her, blocking the steps and causing her to pause where she stood.

"I am not in the habit of repeating myself," Celeste said coolly. "Nevertheless, I will give you one more opportunity to explain yourself. What are you doing here?"

"My clan was summoned to give representation at this meeting," Marion replied, her eyes widening innocently. "As were all of the oldest clans."

"That invitation was sent to your daughter Peyton, not to you," Celeste said, "or did you not bother to read it properly?"

"Yes, but my daughter is unable to attend," Marion replied. "She is recovering, you see, having recently given birth to my first grandchild. A girl, in fact."

I felt my jaw drop. I'd completely forgotten that Peyton had been expecting a baby, though I'd seen her at Róisín's wedding several months before, round-bellied and supremely smug in a rose-colored bridesmaid dress. Not that I'd been expecting to be invited to a baby shower or anything, but the news still felt like a blow out of nowhere. As I absorbed the shock, all around me there arose an obligatory flurry of excitement at this news. The news of a child was always traditionally cause for celebration, particularly in a culture that was so focused on maintaining the continuation of bloodlines. But the birth of a girl was met with even more fanfare, given the potential to carry on the Gateway. Courtesy bound Celeste to respond accordingly.

"Please allow me to extend Fairhaven's deepest congratulations to the rest of your clan on this happiest of events," Celeste said, her lips barely parting to allow the words to escape. "And of course, we understand why your daughter could not join us. However, your clan is not limited to you and your daughter. Alternate representation ought to have been agreed upon by your clan."

"It was," Marion said, spreading her arms in a presentational gesture. "Given the seriousness of events transpiring here, my clan did not feel comfortable sending anyone less experienced than a former Council member. And so here I am."

"Your clan does not have the right or power to overlook your banishment from these grounds," Celeste said, her voice rising now. "Your very presence here is an affront to the Council and our laws. Unless you choose to remove yourself this instant, I will see to it that you are escorted in the swiftest possible manner not just from the castle, but from the grounds as well."

"Yes, I thought you might say that," Marion said, still, inexplicably, smiling, "which is why I am lodging a formal request to have my banishment reviewed by the International High Council."

Again, an uproar ensued. But, I noticed, not everyone looked surprised to hear Marion's pronouncement. Up in the benches, Patricia Lightfoot was smiling down on the proceedings like she'd just found her favorite show on television, and she wasn't the only one. I spied many of Marion's former cronies smirking and smiling both in the benches and amongst the crowd. What the hell was going on here? Had this been planned?

But beside me, Karen had figured it out. She leaned in toward me and whispered in my ear, "Do you see what she's done?"

"You mean besides thrown a stick of dynamite into this meeting and completely derailed it?" I whispered back.

"Well, yes, but it's more than that. This is a power play," Karen said.

"Everything Marion does is a power play," Milo pointed out.

"Yes, but she's taken a huge gamble this time, and I think it might just pay off," Karen said. "By appealing directly to Havre des Gardiennes, she's—"

"Hold on, what's Havre des Gardiennes?" I asked.

"It's the home of the High Priestess of the International High Council, the oldest seat of Durupinen power," Karen explained.

"And by involving the leadership there, Marion's got Celeste completely cornered."

"How—?" I asked, but Celeste was speaking again, and I broke off to listen.

"You do, of course, have every right to appeal," Celeste said, in a valiant show of keeping a grip on one's patience, "as indeed you were informed when your banishment was instated. That appeal does not entitle you to re-enter the castle in the meantime. My order that you vacate the grounds stands, and I highly recommend you heed it."

"And I highly recommend you reconsider," Marion replied, the steel glinting in her tone now, all trace of friendly banter gone, "before you find yourself in rather an awkward predicament."

Celeste bristled. "Explain yourself at once, and do not dare trifle with me, Marion."

Marion shrugged. "I've simply come as a courtesy to you, High Priestess. I've brought a copy of the appeal request with me, for your records. It is identical to the one that one of my Caomhnóir is on his way to hand-deliver to the International High Priestess herself."

Celeste's face suddenly looked to be carved of stone. Her hand closed over the edge of the lectern, her knuckles tense and white.

"Of course, I felt it prudent to explain exactly why this was a critical moment for my clan to be duly represented at Fairhaven, and so I included a detailed description of the current situation as it stands," Marion said. She stood silent for a few moments, relishing the effect of these words on Celeste and the rest of the Council.

"All those who have been privy to the situation at Fairhaven have been instructed not to breathe a word of it outside the walls of this castle," Celeste replied, and though her voice was quiet, it was fierce with anger.

Marion's eyebrows rose in a look of mock innocence. "Is that so? It seems someone's been rather naughty, then."

"From whom did you learn of the goings-on at Fairhaven?" Celeste asked.

My eyes shot straight to Patricia Lightfoot, whose face was the picture of passive disinterest, before returning to Marion.

"I'm afraid I'm not at liberty to say," Marion replied, shaking her head regretfully. "But I must say I'm rather surprised at you,

Celeste, keeping the truth of what's been going on at the castle from the general clan membership and the international leadership as well. I can't imagine they'd have much faith in your continued reign if they knew."

There it was. Check and mate. Celeste knew it as well. I could see the internal conversation happening inside her head as though she was speaking the words aloud. If she sent Marion away from the castle, Marion would be sure that the International High Council was told all about Savvy and the Geatgrima, and Celeste would surely be raked over the coals for having kept it a secret. On the other hand, if she caved to Marion's blackmail and allowed her to stay, even temporarily, she would be publicly humiliated and subject both herself and the rest of us to whatever machinations Marion could orchestrate while within the castle walls. And there was no doubt that, if Marion was allowed to stay, she would waste not a single moment to regain what power and influence she could muster. She was not going to get another opportunity like this, and she knew it. And so now Celeste had to decide; would she rather face the wrath of the International High Council, or take her chances with Marion back in the castle.

I watched the decision form on her face, watched her arrange her features carefully before she spoke. "Very well, Marion. I do not deny that all clans should have the chance to weigh in on what is happening here, as it will surely affect us all. I do not approve of the manner in which you have chosen to make your case for appeal, but you are entitled to make it. If you agree to delay your correspondence to the International High Council until such time as I am prepared to brief them on the happenings here at Fairhaven, I will allow you to represent your clan at these meetings on a temporary basis. The matter of permanently lifting your banishment can be decided when we've weathered the storm of whatever is brewing in the courtyard. Does this arrangement suit you?"

Marion's face broke into a wide satisfied smile. "Oh, yes, High Priestess. It suits me very well, indeed."

"It is settled, then," Celeste said, a note of bitterness in her voice. "Kindly make the necessary arrangements to have your Caomhnóir return with your appeal, and then take your place in the assembly. We still have much to discuss."

GAMEPLAN

"**S**HE'S UP TO SOMETHING," Hannah shrieked, flinging her Council notes down on the coffee table in frustration.

The Council meeting had dragged on for another hour after Marion's dramatic entrance, leaving all of us to sit and stew in our fury until we were at last released to go and vent them. Though she had said little else, Marion had taken great pains to catch both my and Hannah's eye, bestowing a wide, gloating smile upon each of us before returning to her favorite pastime of whispering amongst her little collection of minions, who seemed all too eager to latch themselves back onto her now that she had blackmailed her way back into relevance. Karen had just enough time after the meeting to take both Hannah and me aside and beg us to keep away from her.

"I don't know what game she's playing now, but I don't want you two taking her bait, do you understand?" Karen said, in tones that suggested we were still scared teenagers rather than a Council member and a Tracker.

"Don't worry, Karen, we have no desire to get entangled with her again," Hannah assured her. "Just go take care of what you need to do with Grandfather. We'll give Marion a wide berth until you get back."

I just nodded. For once, Marion was the least of our troubles, but Karen didn't need to know that at the moment. Now, back in our room, we sat huddled together, Milo, Flavia, Hannah, Kiernan, Finn, and I, all together again and free to speak for the first time since I'd awoken from the Rifting.

"Of course she's up to something," Milo replied. "She's still breathing, isn't she?"

"More's the pity," Finn grumbled. The fact that he was actually related to Marion made the brazenness of her machinations even harder for him to swallow.

"What are we going to do about it?" Hannah asked, arms crossed.

"What can we do about it?" I countered. "She's here, and Celeste is letting her stay. I think our best bet is just to try to stay out of her way."

"I can't believe Celeste caved to that kind of blackmail," Hannah said, shaking her head in disgust. "I never would have expected that of her."

"Heavy is the head that wears the crown," Finn quoted with a resigned shrug. "Celeste is under a lot of strain. Even the best of leaders can crack under the pressure. We just have to press on and hope that she can see clear to make the right decisions moving forward. We can't do her job for her."

"I don't think the High Priestess underestimates Ms. Clark's arrival," Kiernan offered. "When I left to come up here, Seamus was already making arrangements—at Celeste's explicit command—to arrange a security detail tasked with keeping Ms. Clark under surveillance at all times. She won't be able to sneeze in this castle without the Caomhnóir alerting the leadership."

"Let's hope so," Finn said, nodding his approval of this plan. "Though Marion can do more damage with a conversation than most people can with a weapon. She's going to be trouble regardless."

"Let's try to focus, okay?" I said, trying to keep the irritation out of my voice. "It feels strange to say it, but Marion is far from my biggest concern right now."

"Right," Finn said, stopping his pacing and rejoining me on the sofa. "I concur. Let's decide what's to be done next."

Hannah gave a grudging nod and sank down onto the arm of the chair Kiernan was sitting in. He gestured for her to take the seat, but she waved him off.

"Flavia, do you want to fill everyone in on what you discovered in the library today?" I said, turning to her. Flavia cleared her throat and assumed her official librarian voice. As succinctly as she could, she recounted the story of the young Durupinen girl and the Geatgrima at Whispering Seraph. By the time she had finished, Hannah's hands were pressed over her mouth in horror.

"That poor little girl," Hannah whispered.

"So, this has happened before," Finn said. "At least, it nearly happened before."

"It sets a precedent for Durupinen being mysteriously drawn to a Geatgrima repeatedly and without the ability to resist it, yes,"

Flavia confirmed. "And then, of course, Irina was drawn to the very same place several decades later."

"Irina?" Kiernan asked, and Hannah launched at once into a whispered explanation of our experiences with the troubled Traveler Walker.

"Is that the only example you can find?" Milo asked.

Flavia nodded. "And I'm not the only one looking. The entire contingent of Northern Scribes will be sure to uncover it eventually. For now, I've kept the information to myself, just in case Jess needed it. I can't guarantee someone else won't stumble across it."

"I think Savvy is one of the Sentinels that Agnes spoke of," I said, voicing aloud, at last, my theory. "And I think that means there will be others."

Hannah's eyes grew wide. "Others?"

"There are Geatgrimas and Durupinen all over the world," I said. "Sentinels. Plural. I think Savvy is just the first—or at least, just the first that we know of."

"What does it mean?" Milo asked, his eyes wide and frightened.

"It means we don't have any time to waste. I've got to start delivering the message Agnes gave to me," I said.

"Who were they again? The people you're supposed to tell, I mean?" Milo asked.

I counted them off on my fingers. "The High Priestess of the Traveler Clans. The Keeper of the Elementals. The High Priestess of the International High Council."

"Did... do you think it matters who you tell first?" Flavia asked, grimacing as though she thought it might be a stupid question.

It didn't sound like a stupid question to me. I considered it. "I'm not sure, but that's the order she said them in, so maybe I ought to go to them in that order, just to be safe. But how the hell am I supposed to get into the Traveler camp?"

"What do you mean, how can you get into the Traveler camp?" Milo asked, laughing incredulously. "We've got Flavia; she can get you in."

Flavia shook her head. "Not anymore," she said, and though she smiled sadly, her voice had a definite tremor in it. "Once upon a time, perhaps, but now I've been properly banished. I would be able to *find* the camp, certainly—even if they've moved it in my absence, I know the patterns and signs to follow to the new location. But I can't get us over the border to speak to anyone. In fact, my presence will almost certainly count as a strike against you before you've even stated your business."

Hannah looked shocked. "You're kidding! But... I thought blood meant more to the Travelers than anything."

"And so it does," Flavia said. "But *I* was the one who broke that bond of blood by choosing to walk away. For Travelers, there can be no greater betrayal. You'll have to find another way in, I promise you."

"And I'm even less welcome than you," I said. "After what I did to free Irina, Ileana would probably arrest me the moment I set foot over the border, unless I have some kind of protection."

"You'll have me," Finn said fiercely, squaring his shoulders.

"And me," said Kiernan, sharing a nod of solidarity with Finn.

"While I appreciate this show of burly manhood, I meant Traveler protection. I'm not going to be able to secure an audience with Ileana on the merits of your brawn alone. I'm going to need Traveler blood on my side."

"Oh sure, no problem, we'll just borrow one of the dozens of Travelers walking around Fairhaven and ask them to help us," Hannah said, a bit hysterically.

I didn't reply. I'd just remembered something—something that might just solve our problem.

"What are you smirking at?" Hannah snapped, seeing the look on my face.

"Well, we might not have any other Traveler friends at Fairhaven, but we have got one a bit farther away, and I think it's time to give her a call."

§

I spotted Annabelle the moment I entered the crowded café. Her glorious mess of tawny curls marked her location like a neon sign. She looked up as I entered, and the smile on her face, while genuine, was a bit grim.

"Hi, Annabelle," I said, as she stood to embrace me.

"We really must stop meeting like this," she said as she planted a hasty kiss on my cheekbone. She pulled back to look at me. "Christ, you look like hell."

"Thanks," I said dryly. "Did you order already?"

"I'm three cups in," she said, gesturing to the half-drunk mug of tea. "I was able to catch an earlier flight, and I just couldn't stand sitting around my hotel room, so I've been here since noon."

"I'm sorry for all the secrecy. I didn't know who else to call."

"Don't apologize. Just sit. Coffee?"

"An espresso. Thanks," I replied gratefully, sinking into the seat opposite. A light drizzle had started on my walk from the underground, and now the raindrops were running down the windows of the café like tear tracks. I watched the world beyond the glass grow blurry and dull, watched umbrellas bloom like flowers on the sidewalks as the drizzle gave way to a shower.

"Here you go," Annabelle said, plunking my espresso in front of me and sliding back into her seat. She had chosen a tiny table crammed between the back wall and a crowded bookshelf—as secluded a spot as she could muster in public. "Did you want a sandwich or something? You're so pale."

"No, the coffee's good for now, thanks," I said, taking a long sip. It burned all the way down, but I didn't mind. "Thank you for coming all this way. How are Iggy and Oscar and the rest of the team? How's the shop doing?"

"Jess, everyone's fine, but I didn't fly across the ocean to shoot the shit with you," Annabelle sighed, exasperated. "You said you needed my help, so here I am. What's going on?"

I took another sip of my coffee and set it down in the saucer. "What do you know about Rifting?" I asked her.

Her eyebrows shot up in surprise. "Uh... a fair bit. Obviously, I was there when you Rifted in the Traveler camp, although I didn't participate myself. And my grandmother used to tell me some pretty fantastical stories about when she and her cousins used to do it."

"Well, I've got a Rifting story, too, and I doubt it's one your grandmother told you," I said. Then I took a deep breath and told her everything—about Savvy and the Geatgrima, about following the clue in the tapestry to the *príosún*, about the Tansy Hag and her cryptic warnings, and finally about what happened to me in the Rift. She did not interrupt me once, but her demeanor grew more and more tense until, when at last I'd told her everything, she might have been carved from stone.

"Annabelle?"

"Just... give me a moment," Annabelle murmured, giving her

head a shake. She picked up her cup of tea, long-cold, and drained it in a single gulp. She stared down into the empty china and sighed. "Damn it, I wish this was something stronger."

I gave a shaky laugh. "Yeah, I probably should have had you meet me at a pub, huh?"

"Who else knows about this? Who else have you told?" Annabelle asked, still staring into the cup as though there might be some tea leaves swirling in the bottom that could help her make sense of the madness she'd just heard.

"Finn, Hannah, and Milo, obviously. Flavia, too—she's at Fairhaven now. I don't know if you heard, but she—"

"Yeah," Annabelle said with a grimace. "I heard. Banishment is the kind of gossip everyone hears about, even the lowly Dormants. You haven't told anyone else? No one in leadership?"

"No."

"Good. That's good," she said, still staring into her cup like a crystal ball. "They'll never believe it, and even if they do, they'll never accept it. To the Durupinen, their gift is absolutely sacred. There will be outright mutiny if you tell them that gift is nothing but a lie."

"You... you actually believe what I just told you?" I asked, incredulous.

Annabelle looked up from her cup for the first time and looked me square in the eye. "Of course I do. You didn't call me all the way to England to lie to me, did you?"

"Well, no, but still..."

"Rifting is a deep part of Traveler tradition, and it is understood that what you discover there is far truer than a dream—a sacred knowledge and understanding that cannot be achieved in any other way. If Agnes Isherwood was able to reach you there—however implausible that sounds—you have to heed her warning. Not to do so would be a betrayal of what the spirit world has trusted you with."

"That's... pretty much what Flavia told me after she got over her shock," I said.

"So, what do you need from me?" Annabelle asked. "How can I possibly help?"

"I have to get into the Traveler camp," I told her. "I need to get an audience with Ileana."

Annabelle's eyebrows pulled together in confusion. "But you've met with her before. Can't you just request an audience?"

"Not likely," I said with a sarcastic smile. "She knows I got Irina out."

Annabelle gasped. "But... how could she possibly..."

"She never figured out how, but she knew that I thought their ruling was bullshit. Finn and I left the camp at the same time Irina went missing. She can put two and two together, even if she can't prove it."

"Does she know that Flavia and I...?"

I shook my head. "No. Like I said, she never figured out how we did it, and since no one knows that you're a Walker, no one has any reason to think you could be somehow involved."

Annabelle's expression cleared, but only for a moment. "So, have you been banished, too?"

"Not exactly," I said. "Without being able to prove I'd committed a crime against the Travelers, she couldn't banish me. And anyway, to banish me would have been to admit that her iron fist had been overruled, and I don't think her pride could take a public blow like that. But she found another way to exact her revenge. She found out that Finn and I were involved with each other, and she told Celeste. That's why Finn was reassigned to the *príosún* last year."

"I... you... *oh!*" Annabelle shook her head. "I had no idea you two were..."

"Yeah, well, apparently you were the only one who didn't," I said with a sardonic smile. "I've been told we were spectacularly shitty at hiding it."

"You're right then, you'll never get over the border by yourself," Annabelle said, biting her lip.

"But you've been back several times, haven't you?" I pressed. "You've got connections there now, right? Family that you've reconnected with? If you came with me, vouched for me..."

Annabelle was already shaking her head. "I'm not sure that will matter. She will have told the Caomhnóir to deny your entrance. You may even be detained if you do somehow manage to get across."

My heart sank. "You don't think they'd let me through with you?"

Annabelle smiled sadly. "Jess, I'm a Dormant. I'm like the distant relative at a family reunion that everyone is polite to, but no one can quite remember how she's even related to the family. They tolerate me because of the blood connection, but I'm not legitimate enough or important enough to get you over that border, let alone into a private audience with the High Priestess. We're going to have to come up with a different plan."

I slumped back in my seat, gazing back out at the rain, which had turned into a downpour. "You *were* my different plan," I admitted with a sigh. "It's starting to feel like the task Agnes set me is impossible."

"That's just about enough of that out of you, Ballard!" Annabelle snapped, evoking, as she did so, a string of memories of our mutual friend David Pierce, who never failed to call me exclusively by my last name, and usually with the same impatient tone and a sprinkling of gratuitous profanity. "I didn't fly all the way over here to watch you give up the moment you hit an obstacle. That's not the Jess I know, and I refuse to accept any other sorry substitute. I want the real thing. I want the fire and the determination and the attitude that convinced me to hate you for the first six months I knew you!"

I blinked, and then looked quickly around to make sure she hadn't attracted too much attention with her sudden outburst. "I... okay," I muttered. "Can you please stop yelling at me now?"

Annabelle narrowed her eyes but deigned to lower her voice. "Look, what I'm saying is, nothing about this situation is logical or rational, and I think the way forward is going to follow suit. Take a page out of Agnes' book. She needed to get this message to you, which should have been completely impossible, and damn it, *she actually did it*. I have a feeling you're also going to have to think outside the box—test the limits of what's possible—in order to carry that message forward."

"But how?" I asked, feeling defeated but trying to keep it out of my voice.

"You'll be able to answer that question by asking yourself another one: why me?" Annabelle said.

I snorted. "Believe me, I ask myself that question about five times a day."

Annabelle rolled her eyes. "Don't you understand what I'm getting at here? Agnes could have opened that second door into any time or any place, I'd bet, making it possible to meet almost anyone.

But she wanted you to be standing on the other side of it. So, you need to ask yourself—what is it about *you*?"

"My winning personality? My edgy misfit fashion sense?"

"Be serious, Jess."

"I *am* being serious. I am the last person who should be trusted with this task. No one's going to listen to me. I can't even get near Ileana without getting myself arrested. The rest of the Northern Clans are inherently suspicious of me because of the Prophecy. Why couldn't Agnes have chosen Flavia? Or Hannah? Or literally *any* other Durupinen, for that matter? It shouldn't be me!"

"But it *is* you! Now, answer the damn question! What is it about you that helped you escape death in that Traveler camp? What was it that allowed you to traverse right through that Geatgrima and into the Aether to prevent the Prophecy from coming to pass? And what was it that allowed both of us to save Irina from a fate worse than death at the hands of the very woman you need to deliver your message to?"

"You... wait, are you talking about Walking?" I asked with a sigh. "Annabelle, I've already thought of that. I can't get over the border in Walker form. Their Castings were set up that way, to make sure that Irina couldn't escape."

"And yet, Irina Walked right out of the Traveler camp, if you'll recall," Annabelle pointed out, a smile slowly blooming on her face.

"She didn't just Walk out," I snapped. "She had to use your body, that was the only way to—"

And just like that, the answer that should have been obvious from the very beginning, the answer hiding behind my panic and exhaustion, finally revealed itself. I did need Annabelle, but not just because she was a Traveler. I needed her because she was a Walker. If Irina could get over the border in Annabelle's body, then so could I.

"Are you really willing to do that?" I whispered.

Annabelle arched one incredulous eyebrow. "I was willing once before, wasn't I?"

"Yes, but... " I licked my lips which had suddenly gone dry, "that was different. You got Irina out of the camp without anyone ever learning that you were a Walker. If you do this, your cover is blown. Ileana will find out what you are. Are you really prepared to let her have that kind of information about you?"

Annabelle shrugged nonchalantly, as though we were discussing whether she wanted to order another cup of tea. "I've spent a long time on the outside looking in at what should be my own flesh and blood. I'm sick of them treating me as a mere Dormant who can be disregarded and cast aside. Let them see what I can do, and damn the consequences."

"Ileana won't let a true Walker slip through her fingers. She'll want you—want to recruit you. To weaponize you," I insisted.

"Let her try," Annabelle said, the fire in her voice matching the fire in her eyes. "I am not her plaything. She could have had my allegiance once, but she turned her nose up at it. Let her come begging for it now."

I felt a smile starting to blossom on my own face. "This is nuts, you know that, right? This plan is absolute madness."

Annabelle raised her cup to me as though in a toast. "My very favorite kind of plan," she said.

§

When I finally left the café an hour later, the knot of tension in my chest had loosened just enough for me to feel like I could take a deep breath for the first time since I'd come out of the Rift. I had a plan—well, I had half a plan, anyway. I had another ally in my corner. I was one step closer to doing what Agnes asked of me, one step closer to finding a way to help Savvy.

It was the weekend, and so the streets of Notting Hill were overflowing with crowds of tourists visiting the famous open market, apparently undeterred by the weather. I skirted the main drag, cutting down some side streets on the way to my flat. Not that it felt much like my flat anymore—we hadn't lived in it for months. But the fact that it had lain vacant for so long had actually proven the perfect cover story for my trip to London. If anyone asked where I was, they were to be told that I was in London, meeting with a realtor about the possibility of listing the place to be sublet for a while. And since I didn't want to risk the chance that any nosy Durupinen might check up on that story, I had actually contacted a realtor and set up an appointment. An appointment for which, I realized as I glanced down at my watch, I was running about five minutes late.

I rounded the last corner and found the man standing on the sidewalk in front of the house, snapping cell phone pictures and jotting some notes down on a legal pad he was carrying in a leather folder. He looked not much older than me, wearing an impeccable burgundy suit, a blue bowtie and a matching pocket square, and standing beneath an enormous plaid umbrella. He looked up when he heard me approaching and broke at once into the kind of smile usually only seen on game show hosts.

"Jessica, I presume? Smashing to meet you. I'm Basil Fenwick, we spoke on the phone?" he said, all the while still smiling in an almost manic way. I took the hand he thrust out toward me and shook it. He had the most perfect fingernails I'd ever seen on a man and he smelled like he'd just gone on a testing spree of men's colognes in a department store.

"Uh, hi, Basil. It's nice to meet you, too," I said. "And thank you for agreeing to meet with me on such short notice."

"Not at all. Delighted, delighted, I assure you," Basil replied with an affected little bow. "Shall we head in, then? This weather is absolutely frightful!"

I smiled. "Sure. Right this way."

"Once more unto the breach, fearless leader!" Basil replied, giving me a salute and stepping dramatically aside for me to pass by him up the steps and swinging the umbrella up over my head to keep me dry as I fumbled around in my purse for my keys.

"I must say, the place looks brilliant from the outside, and from your description, it should get snapped up right away. This neighborhood is quite in demand, you know, and there aren't many flats to let at the moment," Basil prattled on as I finally dug my keys from where they'd buried themselves in the deepest corner of my bag.

"That's good to hear, Basil," I said. "I'd like to get someone in here quickly. I feel bad, just letting it sit empty. It's a great space."

Basil started on a lengthy monologue about "kitchen/diners" and "snugs" and "double aspects" but I had stopped listening. I'd just taken a closer look at the door and knew at once that something was very wrong. The once gleaming brass of the lock hardware was badly scratched up around the keyhole. As I leaned closer to examine it, I also noticed damage to the wood along the edge of the doorframe where the deadbolt was located. My heart began to pump forcefully. I reached out a shaking hand and tried the doorknob. It turned easily and the door swung open. __

Basil, still monologuing enthusiastically like he was hosting House Hunters International, noticed none of this. I paused on the threshold as he crowded up behind me, clicking away with his camera phone and complimenting the moldings. This was one of those moments when what I decided to do could get someone killed. What if there were Necromancers upstairs right now, lurking around in my apartment, tearing it apart for—what? Information about me? Durupinen artifacts I might have left lying around unguarded? I tried to control my breathing. If they were looking for me—hoping to lie in wait and ambush me when I returned to the flat—they surely wouldn't have been so careless leaving obvious signs of their forced entry? No, they were smarter than that. There was, of course, the chance that they were still here. If I surprised them mid-ransacking, there was every possibility that I could put both myself and poor Basil, still blathering behind me, in serious danger. On the other hand, what if Tia had been back to the apartment? What if she was up there now, being held hostage? Or worse, what if they'd...

I was halfway up the stairs before I realized I'd made a decision, ill-advised or not. Somewhere in the back of my mind, I knew how profoundly stupid it was, but I couldn't make myself care. If something had happened to Tia Vezga, I would never forgive myself for the danger I'd put her in just by being her friend.

There was no point in telling Basil to be quiet—he'd been effusing at the top of his lungs since we'd set foot in the entryway, so there was no chance we were actually sneaking up on anyone. I reached the top of the stairs and found the door to the flat hanging crookedly on its hinges, wide open and obviously forced. What I could see of the flat's interior was in absolute shambles—furniture overturned, pillows sliced open, every drawer pulled out and the contents dumped all over the floor.

A sharp intake of breath meant that Basil had arrived on the top step behind me. "Good Lord!" he whispered. "You've been robbed, haven't you!"

"Looks like it," I replied, stepping into the room, listening intently for sounds of the intruders, but it was silent. Beyond the living room and kitchen, the open bedroom doors revealed the same chaos.

"I say, you've got to ring the police!" Basil exclaimed, staring around the place in horror. "I feel obliged to tell you that this will make the place much more difficult to let! I had no idea this neighborhood was prone to break-ins!"

He lifted his phone up as though about to take more photos, but I reached out and lowered his arm. "I don't think these are the kind of photos I want in the listing, so maybe cool it with the photoshoot, okay, Basil?"

I took a few more tentative steps into the living room. I tried to call out for Tia, but it took several attempts before my voice would cooperate. "Tia? Tia, are you here?"

No answer. This did not alleviate my mounting panic.

For the next several minutes, I searched every room, pulling back the shower curtain, lifting the blankets and sheets, opening closet doors. At last, I was forced to conclude, that, wherever Tia was, she definitely wasn't in the apartment.

"What... what are you going to do?" Basil asked, after watching my search of the place while carrying on a steady stream of concerned exclamations under his breath. "I must confess, I don't feel quite right, trying to let the place if this is the sort of—that is to say, I think I'd rather not—"

"You can go, Basil. Thanks for your time," I snapped.

"Right-o, cheers," Basil breathed gratefully and practically ran from the room.

All of a sudden my knees felt like they were going to buckle beneath me, and I quickly sank down onto the tattered sofa. *She's not here because she's not supposed to be here,* I reminded myself. *She hasn't been living here. There's no reason to think anything's wrong.*

But my fingers felt numb as I pulled the phone from my back pocket and clumsily dialed Tia's cell phone number. I held my breath as I waited, my pulse quickening with each ring that went by unanswered.

If she wasn't there... if she didn't answer...

"There you are, stranger!"

I couldn't help it. I burst into hysterical sobs at the very sound of her voice. "Oh, thank you, thank you, thank you, God!" It took nearly a minute for me to calm down enough to start making any sense whatsoever, by which time Tia was starting to get hysterical herself.

"Jess, just tell me where you are and I'll come and g—"

"NO!" I gasped. I took a shuddering breath and mastered myself. "I'm so sorry, I did not mean to lose it like that. I'm just so relieved to hear your voice. I'm so happy you're okay."

"But why wouldn't I be okay?" Tia asked. "Jess, please tell me what's going on, you're really scaring me!"

"I... well, I came back to the apartment to... to get some stuff I left here and I found the door unlocked downstairs, and upstairs the place has been trashed."

"Trashed?" Tia cried, her voice going up about two octaves. "What do you mean, trashed?"

"I mean someone ransacked the place. I don't know if they took anything, or what they were looking for, but it's a total mess in here."

Tia took several deep breaths, and when she spoke again, she was back in a normal register. "Do you think it was them, Jess? Do you think it was the Necromancers?"

I almost lied to her. I almost did it, just to protect her from sharing the fear that was pumping like poison through my veins. But I talked myself out of it. I couldn't do that to her, not after all Charlie had put her through. She deserved the truth.

"Yes," I said. "Yes, I'd stake my life on it."

Tia made a sound halfway between a sob and a squeak. "What should we do?"

"You don't need to do anything except stay away from here," I told her at once. "When's the last time you were here?"

"I haven't been back since I moved over to med school housing," Tia said. "When I came to pack up my stuff, the Trackers were still there doing their investigation about Charlie. That woman Catriona made me turn over everything I had that Charlie had ever used or given me, and asked me a ton of questions. That was the last time I saw it. So that was... what, three months ago now?"

"And when the Trackers were here, I don't suppose they tore the place to shreds in their quest to figure out where Charlie was?" I asked half-heartedly.

"No, of course not," Tia said. "They were being very meticulous—they were even wearing gloves and putting things in plastic bags."

"Okay, then. Well, I'm going to call Catriona and let her know what happened. I need you to promise me that you're going to stay away from the apartment until I tell you it's okay to come back. Is there anything you need from here that I can have sent over to the school for you?"

"Uh…" Tia sounded flustered at being put on the spot in this way. "I… I'm not sure… I… no, I think I have everything I need, honestly. There's not much of my stuff left there, anyway."

"Good. And I… I might have the Caomhnóir or the Trackers assign a security patrol to you," I said. "Not, like, a bodyguard or anything," I added quickly, as Tia began to protest. "Just… just someone to cruise the area around the school."

"I… well, I guess that'll be okay," Tia said, though she still sounded wary.

"I'll find out who they're sending, and text you a photo, so you'll know their face if you see them hanging around, okay?" I added.

"That would be great, thanks," Tia said, sounding relieved. "I didn't want to make myself paranoid if I saw some random guy just lurking around the campus."

"It won't be like that, I promise," I told her.

"Jess… is… I know you can't always tell me everything about Durupinen stuff, but… there's something kind of big going on, isn't there?"

I hesitated only a moment. "Yeah. Yeah, I think there is."

"You have to stay safe, too, okay?" she said, in a tone that was almost scolding.

"Don't worry, I am," I replied.

"Don't you dare patronize me, Jessica Ballard!" Tia snapped, sounding quite suddenly a lot less like my best friend and much more like my mother. "Don't you dare tell me not to worry! Have you met me? I have a post-graduate degree in anxiety! I will never not worry about you. And I am not telling you to 'try' to stay safe, or to 'do your best' to stay safe. I am telling you to STAY SAFE. Do you understand me? I will not be okay if you are not okay. My okayness depends on your okayness, got it?"

"I… I think so?" I said, half-laughing before getting control of myself again. "I promise, Tia."

"Right. That's more like it." She heaved a deep breath, and when she spoke again, she had regained her composure. "So… so in the grand scheme of whatever big thing is going down in the Durupinen world… *are* you okay?"

Was I okay? My entire existence as a Durupinen was based on a lie. One of my best friends was at the center of some cosmic struggle for the soul of the spirit world, and I had no idea if she was going to survive it. I was about to risk my freedom sneaking into a place I was banished from to deliver a message from a centuries dead Seer. And there was a very good chance that, even if I managed to deliver the message, everyone who heard it would think I'd lost my mind.

"Of course I'm fine," I said, repeating the lie I'd heard on more than one occasion from Catriona's lips. "I'm always fine."

WHO WE ARE

———

87

O N THE RIDE HOME from London, I called in to the Tracker office and filed a report about the break-in at our flat, as well as the request for Tia's security detail. I gave all the details to Elin, Catriona's second-in-command, because Catriona wasn't available.

"Well, can you just have her call me back?" I asked. "No offense, but I'd really prefer to speak directly with her."

"She's not reachable at present," Elin snapped, clearly taking offense anyway. "She's gone back to Skye Príosún."

"Skye? Really? When is she going to be back?" I asked.

"Who am I, her mum? I don't know, do I? Do you want to leave a message for her, or not?" Elin grumbled.

After giving her all the details, I hung up with Elin and was preparing to open the connection with Hannah when I thought better of it. She was already so on edge—we all were. I didn't want to unload the news about our ransacked apartment unless I knew she was in a good place, mentally. If I opened the connection, the colors of my mood would flood her at once, and there would be no softening the blow, let alone hiding what happened. No, I would wait to see her in person and use the rest of the drive to figure out how to tell her the truth about what had happened in the least alarming way possible.

When I returned to Fairhaven, however, I couldn't deliver the news to Hannah right away—she was locked up in committee with the rest of the Council, no doubt trying to figure out their next steps in handling the Geatgrima situation. The tension within the castle was palpable. Classes continued, but with a strange, hushed air, as though the Apprentices felt they weren't supposed to be studying at all while a fellow Durupinen was locked in a struggle with the Geatgrima right outside their windows. The Caomhnóir all looked worn out—everyone was pulling longer shifts, and the duties were more onerous. Even the spirits that generally haunted Fairhaven were rarely to be seen within the castle walls. Though it seemed none of them could explain what was happening outside, they were nonetheless drawn to it, and there was a constant ghostly audience hovering over the courtyard like low-hanging cloud cover. One particular member of that spirit cloud detached himself immediately upon realizing I had returned to the castle, and despite the solemn, quiet atmosphere of the castle, his response to my news from London was loud and dramatic enough to require frantic shushing.

"Sorry, I'm sorry!" he hissed, lowering his voice. "But this is crazy, Jess! Necromancers breaking into our apartment and ransacking the place?"

"Well, to be fair, the Trackers haven't investigated yet. Maybe it wasn't the Necromancers at all," I suggested weakly.

"Oh, please, Jess, who the hell do you think you're talking to here?!" Milo scoffed. "Of course it was the Necromancers! The real question, though, is what they were looking for."

"Or who," I pointed out.

Milo shook his head. "I don't think so. If you break into an apartment looking for someone, and they're not there, you don't hang around to trash the place for no reason. You said all the drawers were turned out and all the furniture torn apart, right?"

"Yeah."

"So, that means they were looking for some*thing*, not some*one*," Milo said, crossing his arms and giving a smug look of satisfaction that would have looked at home on Sherlock Holmes' face when he'd cracked his case. "What do you think it was?"

I sank down onto the garden bench, waiting for a spirit to drift by and out of earshot before I replied. "I'm not sure. The problem is, we don't know how much they know."

Milo dropped his smirk and frowned. "What do you mean?"

"Well," I said slowly, trying to lay it all out as much for myself as for Milo, "we know that the Necromancers got some information from the Tansy Hag. She told them something—enough that they know our gift is 'stolen,' because that's what the Necromancer said when he attacked Lucida and carved the mark of the Tansy Hag into her back. But how much did she explain to them, that's the question."

"They knew that Lucida had to be stopped from telling the Council about the mark," Milo <u>said</u>, pulling on a lock of his hair thoughtfully. "That must be why Ambrose followed her to Fairhaven and staged that attack. They didn't want anyone at Fairhaven to find out what they knew."

"And now, somehow, they must realize I'm caught up in it. But how? How could they possibly know that? No one knows I spoke to the Tansy Hag. And no one knows what happened in the Rift except for the people in the room when I woke up—well, and Annabelle, but they'd already broken into the flat by the time I met with her."

"Are you sure no one at the *príosún* knew that you saw the Tansy Hag? That *príosún* is full of people. Isn't there a chance someone saw you?" Milo asked.

"Well," I said slowly. "I had to ask for directions to that spirit cellblock from a Caomhnóir. But I never told him why."

"What about down in the cellblock itself?" Milo pressed.

I shook my head. "There were no guards down there. Only a few other spirits, and not a single one of them was in their right mind."

"What about any other prisoners? Weren't there other Necromancers who had been put back in custody there?" Milo asked.

"Well, yeah, but I didn't actually come into contact with any of them," I said, starting to feel uneasy.

"But there were Necromancers there in the *príosún* when you met the Tansy Hag?"

"Yes."

Milo and I looked at each other, a deep sense of dread blossoming between us. Was it possible, somehow, that word of my meeting with the Tansy Hag had reached Necromancer ears? Did they know that I knew the truth about the Gateways? And exactly how much of the truth did the Necromancers know? This web was getting more tangled, and I was starting to feel like a fly who was stuck in it, just waiting for the spider to show up.

And speaking of vermin...

"Well, now, who have we got here?"

I looked up to see Marion strolling up the garden path with, of all people, Siobhán who, I noticed, immediately dropped her eyes to the ground in apparent embarrassment at being seen in such company. Marion came to a stop, arms crossed, looking positively delighted at the chance meeting. Beside me, Milo was already vibrating with rage, the anger rolling off him in chilly waves.

"Jessica. It's been ages," Marion said with a conniving smirk.

"Not long enough," I replied, standing up and slinging my bag back over my shoulder.

"I'd ask you if you've been keeping out of trouble, but of course, we all know that's not the case. I've heard tales of your exploits while I've been away. You keep quite busy, don't you?"

"Too busy to waste my time listening to anything you might possibly have to say," I said, returning her smile before turning to glare at Siobhán. "Funny, I'd have thought the same of you, Siobhán, but I guess I was wrong about that."

Siobhán looked as though she would have liked to contradict me, but what could she say, with Marion standing right there?

"There's no need to be so hostile," Marion replied, feigning surprise at my less-than-friendly tone. "Siobhán and I served for many years on the Council together, after all. Is it so odd that we would want to catch up?"

I snorted. "Do you think you're crafty? Sly? Do you honestly think there's a single person on these grounds who doesn't know that you're up to something?"

"The proverbial cat strutting around with canary feathers all over her poorly contoured face," Milo added bitingly.

Marion's smooth expression cracked. "Listen to me, you—"

"No, *you* listen to *me*," I said taking a sudden step toward her so that she actually jumped back in alarm, "because you are obviously mistaking me for someone who gives a fuck what you've got to say, and I'd hate for you to keep harboring that delusion. I don't know what you're doing here and I don't care. I don't have the energy or the time to waste on you and whatever petty bullshit you're cooking up. We all know you're drawn to confusion and chaos like an opportunistic moth to the flame, but when the smoke clears, you will still be what you always were: a liar, a traitor, and a grasping, conniving thief. I just hope everyone else around here remembers it."

I shot one last accusatory look at Siobhán, and stalked back toward the castle, Milo hooting and snapping his fingers in my wake.

"Oh, sweetness, I am slain. SLAIN!" he cried, cackling madly. "The look on her face! It was a thing of beauty. I wish I had a picture of it so I could carry it around in front of my eyes and look at nothing else for the rest of my afterlife."

"It was stupid," I muttered. "I let my temper get the better of me, and now she's one more thing I'm going to have to worry about."

"It wasn't stupid, it was brilliant," Milo insisted. "And not just because it was satisfying to watch. Like, I kept reaching for my popcorn. But seriously, Jess, I think someone needed to call her on her bullshit, to make sure she knows that she's not fooling anyone."

"I hope that's true," I said. "And what the hell is Siobhán doing walking around with her? She's supposed to be Celeste's second-in-command."

"Second-in-command doesn't mean they always agree with each other," Milo said.

"Yeah, but it should mean that she would never betray her, and listening to anything Marion has to say feels like a betrayal to me."

"Maybe it's not as bad as you think."

"Maybe it's *exactly* as bad as I think."

"Well, like you said, you don't really have time to worry about it, do you?" Milo said. "Let Celeste and the others manage Marion. Let's focus on Savvy and what Agnes told you to do, okay? Now, tell me what happened when you met with Annabelle. What's the plan? Do you think she can help you get back into the Traveler camp?"

I gave him a wry smile. "You might want to find that popcorn again."

§

The plan was universally acknowledged to be batshit crazy, and yet, no one could come up with an alternative, though Finn quite liked Kiernan's suggestion of gathering a rogue band of Caomhnóir and simply invading the Traveler camp by force.

"What?" he demanded when I gave him a withering look.

"You think starting a war is less dangerous than Annabelle's plan?"

"Less dangerous for *you*," he grumbled. I promptly ignored all the rest of his opinions on the matter.

Flavia, whom I expected to poke a million holes in the plan with her intimate knowledge of the camp, actually seemed rather impressed. "I agree it's completely mad," she said, throwing an anxious glance at Finn, "but I also think it may just work. I can't think of a single Casting or defense that would prevent you."

"Castings aren't the only things that could keep Jess from talking to Ileana," Hannah said. "So many other things could go wrong once she gets inside."

"Yes, but none of those other factors can be predicted," Flavia pointed out. "Happenstance is happenstance, whether Jess sneaks in alone or whether a battalion storms the borders."

"We can't control everything," I said over everyone's continued protests. "We just have to plan the best we can and hope luck is on our side."

Finn settled into disgruntled submission, but Hannah couldn't let it go. She spent the next few days of preparation trying almost constantly to convince me, in one way or another, to abandon the plan. I found myself actually avoiding her, hiding away up in Fiona's tower, helping her restore Agnes' tapestry while I waited for word from Annabelle that she had obtained permission from the Traveler Council to visit the camp. When that word finally arrived three days later, and I was packing to leave, Hannah had still not let up.

"This is nuts," Hannah announced.

"I think that fact has been pretty well established by literally everyone," I said, rummaging in my top drawer for two matching socks.

"But somehow it didn't dissuade you at all?" Hannah asked, her voice rather tart.

"Oh, come on, Hannah, you know Jess only does things the hard way," Milo joked. "It's kind of her M.O." Hannah gave him a furious look and he fell silent.

"What choice do we have, Hannah?" I asked with a weary sigh, settling on two socks that nearly matched and sitting down to pull them onto my bare feet. "It's the only way in. It's kind of... well, crazy, but it will work. It's got to."

"And what if you actually manage it—what if you get yourself across the border in Annabelle's body and into Ileana's tent? What if you tell her exactly what Agnes told you to say and she has no idea what you're talking about? Or worse, what if she does, but she doesn't believe it?"

I did not reply right away, choosing instead to make rather a performance of ensuring the seam across the toe of my sock was straight before answering. She was voicing the very concerns that had curled up into lumps in my throat, choking me every time I thought about them.

"It doesn't matter."

"What?!"

"You heard me."

"Jess, how can you say that?"

"Because it's true! It doesn't matter. I still have to go. I still have to tell her. I don't know what she'll say, or what she'll do, but that doesn't change anything, Hannah!"

"Or it could change *everything*!" Hannah burst out, tears springing into her eyes.

The sudden onslaught of tears caught me off guard, and I faltered. "Hannah, what... why are you crying?"

"Never mind," Hannah sniffed, turning from me so that she could wipe the tears angrily from her face. She flicked them away off the tips of her fingers, as though they had betrayed her. "If you don't already know, I'm not sure that I could even explain it to you."

"What the hell is that supposed to mean?" I asked, defensiveness rearing up in me. "Why wouldn't I understand?"

"You just won't."

"Try me."

Hannah took a deep breath, and when she looked at me, her expression was wary. "You and I have never felt the same about being a Durupinen. For you, becoming a Durupinen was something that happened to you. It dropped down like a bomb on you out of nowhere. It took the world you knew and turned it into something unrecognizable and scary. You had to find a way to make room for it—to accommodate it, and you've always resented that. You probably still do."

I shrugged defensively, feeling suddenly attacked. "I... well, yeah, but you don't have to make it sound so..."

"I'm not judging you, Jess. *Anyone* would feel that way, if that's how their gift came to them. But for me, it was the complete opposite. My connection to spirits was there from my earliest memories. It was an inherent part of me—of my world. I clung to it because it was the only constant, even if it was a constant that isolated me from others. It was the biggest unanswered question in my life, and when the Durupinen came along to explain it at last, it was the single greatest moment of my life because finally—*finally*—I understood who I was. And not only that, but who I was wasn't something to be ashamed of or hidden or managed with medication. It was important. It was wonderful. The Durupinen walking into your life meant you lost yourself. But when they walked into mine, I was found."

I sat stunned into silence. I'd never, not once since I'd met her, stopped to consider how completely opposite Hannah's view of the Durupinen must be, at its heart. I mean, I'd always known her life had been terribly different from mine, that spirits had essentially made her life as a ward of the state a veritable hell, but I'd never translated that any further—never realized that it was this, perhaps, that made it so much easier for her to put her trust in Lucida when Lucida was trying to manipulate her. From my perspective, the Durupinen had hijacked my life. From Hannah's, they had rescued her from hers.

"So, you see, Jess? You have to understand that you're charging off hellbent on destroying the one thing that's ever made my life make sense—the one thing that helped me to come to terms and understand who I am."

"I'm not hellbent on destroying anything!" I cried, stung. "I'm trying to save something!"

"But I'm the collateral damage!" Hannah cried, sounding quite hysterical now. "Being a Durupinen is who I am! It's who all of us are! And if you do this—if our gift gets taken away, then who am I? WHO AM I, JESS?!"

Her voice rose to a shriek and she burst into wildly hysterical sobs. Milo and I stared at each other, stunned. Then, before I knew what was happening, because I could not bear to hear those sounds coming out of my sister, I was across the room with my arms wrapped around her, stroking her hair and murmuring her name over and over again. Milo followed, enfolding both of us in the cool comfort of his embrace.

"I'm so sorry. Hannah, I'm so sorry. Ssshh, please stop crying. I'm sorry, I'm sorry, I'm sorry," I repeated into the thick, dark waves of her hair. "Forgive me, Hannah, I had no idea."

We sat there, the three of us, rocking together like a boat in the storm of her grief. She was mourning, I realized. Mourning for this part of her identity that was so central to accepting her own worth. I realized that, at some level, all of us would have to reckon with the missing piece, even those of us who had never wanted it to begin with. Gradually, the tempest blew itself out.

"I'm sorry," she muttered like an echo after the last of the hitched breaths and sniffs died away.

"Hannah, don't apologize, please…"

"No, I wasn't honest with you. I should have told you about these feelings when I first started having them, but I was ashamed of them, ashamed of myself."

"What do you have to be ashamed of?" I asked.

"Because this is selfish. I'm selfish."

"Excuse me, but I got all the selfish genes in this family," I told her with a shake of my head. "You're like, the least selfish person I know!"

"What could be more selfish than wanting to keep a gift that isn't even mine, even if keeping it could mean the complete destruction of the links between our world and the spirit world? Why aren't I thinking of Savvy and what's happening to her? Why aren't I thinking of all the spirits that could get trapped here forever? Why can I only seem to think about myself and what I'm going to lose?" Hannah asked, and though she didn't seem to expect a reply, I gave her one anyway.

"You aren't selfish. You've helped so many spirits. You've used your powers for good."

"Sometimes," she said softly. "I *sometimes* used them for good."

"You *ultimately* used them for good," I corrected her. "One misstep doesn't erase all the good you've done. Our mistakes help shape us, but they don't define us, Hannah. If they did, I'd just be a walking mistake with a big mouth and over-processed hair."

Hannah made a soft sound that might have been a chuckle, but it was hard to tell.

"Anyway, it's not selfish to want to keep helping others, or to keep being the person you've become, especially after you fought so hard to find her," I said. "It took me a long time to accept what I am, and even longer to be any good at it, but even I don't like the idea of giving it up."

Hannah looked me in the eye for the first time since breaking down. "You don't have to say that just to make me sound less awful."

"I'm not just saying that!" I insisted. "It's true. I'm not happy about any of this. I don't want to destroy this entire system—well, okay, I want to destroy large swaths of it, obviously, because I get fed up with the bullshit of regulations or social etiquette or who's allowed to do what job. But at its heart—at its core—I've always believed in what we do. I've never wanted to stop doing Crossings or helping spirits who are lost and confused. That part's always been easy—and sometimes even wonderful."

"What if it all just vanishes?" Hannah whispered, speaking aloud the real question at the heart of her terror. "What if we do what Agnes wants us to do, and restore the Gateways to the Geatgrimas and then we're just... empty? What if we have no purpose?"

"But we did have a purpose, even before we took the Gateways into our bloodlines," I told her. "Don't you remember what Agnes told me? The Durupinen already existed as a sisterhood. We could see and communicate with spirits. It was our role to guide them to the Gateways, and to watch over the Geatgrimas. We were already sensitive."

"But what if we lose that, somehow? What if we restore the Gateways, and suddenly we can't see spirits anymore? What if... what if I lose you, Milo?"

Milo's face twitched as he fought to bring something huge and awful under control. After what seemed like a Herculean effort, miraculously, he managed a smile. "Sweetness, you need to understand something. There is nothing in this world or the next that can take me from you. Not in life, not in the afterlife, not ever."

"But how do you *know?*" Hannah whispered desperately.

"Because I just do. We are Bound. I understand it and feel it in ways you can't imagine because your body gets in the way, but you just have to trust me on this. This," and he gestured to the space between them, to the invisible connection of the Binding, "doesn't bend. It doesn't break. It only deepens. When two souls are linked like us, let the universe do its worst, sweetness. We got this. You and me."

Hannah gave him a watery smile before bursting back into tears. I let Milo comfort her now, extricating myself gently from Hannah's embrace and sliding away across the couch before laying my head back and closing my eyes.

She was right of course. She always was. I was charging ahead with this mission recklessly, as was my general approach to life, and I hadn't really stopped to think about what the fallout might be—not really. And there was probably a reason for that. If I stopped for too long, thought too much, considered too much, then I'd probably talk myself out of it. It was as though Agnes had handed me a lantern and pushed me out onto one of those foggy moors that roll through the English countryside. I could only see a few feet in front of me, could only take a few steps at a time. She set me on the path, but now I had to trust that the rest of the journey would become clear as I went, that I would know what to do when I came to a fork or, perhaps, even lost the path altogether. That lantern would not allow me to see the final destination—only the next step that would lead me there. I had to trust—in myself, in Agnes, and maybe even in a greater reason that I'd never been confident had existed at all.

The more I thought about it, lying there next to Hannah, the more I wished I could just go back to plunging recklessly through things.

At last Hannah unburied herself from Milo's shivery comfort and turned to me again. I was relieved to see that some of the animal panic had left her eyes, and when she smiled, her face fell easily into the familiar lines of the expression.

"Okay," she said, with a deep breath. "I'm... I'm okay now. I won't freak out on you again, I promise. I just... I guess I just needed to get that out."

"I'm glad you told me," I said. "It's important for us to be on the same page. I can't do any of this without you."

"You won't have to," she said, reaching out to squeeze my hand. "I trust you, and I'm with you."

"Me too," Milo said.

"Well then, I guess I'd better get going," I said, hoping my smile looked more confident than it felt. "I'll hop into the connection when we get there, and I'll stay in touch as long as I can. Once I'm Walking, though, all bets are off."

"I would still feel better if Milo went with you," Hannah said, biting her lip. "Then he could stay in touch with me so I know what's happening."

"We've already talked about this," Milo told her in a soothing voice. "I can't go—it's too risky. The Travelers already know me, and they know who I'm Bound to. Seeing me will just alert them to the fact that something's up."

Hannah pouted. "I know. Just being selfish again."

"For the last time, you are not selfish," I yelled. "And I will let you know what's going on the second I reconnect with my body, okay?"

"Yeah, okay," she muttered. "Just, please, be careful, okay?"

"Always," I said as I stood up and slung my backpack onto my shoulder.

BODY SWAP

I'D ONLY MADE IT TO THE END of the corridor before Milo caught up with me.

"Mind if I walk you down?" he asked.

"Not at all," I said, "although I kind of figured Hannah might need a bit more time snuggled up to her best little coping mechanism."

"She decided to go down and have lunch with Kiernan instead," Milo said. "He just sent her a text that he's between shifts."

I raised my eyebrows. "So, something seems to be happening there, doesn't it?" I said.

Milo nodded with a little smirk. "It's healthy for her to have a pair of live arms to run to when she's upset."

"And you're okay with that?" I asked, eyeing him shrewdly.

He looked up, surprise all over his face. "Of course I am! Hey, I know what this is. I have no interest in holding her back from human experiences just because I'm not going to get to experience them myself. Seeing her happy makes me happy. Always has. I don't care if I'm the one making her happy."

"That's sweet Milo, but it's got the potential to leave you waiting in the wings an awful lot," I said softly.

He snorted. "Honey, please. Milo finds his light regardless of the stage. I'll be just fine, don't you worry about that. Anyway, thanks to Milo's Closet, I've got more attention than even I can handle."

It was my turn to snort. "Please. We all know that level of attention does not exist."

Milo chuckled, then changed the subject. "How is Finn coping with all of this?" He gestured to the bag slung over my shoulder, and I knew he was referring to my journey to the Traveler camp.

"He's nervous. He really wanted to send a Caomhnóir with me, but I talked him out of it. It would have been way too much of a giveaway, seeing a Northern Clan Caomhnóir assigned to protect a Traveler Dormant. Ileana would have been tipped off at once that something wasn't right. Besides, he can't reassign a Caomhnóir to me now, not with the Caomhnóir leadership on high alert and the

Council in a panic over Savvy and the Geatgrima. The last thing we want to do is draw attention to a trip I'm probably not even supposed to be taking."

"Do you think you're going to get in trouble once they find out where you've gone?" Milo asked.

I turned a sardonic smile on him. "Does it matter?"

He smiled back. "I guess not. We're all in trouble if you don't go."

"Hey, listen, thank you for talking Hannah down back there," I said.

Milo shrugged. "It's what I do."

"I know, but sometimes it's got to be harder than others," I said gently, trying to catch his eye. "Especially when you're freaking out a little yourself."

Milo looked up and smiled sadly. "Was it that obvious?"

"Not to her," I said. "She was too distraught."

Milo nodded. "That's good. I really didn't want her to know."

"You're allowed to be scared too, Milo," I told him. "It's not only Durupinen lives that are going to change around here."

Milo's whole form trembled. "If I lost her, Jess…"

"I know."

He looked up at me, his eyes asking for a promise I couldn't make. Then he looked away again. "I don't want to lose you either," he said in barely more than a whisper.

It was my turn to swallow back my fear, to push it deep down and hold myself together just long enough to get out those two words he and I both needed to be true.

"You won't. As a wise Spirit Guide once said about five minutes ago, you just have to trust me on this."

§

Down on the grounds, Finn met us by the border behind the barracks. His face was so rigid with stress that he looked like he'd been carved of stone.

"I've altered the Casting by your exit point so no one will be alerted to your leaving, but it's just a temporary interference that will wear off soon, so you'd best head along quickly."

"Wow. I guess being part of the Caomhnóir leadership does have its perks," I said, turning to Milo with a grin. "Remember all those times we had to get cozy just to get over the border?"

"Vividly," Milo replied.

"Is everyone briefed on the cover story?" Finn asked, clearly plowing on with his mental checklist.

"Yes," I assured him. "Flavia, Kiernan, and Hannah all know that if anyone asks for me, I've gone to London to meet with another potential sublet for our flat in Notting Hill."

"Have you heard from Annabelle?" Finn asked.

"Yes, she texted me. She's already arrived. She'll be waiting for me at the turnoff to the private road," I told him.

"You'll keep me posted?" he nearly barked.

"Of course," I said, ignoring his curt tone, which I knew had nothing to do with me and everything to do with all of the protective impulses he was repressing. I took a step forward, raised myself onto my tiptoes, and planted a long, tender kiss on his lips. I felt his entire body shudder, and then relax. "I will protect myself the way you would want me to. And I will be back just as soon as I can."

"That's all I ask," he whispered, running a long finger along the curve of my jaw.

"Piece of cake," I replied, pecking him on the lips once more before turning and heading down the slope.

I tossed my backpack over the top of the low stone wall and then climbed awkwardly over it. As I did so, I felt a shiver of energy pass over me, like a breeze, but charged, and I knew that I was now over the boundary line of the grounds and beyond the reach of the Castings. I expelled a breath I didn't realize I'd been holding, scooped up my bag, and set off. I jogged along the curve of the dirt road to where it disappeared around the corner of a hedgerow. I rounded the bend and found Annabelle's car pulled over on the shoulder of the road, half in the grass, the engine running. She stood in the road beside it, pacing and fidgeting anxiously with the collection of bangles on her wrists.

"Annabelle!" I called.

She jumped, startled, pressing a hand to her heart. "Jess. Thank God. I was starting to worry."

I glanced at my watch. "I'm only five minutes late."

Annabelle scoffed. "Five minutes is a lifetime on a dirt road by yourself."

"Sorry to keep you waiting," I said, but she was already waving away my apology and gesturing <u>for</u> me to get in the car. I obliged as quickly as I could, and we set off down the road, the tiny rental car bumping and groaning with every pothole and rut.

Annabelle didn't speak until we reached the motorway—it was as though she thought someone would somehow catch us making our getaway if we dared utter a sound inside our own car. She checked the rearview and sideview mirrors obsessively, clearly convinced a pursuing vehicle would be revealed at any moment.

"No one's going to follow us, Annabelle," I tried to reassure her. "I'm not technically breaking any rules here. I'm at perfect liberty to leave the grounds whenever I want. I'd just rather not call unnecessary attention to it, that's all."

Annabelle scoffed again. "Not breaking any rules *yet*," she corrected me. "In a few hours' time we'll be breaking nearly every Traveler rule currently in existence and maybe even spur the creation of some new ones."

"Fair point," I said with a sigh. "Well, the Travelers already think I'm a manipulative traitor, so I may as well play the part fully, right?"

"Go big or go home," Annabelle agreed. "We've got a long drive ahead of us, so let's review the plan. I have no interest in winging any of this operation."

Entrance into the camp could only be made by formal request. Any unannounced arrivals at the boundary of the camp would be treated with suspicion and additional scrutiny, and that was the last thing we needed. Annabelle had sent her formal request to visit under the guise of passing along some of her grandmother's old letters and photographs to her relatives in the camp. The request was approved by the Traveler Council without incident, and the arrangements were made that Annabelle would meet a Traveler Caomhnóir on the northern boundary of the camp to be escorted within grounds. To maintain secrecy and protect their camp, the Travelers insisted that visitors arrive under cover of darkness when possible. Annabelle readily agreed to this stipulation—the darker it was, the harder it would be for any of the Travelers to spot anything odd about Annabelle's appearance or demeanor—or rather, my appearance and demeanor, since I would be the one occupying Annabelle's body and attempting to impersonate her.

Over the past two weeks, I had diligently studied and memorized the pages and pages of information Annabelle deemed important for me to know if I was to escape detection. I learned the names and appearances of a dozen of her relatives from a set of flashcards she made for me, including photographs, names, and how each person was related to everyone else. I practiced a list of basic Romany phrases until I could pronounce them perfectly. Annabelle taught me how to fluidly slip them into conversations so that I would appear comfortable switching back and forth between the languages. She drilled me on proper etiquette—how to show deference to Council members, the appropriate ways to greet people and show affection. She drew me a map, which I committed to memory, that showed the layout of the camp, including the wagon where she typically stayed, as well as which wagons belonged to her Traveler family members.

"But what's the point of memorizing this if things have been moved around since the last relocation?" I asked her.

"Then it's all the better for you to have this information. If you expect things to be in the previous location, your confusion only reinforces the idea that you're me and that you've been there before," Annabelle insisted.

By the time we had reached the turnoff that would lead us to the edge of the wood where the Traveler camp was ensconced, we had reviewed ad nauseam every single scenario we could conceive of that might occur before I had a chance to see Ileana, and how I might navigate it. All of this was really just to distract us from the fact that we had absolutely no control over what happened once I entered the camp, and that we had no way to predict what other people might do or say. In other words, we were staving off the panic with distraction—but no amount of distraction could keep us calm as we killed the engine, stepped out of the car, and concealed ourselves behind a nearby clump of bushes.

"This is it, then," I said. "Are you ready?"

Annabelle gave me a smile, though it twitched nervously at the corners. "Our chances won't get any better. Let's do it."

I pulled two Soul Catchers from my pocket and we took turns tying them onto each others' wrists. Flavia had made them for me, desperate for some way to help, given that she couldn't get me into the camp. She had done some research and imbued them with a secondary, somewhat experimental Casting that was meant to ease the disorientation that resulted <u>from</u> inhabiting an unfamiliar body.

Annabelle and I settled ourselves down in the grass side by side and pulled out the Swiss Army knives Finn had procured for me from the Caomhnóir barracks. Annabelle turned her face toward me, nestled in her magnificent nest of auburn hair. She nodded, her face set and determined.

"Together," she whispered.

A moment before, I wasn't sure I'd be able to coax the words of the Casting from my lips, but knowing that another person was about to slip the same physical bonds and occupy the same spiritual space eased my nerves. Our voices in perfect synchronicity, we recited the Casting that would allow us to leave our bodies behind us:

> *"Sínim uaim thar dhorasmo choirp*
> *Ach an eochair coinním fós,*
> *Bheith ag Siúl tráth i measc na marbh*
> *Agus filleadh ansin athuair."*[1]

Instant, unparalleled freedom. I felt myself soar away, leaving every physical impulse far below me in the grass. It took me a few moments to adjust how I related to the world—how to see without eyes, to hear without ears, to feel without physical sensation; but when I did, I heard a whoop of joy and saw Annabelle sailing through the air beside me, her Walker form iridescent as a rainbow reflection on rippling water.

"Be careful," I warned her, even as I fought the impulse to whoop myself. "We don't want anyone to hear us."

"Right," Annabelle replied, still breathless and giddy. "It's just... I almost forgot what this feels like. I think I was too nervous last time to really appreciate it."

"I think that's part of what protects us," I said, allowing myself a low swoop through the air, but being careful to keep myself below the canopy of leaves above us. "The fact that we can forget. Irina couldn't stop obsessing about this feeling, and it's what ultimately destroyed her."

Annabelle's smile slipped, and she floated to a stop. "Yeah, good point. Don't want to enjoy it too much," she whispered to herself in admonishment.

---

1. I reach beyond my body's door and yet retain the key, to Walk awhile amongst the dead and then return again.

Together we drifted down toward the bodies we'd left in the grass. They looked strange, the way bodies in caskets look more like objects than real people. Our faces were utterly still, though they still bore the expressions of stress and anxiety they'd borne when we'd inhabited them. I knew that within that body, a heart was still beating rapidly, muscles were balled up with tension, a brain was waiting to torture itself with vague intangibles. It was not a pleasant thought, subjecting myself to that environment again just moments after freeing myself from it, but there was no time to indulge my preferences, not when so much hung in the balance.

"Are you ready for re-entry?" I joked weakly.

Annabelle's face was stricken with the same reluctance I was feeling, but she quickly composed herself. "Yes," she said, and then she smirked. "I'll let you take her for a spin but take good care of her."

I grinned back. "Ditto."

I looked down at Annabelle's motionless body and visualized myself inside it. The moment I did so, I was drawn irresistibly toward it, my consciousness instantly manifesting my visualized movement. I braced myself for impact.

The sensation was utterly bizarre, an uncomfortable combination of dizziness and the feeling of a foot being squeezed into a too-small shoe. Everything about it felt wrong—the mental space felt sticky, like my thoughts were swimming in honey. The physical space felt hostile, immediately on the verge of rejecting me. I was a parasite—an intruder who had taken this body hostage.

This feeling, powerful in its initial impact, lessened as I calmed myself. I visualized my consciousness flowing through Annabelle's body like water, filling it up, until I could feel no space between her and me. At the same time, I imagined a million different points of connection within her that I could attach myself to, like the strings on a puppet, but much shorter, much more tightly controlled. It was after I had established those connections that I finally managed to connect my mental impulse to a physical response. I opened Annabelle's eyes.

It took several seconds for my vision to clear, for the blurriness to recede. When at last it did, I found myself staring up into my own face. I shrieked in surprise.

"Sssshhhh!" I hissed. Or rather, Annabelle hissed through my lips.

"Sorry," I muttered, "But you scared the hell out of me, standing over me like that." The words struggled slowly forth, slurred and difficult to manipulate, like my mouth was full of marbles.

Annabelle chuckled. "You sound drunk."

I frowned. "This is hard, okay? Your body doesn't want to cooperate. Not that I'm surprised." I glared at her—or rather, I tried to. I couldn't tell if the facial muscles were obeying me or not. "You sound almost normal. Why is it so much easier for you?"

Annabelle shrugged. "I'm not sure. Some of us are just naturally talented, I guess." However, even as she said it, she wobbled and fell over into the grass. I snorted. She managed to successfully stick my own tongue out at me.

"This is so freaky," I said, watching her struggle a bit to get to her feet. "Seeing pictures and videos of yourself—even seeing yourself in the mirror—does not prepare you for seeing yourself like this—standing right in front of you."

"Tell me about it," Annabelle said, staring back at me with a slight shake of her head. "My God, I really must find a new anti-wrinkle cream. Obviously the one I'm using is complete crap."

I grunted and groaned as I moved awkwardly first into a sitting position and then, staggering, to my feet. I felt like the earth was moving beneath me, like I was a seal trying to balance on a ball. It took several minutes of lurching around like a baby taking their first steps before I'd managed to get the hang of it.

"Clearly, we should have practiced this ahead of time," I said, managing to walk a nearly straight line between two trees, then gripping one of them for support as I attempted to turn around.

"No time for that now," Annabelle said, watching me with a critical eye. "You keep leaning to the right for some reason. Concentrate on keeping the left side in line with the right."

I spent several minutes doing just that, focusing my energy on balancing the tug on those hundreds of points of connection between my spirit and Annabelle's body, until the movements became more fluid, more natural.

"That will have to be good enough," Annabelle said, looking down and checking my watch. "We've got to walk nearly a third of a mile around this grove to meet the Caomhnóir who's escorting you in. You can practice a bit more on the way."

"Are you coming with me?" I asked, hearing my panic clearly even through Annabelle's naturally honeyed tones.

"Part of the way, yes, but I can't very well let myself be spotted near the border—the whole point of this plan is to keep you hidden," Annabelle replied. It was bizarre, listening to my own voice try to reason with me. "But I'll be close by, and you can always reach me by text."

"If I manage to find a signal," I pointed out. "Okay, well, I'm officially just stalling for time now, so let's get moving," I said. "The sooner I get in there, the sooner I can get out, right?"

"In theory, yes," Annabelle muttered.

We set off along the western side of the road, keeping the Travelers' grove in view on the eastern side, but taking care to stay out of sight. At last, we reached the spot where Annabelle had arranged to meet the Caomhnóir.

"Perfect," Annabelle whispered. "Right on time." She reached out and squeezed my shoulder. "Good luck. Don't invite conversation. Keep your answers short. Try to stick to the topics we talked about. When in doubt, revert to what you know about me—talk about my shop back home, the ghost hunting team, any subject you feel comfortable with that doesn't require you to make shit up on the spot. Beg off as soon as you can with a headache and find your way to Ileana's tent. After that, just use your head."

"You mean your head," I replied with a weak chuckle. Annabelle managed half a smile in response.

"It's going to be okay," she told me. "Agnes Isherwood knew what she was doing."

"I'm glad one of us does," I said. I reached out, gave my own hand a squeeze, and felt the thrill of connection. Then, reluctantly, I pulled away from her and turned this strange new vehicle toward the road, wanting to look back, but focusing instead on moving smoothly forward, putting one unfamiliar foot in front of the other.

By the time I reached the far side of the street, a lone figure had appeared in the shadows that crowded the edge of the Traveler grove. He kept himself so well hidden, so still, that if I had not been looking for him, I could surely have passed within a few feet of him and never noticed he was there. As he stepped out into the fading twilight, I realized that I knew him.

"Fennix!" I cried in surprise.

Fennix narrowed his eyes at me and nodded. He was one of Flavia's friends—I had met him the last time I'd been to the Traveler camp. He had been part of the rowdy young crew who'd convinced me to Rift for the first time. Of course, for them, it had all been a lark—just something to do when the boredom of the encampment began to drive them mad. For me, of course, it had altered the course of my life, allowing me to find the only way to save Irina, but also leading to my long and torturous separation from Finn. Fennix looked much the same as the last time I'd seen him—barrel-chested, with a wide-featured, pockmarked face and thick black hair barely restrained in a bun on the back of his head. But he looked different, too—older, more serious. Based on the fact that he was meeting me on his own, he must have passed his Caomhnóir training at last.

"That's right," he said. "Have we met?"

I froze for a moment, horrified by my error. For God's sake, had I already blown my cover with the first damn word I uttered? I dug quickly through my knowledge of Annabelle's family tree. "Um, Mina pointed you out to me. She's my second cousin on my grandmother's side."

Fennix's suspicious expression cleared at once, replaced by a flush of embarrassment. "Oh, right. She... uh... she told you about me, huh?"

I suppressed a smirk. Mina and Fennix had been very friendly around the fire when I'd last hung out with them. Apparently, I now had some kind of gossip leverage over the Caomhnóir escorting me into the camp. Score one for Jess.

"Oh, yes," I said, deciding to keep it vague. "You know how she likes to talk. Anyway, thank you for meeting me."

Fennix shrugged, looking moody. "I was assigned. I didn't ask for the job." The way he said it made me realize that escorting a mere Dormant into the grounds was considered a poor assignment. Although I wasn't actually Annabelle, I felt resentful on her behalf.

"Lead on, then," I said, gesturing forward.

Fennix turned without another word and stalked off through the woods. The walk was treacher<u>ous</u>, no less so because I was so clumsy in my ability to maneuver Annabelle's body. Fennix wore no shoes, and yet he seemed utterly unconcerned with staying to any visible path. He padded deftly over tree roots and through low brush, barely making a sound as he moved. I was sure this was a skill valued in a Traveler Caomhnóir, being able to move swiftly and silently through the woods. I, on the other hand, blundered about so badly that I sounded like an elephant crashing through the undergrowth. Practicing moving about in the clearing had been difficult enough, but it had not prepared me for this. I tripped several times, once landing right on my face, and causing Fennix to grumble and swear under his breath as he slowed his pace over and over again to compensate for me.

"Sorry," I said, picking myself up for the fifth time. "I'm not used to walking through the woods like this."

"Settlers rarely are," he growled.

I knew this was meant to be the direst of insults to anyone with Traveler blood, but I didn't rise to the bait. The last thing I needed was to piss him off still further. I bit my tongue and took heart in the fact that I could now smell the smoke from a campfire; we were close.

At long last, we broke through to the clearing in which the Traveler encampment was nestled. It was an entirely different experience, sensing the place through Annabelle's body. The sights and smells and sounds were familiar to me, but there was a deep connection to them that seemed to tingle in every cell of the temporary vessel I now occupied. I recognized the sensation, for it was the very same one I had when I'd looked out over the rolling hills of the Cambridgeshire countryside for the first time. I smiled, happy to realize that she had forged this kind of connection with the Traveler camp. The smile faded, however, as I realized how irreparably I had the potential to fuck it all up for her.

"You know where you're going from here?" Fennix asked, clearly eager to get rid of me.

"Sure, not a problem. I assume Zina and the other Boswells are still on the north side of the central fire?"

Fennix nodded curtly and stalked off, clearly glad to be rid of me and, luckily, seemingly oblivious to the fact that I wasn't who I claimed to be. I took a long, deep breath and blew it out slowly.

Okay. I was in.

THE MESSENGER

I LOOKED AROUND for a familiar face from Annabelle's family tree. Now all I had to do was convince Annabelle's relatives I was, in fact, Annabelle, and somehow make contact with Ileana. I had absolutely no idea how I was going to pull the second half of that plan off, but there was no time to dwell on it. Luckily, the first half of that equation began to work itself out in the form of a short, buxom woman with a cheerful smile and cheeks as red and round as apples who came hurrying over to me from the central fire, wiping her hands on her apron and pulling me into a hug that made all of Annabelle's bones crack in protest.

"Annabelle! There you are!" she cried. I recognized her right away from Annabelle's descriptions and photo album as her great-aunt Zina. Zina held me out in front of her and examined me like she thought I might have brought the chickenpox in with me.

"How are you keeping? Your journey was good? No trouble at the border from those upstart Caomhnóir? This young batch is such a gang of jumped up little buggers, aren't they? Such insolence, such insolence. Come warm yourself up, now, you must be frozen." She asked all her questions so quickly that I couldn't tell if she actually wanted me to answer them, or if it was simply a formality to ask them.

"I'm... I'm fine, thanks," I said, in an effort to blandly answer all of her questions at once. I scanned my memory for all of the facts I had memorized about Annabelle's family and seized on something specific to ask, and remembered something about Zina's husband. "Um, how is Mariuz's gout? He could hardly walk when last I visited."

Zina rolled her eyes and spit on the ground. "Oh, that man. Such a fool. If he laid off the drink, his gout would be fine, but will he listen? No! He prefers to suffer rather than give me the satisfaction."

I laughed. "Well, that's men for you."

"Why I put up with the fool, God only knows. Perhaps I like to suffer, too, eh?" Zina said, and then threw back her head and roared with good-natured laughter.

I laughed too, though not too loudly, since it wasn't my husband we were roasting. When Zina finally calmed down, I took my chance to cement my legitimacy in the Traveler circle. "I brought the pictures I told you about, the ones I found in my grandmother's trunk," I said, reaching into Annabelle's beaded bag and pulling out a small, crumpled paper sack of photographs. "I thought you might like to have them for the family history you're working on. There are some great ones of the Boswells in here."

Zina grabbed the packet excitedly from me, and then gave me two kisses on each cheek. "Thank you, Annabelle, this is wonderful!" she said, eagerly tearing into the bag. Within moments she was cackling again and hurrying off around the fire to share the memories the photos had dragged from the past and into the present. I heaved a sigh of relief. It felt as though my infiltration had been successful. All I needed to do now was figure out how to slip away to Ileana's tent—though this was likely going to be much more difficult than what I'd managed to accomplish so far.

I slumped down into an empty folding camp chair, and almost instantly, someone handed me a steaming mug of something that made me dizzy with its heady fumes. Intoxication was definitely not going to help my abysmal coordination skills in Annabelle's body, so I simply nodded and pretended to drink. Within moments, though, I nearly spilled the entire contents all over myself as a wriggling little creature climbed under my chair and hid in the folds of my skirt.

"What the hell—?" I began, but was quickly shushed by a high, fluting voice.

"Shhhhh! I'm hiding!"

I froze, looking around to see if anyone had noticed, but no one was paying the slightest attention to me anymore, now that Zina was making her highly animated rounds with the photographs. Surreptitiously, I leaned down and pulled at the hem of my skirt.

A small girl of about six or seven years old was crouching beneath my chair, giggling madly. She had a wild tumble of dark curls and a smile that was missing several prominent teeth. I couldn't help but smile back at her.

"And am I a good hiding place?" I asked her.

She shrugged. "You're the Dormant. Most of the kids won't go near you because they're too scared. So yeah, you're a good hiding place."

I probably should have been indignant on Annabelle's behalf but, to be honest, the little girl's pluck had disarmed me. I smiled again. "But you're not scared?"

The little girl gave me an appraising look. "You don't look frightening to me. Just kind of tired."

I laughed out loud at that. "I am tired. And don't worry, I won't give you away."

The girl smiled broadly. "Cheers!" she said brightly.

I allowed the giggling little thing to hide under my chair for a few more minutes, watching several children go by in obvious pursuit. She was right—none of them so much as looked at me as a potential hiding place. At last, the little girl ducked out from under my skirt, peeked around and, determining the coast was clear, climbed out from under my chair.

"Thanks! I never win this game!"

"Really?" I asked her. "You seem like a really good hider."

She grinned. "They're all bigger than me. But I showed them, didn't I?"

"You sure did!"

With one last brilliant smile, she took off between two nearby wagons and disappeared. I chuckled, glad to have helped the underdog scrape a win. Not a minute later, a woman came searching through the raucous gathering.

"Naomi? Naomi! Heavens, where has that blasted child got to?" she grumbled to herself, peering through the crowd.

"Lost her again, have you?" another woman called out with a broad smile. "She's trouble, that one!"

"She's not trouble!" the first woman snapped. "She just likes to be included with the older children." She headed off in the direction the little girl had vanished. I decided in that moment that Annabelle, though eager to establish her place amongst the Travelers, was not a dirty rotten snitch, and trusted that the child would eventually answer her mother's calls.

Sure enough, a little while later, I watched as Naomi was led back through the central gathering area, rolling her eyes and pouting as her mother shouted her way through a stern lecture. Poor kid. I hoped she'd at least outwitted the big kids she'd been playing with.

Being inside Annabelle's body was like captaining a ship I'd never seen before; much of it felt unfamiliar, but certain impulses are universal, and I recognized one of them right away: hunger. I was ravenous—or rather, Annabelle was ravenous, and as I was in charge of her body for the moment, it was my job to feed her. Luckily, plates and bowls and trays of food kept being passed along through my hands, and so I made sure to snatch a hunk of bread and a small bowl of stew for myself as they made the rounds of the bonfire. Dunking the bread into the stew and eating it was akin to heaven, I realized, as the physical and mental processes synchronized with each other.

I had barely taken a few bites, however, when a young woman slid into the seat beside me, her eyes wide and anxious. It was lucky that my mouth was full of food, or I would have completely given myself away by blurting out her name in surprise.

"Hi. We met once before, but you might not remember me. I'm Jeta. Flavia's cousin?" she said, rather breathlessly.

I, of course, knew Jeta much better than Annabelle would have. I first met her in the Traveler camp when I returned to testify at Irina's trial. It was she who had drawn the intricate artwork upon my hands and arms the first time I Rifted. And then, after Flavia had been banished for choosing a career in the outside world rather than her prescribed role in the Traveler camp, Jeta had traveled to London monthly to complete their Crossings and I met her once again. This was when Flavia was kidnapped and held hostage by Charlie Wright, and so Jeta had spent most of that visit in deep emotional distress for the welfare of her cousin. After having consoled her through this extremely trying event in her life, I felt quite close to her, but of course, I couldn't give that impression while occupying Annabelle's body. Instead, I worked to keep a politely distant look on my face as I replied to her.

"Yes, of course I remember you. How are you, Jeta?"

The girl shrugged, attempting a smile and looking, in my opinion, rather thinner and more drawn than the last time I'd seen her. She tucked her hair behind her ear. "I'm... I'm okay, I guess. It's really strange, not having my cousin here anymore. I'm... I'm not sure how much you know about her situation right now?"

I decided on the spot that it would be reasonable for Annabelle to be in touch with Flavia. After all, they were both Traveler outcasts, in a way, and they had spent quite a bit of time together when we had all worked together to free Irina from the camp.

"Yes, we've been in touch," I said carefully. "Mostly by email. Why?"

"Well, it's just..." Jeta bit her lip and looked anxiously around the fire, as though worried someone would suspect the content of our conversation. "I'm not permitted to contact her, outside of our monthly Crossings, which are to be performed in the presence of witnesses. I can't ask her how she's getting along or... or how she's coping..." Jeta's voice grew thick with repressed tears. "I just wondered whether you knew if she was all right. I'm so worried about her, after what that Necromancer bastard did to her..." She gave a gasp and pressed her lips together, lest she succumb to very public—and very obvious—tears.

It took me a moment to rein my own emotions in enough to give a controlled reply, but when I spoke, I was relieved to find that Annabelle's voice was quite steady. "She's fine. Truly. She's been staying at Fairhaven, and they have given her the full measure of their protection. She has been given a post in their library, assisting the other Scribes. Physically, she has recovered. Mentally—well, she's making great progress," I said. I was determined not to lie to her.

Jeta gave a sound that was half-laugh, half-sob. "Thank God for that," she whispered, then looked up at me curiously. "And she told you all that? She hasn't even confided in me."

I chose my words carefully. "I think it's comforting for her to confide in someone who also understands what it's like to be an outsider around here." I gestured around the fire. "I'm allowed to visit, of course, but I'll never be one of you—not really. Flavia is just coming to grips with that feeling, and having someone to talk to about it makes a difference. It's not easy, being homesick for a home that doesn't want you anymore."

"It's not true that we don't want her," Jeta muttered fiercely under her breath. "It's the Council and the High Priestess. They're so... so *stubborn!*"

I thought of our own Council back at Fairhaven, hiding the truth about Savvy rather than seeking the help of the International High

Council. "Yes, well, leadership is very often like that. Especially in a society that clings desperately to so many traditions."

Jeta looked like she half wanted to contradict me, but after a moment of internal struggle, she sighed and nodded instead. "It's not easy, this life. So much pride. So much fear."

"You had to band together to survive for so many centuries. Loosening those bonds—even when they begin to feel like restraints—is never easy. Give things a little time."

Jeta nodded, though without much hope in her expression. "If you talk to her when you get back, tell her... tell her I miss her, will you?"

"Of course I will," I promised.

Jeta thanked me, and then slipped away through the crowd, which was growing raucous. Zina had launched into some story that had a large knot of people in stitches. Pretending to listen and laugh along, I tried to plan out my next move.

I knew where Ileana's tent was, of course. Finding my way to it would be simple enough. Avoiding attention and awkward questions along the way was more of a problem. As an outsider, I couldn't possibly have been more of a spectacle, and everyone I passed would remember seeing me, since visitors were so few and far between in a Traveler camp. And finally, there was the problem of finding my way into the tent. I couldn't just stroll in, of course. Ileana's tent was heavily guarded, and I was the last person in the camp they'd allow inside for a quick word. I also couldn't just hang around the place, hoping to catch her on her way out. My presence would be missed around the fire, and instantly questioned in proximity to Ileana's tent. No, I would have to make a formal request for an audience and hope it was honored, though goodness only knew how long Ileana would make me wait. We had agreed that I would remain in the camp as long as it took to deliver Agnes' message, but I didn't want to leave Annabelle stranded in the woods trapped in my body for days, nor did I fancy occupying her body any longer than was absolutely necessary.

I stood up, picked up Annabelle's bag, and flung it over my shoulder. My best bet was to pretend to turn in for the night, and then make my way down to Ileana's tent to request an audience. Then I had no choice but to wait and hope she was feeling generous with her time. I snorted. Fat chance.

"Auntie? Auntie Zina?" I called out. Zina turned from her captive, roaring audience at the sound of her name. "I'm going to turn in, I think. I had a long flight and a long drive, too."

Zina bustled over to me, kissed me twice on each cheek, and gave my face a little pat. "You crazy Settlers and your airplanes. It's not natural, you know. If God meant for us to soar through the air, he would have given us wings."

I nodded but did not reply, though as someone who absolutely hated flying, I completely agreed with her.

"You know where you're staying, yes? Everything you need is all ready for you."

"Yes, I know. Thanks, Auntie. I'll see you in the morning."

"Sleep well, Annabelle. And thank you for the photographs. We have so few."

I set off down the path to the south of the fire, toward the section of the camp where the Boswell wagons were set up in a semicircle around a single cooking fire and set of picnic tables—the Traveler version of a little family neighborhood. Just behind the first row of wagons, a smaller wagon was parked under a tree. If the clans were on the move, it was used to house the family's outdoor trappings—laundry lines and benches and chairs and cookery and tents and such. But while the clans were camped out for a long stretch, it became a sort of bunkhouse for additional sleeping space. Because of my arrival, the children who usually escaped to the bunkhouse for bedtime would bunk up in the main wagons with the rest of their families, leaving the Dormant to sleep on her own. It was an arrangement that conveyed both hospitality and a certain wariness for outsiders. It also earned me a few dirty looks from a couple of the Boswell children who were playing by the fire. I shrugged an apology at them and stepped up into the wagon to ditch my things. The interior of the wagon was almost entirely taken up by bunk beds, two on each side and one on the far end, which had been crammed with bundles of clothing and baskets of dishes and cutlery. I slid Annabelle's bag into one of the lower bunks and pulled out my phone. A quick look at the screen confirmed what I suspected would be the case: I had no service in this God-forsaken wilderness. It looked like Hannah, Milo, and Finn would have to wait to get an update, which was just as well, given all I'd accomplished so far was getting over the border, tripping a lot, and providing a hiding spot for a mischievous seven-year-old.

A knock sounded on the outside of the wagon, and I quickly pocketed my phone. I poked my head out of the door to see a Caomhnóir standing there, looking grim—which, to be fair, was a standard Caomhnóir facial expression. Still, it was with trepidation that I asked him, "Can I help you?"

"The High Priestess has requested that you meet with her in her chambers at once," the young man said, looking not at me, but straight ahead, like a soldier at attention.

"Are you serious?" I blurted out.

The Caomhnóir frowned at the question. "Yes. Quite serious. I am to accompany you. Would you come with me, please?"

"But why does the High Priestess want to see me?" I croaked.

I finally aggravated the Caomhnóir into looking directly at me. "The High Priestess does not share such information with Guardians. The reason should not matter. You have been summoned. That is all you need to know. Now, I say to you again, come with me, please."

My thoughts were buzzing so loudly, I could hardly calm myself down enough to remember how to put one of Annabelle's feet in front of the other to follow the man. All at once, my heart was in my throat. I should have felt thrilled that the opportunity I was hoping for had just fallen right into my lap, but I didn't. I felt dizzy with fear. This was not a coincidence. There was no way in hell I was this lucky. Something was wrong.

She knows, I told myself. Somehow, someway, she knows.

The Caomhnóir took a very circuitous route to Ileana's tent—it seemed he was as eager to avoid prying eyes and awkward questions as I was. This was fine with me, as it gave me more time to try to figure out what the hell I was going to do, what in the world I was going to say. At what point should I reveal that I am actually Jess Ballard, if at all? Was it safer to allow her to think that Annabelle was delivering the message? Should I perhaps pretend to be Annabelle, but claim that Jess had given me the message to pass along? Should I just blurt it out the moment I saw her, or should I wait and see why she wanted to see me? Play along? Observe the niceties? Every new possibility exploded in my head like a firecracker, disorienting me, confusing me; so that when we arrived at Ileana's tent, I barely knew how to stand up straight, let alone what I was going to say to her if I managed to get inside without falling over.

The Caomhnóir pulled back the tent flap, stood aside, and barked, "Dormant of the Boswell Clan, Annabelle Rabinski, requests permission to enter."

"Permission granted," came a familiar croaky voice.

Out of options and out of time, I entered the tent, legs shaking like mad.

The last time I set eyes upon Ileana, she was flushed with victory, having just used her influence and sway to separate Finn and me, seemingly forever. As I had watched her walk away from me that evening into the Fairhaven twilight, I could not conceive of hating any human being more. Now that hatred was playing second fiddle to my fear, which was raging out of control in my chest, nearly choking me.

Ileana was perched upon her elaborately carved throne, the star attraction in the center ring of her very own big top tent. All around her, rich silks and velvets hung in luxurious swaths. Gorgeous antique furniture and priceless heirlooms of her clans occupied every corner, every shelf, and thick Persian rugs had been laid out on the ground beneath her bare feet. A massive black raven, lamplight glinting off his glossy feathers, stood beside her on a golden perch, eyeing me reproachfully as I came before them.

"High Priestess," I mumbled, forcing Annabelle's body into a kind of awkward bow. "You asked to see me."

"Yes, I certainly did," Ileana said, cocking her head to one side as she looked at me, much in the way her bird did. "How was your journey, Dormant?"

I swallowed back resentment at the fact that she did not use Annabelle's name, and instead, forced a smile as best I could. "It was long but uneventful, High Priestess. I am glad to have arrived at last."

"Yes, I'm sure you are," Ileana replied. She reached out, picked a nut out of the bowl at her side, and crushed it with her hand before extending the pieces to her bird, which pecked fitfully at it for a moment or two before turning up its beak at the offering.

"It... it is very kind of you to inquire after my trip," I said when

Ileana did not continue. "I did not think the High Priestess would deign to trouble herself with the comings and goings of a Dormant."

"On the contrary, I find your comings and goings to be most fascinating," Ileana said, brushing her hands together so that the remnants of the nut fluttered to the floor at her feet. "Most fascinating indeed. Please remind me, what was the purpose of this trip?"

"I... I wanted to pass along some old photographs I found amongst my grandmother's possessions," I said, deciding for the moment to stick to the official story, at least until I understood what Ileana was up to.

"Oh, yes, that's right. Zina brought us your request. Strange, I thought, to come so far just to deliver a few scraps of paper."

"Zina is working on a clan history of the Boswells," I explained. "The photographs included many of her relatives, and even some of Zina herself when she was very young. I thought they would be a good addition to her project. After all, I have no use for them."

"Oh yes, I'm sure Zina will appreciate them," Ileana said, waving her hand dismissively. "And when you've finished cozying up to your relatives? What do you intend to do then?"

I tried to look politely puzzled, but my fear was peaking and, honestly, Annabelle's face could have been spastically twitching at that point and I would have been powerless to stop it.

"You must think me a fool."

"I'm sure I don't know what you mean, High Priestess," I replied, after several long moments of trying to find my voice.

"Don't you?" Ileana asked. She did not look at me, but stared thoughtfully at her own gnarled forefinger, stroking the glossy black breast of the raven upon the perch.

"No, I don't," I admitted, for I truly did not.

"Even behind the disguise of Traveler form, a true Traveler can always sniff out the stench of an outsider."

My borrowed heart was racing now as my mental terror flooded through the connections to my physical form. "Is that so?" I hedged, determined not to give up the disguise until it was absolutely too late.

"Oh, yes," Ileana said, still lazily stroking the bird which seemed, for the moment at least, to be tolerating her attentions. "Not the young ones, of course. They have no proper pride, no appreciation for the ancient arts. But for those of us who truly understand what is owed to our blood and our gifts—those of us who never let our guard down, never sleep upon the surety of our safety and our secrecy—we always know."

I did not reply. My mind was racing, struggling to think ahead to my next move, my next gambit, but it was like sitting in front of a chessboard blindfolded. I didn't know where any of the pieces were. "And what is it you know, exactly?" I finally managed to ask, not quite able to control the tremor in my voice.

Ileana looked up, stared me straight in the eyes, and it was as though I was standing before her, utterly bare. "I know you have betrayed us. I know that you claim loyalty to our blood while continuing to consort and traffic with one of our enemies."

I said nothing because this answer didn't make sense. Claimed loyalty to their blood? When had I ever done that? And what enemy was she talking about? Was it possible she didn't know who I really was after all? Maybe I had misunderstood her.

Ileana glared at me while I worked through these frantic thoughts, but when I still did not reply, she plowed on. "Now, as I said, you might think me a fool, but I *know* you to be one. For only a fool would dare to set foot again within our sacred bounds once she had betrayed us. Did you really think I would harbor no suspicions that you were involved in the Walker Irina's escape? After all, you were one of two outsiders in the camp that day, and I knew you to be a friend of Jessica Ballard. I could not prove your involvement, but I vowed to keep a very watchful eye on you after that."

"You've been spying on me?" I asked, trying to sound indignant rather than relieved that she thought I really was Annabelle. Her Walker secret was safe, at least for the moment.

"I've been protecting my people," Ileana said, crossing her arms, which jangled like mad tambourines under her clanking clutter of jewelry. "And it is clear that I was right to do so, for tonight, you have betrayed us once again, Dormant."

I opened my mouth to ask what she meant, but at that moment, Ileana turned a triumphant gaze on the tent opening behind me. The scuffling noise of a struggle sounded behind me and I whirled around to see my own body, bound and gagged, being dragged into the tent.

I looked into those terrified_eyes, and I could see Annabelle staring back out at me, pleading silently for me to help her, to tell her what to do.

"Jessica Ballard is a traitor and a criminal according to our Traveler laws. She has been banished from our borders, and yet you have traveled here with her, knowing what she has done. You've delivered her right to my doorstep. I really ought to thank you."

I tore my eyes from Annabelle and turned back to face Ileana. "Thank me? Why thank me?"

Ileana's face stretched into a wide, grotesque smile, revealing the many gaping spaces where her teeth had once been. "I could not deal with Miss Ballard as I would have liked, once she had left our boundaries and entered under the protection of the Northern Clans. I exacted what little revenge I could, breaking up her little romance, but true justice could not be served. The scales could not be tipped once again into balance. But now that she has crossed illegally into our domain, she has forfeited her protections. I can deal with her as I choose."

"What do you mean, crossed into your domain?" I shouted. "She didn't set foot in your camp. Your Caomhnóir dragged her in!"

Ileana's grin widened even further, making her look like an ancient caricature. She shrugged. "That's not how I remember it. As I recall, she was apprehended within our borders. I imagine my Caomhnóir will testify to the same, won't you, Dragos?"

Dragos did not return Ileana's smile, but inclined his head in a bow that left no room for doubt. He would, without hesitation, lie for his High Priestess.

From the shadows of the back of the tent, a hulking Caomhnóir stepped forward and, in one deft movement, had grasped both of my arms and forced them behind my back. Before I was able to do more than gasp in surprise and pain, he had secured my hands with something thin and hard that bit into my flesh—a zip-tie, maybe? I began to panic, and in my panic, lost some of the control I had gained over Annabelle's body. My words, as I began to shout, were slurred and disjointed. "You can't do this. We came here to tell you something. Something very important, please..."

"I cannot imagine that anything a pair of traitors would have to say would be of even the slightest interest to me," Ileana said with an unconcerned shrug. She was already turning away from us, flicking a hand languidly over her shoulder. "Lock them up. Irina's old haunt should do nicely for them, seeing as it's their fault it's currently unoccupied. You should find an adequate collection of chains and ropes to ensure they behave themselves."

The Caomhnóir holding my arms began to drag me backward toward the tent flaps. Behind me, I heard the scuffling struggle of Annabelle likewise being dragged from the tent. My mind threw itself into a panic. Once I was locked up, I might never have another opportunity to speak to Ileana. She might decide to lock me up and forget about me, like she tried to do with Irina. This might be my last chance to get Agnes' message to her. There was no way to do it without the two Caomhnóir hearing it as well, but what choice did I have? I dug my heels deep into the dirt floor of the tent and focused every ounce of mental energy I had on forcing those six crucial words out of Annabelle's lips:

"The Sentinels have begun their watch!"

Ileana froze on the spot, her shoulders rigid, one hand paused in the air, reaching toward the raven to stroke it again. The hand began to tremble. She slowly lowered it and turned to face me. Her face was an ancient mask of shock and horror.

"What did you say?" she whispered hoarsely.

"The Sentinels have begun their watch!" I repeated in a breathless voice.

A shiver passed over Ileana's features—for a moment, it seemed she would speak to me. She was staring directly into my eyes, burrowing into them, right past the veil of my disguise to the soul hiding behind it. In that fraction of a moment, I felt I had not a secret in the world those eyes could not divine.

And then...

"Take them away. Lock them up. Tell no one," Ileana whispered, and turned her back on us once more.

UNLIKELY ALLIES

"SHE KNOWS."

"You think so?"

"Absolutely. Didn't you see the look on her face when she heard Agnes' message? She knows."

"Then why do you think we're still rotting away in here?"

"Here" was Irina's old cage, a makeshift prison fashioned from a dilapidated Traveler wagon so filthy and run down it would have been unfit for a wild animal, let alone a human being. In the year since Irina had occupied it, the forest had started to claim it as its own. Some kind of creeping vine had wound its way through the wheels and up through the holes in the floor. Spiders had festooned the shadowed corners with elaborately spun webs. Something small and furry had built a nest of dead leaves and twigs in the space between the open door and the wall. Faded runes still graffitied every inch of the interior, and though none of the markings looked fresh, some of the Castings were still active. The force of their magic pressed down on us like weights, making my chest feel heavy and my head pound. Even if the Caomhnóir had not searched us and confiscated the rest of the Soul Catchers, I don't think we would have been able to Walk and re-enter our own bodies, even if we had dared to try it.

As soon as we'd been pulled from the tent, Annabelle and I had both been gagged, so that our screams wouldn't alert the rest of the Travelers to our presence. The gags had only been removed when we'd been securely chained up inside the abandoned wagon, which was far enough from the main encampment that I doubt shouting and screaming for help would have done any good at all. But I knew enough about Travelers to know that there were no secrets in a Traveler camp, and it was only a matter of time before the rumor of our imprisonment would be spreading from wagon to wagon like wildfire. At the very least, Annabelle's relatives would be looking for her in the morning, and it wasn't likely they would buy any kind of lame cover-up story that might occur to the Caomhnóir. No, every Traveler would know who was locked in this wagon by first light, I was certain of it. They'd be crowding the edges of the clearing, trying to bribe the Caomhnóir guarding the perimeter and gawking for a peek at the Northern Girl in chains while they finished their morning coffee. So much for my plan to keep my mission from Agnes a secret.

Once again, I had screwed things up beyond the reasonable hope of repair. Classic Jess.

"Jess, are you listening?"

"Huh? Sorry, what?"

"I said, why do you think Ileana locked us up here, if she understood your message?" Annabelle asked.

I shook my head. "I don't know. I just don't know. Maybe I scared her. Maybe it just caught her off guard. Maybe she didn't want to say anything in front of the Caomhnóir—God knows *I* would have preferred if they hadn't been there, but I wasn't sure if I'd get another chance. But she knew, Annabelle. She definitely knew."

"What... what does it mean?" Annabelle asked softly. "Are you allowed to tell me?"

"Even if I wanted to, I couldn't," I told her. "Agnes didn't explain it. She just told me who to give the message to. She promised me they would know what it meant."

"You don't think... maybe she's going to try to bury it, do you? Just leave you here so that no one ever finds out?" Annabelle's tone was calm, but it was forced, too. I could tell she was steeling herself for the very real possibility that she would never get out of here.

Her words fell like lead inside of me. What if Annabelle was right? This was always the danger, wasn't it? This was why the truth had been so closely held, not just to protect it from the Necromancers, but to protect it from the Durupinen themselves. After so many centuries of power, prestige, and tradition, what Durupinen in her right mind, especially one in such an influential position, would want to give all of that up? Why wouldn't she just bury it deeper, so that no one would ever discover it again?

But the answer whispered itself to me, in a voice very like Agnes'. *Because it had already been buried too long. They cannot run from it now. It has found them at last.*

"It's possible," I finally managed to reply. "But even if she does, I don't think she'll be able to hide it for long. Pandora's Box is open."

I dropped my head onto my knees. "God, Annabelle, I am so sorry I dragged you into this. It's all my fault."

"Stop that," she snapped, and even in my own voice I could hear her familiar exasperated tone, like at any given moment she would decide to stop tolerating me permanently. "Wallowing in self-pity won't get us out of here. Now, think. What's our next move?"

I tried to concentrate through the constant Casting buzz. "Fuck, Annabelle, I don't know. I can't reach anyone at Fairhaven because I can't use the connection unless I'm in my own body. There's no one here in the camp that's going to help us, unless you think one of your relatives might...?"

She raised one of my own eyebrows at me, which incidentally, made me look like quite the bitch. "Choosing a distant Dormant relative over the orders of the High Priestess? Not a snowball's chance in hell." She laughed. "I've persisted in returning here to get back to my roots, you know, but the truth is, it's been futile. The Travelers have got a crust I've never been able to crack, no matter how many stories about my grandmother I tell or how many of her old photos and trinkets I parade back here. I've only ever been tolerated. I expect some of them will even be relieved to know they'll no longer be required to make the effort to accommodate me."

"Not all of them. That one woman—Zina?—she seemed pretty excited to see me when I was pretending to be you."

Annabelle smirked. "She's the exception to the rule. She was my grandmother's niece. She actually remembers my grandmother before she ran off to marry my grandfather."

"One exception might be all we need," I pointed out, grasping a bit desperately at this tiny ray of hope.

Annabelle didn't reply. She just stared forlornly down at my knees, as though she was wondering if she'd always be forced to occupy a body in ripped black jeans.

I opened my mouth, hoping that I might find the right words to comfort her, to tell her just how sorry I was to get her into this mess, and that I would find a way—somehow—to fix it. But I was spared the struggle, for I caught a movement out of the corner of my eye and was so distracted that I forgot all about apologizing.

A Caomhnóir was running from the northern perimeter of the clearing, waving his arms in an effort to flag down the Caomhnóir that was patrolling the southern side. The speed at which he was moving was notable, as was the franticness with which he waved his arms, but honestly, the thing that gave me the most pause was the size of the Caomhnóir—he was incredibly slender and slight, his uniform ill-fitting and hanging from his limbs as he sprinted around the edge of the clearing. I could not remember seeing any Caomhnóir amongst the Travelers who was so slight of stature, so delicate of build.

Annabelle followed my gaze and had also spotted him now and, like me, was utterly nonplussed. "What the hell...?" she whispered as she watched the figure close the last few yards between himself and the other guard.

The small Caomhnóir, whoever he was, had his fellow on the ground in one swift, fluid motion that caused both Annabelle and me to gasp aloud. Before the felled Caomhnóir could so much as cry out, his attacker brought his elbow down on his face with a resounding crunch, and the Caomhnóir on the ground moved no more. The tiny Caomhnóir then slunk from shadow to shadow like a lithe predator, closing the space between himself and the wagon bound by catlike bound, until, with one last graceful leap, he landed on silent feet. Annabelle and I both struggled to stand. Annabelle had gathered up a handful of her chains to use as a weapon. All I had managed to do was put my hands feebly out in front of me to protect myself.

"D-don't come any closer!" Annabelle stammered breathlessly.

"I can hardly break you out of here if I can't come any closer, Jess," said a familiar, bored voice.

My heart was in my throat. I could barely choke out my next words.

"Catriona?! Oh my GOD! What... how... what are you doing here?!"

At the sound of her name, Catriona pulled the rough woolen hood from her head to reveal her cascade of golden blonde hair. She looked at me in utter confusion.

"Yeah, that's right. Have we met?"

For a split second, I couldn't understand why she was asking me such an absurd question. Then, I remembered that I was inside Annabelle's body, a fact that Catriona could have absolutely no inkling of.

"Cat, it's me! It's Jess. I Walked, and then occupied Annabelle's body. I'm trapped in here," I explained.

Catriona narrowed her eyes at me. "That's not possible. If you're Jess, then who's in there?" she asked, pointing at my body.

"That's Annabelle. You know her, she was part of your investigation into David Pierce. She's part Traveler."

Catriona opened her mouth, undoubtedly ready to unleash a snarky, dismissive retort, but then she froze, her mouth half open. Cautiously, she took first one, then several steps forward, looking deeply into Annabelle's eyes. I saw the exact moment when she recognized my spirit behind them. "Jess?" she whispered, her eyes darting now to my body, as though it was a dangerous object she dare not touch.

"Yeah, it's me," I told her, and watched the truth expand like a small bomb, dilating her pupils and turning her pale.

"So, does that mean... the Dormant...?" she pointed a shaking finger at my body, and Annabelle within it coaxed my hand into a sheepish sort of wave.

Catriona's eyes went as wide as saucers. "But how... how did you..." she swallowed convulsively. "I'm starting to think that I don't even want to know what I've just gotten myself into. But tell me anyway."

Glancing nervously over her shoulder, she seemed to decide that we were too exposed, even with the clearing deserted and the single guard unconscious in a heap in the grass. She shoved with all her might against the ancient sliding door of the wagon so that it squealed along its track and closed maybe another foot and a half. It wasn't much, but she seemed satisfied with the additional coverage. She folded herself into the newly created shadows and began to examine my chains, and then Annabelle's. "I'll work. You explain," she said bluntly.

"Annabelle is a Walker, too," I said, the words tumbling out over each other in my relief at seeing a friendly face. "She figured it out last year when I was here for the Walker Irina's trial. And yes, before you point it out, we know that a Dormant shouldn't be able to have any such abilities, but it happened anyway; and so all formerly accepted rules about Walkers and Dormants are now outdated garbage, okay?"

I watched as Catriona made the enormous mental effort to

swallow this news whole and, admirably, she managed to choke it down. "Right, then," she said at last, and continued her examination of the chains.

"How did you know I was here?" I asked her as she worked. "Nobody knew that I'd left."

Catriona gave me a withering look. "Did you really think, after the conversation we had, that I wasn't going to keep tabs on every single move that you made? I've had people tracking you since you left the grounds."

"Of course, you have," I muttered, barely refraining from rolling my eyes. It probably wasn't the best idea to roll my eyes at the person who was, at that moment, attempting to free me from bondage.

"I would have done it myself, obviously, but I was... otherwise engaged. Then I was informed that you had been tracked to the edge of the Traveler encampment. I knew then that I had to get personally involved."

"Why?' I asked.

"Because I was one of only a few people who knew how dangerously close you'd been to being charged with high crimes against the Travelers," Catriona snapped at me. "Your status in the Northern Clans was all that saved you from extradition back into the forest to face their justice. I have it on good authority that Celeste herself had to intervene, and that the banishment of your loverboy was the price of your freedom."

Anger reared inside me like a feral animal. "Are you kidding me? How dare she accuse *me* of crimes when *she's* the one who—"

"Jess, save your indignation for someone who needs to hear it. You're preaching to the choir, okay? Blast... this... bloody... ah, here we are!" Something deep inside the lock gave a screechy, rusty click, and the shackle around my left ankle fell away. Catriona kicked it away from me and moved on to the right ankle.

"But how did you know we needed help?"

"I had staked you out and saw you get captured," Catriona said. "Or rather, I saw *her* get captured." She pointed to Annabelle, who was hanging on every word of her story. "And once she'd disappeared into the camp, I knew I was her only hope of getting out."

"How the hell did you get in here?" Annabelle asked her. "The borders are sealed with Castings. Every intruder, living and spirit alike, set off all the Caomhnóir defenses."

Catriona held up her left wrist. Upon it was a strange set of braided leather bracelets. "I borrowed these."

I squinted down at them. "What are they?" I asked, but even as the question left my lips, I thought they looked familiar.

"The Caomhnóir wear them. It allows them to cross back and forth over the borders without tripping their own intruder Castings," Catriona said.

"Borrowed it? From whom?" Annabelle asked.

"I set a little trap for one of the Caomhnóir patrolling the border. Turns out he couldn't resist the chance to help a damsel in distress."

I grinned. "What did you do?"

Catriona shrugged, smirking. "I popped the bonnet on the car, popped the top few buttons on my blouse, and adopted an expression of general feminine helplessness. Bob's your uncle, he was unconscious, bound up, and all snug and cozy in the boot—but not before I had these for my own. Honestly, what a complete git."

I wondered silently if the Caomhnóir now trapped in the trunk of Catriona's car was Ruslo, a young Caomhnóir who had fallen victim to a similar ploy by Irina once and nearly gotten himself killed. If he'd made the same mistake twice, there was no doubt he'd be stripped of his post and relegated to the lowest of drudgery. I tried to give a shit but found I just couldn't.

The second set of locks sprang open and both of my legs were at last free. Catriona unwound the excess chain from around my body and sliced cleanly through the bonds around my wrists with a lethal-looking knife I also recognized as a Traveler Caomhnóir accessory.

"I don't suppose you're going to tell me why you're here, of all places—unless of course you harbor a burning desire to rot in a remote forest prison for all of eternity that I simply didn't know about, in which case, this little excursion makes perfect sense," Catriona said.

I rolled Annabelle's eyes. "You already know I can't tell you that."

"I know circumstances have changed since we last spoke," Catriona said through her teeth as Annabelle's ankle chains fell away. "How many times do I have to rescue you from certain peril before you trust me, Jess?"

I bit my lip. She had a point. I wasn't going to be able to get out of here without her help, and I couldn't deny that she'd saved my life nearly as many times as Finn had by now. She was practically my honorary Caomhnóir at this point. I heaved a deep sigh. "Let's concentrate on getting back over the border," I finally said, choosing to stall rather than commit. "There will be time for explanations later."

Catriona narrowed her eyes at me, but didn't argue. Annabelle let out a long, low groan of relief as she cut the last of the ropes away. Catriona helped her to her feet and held on to her arm to steady her as she stretched and massaged some feeling back into her—well, *my*—limbs. Once she had relieved some of her physical discomfort, though, she turned back to me, tense as ever. "What's next?" Annabelle asked.

"Let's get back into our own bodies," I said. "If we do it quickly, there's still a chance we can get out of here without the Travelers ever discovering that you're a Walker."

Catriona looked between us, mystified. "You mean they caught you both, arrested you, and imprisoned you without ever realizing you're occupying each other's bodies?"

"Yes," I said. "I still can't believe it myself. Do you still have the Soul Catchers?" I asked Annabelle.

She shook her head despairingly. "No. I'm sorry, Jess. I tried to hide them, but that Caomhnóir ambushed me. He took the Soul Catchers and the Casting bag, too."

"It's okay," I told her, even as I fought back my own panic. It would be so much harder to move effectively back through the woods still blundering around in an unfamiliar body.

"I guess it's a good thing I brought these, then," Catriona said, holding up a fistful of tangled woven bracelets. I gasped in shock as I recognized the familiar patterns and colors of Soul Catchers.

"What... how did you...?" I murmured weakly, holding out my hand and allowing Catriona to drop one of the bracelets into my shaking fingers.

Catriona heaved a long-suffering sigh. "Honestly, it's as though you think me incompetent at my own job. What else would I bring when tracking a Walker to the place where she once learned how to Walk?" Then she turned and handed a Soul Catcher to Annabelle, letting out a snort of incredulous laughter. "Although, I didn't realize I was tracking *two* Walkers, so the fact that I've got enough for both of you is sheer bloody luck."

Knowing that we could be discovered at any moment, Annabelle and I worked quickly, tying on the Soul Catchers and borrowing Catriona's blade to cut through them when we slipped out of each other's bodies. The sense of relief I felt soaring up above Annabelle's body was astronomically more satisfying than the relief I felt slipping the bonds of my own. Her body had been as close to a prison as I had ever experienced—a constant state of psychic discomfort and sensory confusion. It was with definite reluctance that I faced the prospect of returning to my own body, lying empty now upon the floor of the wagon. It took several seconds of grappling with logic and memory until I was able to convince myself that returning again to my own body would not be the torturous experience that occupying Annabelle's body had been. I forced myself to remember Irina and the way she had detested and scorned the very idea of entering any body at all, even her own. It was, in part, my fear of embracing Irina's madness that cleared my mind and ultimately forced my decision to rejoin with my body.

The first breath with body and soul rejoined was like an awakening. Every sense was on fire with the ferocity of the returned sensation. By the time I had recovered from the overwhelming shock of it all and focused myself on my surroundings again, I found Catriona with her back pressed to the wall of the wagon, and Annabelle gasping on all fours trying desperately to regain her bearings.

"That was... intense to watch," Catriona managed after a few moments. "Are you both quite well?"

"I... I think so," Annabelle gasped. She looked up and caught my eye, grinning. "But I'm never occupying such hostile territory again."

I found it quite easy to grin back, glad to have full control over my body again. "Hey, now. I am an impeccable host. I'm thinking of listing this bitch on Airbnb. Single guests only, no pets."

Annabelle collapsed in a fit of exhaustion-induced laughter, but Catriona broke in impatiently. "As much as I appreciate this kind of niche humor, can we save the jokes for another time? We really need to focus on getting out of here."

"Right," I said, rising awkwardly to my feet but, once there, finding myself quite steady. "You're right. Sorry. What do we do now? What's the game plan?"

"I'm not sure I have a game plan," Catriona admitted. "This entire night has been an exercise in my improvisation skills. Don't let my genius at such exercises fool you. We'll need to think on our feet to get out of here."

"Okay, you're the boss," I said. "You managed to get in here without getting caught, which is more than I can say for the two of us, even with our insider knowledge of the camp, so we'll take our lead from you."

Catriona closed her eyes and held up one hand. At first, I thought she was doing something of a mystical, Durupinen nature—reaching out through her spirit connection or trying to sense one Casting or another. But, instead, she muttered. "Give me a moment to savor this complete lack of insubordination on your part."

Given as she'd just likely saved both of our lives, I swallowed my snark and let her have her requested moment. Then she opened her eyes. "Okay. I think our best bet is to move out of the grove on the west side. I can communicate the coordinates to the car, and they can meet us on the border. I can cross it without setting off the Castings, but once you do the same, we'll only have a minute or two before we have Caomhnóir on our trail, and I'd prefer to be several miles down the road by the time that happens."

"Communicate back to the car?" I asked. "But who—"

"Let's not waste any more time," Catriona hissed. "I don't know how long we've got before Sleeping Beauty over there wakes up." She hitched her thumb over her shoulder where the Caomhnóir she'd attacked still lay motionless in the grass.

As quietly as we could, we dropped to the ground in front of the wagon, bypassing the old and rotting steps and running at a crouch to the far side of the wagon, so that we could no longer see the fallen Caomhnóir, nor the path that led back to the main encampment. Thankful for the cloud cover that kept the clearing protected from the searchlight brightness of the full moon, we darted into the trees and made for the border of the grove.

It was very slow going. Every snap of a twig caused us to freeze in terror for several moments. Catriona, for all her expertise, was definitely on edge. I'd never seen her so jumpy, and we'd been in some pretty tense situations together. Annabelle and I hung back, letting her choose the path through the trees, grateful to be moving in a much more coordinated manner, rather than the drunken stumbling that was all I'd been able to manage in Annabelle's skin.

We all seemed to be holding our breath, waiting for the inevitable echoing cry of "Escape!" or "Guardian down!" or something similar that would raise the alarm and turn the forest into a minefield of potential enemies, but no such shouts reached our ears. I could have cried at the realization that the trees were beginning to thin, that the road was nearly within sight.

Catriona stopped to huddle over her phone, texting our coordinates so that the car would meet us when we exited the woods. She turned back to us, fingers to her lips. "When you see the car approach, don't hesitate—run straight for it and jump in the back seat. We are no less safe in the open beyond the border than we are here in the woods—we will be exposed, and Traveler jurisdiction will permit them to attack the vehicle if they witness a violation of their laws in progress."

Annabelle and I nodded. Another snap of a twig and a flutter of wings caused me to clamp my hand down over my mouth to stifle a scream, but it was only a crow, shooting up through the canopy and bursting like the negative of a firework against the night sky.

When at last we broke through the remaining fringe of trees, it was barely a second before the hum of an engine and the glow of headlights rolled into view, temporarily blinding us after the gloom of the forest. As the car—one of the Caomhnóir SUVs, by the look of it—pulled up beside us, Catriona turned to me, took me by both shoulders and said, "Don't freak out."

"Freak out? Why would I...?"

"Get in, losers," came a familiar velvety voice from the darkened interior.

I turned to Catriona, eyes wide. "What the ever-loving fuck is Lucida doing here?"

"It's a long story," she said. "I'll explain when we're safely on the freeway. Just get in the bloody car."

Still stammering and spluttering, I hurried after Annabelle, who flung the car door open, and slid into the back seat behind her. It wasn't until Annabelle had put her seatbelt on and heaved a huge sigh of relief that she realized who was in the driver's seat.

"What the hell? What the HELL?" she cried, her voice rising in a shriek. She fumbled around in the dark for her seatbelt, as though she was going to leap from the vehicle.

"Annabelle," I cried. "Annabelle, it's okay!"

But it was not okay, and Catriona should have realized it. The last time Annabelle had seen Lucida, Lucida had been working with the Necromancers. The Necromancers had broken into Annabelle's apartment and tortured her for the better part of a week, leaving her hidden in plain sight within the confines of a cage made of dismembered spirit fragments. The last Annabelle had known of Lucida was discovering that she had been in on that plot. It took every ounce of strength in my body to keep Annabelle seated and to force her to look me in the eyes.

"Annabelle, look at me. LOOK AT ME," I commanded.

As Annabelle's eyes found mine, her animal terror sharpened into rage. "Jessica Ballard, what in the name of all that is holy am I doing riding in a car driven by *that woman?!*"

"I have no idea, but you have to trust that everything is going to be—"

"Trust? TRUST?!" Annabelle positively shrieked. "Jessica, so help me God—"

"Okay, okay, I know, but I'm not asking you to trust her!" I cried. "Trust me, okay? Just... just trust me! That's it! You can do that, right?"

Both Lucida and Catriona were staring tensely into the rearview mirror. Annabelle looked, for a split second, like she was about to tell me that she absolutely could not do that, and that I was insane for even asking her, but then she held my gaze for a moment, and I felt her body relax slightly, settling back into the seat. Her hands pulled away from the seatbelt buckle, folding instead into a white-knuckled ball in her lap.

"Yeah," she said quietly. "Yeah, I can do that. For right now, I can do that."

I nodded encouragingly at her but left my hand on her shoulder as a physical reminder of what she had promised me. Then I looked up into the rearview mirror and nodded at Lucida and Catriona, both of whom looked visibly relieved that we weren't going to have to physically restrain Annabelle from exiting the car. Catriona wrenched the Caomhnóir hood from her head, shook out her hair as though it had been suffocating, and murmured, "Get us back to the freeway. We can figure out our next move from there."

"You're the boss, boss," Lucida replied, pulling deftly out into the middle of the road, easing onto the gas to accelerate while avoiding the screeching of tires and revving of engines that typified a getaway.

Catriona then turned to me. "What is our next move? What in the hell is happening?"

I opened my mouth to answer her, not sure what I was going to say. The truth was, I had no idea what to do next. No idea where to go. I needed time. Time to think, time to—

"LOOK OUT!" Annabelle screamed, pointing out the windshield.

Every face turned in time to see a woman's figure standing in the middle of the road, arm outstretched as though she could stop the oncoming car with the sheer power of the gesture. Lucida slammed her foot down on the brake, at the same time veering wildly to the right to avoid mowing the woman down. We narrowly missed a massive oak tree and came to rest in a ditch so deep that I slid straight across the back seat and pinned Annabelle to the car door.

"Everyone all right?" Catriona called at once, to which there was a grumbling chorus of assent. Catriona turned, kicked her door open, and hoisted herself out of the car, which lurched awkwardly at the weight shift. Then she reached a hand in and pulled Lucida from the driver's seat before heaving my door open and pulling first me and then Annabelle up onto the road.

They all started to examine the car, but I stepped further out onto the road, peering into the gloom for the woman who had caused us to crash. As my eyes adjusted, the figure strode forward through the fog, her expression as cool and unruffled as though she had daily brushes with death.

It was Ileana.

I squashed an impulse to run. Run where? She owned these woods and they were crawling with her Caomhnóir. One word from her, and we'd have the whole lot of them descend upon us—I was shocked she wasn't surrounded by a small army of them already. But no, she approached me as a solitary figure, coming to a stop just a few feet away. Defiantly, I stood <u>my</u> ground. Just behind me, I heard

Catriona and the others whispering, having finally realized who we had nearly hit.

"Jess..." It was Catriona's tense voice that broke the silence.

"It's okay," I replied, with more certainty than I felt. "Let me talk to her."

"But—"

"Just... give me a second, okay?" I hissed, looking over my shoulder at her. "Please."

Catriona bit her lip but nodded. Annabelle hovered beside her, shifting nervously from one foot to the other, her teeth chattering with cold and fear. Lucida skulked back in the shadows near the car. She had surreptitiously scooped up a large, broken branch from the ground and was wielding it in her hand like a weapon, clearly ready to fight our way out of the situation.

Having no weapon but my big fat mouth, I prayed I could talk our way out of this mess.

It was Ileana who spoke first, though.

"It was you, wasn't it?"

I mulled this over. "You'll have to be more specific," I answered at last. "I like to know exactly what it is I'm being accused of before I take full credit."

"The Dormant spoke the words to me, but it was you, wasn't it? You were meant to be the messenger."

"What messenger?"

"The one who was tasked to find me. The one into whose ears the words were spoken: the Sentinels have begun their watch. It was you, wasn't it?" Ileana asked, her teeth clenched.

I threw a glance back at Annabelle, who seemed to be making a motion like she wanted me to come back to the car. I tried to smile at her, to reassure her that everything was fine, even though it most likely wasn't fine at all. I turned back to Ileana. "Yes. That message was given to me," I told her.

Ileana closed her eyes for a moment, as though these words were some kind of physical blow to be absorbed, the confirmation of a worst fear. "Why did you allow the Dormant to deliver it?"

I swallowed. "You didn't give me much choice," I said. "I knew I had to get the message to you, but I was banished from the grounds of the encampment. I thought perhaps, if you heard it from Traveler lips, instead of mine, you might <u>actually</u> listen."

"The lips of deception from whom truth must spring," Ileana whispered, the words barely audible in the night's foggy stillness.

"What does that mean?" I asked.

"Those words are mine to fathom, not yours," Ileana snapped. "Nowhere in the lore of this day did it demand I give everything to you."

I longed to protest. I didn't want anything from this woman. Well, okay, that wasn't entirely true. I wanted her to believe me. I wanted her to act. And it was only now that I came to appreciate exactly how much that would cost her.

"How did you come to hear those words, and how did you know to deliver them to me?" Ileana asked.

"I followed a trail of clues laid out for me by Agnes Isherwood."

"The Northern Prophetess," Ileana whispered, eyes wide, her expression almost reverent.

"Yes."

"How do you know the clues were yours to follow?"

How did I know? Because I'd somehow time traveled and laid the clues for myself. But there was no way in hell I was telling Ileana that, not if I wanted her to take me seriously. "That is mine to fathom, not yours," I said, throwing her own words back in her face.

Ileana seemed to swallow back something large and bitter—probably her pride—before continuing to her next question. "What did you find at the end of this trail?"

"The clues made it clear that I had to go Rifting," I said.

"Rifting?!" Ileana cried indignantly. "You're not a Traveler, how could you presume to—"

"Hey, I'm not the first Settler to go Rifting and I sure as hell won't be the last, so if I were you, I'd save the righteous indignation for shit that really matters. Unless I'm very much mistaken, the Durupinen world is basically on fire right now, so let's keep things in perspective, okay?"

Ileana raised her chin into the air and gestured haughtily for me to continue.

"It was the Tansy Hag who taught Agnes how to do it. I assume," I said slowly, seeing the look of sudden shock on Ileana's face, "that you've heard of the Tansy Hag?"

"A children's tale," Ileana whispered. "An invention of ignorant

Settlers, meant to demonize us and frighten people away from our encampments."

"Yes, but based upon a real woman, a Traveler Durupinen who lived centuries ago, during Agnes' time. Her spirit is still imprisoned in the deepest bowels of Skye Príosún."

Ileana's face went, if possible, still paler. "A Traveler spirit in a Northern *príosún*? Impossible. This cannot be. It flies in the face of our autonomy—our treaties—our very—"

"Well, it's true," I snapped, all patience gone. "When this is all over, I'll take you there myself if you like, and prove it to you. You can take it up with the Council, not that you seem to treat Traveler prisoners any better here, from what I've seen."

Ileana swelled with indignation. I decided to pivot back to the topic of Rifting before I lost my chance. As much as this woman and I loathed each other, I couldn't afford to alienate her now.

"Agnes left special instructions on how to do it—on how to reach a second, deeper door that she herself had created within the Rift."

"Second door? What is this nonsense? There is no second door," Ileana whispered.

"Maybe not for you," I replied. "But there was when I went through into the Rift. Agnes Isherwood was waiting for me there. She was the one who told me the truth. She was the one who gave me my instructions. She's the reason I'm here. She told me you would know what the message means, and what we have to do next."

Ileana's left eye was twitching. Her hands were shaking. I took an involuntary step back from her, unable to suppress the feeling that she was about to jump on me and claw my eyes out. But whatever battle was waging inside her was waged entirely in silence. She took a deep breath. She steadied her hands. And when she looked at me again, the usual sparkle of hatred that gleamed in her eyes just for me had been replaced with a steely determination.

"I do know what it means. And I know what to do next," she said. "But first I need to know, am I the first to whom you've delivered this message?"

"Yes," I said with a sardonic smile. "Believe it or not, I thought you would be the easiest one to reach."

"You weren't wrong," Ileana said grimly. "Have you told your High Priestess?"

"No."

She narrowed her eyes at me. "The most important revelation in our long and storied history, and you spoke not a word of it to the leader of the Northern Clans?"

"No."

"Why not?"

"Because those were not my instructions," I replied. I could be vague, too.

Ileana snorted, eyeing me beadily, still trying to ascertain if I was telling the truth. I couldn't tell whether she believed me or not.

"What of your companions? Do you trust them? How much do they know?"

I hesitated before answering. By this time, I trusted both Annabelle and Catriona with my life. Lucida was another matter... on the one hand, she was *Lucida*. On the other, I never would have found the Tansy Hag or discovered the meaning behind Agnes' clues without her. She was bound up in this just like I was, whether I liked it or not.

"They know as much as I've had to tell them, and no more," I said at last. "And yes, I trust them a damn sight more than I trust you."

"Very well then," Ileana said. "There is no time to lose. Now that the wheels are in motion, it's only a matter of time before all hell breaks loose. We will take your car."

I blinked. "Our car?" I asked. "To... to where?"

"We have a visit to pay," Ileana said, "to the Keeper of the Elementals."

THE KEY AND THE TRUTH

"T HE KEEPER OF THE ELEMENTALS?" I breathed. "You… you know how to find them?"

"Yes," Ileana said, though it was clear the thought gave her no pleasure. "But the journey will be difficult, and there are a few things I must do to prepare. Come back to the camp. I shall have the Caomhnóir see to your vehicle."

I looked back at Annabelle and the others. Annabelle was shaking her head violently at me, while Catriona and Lucida had both settled into defensive poses, ready to fight.

"You… you expect us to go back within the borders of the camp? After what you did to us for daring to set foot in there in the first place?" I asked, half-laughing, though there was no humor in the situation.

"You have my word that none of you will be harmed. You will not be detained. But you will want to eat and rest up before we leave," Ileana said.

"I have your *word*?" I asked, and there was a definite edge of panic to my laughter now. "You could sign a contract with the Devil himself in your own damn blood and I still wouldn't trust you. I was chained under your orders less than an hour ago. What's changed?"

Ileana stared at me as though the question was absurd. "Everything has changed, Northern Girl. Everything."

And I understood. This was bigger than either of us now. How we felt about each other, what had passed between us— all that was gone now, swept up in the current of this new storm. We would have to weather it together, or not at all.

I turned back to the others who were staring, mystified, at this prolonged conversation between myself and the woman who, until moments ago, had been my captor. I walked back toward them, trying to give a reassuring smile. "It's okay. She's going to come with us," I told them, and then braced for the outrage.

"Come *with* us?" Catriona gasped.

"You can't be serious!" Annabelle hissed.

"Come with us *where*, mate? You haven't even told us what the bloody hell is going on!" Lucida added.

"You're right, I haven't," I said, turning to Lucida. "And I don't owe *you* any explanations until I find out what the hell *you're* doing here, because in case you've missed it, you were most definitely *not* invited." Lucida had the good sense to look abashed, and I addressed the others. "Look, none of you are obligated to be involved in any more of this… this mess I've gotten myself into. You can get in the car and leave now, and I won't blame you in the least. But I have to keep going, and Ileana has to come with me."

"There's no way I'm leaving you to the mercies of that woman," Annabelle said at once, tossing her fiery hair and crossing her arms.

"Trackers don't abandon each other," Catriona said without hesitation.

I looked at Lucida. "If I can be of use, I'll tag along as well," she said, rather meekly for her.

I nodded my gratitude to all three of them. "Thank you. And I'll explain everything… well, not *everything*, but I'll explain what I can, okay? But first, we've got to go back to the camp."

I waited for the second round of incredulous protest to pass.

"Ileana has to prepare for the trip. She gave me her word that we'd be safe," I said.

"Her *word?*!"

"You've got to be bloody joking!"

"I just risked my neck to get you out of that place, and we're just going to stroll casually back in?! What's to stop her from arresting us all the second we cross back into her territory?" Catriona hissed.

"Look, you don't have to trust her. Trust *me*," I said for the second time in the last fifteen minutes. "But if you want to join me on the next leg of this catastrophe, you have to come back to the camp with me. Now." And without waiting for a reply, I turned back to Ileana and gestured toward the camp.

"Lead the way, High Priestess," I told her, and marched right back into the woods, not even stopping to see if the others would follow.

§

And so, in one of the most bizarre plot twists of my life, twenty minutes later I found myself sitting in Ileana's tent once again, this time as an invited guest, sipping on a heavy pottery mug of herbal tea and smirking at Dragos, whose scowl made it clear that

144

he did not fully understand why I was suddenly no longer a prisoner, let alone why he was now being commanded to bring me tea. I made sure to smile smugly at him every time he caught my eye—I still hadn't forgotten how roughly he had dragged me through the woods, how much obvious delight he'd taken in chaining me up in Irina's former cell. Several times, I considered "accidentally" spilling the tea just so I could watch him clean it up.

I might be exhausted and scared and confused, but that was no reason to waste an opportunity to be petty.

At first, Ileana's tasks seemed dull and commonplace; why did she insist I return with her to the tent just to watch her dictate orders to Dragos and fill a tattered old carpet bag with equally tattered and old belongings? Couldn't I have stayed with Catriona, Lucida, and Annabelle, who were currently gathered around one of the Traveler bonfires at the center of the camp, being amply supplied with food, wine, and an impromptu concert of Romany music? But then, Ileana snapped the bag shut and beckoned me over toward the ancient carved throne upon which she always sat whenever I had been summoned for an audience with her.

"Every High Priestess, upon her coronation, has sat upon this throne," she told me, her voice deep and husky with emotion. "And each of us has been charged with a host of sacred duties to carry out while this throne was still ours to sit upon. There has always been a single duty—mysterious in its origin, but tantamount in its importance—that every Traveler High Priestess has been told of, but that none has ever yet had to perform. Until now."

She turned toward Dragos and barked, "You will leave us. Now."

Dragos stepped forward, his face full of resentment, protestation poised on his lips, but Ileana made a sound, somewhere between a growl and a grunt, and thrust a hand out toward him, pointing her long jagged fingernail as though it was a deadly weapon. I had heard stories of witches and "gypsies" and the curses they could cast upon you with a single word, a single gesture. Whether they were true or not, I could not say, but in that moment Ileana was so terrifying that Dragos took a hasty leap backward, dropped his eyes to his feet, and fairly fled the room without so much as a word.

Snorting with disgust and muttering something about "insubordination," Ileana reached a gnarled, arthritic finger down to the front of the throne's seat to the carved wooden panel just below the faded tapestry seat cushion. With a single sharp jab, she pressed upon a knot in the wood, the center of which was set with a huge ruby that sparkled in the lantern light. The knot receded into the wood, setting off a strange series of clicks and whirs that seemed to be coming from inside the throne itself. Then, with a long, drawn-out squeak of protest, the entire front panel of the throne pushed slowly outward, revealing a hidden compartment within it. Her face was just as full of wonder as mine, to see the drawer appear.

"I've always wondered," she whispered, more to herself than to me, and sounding for a moment like a child who had just discovered that some small bit of magic was real, "what would happen if I ever had the chance to push that button."

She reached a shaking hand forward and picked up the only object within the compartment: a massive skeleton key made of heavy black iron, and hung upon a golden chain.

"What is it for?" I asked. "What does it open?"

Ileana looked at me. "I do not know," she whispered. "But when the messenger comes bringing word of the Sentinels, I'm to bring it to the gathering of the Three."

"The Three?" I asked, though I already felt a stirring in my chest at what it might mean.

"The High Priestess of the Traveler Clans. The Keeper of the Elementals. The High Priestess of the International High Council," Ileana replied, confirming my suspicions.

"And then?" I asked.

Ileana shook her head. "No one knows," she answered.

"What about the Sentinels themselves?" I asked her. "Do you have any idea who they are, or what the reference might mean?"

Again, Ileana shook her head. "They will rise at a time of great peril to our clans. That is all I know. When signs started pointing to the fulfillment of the Prophecy, when you arrived at our encampment that first night, seeking refuge, I was sure, then, that the time of the Sentinels was upon us. I kept waiting for the messenger to come, for the words to be spoken, my finger poised upon the button, sure that the moment had come at last; for what could bring more peril to all we hold dear than the Prophecy?"

My heart thundered in my chest. Was it the right moment to answer that question, or ought I to wait? Perhaps, when all of The

Three were gathered, it might be safe to tell her? Yes, surely that was the right time.

"You'd best get some rest," Ileana said, foisting on her stern demeanor as easily as flicking a light switch. "We have a long journey ahead of us. The Caomhnóir will see to it that your vehicle is in fine working order for the trip."

"Where exactly are we going?" I asked.

"To a small village called Pluckley in the county of Kent. There is a wood there—deep within it is where we will find the Keeper of the Elementals."

I shuddered. Ileana narrowed her eyes at me. "Heard of the Elementals, have you?" she asked.

"Heard of them?" I snorted. "I've come face to face with one. Twice. It's not an experience I have any desire to repeat."

Ileana nodded at me, evidently impressed with my pluck. "Well, you're going to repeat it and then some. But with a bit of luck, we may just come out of it unscathed."

I rolled my eyes. "That's very reassuring, thanks."

Ileana took the golden chain of the key and hung it around her neck, tucking it down into her bosom and cloaking it beneath her many shawls and scarves. "Out with you, then," she barked, pointing to the door. "We leave at first light."

§

I found Annabelle alone on a bench by the central bonfire, a mug of something hot in her hands and an untouched plate of bread and stew beside her.

"Hey," I said, sitting down beside her. "You going to eat that, or what?"

"Help yourself," she said. "I'm not hungry."

She was staring across the fire to the other side, where Catriona and Lucida sat huddled in conversation over a jug of wine.

I dipped the bread into the thick brown gravy and wolfed it down. It was earthy and spicy and delicious, whatever it was.

"No one will talk to me, apart from my Auntie Zina, and she's just trying to pump me for gossip," Annabelle said dully. "They all must know by now that we were detained."

I nodded. "I think Dragos and the other Caomhnóir probably had something to do with that. They're royally pissed off that we've been released. I expect they've told the others just to vent their frustrations at Ileana."

Annabelle gave a mirthless laugh. "It would have come out anyway." She gave one last, wistful look to a nearby knot of Travelers who sat laughing together, like it was the cool kids' table in the cafeteria, and then turned to me. "So, what's going on? What's happening now?"

"Ileana wants to leave at first light," I said. "We're traveling to some village in Kent, where the Keeper of the Elementals lives."

"And when we get there?" she asked.

I shrugged. "I have no idea. Ileana seems to know where she is and how to get to her. So we'll let her lead the way, and then I'll deliver Agnes' message. I have no idea how it will be received, but we've already been bound, gagged, and shackled while trapped in each other's bodies, so it can't really get worse than that, right?"

Annabelle managed half a smirk before her face fell back into lines of misery. "And you're still sure you want her to come?" She jerked her head in Lucida's direction.

"She's not my first choice," I admitted. "But she's in this, Annabelle. The Necromancers cut the mark of the Tansy Hag into her flesh. I would never have found the clues hidden in the Skye Príosún if she hadn't led me to them."

"You know who she worked for," Annabelle said through gritted teeth. The mug in her hand trembled. "You know what they did."

"I haven't forgotten." I murmured. "I promise you, I haven't. Lucida is... well, it's complicated. I haven't forgiven her for her role in the Prophecy, and for what she did to Hannah, and I probably never will, but... well, she saved my life since then. She didn't have to, but she did. I don't know what it all means except that sometimes—maybe even most of the time—people are messier than we perceive them to be. It's not black and white. Mostly, it's just... grey."

Annabelle did not reply. She just stared down into the steaming depths of her mug for a few moments before knocking the contents back in a single swig. A deep, heady aroma drifted toward me, and I realized she was drinking the same kind of mulled wine that Flavia and her friends had passed around the night I had Rifted for the first time. I crammed another hunk of stew-soaked bread into my mouth and stood up. "I'm going to fill Catriona and Lucida in on the plan. Do you want to come with me?"

Annabelle shook her head. "I'll walk with you that way, but I think I'm going to turn in."

I gave her shoulder a squeeze and we set off together around the perimeter of the bonfire circle until we reached Catriona and Lucida. They broke off their conversation at once when they saw us coming. Lucida stood up, handing a bottle of wine to Catriona.

"I've got to find the loo," she announced, and then with a laugh turned to Annabelle. "This Traveler wine, eh? Strong stuff, don't you—"

SMACK. Annabelle had pulled back her arm and slapped Lucida across the face as hard as she could. Lucida staggered, bringing her hand up to her cheek and staring at Annabelle in utter disbelief.

"That was for David," Annabelle growled, her chest heaving. "Do not presume, because I am tolerating your presence on this journey, that you are permitted to speak even a single word to me. Ever."

Lucida straightened up, dropped her hand, and assumed a blank expression. She nodded to indicate she understood, and then turned to Catriona, whose mouth was hanging open.

"Right, then. Think I'll turn in," she murmured. She ducked between two Traveler wagons and out of sight.

Annabelle exhaled slowly, a flush of anger receding from her face. "Good night, then," she said to Catriona and me, before stalking off in the opposite direction.

I turned to Catriona, who looked as though she was about to call out after Annabelle. "Don't," I advised her. "You know what the Necromancers did to David Pierce. Lucida should count herself lucky Annabelle didn't kill her on the spot."

Catriona swallowed back her reply, and swiftly changed the subject, assuming her professional tone of Tracker formality. "What's going on, then? What did Ileana say? Are we heading out soon?"

"Relax. We're not leaving until dawn. But there are some things I've got to tell you first. If you're going to come along for this ride, you deserve to know what you're signing up for."

"About bloody time!" Catriona said, shifting down the bench to make room for me.

"But before I tell you what I can, I need some answers, too," I said, sitting down beside her.

"Like what?" Catriona asked.

"Like what in the actual hell is she doing here?" I said, nodding toward the spot where Lucida's form had just vanished into the shadows.

Catriona sighed. She offered her cup to me and I took it. She refilled it with wine for me and began to talk. "Do you remember that I told you I'd gotten a call from Lucida? The first call she'd made to me since she'd been imprisoned?"

"Yeah," I said. "You said she wanted details about me, if you'd heard anything about what I'd been up to since I'd been back."

"That's right," Catriona said. "And by the time I'd returned to the Tracker office after I'd found you, she'd called again. I knew something was dodgy. Two phone calls in as many days after five years of silence? As soon as the general assembly meeting was over, I excused myself on Tracker business and set out for Skye Príosún."

"I'm surprised Celeste let you go, with everything that's going on at the castle," I remarked.

"She nearly didn't. But I'm no use at Fairhaven sitting around, watching and waiting with everyone else, and I told Celeste as much. We're still trying to sort out the mess at the *príosún* anyway, let's not forget that." She gave me a resentful glare, as though I had abandoned her, which, to be fair, I had. I'd taken a leave of absence from the Trackers to help Fiona with her recovery, and then I'd abandoned Fiona as well to follow Agnes' clues.

"So, what happened then? When you got to the *príosún*?" I asked in an effort to get the conversation back on track.

"When I checked in with the guards there, they told me that Lucida was behaving like a total nutter—refusing to eat anything brought to her cell, refusing to be escorted anywhere by Caomhnóir, and threatening to attack anyone who came near her. They were worried she'd starve herself to death. Lucida hadn't mentioned anything like that when I'd spoken to her. All I'd gotten from her were endless, obsessive questions about you. Obviously, I went right down to see her. She was in better shape, physically, than I'd feared, but mentally—she was beside herself with panic. She was convinced that the Caomhnóir were going to try to kill her."

I raised my eyebrows "Why?" ___

Catriona threw her hands up in frustration. "That's what I said. I said, 'Lucida, that's crazy, you've been in here for more than five years. Why would the guards suddenly want to do you in?' She said it was because of the Necromancers. Now that they had infiltrated the Caomhnóir, she couldn't trust the *príosún* guards anymore. I told her repeatedly that all of the compromised Caomhnóir had been removed, that all of the current guards were either cleared of wrongdoing by the Trackers or else brand new to the *príosún*—on assignment from other clans around the world while we sorted this mess out. But she wouldn't be swayed. She just kept babbling on and on about how she knew too much, and that the Necromancers would never rest once they heard she'd survived the attack at Fairhaven."

"You already knew she was freaked out," I pointed out. "Remember how she kept asking for additional protection at Fairhaven when she heard the Necromancers were coming to testify before the Council? Well, she was right about that, wasn't she?" Indeed, it had been Lucida's murder of Ambrose, my own former Caomhnóir and Necromancer convert, who had snuck back onto the grounds bent on revenge, that landed her back in Skye Príosún in the first place. Lucida had refused to defend herself against the charges of killing him, but it was clear that he had initiated the attack, and that she had killed him in self defense.

"Yes, I daresay she *was* right about that, although we have no evidence that Lucida was the intended target of that attack. She could simply have been in the wrong place at the wrong time."

I didn't reply. This theory felt like a hell of a stretch to me. Lucida escapes from the castle because she's terrified of a Necromancer attack and then, no sooner does she reach the border of the grounds then she happens, purely by chance, to fall victim to a completely unpremeditated Necromancer attack? Not likely, but Catriona, ever the Tracker, would hold on to every conceivable explanation until the hard evidence ruled them out one by one.

"Anyway," Catriona went on, "once she was back in the *príosún*, she felt no safer than she did at Fairhaven. I would even venture to say that being locked up again only served to amplify her paranoia. By the time I went to see her, she was out of her mind with terror. I'd never seen her so unhinged, and I've seen her at her absolute worst. I knew I couldn't leave her there like that. Not... not after everything we've been through."

"You left her there for five years," I said, surprising myself with the bluntness of the observation that sounded much more like an accusation than I had intended. But if Catriona was hurt by my words, she absorbed the blow without so much as flinching. She nodded, allowing for the truth of it to expand between us before replying.

"When Lucida was first sentenced to her time in Skye Príosún, she accepted it. She didn't beg and plead for mercy. She didn't try to make deals or sacrifice others to lessen her punishment. She met her consequences with far more grace than I'd known she possessed. Honestly, I sometimes wondered how she'd turned traitor in the first place, if she had that much character hiding in there to begin with. Regardless, she betrayed not a bit of fear or regret when they marched her away to Skye, and I never once pitied her. I was full of self pity, mind, but for Lucida? Not a jot." Catriona shook her head. "But this? This was something else entirely. I've never seen her like that. I knew I had to get her out."

I blinked. "Get... get her out? Do you mean... Catriona, please don't tell me you're on the run right now."

Catriona didn't reply. I groaned.

"Oh, my God. You have got to be kidding me. You have got to be fucking kidding me."

"Look, I didn't break her out," Catriona said hurriedly. "Not... not the way you're thinking. It wasn't some kind of swashbuckling adventure where we fought our way out. I just... I forged some transfer papers for her. I told the guards that she was being transferred to another *príosún*, and just walked her out in cuffs. It could be weeks before they discover that she's been broken out."

"But when they do, the entirety of the Caomhnóir and Tracker forces will be after you, Cat!" I cried. "My God, everything you've built, your career, your place on the Council... is it really worth it?!"

"Would it be worth it to you if it was Hannah?" Catriona asked.

I looked up at her and saw, to my shock, that there were tears glittering in her eyes. Her face was transformed by the emotion, her expression a silent plea for understanding.

"Yeah," I admitted at last. "Always." I realized in this moment that several nearby Travelers were staring at us, and I hastened to lower my voice. "Look, I get it, I do; but if the Trackers are now after you, they're going to be after me, too! It's one thing if you want to sacrifice yourself for Lucida, but now you've dragged me into it! I'm trying to fly under the radar here, and you've just put a giant target on my back!"

"I know," she said, her voice trembling with a desperation I'd rarely heard there before. "I know, and I'm sorry, but—"

"It's going to take more than an apology to fix this, Cat!"

"She showed me, Jess. She showed me the mark of the Tansy Hag."

I froze. My heart, thumping in my chest a moment before, seemed to go still.

"She showed you?"

"Yes."

"Did she tell you what it means?"

"I know the Necromancers cut it into her flesh," Catriona hissed. "I know that they think it's some kind of evidence of our great crimes. I know they think they've discovered a secret that's going to take our power from us. And I know that, whatever it is, it's part of the reason you're here. So if you can shed some light on any of that, now would be the time to do it."

I dropped my face into my hands. This was too hard. Too hard to know what to tell, and what to keep secret. Agnes never gave me any guidance for this, for who to trust and who to keep in the dark. If I'd been able to stay in the Rift just a little bit longer, would she have sworn me to secrecy, made me promise to take her words to the grave? Or would she have told me to gather my own army, to use every resource at my disposal to make sure that I was able to carry out her orders? Surely, if she trusted me with this task, she trusted me to make the decisions along the way to carry it out? I had to believe this was true, and so that meant I needed to decide: who were my allies in this, and did I trust them enough to tell them the whole truth?

I looked into Catriona's face and found that the answer to that question came surprisingly easy.

I handed the mug of mulled wine back to her. "Here. You're going to need this," I said, and plunged headfirst into the story.

By the time I had finished, the mug was still clenched tightly in her hand. She had not taken a sip. She had not spoken. I'm not sure she had even blinked. It took several moments of loaded silence before she managed to respond.

"All my life, I wondered," she whispered at last, "why it was that the Geatgrima drew us in so powerfully. It stood there, a mere symbol, and yet it felt like so much more. My God, it all makes sense now."

I exhaled with relief. "You believe me, then?"

Catriona looked as though the question I had asked her was absurd. "Why in the name of the Aether would you make something like that up? What possible motivation could you have?"

I shrugged. "I'm sure others will think of a million reasons not to believe it."

"Well, I'm not others," Catriona said. She looked down at her own hands for a moment, as though she had suddenly found a stranger's hands attached to her wrists, then knocked back the entire mug of wine in a single go. She looked back at me, her expression deadly serious. "Many of the Durupinen are going to fight this. Right to the very highest ranks."

"I know."

"Some of them will try to bury this, and you with it."

"I know. I thought you might be one of them."

Catriona's lips curved into a sad half smile. "There was a time not that long ago when I surely would have been. But I've seen too much of our world start to crumble. Since the Prophecy came to pass, we've been coming apart at the seams. The leadership doesn't want to admit it, but it's true. I'm in the trenches every day as the head of the Trackers, and I've never seen such upheaval and chaos as I've seen in the last few years. It was as though the Prophecy had upset something incredibly delicate, something forgotten and fragile, and we've been frantically trying to keep it from shattering every moment since. And now it all makes sense. We've been living on borrowed time, perhaps for centuries, without even knowing it. And by fighting so desperately to keep things as they are, we've been waging war against how they ought to be. That has to end, and it has to end now."

"Do you think I did the right thing, keeping this from the Council and from Celeste?" I asked her.

"Oh, yes," Catriona said, nodding her head sagely. "You'd never have made it out of the castle, I <u>guarantee</u> it."

"So, you'll stay? You'll come with us?" I asked.

"Of course. As much as I've struggled with what the Durupinen have done to Lucida, I've never doubted that being a Durupinen is the best of who I am. Now I know what I need to do to truly fulfill that purpose, as it was always meant to be fulfilled, and I'm going to bloody well do it."

"What about the castles? The money? The power structure? The traditions?"

"Tear 'em down," Catriona said. "Tear 'em down and watch 'em burn. They were always the worst of us anyway, weren't they?"

I smiled. "Yup. They really were."

AT THE RUINS

A LTHOUGH MY BODY ACHED with exhaustion and I could hardly keep my eyes open, I did not fall immediately into bed when I returned to the wagon where Annabelle and I would be staying the night. Instead, I opened the connection and found two frantic and familiar energies waiting for me.

"Jess, thank God! What took you so long?" Milo sighed.

"Sorry, it's been a little crazy, but I'm fine," I said.

"If we hadn't heard from you soon, I wouldn't have been able to stop Finn from coming after you!" Hannah said, and I could feel the rolling waves of her anxiety fill my head like the sea. "He's going spare, Jess. What's happened?"

By the time I finished filling them in, their shock had turned my mental space into a barren, echoing void. It was actually rather peaceful, until they began to process the details.

"Lucida? Are you serious?"

"Ileana is coming with you? After she imprisoned you like that?"

"At least she believed her!"

"Yeah, but what if it's a ploy? What if she turns on her?"

"You guys, please, the speculation is not helping," I said wearily. "I've asked myself all the same questions. It doesn't matter. There's only one way forward. I have to keep going. But there is one thing I need you to do for me."

"What is it?"

"Yeah, how can we help?"

"I need you to find Finn and fill him in on everything. And I need you to tell him he has to meet me in Kent."

"You want him to come?" Hannah asked.

"Yes. I think we're going to need a Caomhnóir, and Ileana is refusing to bring one from the Traveler camp. She doesn't want anyone else here to know what's happening, and I can't say I blame her, but it leaves her unprotected. Finn has experience with Elementals and I don't think we're going to be lucky enough to meet someone called 'the Keeper of the Elementals' without encountering at least one."

"Not to mention the fact that he'll probably take it upon himself to show up anyway, once he realizes you're about to walk into a forest full of Elementals with Ileana and Lucida, of all people," Milo pointed out.

"Exactly. So, let's salvage a little bit of my dignity and invite him before he can crash the party, okay? I'll feel better if he's there, anyway. Now what's happening at Fairhaven?"

"As far as Savvy, nothing seems to have changed, but amongst the Council there have been… developments," Hannah said carefully.

"Developments?" I asked, all sleepiness gone in an instant. "What kind of developments?"

"People aren't happy with Celeste's 'wait-and-see' approach," Hannah said. "Patricia Lightfoot is heading a faction to try to garner enough support for a no confidence vote."

"A no confidence vote?" I repeated. "You mean she's trying to get Celeste removed?"

"Well, it would be the first step," Hannah admitted. "If there were a no confidence vote, and Celeste lost, they would be able to hold an election to officially run someone to oust her. And… well, I'm sure you can imagine who has her power-hungry little eyes on the candidacy."

I didn't need to imagine. I knew.

"Marion."

"Of course," Milo replied. "Does that woman even exist if she's not causing as much trouble as absolutely possible?"

"She can't possibly be eligible. She's not even on the Council," I pointed out.

"I asked Keira about that, and she says it doesn't matter. There's a loophole. Because of the manner in which Marion lost her seat, she can use the election as an appeal. By voting for her, people will be giving their approval for her reinstatement."

"But that doesn't mean you'll lose your seat, will it?" I asked with a gasp. Hannah had fought tooth and nail to be elected into the seat that Marion had been ousted from.

"No, because that's not the seat she wants anymore," Hannah said, and the acid in the reply was like fire inside my head. "She's got her sights set higher now. Although if she were to gain the High Priestess' seat, there's no doubt she'd use it to make my life hell."

"And there's nothing Celeste can do to stop her? No rules she can invoke? No appeals she can make?" I asked, incredulous.

"No. A no confidence vote trumps all other decrees," Hannah replied. "Her only avenue is to appeal to the International High Council, and of course you know why she won't do that. She's afraid the Northern Clans will lose autonomy if the International High Council gets involved."

"Which is really just another way of saying she's afraid she's going to be stripped of her own power," I growled, "which makes her little better than Marion at this point. So, what's Marion doing, then? She can't possibly be openly campaigning."

"She's doing what she does best," Milo replied. "She's floating around like she's queen bee again, swarming around with her little cronies and buzzing about for support. Quietly, of course, but everyone knows what she's doing."

"But people couldn't wait to distance themselves from her when she lost her seat," I thought desperately. "Why the hell would they want to form an alliance with her now?"

"They see it as an opportunity," Hannah said. "The pendulum has swung back in her favor and they all can't wait to climb back on her coattails. They'll abandon her in an instant if she loses, but they're willing to gamble on her in the short term."

"You know what? I'm starting to understand exactly why we've held onto the Gateways for so long," I said, my anger seething. "Drunk on our own power from day one, and we haven't learned a damn thing, have we?"

"Apparently not," Hannah replied. "But the thing is, Jess, even if they lose the no confidence vote, they'll have called together the entire Northern Clans to Fairhaven to hold it. It's just like the Airechtas, every single clan needs to be represented. It will be impossible to keep the situation with Savvy a secret anymore. The word will spread like wildfire and the International High Council will find out anyway. Marion and the others are counting on the fact that they will strip Celeste of her authority for keeping it from them."

"So, Celeste loses power either way," I said, shaking my head. "Those fucking vultures, just circling and biding their time, ready to attack at the first sign of weakness."

"Pretty much," Milo said. "But the point is, you're on the clock now. It's only a matter of time before the entire Durupinen world knows about what's happening with Savvy, and once they do, we won't be able to control the narrative... or the fallout."

"Right," I said, taking a deep breath. "So, no pressure, in other words."

"Yeah, I mean, take your time, no rush," Milo replied, and inside my head, I felt the gentle, warm nudge of the joke quickly washed away in our mutual flood of anxiety.

A few minutes later, after many promises of regular updates and lengthy emotional goodbyes, I finally lay my head back upon the pillow in the wagon's top bunk, listening to Annabelle's steady breathing and my own pounding heart. I closed my eyes and tried to focus in on the blood in my veins, to the tenuous, ancient connection within it that bound me to Agnes and to my sister, and to so many other Durupinen over the centuries—I tried not to think of any part of that connection as stolen. And as the connection in my blood sang to me its ancient song, I sang back to it, softly.

"I'm doing my best. Please help guide me. Help me to make the right choices."

The connection in my blood sang back, and though I could not understand the words, there was a familiar comfort to it, and before long, it had sung me to sleep.

§

I woke so suddenly, so completely, that I wondered if I had even been asleep at all. Voices were shouting outside the wagon. I rolled over and squinted at my watch. It was two o'clock in the morning. I'd barely been asleep for two hours.

I sat up, forgetting where I was and cracking my head on the low wooden ceiling. Cursing, my eyes watering, I slid down out of the bunk just as Annabelle sat up, looking around sleepily and mumbling, "What is it? Is something happening?"

"I don't know," I told her, sliding my feet into my sneakers. "I can hear a lot of people out there. I'm going to check it out."

"Wait for me, I'll come with you," Annabelle said, remembering to keep her head low as she rolled out of her own bunk.

I lifted the latch that held together the two halves of the Dutch door and pushed the top half wide. Outside our wagon, a group of perhaps a dozen Travelers were huddled together, two holding torches, the others lanterns of <u>various</u> shapes and sizes. An older

160

woman, her head wrapped in a bright red scarf, was gesticulating enthusiastically, pointing in various directions and sending the other Travelers scurrying off to wherever she indicated.

"Auntie Zina?" Annabelle called out, and the woman looked up. "What's going on?"

"It's Vashti's little girl, Naomi. She's gone missing from their wagon and no one seems to know where she's gone off to. We're searching the woods," Zina replied. Vashti stood beside Zina, clutching a shawl around her shoulders, eyes red and swollen from crying. Zina had thrown her arm around the woman and was rubbing her arm consolingly. I recognized Vashti at once as the mother of the little girl who had hidden beneath my skirts at the campfire.

"Let me help," Annabelle said, pulling the latch on the bottom of the door and hurrying down the steps. "I can help look for her."

Zina looked skeptical but shrugged, reaching into her pocket and handing Annabelle a flashlight. "Suit yourself, but we can't be looking for you as well if you get yourself lost in the woods."

"I can look after myself, Auntie," Annabelle shot back, sounding a bit petulant. "I want to help."

"Very well. The child is wearing a blue nightgown and her red wellies are missing, so she's likely wearing those, too. Take that path north but be sure to turn back if you reach the river. It's swollen this time of year, and it's not safe to search it in the dark."

"Naomi knows better than to go near the river. She's scared of the current," Vashti sniffed in a quavering voice. Zina nodded and rubbed Vashti's arm vigorously in reply.

"That's right, love, that's right. Don't worry, we'll find her. Fan out now, everyone."

I descended the steps as the group dispersed and joined Annabelle. "I'll come with you," I told her. "I want to help, too."

"You don't have to do that," Annabelle said. "You should try to get some sleep."

I rolled my eyes. "Like I can sleep knowing there's a little girl lost in the woods out here? Don't be ridiculous. I'm coming. Hang on, though, I'm going to grab one of the lanterns from the wagon."

A few minutes later, Annabelle and I found ourselves deep in the nighttime forest, surrounded by velvety darkness, wind-rustled trees, and the echoing shouts of the missing girl's name. Behind us, back at the camp, surely everyone must be roused by now, drawn out of their slumber by the ruckus. Above our heads, bats swooped through the trees, and around our feet, small nocturnal creatures scurried away from the beams of our searchlights. Every minute that went by dug the hollow of dread in my stomach a little deeper. Where could the child have gone? What might have happened to her?

"Traveler kids must know better than to wander off from the camp, right?" I asked in an effort to distract myself as the 'what if's' began to creep up on me. "They must teach them that from the cradle."

"Yeah, but you know how kids are," Annabelle replied, squinting into the darkness. "Some of them have to test the limits, just to see. It's like when your mom tells you not to touch the stove because it's hot. There's always one little bugger who just *has* to know how hot it really is."

I chuckled. "I was totally that kid. Until I got old enough to notice my mom was more likely to set the place on fire than I was, and then I realized I needed to watch out for both of us."

A whoosh and a shiver indicated that a spirit had passed by us overhead. This was nothing unusual; much like Fairhaven and any location where Durupinen congregated, spirit activity was heightened in the woods surrounding the Traveler camp. So it wasn't until the third spirit swooped over us, sailing off in the same direction, that Annabelle and I really took notice.

"That's... strange," I said, watching the silvery glimmer of the third spirit disappear into the trees ahead of us. "What do you suppose that's about?"

"I'm not sure," Annabelle said, though she looked wary now. "But I think it means we should keep going."

We continued down the same path, hyperaware now not only for signs of Naomi, but for spirit presence as well. So when two more spirits sailed into the path ahead of us, we did not waste the opportunity to question them.

"Hello!" I called out. "Excuse me?"

One of the spirits turned to me in surprise. He took the form of an elderly gentleman in a long robe that might have been a monk's garb.

"Where are you going?" I asked.

The spirit blinked at me several times. I could not be sure if he'd understood me or not, until he muttered something that sounded like Italian, pointed up the path ahead of us, and continued on his way.

Annabelle looked at me, eyes wide. "That was... interesting."

I nodded. "Did you see that he didn't even notice me until I called out to him?"

Annabelle smirked. "Do you get this put out every time a man doesn't notice you?"

"I'm not put out," I said, "I'm intrigued. It's not often that a ghost can float right past a Gateway without even giving it a passing glance. That must mean there's something pretty damn intriguing up this path."

Annabelle stared at me, and I could read the fear in her face. "Do you think... Naomi?" she whispered.

"Let's find out," I replied. "Let's follow them."

We hurried our pace to keep the spirits in sight. After several minutes, they veered from the path and into the thick vegetation of the forest, and it became much more difficult to follow them. We scrambled over clumps of bushes and fought our way through branches grown so close together that they formed thick, leafy barriers. Tree roots tripped us every few steps, and the ground between them grew wet and spongy with moss. The faint, translucent glow of the ghosts drifted further and further ahead of us. If we had to go much further, we would lose them completely, and then I doubted we'd ever be able to find our way back to the encampment.

"Jess."

I picked myself up, swearing from the ground for what felt like the hundredth time and turned to see Annabelle white faced, holding a muddy red boot.

My heart sped up. "We must be getting close," I told her. "Let's keep moving."

But I'd only pressed forward a few more feet when I met a tangle of branches, vines, and foliage so dense that I could not break through it. It was as though the forest itself had built a wall between us and whatever was on the other side. Annabelle stumbled to a halt beside me and began pulling and tugging at the foliage as well.

"What in the world..." she panted. "How do we get through?"

I held up my lantern, gazing around, but the dense, leafy wall stretched for as far as I could see in the flickering light. I hesitated to change directions; what if we lost our way? I turned to the nearest ancient tree trunk, wondering if I might be able to scale it, when I stepped on something smooth and slippery. I looked down.

Another shiny, red wellie, spotted with mud.

As I bent to pick it up, I noticed a hole, perfectly round and child-sized, in the dense barrier of foliage. I blinked, wondering for a moment if a white rabbit with a waistcoat and a watch was going to pop out of it and announce that he was, in fact, very late. Then I shook my head to clear it.

"Annabelle! Look!"

I handed her the boot, then showed her the little tunnel.

"Do you suppose we can fit through it?" Annabelle asked.

"Only one way to find out," I said and, dropping to my hands and knees, attempted to wedge myself through it.

We definitely brought the wrong twin for this job, I thought to myself, thinking of my tiny sister as I forced my proportions through the entanglement, snaring my hair, ripping my clothing, and scratching up every exposed bit of skin. After much struggling and a fair amount of cursing, I forced the top half of my body through the tunnel and felt a frigid wind hit my raw face.

The tunnel opened into a small, circular clearing, with monstrous trees arching high on all sides, coming nearly together up above us like the arches of a natural cathedral, but for a round hole at the very center, through which the full moon shone like a celestial spotlight. And in its milky beam, a small child stood, her long, dark hair adorned with twigs and leaves, her blue nightdress washed out and shredded from a long and treacherous journey through the snatching and grabbing fingers of the wilderness.

"Naomi."

But the child did not turn. She could not. For before her stood a dais, and upon the dais, the crumbled remains of what was, unmistakably, a Geatgrima. And flowing between them, the girl and the ruin, was a glowing current of pure spirit energy.

"Oh, God, no," I whispered.

"What? What is it? Did you find her? Let me through, Jess!"

I slid the rest of my body through the tunnel and struggled to my feet, never taking my eyes off of the girl. I barely registered when

Annabelle finally fought her way in to appear at my side, hardly took in a word of her frightened exclamations. It wasn't until she rushed forward, arm outstretched to pull the child back from the dais, that I regained enough sense to reach out, grab Annabelle by the back of her sweater and yank her backward.

"Don't! You can't touch her!"

"But Jess, something's wrong, something's happening to her!"

"I know, but you mustn't touch her! It's too late, Annabelle, we can't help her now."

Annabelle turned a devastated expression on me as memory caught up with reality. "This is what happened to your friend Savannah, isn't it?"

"Yes," I said, a lump rising in my throat.

Annabelle turned over her shoulder and, before I could stop her, she started screaming for help, her voice reverberating through the trees, echoing and shattering and echoing again, until it seemed the forest itself was crying out for help for the little girl.

I stepped forward, walking slowly around until I could see Naomi's face. It was arresting to see that the very same expression could exist on two such completely different faces as this child and Savvy. An identical look of utter tranquility, of pride and duty—of... *peace.*

"It's all right, Naomi," I whispered to the girl. "Don't be afraid. Everything is going to be okay." She didn't appear afraid, of course; it was my own fear I was trying to soothe. Naomi's face remained unchanged, her connection with the Geatgrima all-consuming. She was no longer just a child, lost in the woods. She was a Sentinel now.

I stepped back from the girl and turned my attention now to the Geatgrima. It was truly ancient, little more than a pile of rubble upon the dais, which was itself crumbling to dust, creeping vines and weeds forcing their way up between the stones. I knelt down and examined the largest of the remaining stones. Just there, behind a tangle of ivy, the faintest impression of a marking, worn almost to nothing by hundreds of years of rain and wind and time: the mark of the Tansy Hag.

Meanwhile, around the edges of the clearing, voices were growing louder, followed by the dull thuds of axes and knives as Traveler Caomhnóir cut and hacked through the forest's defenses of the sacred space. At last, the Travelers swarmed the clearing, all of them stopping short upon the revelation of the moonlit scene before them. It seemed as though the entirety of the camp had joined in the search—I even spotted Catriona and Lucida's wary faces near the back of the crowd, unsure whether they really ought to be there, and yet too curious not to follow.

"Naomi!" a desperate voice cried out, breaking the silence. Vashti, the girl's mother, had at last broken through. She rushed forward as Annabelle had done, but was held back by a dozen hands at once, all shushing and soothing and restraining in a chorus.

"You mustn't touch her, Vashti."

"Keep back, love."

"There, there, now. You mustn't do anything foolish."

Vashti's cries for her baby filled the clearing, rising to a keening so pure that it raised the hairs on the back of my neck and sent birds scattering from the trees above us.

"Let me through. What has happened here?"

Ileana had arrived at last, her raven swaying upon her shoulder. Flanked by Dragos and a second Caomhnóir with a jagged scar running the length of his face. The crowd of Travelers parted for her, drifting to either side, all of them gazing at her, desperate for answers. Ileana's expression as she laid eyes upon the child and the Geatgrima was inscrutable. She walked the total circumference of the clearing, examining the scene from every angle. She stared up into the face of the moon, as though it was speaking to her, whispering words carried to her on the breeze that none of the rest of us could hear. At last she stood so near Naomi that the gathered company drew in a collective gasp. She stared into the child's face, and examined the pulsing glow of her connection to the Geatgrima. Finally, she straightened up and surveyed the captivated crowd.

"Who found her like this?" she asked.

"We did," I replied, the sound of my own voice making me wince. "Annabelle and me. We heard the others outside our wagon organizing a search party, and we volunteered to help."

"How did you know to come here?" Ileana asked, the raven upon her shoulder cocking its head in an accusatory way.

"We didn't know to come here," Annabelle replied, raising her chin defiantly at the insinuation in the question. "We were sent down this path by my Aunt Zina. We followed her orders."

"This is true," Zina piped up from the midst of the crowd, where a distraught Vashti sobbed inconsolably into her shoulder.

"But you left the path," Ileana said. "Why?"

I pointed up to the sky, where nearly a dozen spirits now hovered over the clearing. "We followed them. After four of them passed us, all traveling the same way in the forest, we felt it was worth investigating. We also found her boots along the way."

I held up the pair of little red wellies. Vashti sunk to the ground, weeping into Zina's skirts.

"How did the child find the Geatgrima?"

She asked the question to the group at large, but no one answered.

"This site has been lost for many years. How did the child find it?"

Again, no answer from the Travelers, but a question rose from my own lips before I could stop it. "You didn't know this Geatgrima was here?" I asked, incredulous.

"Yes, we knew it was here, once," Ileana replied stiffly. "A ruin only, abandoned many years ago when we were forced from these lands by a fire. Our people occupied these forests many centuries ago. We have been drawn back to it over the generations. It has become a bastion of safety in our many wanderings. But the exact location of this monument was lost to us. Until now."

Ileana looked up at the spirits who crowded the sky above us like sentient clouds. Then she crossed the clearing until she was standing right in front of me.

"You know what is happening. You have seen this before."

It was not a question, and I wasn't entirely sure how she knew it, but I nodded. "Yes. At Fairhaven, in our central courtyard. My friend Savannah Todd—you've met her, she was with me when the Necromancers attacked your camp. She is now locked into a connection just like this."

"When?"

"About two weeks ago. She has neither moved nor spoken. No one can approach her."

What little color the moonlight had not leeched from Ileana's complexion now left it.

"And the child?"

I leaned in close to her so that my lips nearly brushed her ear as I replied, "She is a Sentinel now."___

Ileana closed her eyes for a moment. She seemed to be gathering something up within herself—strength, perhaps, or resolve. Then she stepped away from me and spoke to the gathered Travelers, her voice rich with authority. "No one is to touch the child. She is within the grip of the Geatgrima. Dragos, you will organize a watch over her. She is to be guarded, day and night. I will leave in the morning. I must seek consultation on how to proceed."

All of the Travelers stared in shock. Evidently "seeking consultation" was not a thing that the Travelers did very often. Fierce independence from "Settler" clans had long kept them nearly entirely separate from the rest of the Durupinen world.

A very old woman broke away from the crowd, hobbling forward until she stood only a few feet away from Naomi. She looked so frail, so ancient, that it was a wonder she had even managed to follow the group through the forest to the clearing at all. No one put out a hand to stop her. No one spoke. No one even moved. Even Ileana stepped back from the woman with a kind of deference that could only be reserved for an elder—a matriarch.

The woman took the knobbly stick with which she walked and dug its tip into the bare, mossy ground. Next, she slowly traversed the clearing, dragging the stick behind her, so that when she arrived back where she had started, she had created a near-perfect circle within which we all now stood, waiting silently. The woman sank to her knees before the child, placing one gnarled hand upon the ground at her feet and raising the other as though in supplication to the sky. Then, she began to sing.

"Sing" did not do justice to the depth or primality of the noise that reverberated around the space, enveloping it in a blanket of sound that at once warmed me and sent shivers up my spine and into the roots of my hair, but I could think of no other word for it. The melody was full of strange, unexpected intervals woven together in a heart wrenching minor key, rendered all the more haunting in the old woman's ancient husk of a voice.

And then, from the furthest shadows of the group, a mournful fiddle began to play. We all turned to see Laini sawing away on her violin, her back pressed to a tree, her eyes closed as though in prayer. And then the music swept up the other Travelers, and they spread around the clearing and dropped to their knees, creating a second living circle within the first that had been etched into the earth. One by one, they caught up the tune, adding their voices until the music swelled to a full chorus. Annabelle sank to her knees as well, and though she did not know the words or the tune, she clasped her hand around her Auntie Zina's and swayed along. I looked around and realized that only Lucida, Catriona, and I remained standing, intruders in this show of solemnity.

"The song is a promise," came a voice from behind me, and I realized that Ileana had risen from the circle and appeared at my side. "The child protects them, and so they will protect the child. That is the deepest promise of blood."

"But how does the old woman know that the child is protecting them?"

Ileana shrugged. "How do we know anything? Sometimes what we seek to hide reveals itself in ways we do not anticipate. Sometimes the truth, it sings to us."

I did not know what to say, so I turned back to the girl and made my own promise. I would not rest until Agnes' message had been delivered. And if it was within my power, though we shared no Traveler blood, I too would promise to protect this girl—and Savvy, and any other Durupinen who might fall under the Geatgrima's spell.

I would find a way to sing the truth, too.

A BIT OF SHINE

IT WAS A STRANGE and somewhat hostile group that piled into the Tracker SUV the next morning at dawn. The tension in the car, once the doors were closed, was almost overwhelming. Catriona sat in the driver's seat, her eyes, hidden behind giant sunglasses, fixed firmly on the road. Beside her, in the passenger's seat, Lucida sat with her knees pulled up to her chin, looking bleary-eyed and exhausted—her face had still not lost the sharp, hollow look that Skye Príosún had given it. On my right, and as far from Lucida as the tight quarters would possibly allow, was Annabelle, arms and legs crossed tightly into tense knots. On my left was Ileana, who looked as out of place in a car as a fish on a bicycle. She was clutching her many shawls and scarves tightly around her body, as though trying to protect herself from the indignity of modern Settler convenience. And stuck in the middle, trying to keep all occupants of the car at bay from each other, was me, sleep-deprived, skittish, and feeling like the kid who drew the short straw on the most dysfunctional family road trip ever.

It was a trip that almost didn't happen at all. The Traveler Council spent most of the rest of the night in session, anxious to understand what was happening to little Naomi, dragging the Scribes from the vigil in the Geatgrima's clearing into their wagons to begin what was sure to be days upon days of feverish research. When it became clear that Ileana was determined to leave the camp, the fight began over how she should travel and who should accompany her. The fight became all the more fierce when they realized that she had absolutely no intention of telling them where she was going or from whom she was seeking consultation, and that she was determined that no other Traveler accompany her. The protest was particularly strong amongst Dragos and his Caomhnóir contingent, who had a sworn duty to protect their High Priestess and could not fathom allowing her to simply vanish with neither companion nor protection. When it was revealed that she would have both companions and protection, but that it was Northern Settlers, not Travelers, who would be providing them, the ensuing uproar was enormous. Or at least, that was the report that was relayed to us around the fire by Jeta, who had crept round the Council tent and gotten the full story from Fennix, who was standing guard at the entrance. Traveler Council meetings were typically raucous, crowded affairs, open to every Traveler, and generally well attended, but with nearly the entire camp still gathered in vigil around Naomi, only a handful of people had slipped away in order to find out what was going on and inform the others.

"I can't imagine what would be so cataclysmic that the High Priestess would put her life in Settler hands to keep it secret," Jeta murmured, looking at the four of us with a mixture of awe and fear.

None of us answered, which only confirmed, I suppose, just how right she was. She couldn't imagine. None of us could.

The drive from the Traveler grove in Cambridgeshire to the village of Pluckley in Ashford, Kent was only about two and a half hours, but it seemed an eternity trapped in that horribly silent car. I had a hundred questions to ask Ileana about where we were going and who we would be meeting when we got there, but the expression on her face was so fiercely closed off that I didn't dare break the silence. Even Catriona, with whom I was expecting to spend the entire drive assembling facts and formulating detailed plans, didn't dare to take charge in that way, though I could see her biting the inside of her cheek now and then to stop herself from blurting out whatever inner monologue she was carrying on. My only solace during the trip was using the connection to check in with Hannah and Milo.

When I relayed to them what had happened with Naomi, my head started to buzz like a beehive at the onslaught of collective fear, shock, and sadness.

"That poor little girl. That's so terrible, Jess." Hannah's thought was like a long tremulous note played on a violin.

"I know," I agreed. "It sounds from what her mother said like she's been getting out at night. They all thought it was sleepwalking, of course."

"It's just starting, isn't it," Milo said, and there was no question in his words. "It's spreading."

"It may already be happening," I pointed out. "There's a chance that Savvy isn't even the first. If other clans are keeping the word from spreading, like Celeste is, who knows how many Sentinels there are, locked into connection with Geatgrimas right now all over the world."

We all shared in the cold shiver of horror at the thought.

"Finn is on his way down," Hannah told me, when we'd all recovered. "He left about an hour ago. I promised him I'd let you know. When are you going to be able to use a phone again?"

"When we get there, I expect," I replied.

Catriona had demanded that all of us turn over our cell phones to her (except for Ileana, who had never possessed such a contraption and looked vaguely nauseous at the very thought). She had turned them off, removed the batteries, and locked them in the glove compartment. Annabelle was extremely hesitant to do so, until Catriona explained about the ways cell phones could be tracked using GPS data and cell towers. She showed us all a large ziplock bag full of burner phones, which was apparently a normal thing to have in your possession when you were on the run.

"We can use these as necessary, both to keep in touch with each other, or to make any other calls we might deem necessary. They're not for a cozy catch-up with your mum, they're to be used sparingly, and disposed of before we move on," Catriona said.

At long last, we pulled into the village of Pluckley. On any other day, I would have "ooh-ed and "ahh-ed" at its quintessential English country quaintness, but today was not that day. Ileana instructed us to pull through the center of town, past the pub and the little half-timbered hotel and the shopfronts, and directed us into an alley so narrow that it could hardly have been meant for tiny European cars, let alone our massive SUV. I held my breath as Catriona inched our way down the road, coming out along a row of thatched semi-detached cottages that appeared to be private homes, all except one, which had a small, rather grimy sign hanging above the door that read, "Milkweed Teahouse and Lodgings."

"Stop here," Ileana barked, and Catriona grudgingly obliged, pulling around a corner into a wider lane so that we'd actually be able to get the car doors open. Catriona killed the engine and made to exit the car, but Ileana held up a hand. "Stay here, all of you. I'll need to speak to the proprietress first."

Regally, like she was descending a royal coach instead of a comically large vehicle, Ileana lowered herself to the cobblestones and approached the plank front door of the Milkweed Teahouse. We all watched silently as she rapped three times sharply on the wood.

A tiny panel slid open on the top of the door almost instantly, revealing the dark shape of a face peering out into the early morning sunshine. Ileana leaned in close to the door and began talking quietly to whoever was on the other side of the door. After a brief, terse exchange, the little window slid shut and the door opened. Ileana motioned for us to wait where we were, then disappeared behind it.

"I know that woman is a High Priestess, but she is not my High Priestess and if she talks to me like she's addressing a servant one more time, I'm going to throttle her with one of those bloody scarves," Catriona growled, pulling off her sunglasses and tossing them onto the dashboard in disgust.

"Well, you did commit a fair few crimes she's not prosecuting you for, so I'd grin and bear it, mate," Lucida suggested from the passenger seat.

"I don't suppose she's told you why we're stopping here?" Catriona asked, fixing me with her piercing glare in the rearview mirror.

"Nope," I said. "She hasn't felt the need to tell me anything, actually. I'm just along for the ride, like you. Which is ironic, given that I never invited any of you except for Annabelle to come along on this exercise in absurdity."

"Lovely. Well, I hope we're not expected to eat here," Catriona said, scrunching up her face at the thought. "This place looks like it hasn't seen a health inspector since the heyday of William bloody Shakespeare."

"Oh, I'm sorry, were you expecting five-star accommodations while on the run?" I asked politely, pulling out the burner phone and holding it up. "I'm going to text Finn now to let him know where we are. Is that okay?"

Catriona nodded sourly. I sent off a quick message with the location of the place and pocketed the phone again. Then I looked up at Catriona. "How much did you tell her last night?" I asked, indicating Lucida with a jerk of my head.

"Everything you told me," Catriona replied promptly.

"So, we all know why we're here, at least, right?" I asked.

All three heads around me nodded.

"I don't know anything about the Keeper of the Elementals," I said. "All I knew was that I somehow had to get a message to her. Ileana seems to know all about her, or enough to get us to her, anyway. She's only just restraining herself from having us all arrested for crimes against the Traveler Clans, so I'm trying not to piss her off or ask too many questions because we still need her right now. I know she's basically a nightmare, but we all just need to grin and bear it for now. Unless, of course, any of you want off this crazy train. I'm the only one who actually needs to do this, so seriously, now's the time. I have no idea what's waiting for us in those woods. My only request, if you do decide to cut and run, is that you don't tell anyone about what I'm doing."

"I've told you already, I'm with you," Annabelle said at once.

Catriona looked at Lucida, who nodded. "We're not going anywhere. You're going to need all the bloody help you can get."

Annabelle snorted dismissively, but no one responded. We had just spotted Ileana poking her head out of the door of the Milkweed Teahouse. She beckoned us to join her, then slipped back inside. Exchanging wary looks, we all unbuckled our seatbelts, clambered out of the car, and followed her.

Stepping inside the Milkweed Teahouse was like stepping back in time. The interior was so dark that it seemed hard to believe that bright sunlight filled the street outside. Thick purple velvet curtains were drawn over all of the windows, and the only light came from little oil lamps set along the walls and candles upon the tables. The front door opened into a kind of sitting room, which was crowded with small round tables draped in dingy, lacy tablecloths and mismatched chairs of every size and description. On the far wall, a fire crackled in the beehive brick fireplace, and three heavy black kettles hung on an iron pole over the flames. Above our heads, dangling so low that we had to duck under them, were hundreds of bunches of dried herbs and flowers, tied together at the stems with lengths of black ribbon hung from antique nails driven into the beams. The walls were almost entirely covered in wooden shelves, crammed with tattered books and hundreds of china teacups and saucers. I let out a yelp as something furry brushed past my leg, but it was only a tabby cat who had come to investigate the intruders.

As my eyes adjusted to the gloom, I saw that Ileana was standing by the fireplace, conversing with a woman who was bent low, poking at the embers with a fireiron. The woman was wearing a long, patchwork dress and her head was covered in a red kerchief, from which wisps of white hair were escaping. When she stood up, I had to suppress a gasp, for she had the strangest eyes I'd ever seen. They were such a pale milky blue color as to be nearly white, and my first thought was that she must be blind. But then she hobbled forward and fixed each of us one by one with a piercing glare, and it was clear that she could see us just fine. Beside me, Annabelle reached out and clutched my arm in alarm.

The woman surveyed us each like she was trying to get a fair price for us, then turned to Ileana and asked, in a dry, reedy husk of a voice, "And they're Durupinen, all?"

"All but that one, the Dormant," Ileana replied, pointing a dismissive finger at Annabelle. "But she's of the bloodline, and a sensitive at that."

The woman gave a nod of approval and held out her knobbly little claw of a hand. Ileana dropped several large gold coins into it and waited patiently while the woman held each of them up to examine them and then bit them with what few, decayed teeth remained in her mouth. Then she smacked her lips together in a satisfied sort of way, dropped the coins into the pocket of her greasy apron, and rubbed her hands together. "Let us begin, then!" she crowed delightedly.

She started toward us with surprising speed and we all leapt away from her involuntarily. Catriona, whose leap had put several small tables between herself and the strange little woman, cried out, "Excuse me, but who the bloody hell is this woman and where are we and begin *what*, precisely? I'm all for winging it, but I've got my limits."

Ileana, her arms crossed truculently, looked for a moment like she wasn't going to answer. But then she heaved a great sigh and gave in. "This is Abigail Blackwood. She is the proprietress of this fine establishment and the only person who can get us safely into the Dering Woods."

"Is she a Durupinen?" I asked, trying to hide the skepticism in my voice.

"Yes. She's several generations removed from the Gateway, of course, but she continues to do this work for the Durupinen."

"And what work is that, if I'm allowed to ask?" Catriona pressed.

"She's the Shepherd."

"The what, now?" I asked, wondering how we'd somehow arrived at sheep.

"The Shepherd for the Keeper of the Elementals," Ileana replied, as though this was somehow self-explanatory.

"Yes, but what does that mean?" Catriona asked through her teeth, clearly frustrated that she had to work so hard for the tiniest detail.

"It means I keeps the riffraff far away from the truth at the heart of the forest, and I shepherds in them what needs to see the Keeper," Abigail replied, thrusting out her chest proudly.

"Are... are there a lot of people trying to get into the woods out here?" I asked with a slight smirk. Crowd control didn't really seem like it would be an issue in a tiny country village like this.

"Oh, yes. There's lots what come to explore the Screaming Woods," Abigail said with a solemn nod.

"The... the *what* woods?" Annabelle asked, going a bit pale.

"The Screaming Woods, lass. The woods what masks the Elementals from the world."

Annabelle looked at me accusingly, and I jumped in quickly, "I'm confused. I thought we were coming here to enter a place called the Dering Woods?"

"Aye, the Dering Woods is its proper name, o' course," Abigail said. "But them as finds themselves unlucky enough to wander the place at night have christened it anew, and for good reason. The name is famous now, and many a fool who fancies himself a hero marches off into the trees at night, hoping to emerge with a good campfire story."

I looked at Ileana, whose face was twisted with distaste. "Tourist trash and amateur ghost hunters. You know the riffraff she's talking about. Loud, obnoxious, trying to capture evidence of spirits while having the daylights scared out of them by owls and squirrels. Leaving nothing but tall tales, trash and destruction in their wake."

Yes, I did know what she was talking about only too well. And I knew what kind of appeal such a notorious place would hold, once word got out that it might be haunted. Annabelle and I exchanged a look. If Iggy, Oscar and the boys knew there was a place in the south of England that had been dubbed the Screaming Woods, they'd be camped out in a tent in the middle of the place collecting evidence before you could blink. And they were professionals who were respectful of the sites they chose to visit. I could only imagine what random thrillseekers and drunken university kids probably did for a scare in there.

"It makes me job a bloomin' nightmare, and no mistake," Abigail went on, clicking her tongue disapprovingly. "I've done more Castings in the last five years than I've done in the previous sixty-five. The village Council is fed up too, but they won't turn their nose up at that kind of tourist money. Why else would anyone in their right mind come to Pluckley? Unless they's lost, o' course."

"Are you expecting we'll meet other people in the woods tonight?" I asked, wondering how the hell we were supposed to keep our adventure a secret if we were going to wind up on the B-reel of some amateur ghosthunting YouTuber.

Abigail shrugged. "The Council has introduced an ordinance banning folks from spending the night in the woods. There's always a chance some gormless pillock will sneak his way in, but you're more likely to meet them down at the pub after dark these days. That's why you'll wait until dark to venture in."

Lucida, who'd been silent since we'd entered the room, asked the question the rest of us wanted the answer to. "I wouldn't mind a little insight into why they've called it the Screaming Woods," she said quite casually, though I thought I detected a hint of a tremor in her tone.

Abigail grinned broadly, showing terribly blackened gums. "That'll be the Elementals, working their dark magic. Plenty to scream about, when you're made of pure terror, hatred, and sadness."

Beside me, Annabelle seemed to be holding her breath. Even Catriona looked sobered.

"Right, well, I've got plenty of work to be getting on with if you're entering the woods tonight," Abigail said, rubbing her hands together excitedly. "Fancy a cuppa before I get started? This is meant to be a teahouse, after all. I've just taken some scones out of the oven."

I nodded automatically, knowing I should probably eat something, and was halfway into a chair when the phone in my back pocket buzzed, startling me. I knew who it must be; only one person had the number.

"Finn?"

"It's me. I'm outside."

"My Caomhnóir is here," I told the room at large. "He's going to accompany us. I'll, uh… I'll be right back."

I could feel Ileana's eyes burning into the back of my head as I eased open the ancient door and slipped back outside. Finn was just pulling around the corner into the tiny lane. Luckily for him, he'd chosen a much smaller vehicle than the monstrosity we'd driven in, which he swung deftly into a narrow parking space between two of the cottages before jumping out. Before I could even open my mouth to say hello to him, he had pulled me into a fierce hug and kissed me like he hadn't seen me in months.

"Thank God you're all right," he mumbled against my lips.

"I told you I was fine," I reminded him.

"Yes, love, and I know that you would say almost anything to keep me from worrying about you. You'd tell me you were fine while dangling one-handed from a cliff," Finn chuckled. He took me by the shoulders and stepped back so that he could look me in the eyes. "How are you really?"

I sighed. "Tired. Nervous. Freaking out a little."

"Come on. Let's go for a walk," Finn said, reaching out a hand. "Hannah filled me in, of course, but I'd like to hear the full proper story from you now."

Slipping my hand into his was like recharging my soul, and as we set off down the cobblestones, I launched into a full description of everything that had happened from the moment I left Fairhaven. Finn didn't interrupt me with tedious questions or exclamations. He simply listened until I had run out of story to tell, of thoughts to air. By this time, we were sitting at a table outside the local coffee shop, each of us drinking a strong cup of coffee, a small pile of pastries half-eaten between us.

"And this Abigail woman, you trust her?" Finn asked.

"Not even a little, but what choice do we have?" I asked, popping another piece of danish into my mouth. "We can't just charge off blindly into those woods and hope the Elementals will leave us alone. Ileana says Abigail can get us in safely, that she's been stationed here for decades doing just that for generations of Durupinen."

"I hardly think this is a busy Durupinen thoroughfare," Finn said, looking skeptical. "I've never heard of anyone visiting the Keeper of the Elementals. Christ, I didn't know there *was* a Keeper of the Elementals until you woke out of the Rift insisting you needed to visit them."

"We're finding out all sorts of things we never knew about the Durupinen," I said. "Just add it to the list, I guess."

"What do you plan to do when you get in there?" Finn asked.

I shrugged. "I have no plan, other than to deliver my message as quickly as I can. But I've got a theory. I'm thinking the Keeper of the Elementals might have something—some kind of relic that has to do with the Sentinels."

"What makes you think that?" Finn asked, frowning.

"Well, Ileana had that key I mentioned. She doesn't know what it's for, or what it opens, if anything, but she was told that, if a messenger ever came to her with Agnes' words about the Sentinels, that she must take the key with her to the Keeper of the Elementals."

"Perhaps the Keeper of the Elementals is in possession of whatever that key opens?" Finn suggested.

I shrugged. "It's possible. I just hope we can get in and out of the woods with what we need without encountering an actual Elemental."

"And what do you think the odds are of that happening?" Finn asked darkly.

"With my track record? Let's just say I won't be placing any bets on it," I replied.

"And you're really okay with bringing Lucida along on this already dangerous excursion?" Finn asked. "Isn't there enough to worry about, wandering into a forest full of Elementals?"

"Like I've explained before, she's in this, Finn, like it or not. I never would have found Agnes' clues or the Tansy Hag if it weren't for her. We're not friends and we never will be, but she's here for the duration of this."

Finn gave me a long hard look, and finally nodded. "I trust you," he said. "But I'm going to be keeping a careful eye on her."

"Good," I said. "It will save me the trouble of having to do it myself."

"And of course, if we get caught traveling in her company..."

"I know. I know she's probably more trouble than she's worth, as usual," I admitted. "But Catriona saved us, and I feel better having her here, at least. A Senior Tracker, with all her knowledge and resources? I'll take Lucida as an inconvenient accessory to have Catriona along for the ride."

We finished our food and returned to the Milkweed Tavern. I knocked on the door and waited for Abigail's dried apple of a face to appear in the little window at the top. She had to be standing on a stool or something; I knew now that she was about two feet too short to actually reach that window. She stared at me for a moment with those disturbing eyes, and then slammed the window shut and opened the door without a word. Finn and I stepped inside.

"Just one Guardian, eh?" Abigail said, looking Finn over and chuckling. "You're a brave lot, aren't yeh?"

I ignored the comment and surveyed the room. Catriona and Lucida sat huddled at the table closest to the door, the remains of their tea and scones between them. Annabelle had chosen a table near the fire. She'd barely nibbled at her food, and the tea still filling her cup must have been stone cold by now. Ileana was standing in the corner, examining the many books on the shelves near the back of the room. She looked up when she heard us come in.

"Well, well, if it isn't the star-crossed lovers," she said acidly before returning to her books.

Finn said nothing, forcing himself instead into the stiff half-bow that ceremony required of him when in the presence of a superior, though his expression remained stony.

"Finn will be coming with us into the woods," I told everyone, though Abigail was the only one who didn't already know this. "He's had experience with an Elemental on several occasions."

Abigail looked surprised at this. "Is that so, laddie? You've tangled with the foulest of the foul, then. At Fairhaven, I expect? They did insist on keeping one there, though many advised against it. And you look no worse the wear for it. Yes, I won't object to having you along, not a mite."

"I...that is to say... thank you...?" Finn replied, completely wrong-footed as he was caught in Abigail's bizarre gaze for the first time.

"Sorry, I should have warned you about the eyes," I whispered into his ear.

"Yes, you *really* should have," he muttered back.

"Well, I'll not keep yeh all awake while I gather my provisions. It will take hours to get everything together, so you may as well head upstairs and have a good lie down. There ain't no sense in sitting around down here when you could be replenishing your strength for what's ahead. Go on, now, off with yeh."

Everyone looked rather surprised at this sudden dismissal, but then again, we were all beyond exhausted, having slept so poorly the night before in the Traveler camp. No one objected, and instead we all lined up to trudge up the ancient staircase.

I paused at the top of the stairs as Annabelle ducked into the first tiny bedroom on the left. I didn't like the idea of her being alone. "Do you want me to—?"

She rolled her eyes at me. "Of course not. I'll be fine. See you whenever that mad old bat downstairs decides to wake us."

I smiled as she winked at me. "Okay, then. See you soon."

Lucida and Catriona were already disappearing behind the first door on the right. I could see Lucida sitting on the edge of the canopied bed, pulling off her boots wearily. Just past their room was a single shared bathroom for the floor, containing a sink, a laughably tiny bathtub, and what was likely the world's oldest surviving indoor toilet. And in the back corner of the house was one last bedroom, into which was crammed a double bed, a washstand, and a single, straight-back, horsehair chair that surely no person had ever sat in except as punishment. The wide-planked wooden floor dipped badly to the left, and the entire room seemed to creak with every step we took. A painting on the wall of a severe-looking woman in Tudor-era attire glared disapprovingly down at us. I perched myself tentatively on the end of the bed, testing its sturdiness. It groaned but seemed safe enough to lie down on. I slid my tired feet out of my sneakers and laid down with a long sigh, breathing in the musty smell of the blankets and sheets. The bed gave another enthusiastic groan as Finn lay down beside me. I rolled gratefully into the crook of his arm, rested my head on his chest, and was asleep within seconds.

§

It seemed moments later that Finn was shaking me awake. The room was pitch dark, and someone was rapping smartly on the door to the bedroom.

"Yeah?" I called out, sitting up and blinking around blearily.

"Get yerself downstairs, and look sharpish, now," came Abigail's croaky voice. "The time is upon us."

I stifled a yawn and felt around on the little table beside me until I found a tiny lamp, which I turned on. The room became a dim chamber of exaggerated shadows. Finn reached out and squeezed my shoulder.

"How did you sleep, love?"

"Like the dead," I replied. "How long have I been out?"

"About seven hours. It's near enough dark outside now."

"Seven hours!" I cried. "Shit, why didn't you wake me? Hannah and Milo must be out of their minds that they haven't heard from me!"

"No worries, love, I've called them and filled them in. They asked me to let you sleep. If we're going to be spending the night wandering the Screaming Woods, we'd do better to be well rested, don't you agree?"

I sighed. "Yeah. Thanks for doing that. I really was exhausted, not just from the poor sleep last night at the Traveler camp, but the Walking really wore me out too, I think. Were you awake this whole time listening to me snore, or did you get some rest, too?"

"Rest? With that racket going on? Not a chance!" he replied. I threw my shoe at him, but he dodged it easily. Damn those Caomhnóir and their lightning-quick reflexes.

I retrieved my shoe and put it on, and then went to examine the washbasin. Finding a jug full of cold water, I filled the bowl and splashed some on my face in a further attempt to wake myself up. The towel hanging on a hook nearby looked a bit dusty, so I just dried my face off with the sleeve of my sweatshirt. After a quick trip to the bathroom (an experience so unpleasant that I would have preferred to pee in the woods than repeat it) we made our way downstairs.

Annabelle, Lucida, Catriona, and Ileana were standing in an awkward group around the fireplace, watching Abigail add handfuls of dried herbs to a cauldron.

Yes, an actual cauldron. Like, a "bubble, bubble, toil and trouble" style cauldron.

I glanced at Annabelle, who shrugged. She looked much better than when I'd said goodbye to her at the top of the stairs seven hours before, like she, too, had gotten some much needed sleep. She had brushed her hair as well, and pulled it back into a long, loose braid that hung down her back.

"You look better," I told her.

"I feel better," she replied, managing a small, genuine smile.

"That's sorted, then!" Abigail announced, straightening up and wiping her hands on her apron. "So, if I could just have a bit of blood from one of you, we can get started."

I blinked. "I'm sorry?"

"I need blood," Abigail repeated cheerfully. "Well, not yours, Guardian. I'm afraid, in this instance, you're absolutely bloody useless, aren't yeh?" She threw her ancient head back and cackled before continuing. "It's got to be Durupinen blood or the whole brew is naught but rubbish."

"And what exactly are you going to do with the blood when you've got it?" I demanded.

"Into the pot it goes, my lass, into the pot it goes," Abigail replied in a singsong voice. "It binds the Casting, see? Seals it right up, like wax. Then you drink it, luvvie, and it seals you right up, too!"

"I'm still not following," Catriona snapped, nostrils flaring, leaning forward to get a better look at the contents of the cauldron.

"Them Elementals can't get in!" Abigail announced with a near-toothless grin. "Seals up your portals. Closes 'em right off."

"What the blazes does that—" Catriona began, but I thought I finally understood.

"When you meet an Elemental, it doesn't communicate with you out loud. It speaks inside your head. And once it's there, it starts rooting around for all of your negative emotions and memories to feed off of. So this... potion, or whatever it is... will stop them from being able to get into our heads, is that what you're saying?" I asked, turning to Abigail.

"Aye, that's it. Closes the portals," she repeated, as though it ought to have been obvious.

"I don't want this woman anywhere near my portals," Annabelle whispered to me. I snickered.

"So, whose is it to be, then? Just a few drops is all it takes," Abigail said, looking around expectantly, as though we were all going to thrust our hands up in the air and start jumping up and down in our excitement to be chosen.

No one moved. We all just looked at each other, hoping someone else was going to volunteer. Ileana was standing apart, as though this part of the conversation did not pertain to her—as though being a High Priestess meant she could pull rank on things like blood sacrifices. After several seconds of prolonged silence, I sighed and opened my mouth to take one for the team, but—

"Ah, go on then, let's get it over with," Lucida said, stepping forward and rolling her sleeve back.

Catriona looked taken aback. "Lucida, are you sure—"

Lucida shrugged. "What does it matter, really? If it gets us in and out of there safely."

Annabelle was bouncing up and down on the balls of her feet, as though she was longing to protest, and I could understand why; she didn't even want to be in the same room as Lucida, let alone be expected to drink a concoction mixed with her blood. But Abigail was already pulling a knife from the pocket of her apron and holding the blade in the fire to sterilize it.

Lucida did not even flinch when the hot blade was pressed to the crook of her elbow, and watched impassively as her blood dripped lazily down her elbow and into the tiny bowl Abigail was now holding expectantly beneath her arm. Satisfied that she had what she needed, Abigail tossed a length of white bandaging to Lucida, who caught it and began winding it around her arm, applying pressure with her hand where the cut had been made. Then Abigail hobbled back to the fire and tipped the contents of the bowl into the cauldron's belly.

A single curl of purplish smoke rose from the cauldron, releasing a heady, herbal perfume into the air. Abigail reached up and pulled a ladle off a nail on the mantle above the fireplace and pointed to the shelves behind us. "Fetch yerselves a teacup, and be quick about it."

We all hastened to grab a cup—all but Ileana, who stood by expectantly that one would be fetched for her. And indeed, within seconds, Annabelle had plucked a second cup off the shelf and handed it to her.

Without really intending to, we formed a kind of queue in front of the fire. One by one, we held out our cups and Abigail sloshed a ladleful of her concoction into them. The cup quickly became extremely hot to the touch, and I had to adjust my hands to hold it by the handle before I dropped it to the floor. The fumes rising from the cup were dizzyingly sweet, and bits of crushed up herbs floated lazily on the surface. No one made a move to drink it. We were all waiting for further instructions.

Next, Abigail walked around to our backs. She reached up and tugged on Catriona's arm first, so that she would bend over at the waist. Using one, gnarled hand, Abigail brushed Catriona's hair over her shoulder, so that the back of her neck was exposed. Then, pulling a bit of charcoal from her pocket, Abigail drew a rune of protection at the base of Catriona's skull. Catriona flinched at first, then managed to hold still, despite the fact that she had no idea what Abigail was doing or why, for the old woman offered no explanation. Then Abigail went down the line, exposing each of our necks and marking them with the runes. It was one of the runes crucial to Warding, I realized, recognizing its familiar shape as Abigail scrawled it upon Annabelle's neck.

Finally, when each of us had been marked, Abigail stepped back, rubbed her hands together excitedly, and crowed, "Well, what are you waiting for? Bottoms up!"

Catriona caught my eye. "Cheers, mate," she muttered, and knocked the contents of the cup back in a single gulp. I took a deep breath and did the same. All around me, teacups were drained. All around me, mouths and throats were scalded, coughs and sputters and gasps rose up in a chorus. The mixture, though it smelled very sweet, was extremely bitter, with a bite of spice on the back end that cleared my sinuses and took my breath away.

When all the gasping and coughing had subsided, Abigail approached each of us one at a time, tugging us forward, gripping our faces between her hands, and staring into our eyes and then, inexplicably, giving each of us a hearty sniff. Whatever she was looking and sniffing for, she found it, for she gave a satisfied nod before moving on to the next person. When she reached me, she stared into my eyes longer than any of the others. Then she pulled my face so close to hers that our noses were almost touching. I froze.

"You're the Messenger, aren't yeh?" she whispered to me.

It took me a moment to find my voice. "Yes."

"Tread carefully," she replied. "They'll not want you there. It will mean the end of them."

"What?" I asked.

Abigail just nodded. "Tread carefully," she repeated.

Then she stood up and bustled across the room to a large feed sack that clanked when she picked it up. Though it looked quite heavy, she hefted it with ease over her shoulder and then heaved it with a crash onto the tea table before us.

"Choose a tribute," she said, gesturing to the contents of the bag.

"What do you mean, tribute?" Annabelle asked.

"A tribute for the Keeper. She will want tribute. Anything in the bag will do. She likes a bit of shine, a bit of sparkle in the dark forest, yeh know."

We most certainly did *not* know, but one by one we reached into the bag and pulled something out: Catriona, an old costume necklace of glass beads; Lucida, a chipped cut crystal goblet; Ileana, a gemstone bracelet; Annabelle, a set of silver wind chimes; Finn, a polished silver candlestick. I reached my hand into the bag last of all, and pulled from its depths a tiny jewel-encrusted silver revolver, the kind a wealthy woman might have hidden in her handbag or tucked into a garter for protection. I peered into the tiny barrel. The chambers were all empty.

I looked up at Abigail, the question all over my face; surely presenting the Keeper of the Elementals with a potentially dangerous weapon sent the wrong kind of message? But Abigail was nodding approvingly at my choice, so I shrugged and pocketed it uneasily. Abigail picked the bag back up, dumped it unceremoniously on the floor beside the fire, and picked up a lantern.

"Yer as ready as ever you'll be," she announced. "To the Screaming Woods we go."

AT THE HEART OF THE SCREAMING WOODS

TWILIGHT HAD BEGUN to drape itself upon the little village. It was not yet silent; lights bled from the windows of the local pub, and music and chatter echoed into our tiny lane. Cars drove up and down the main road, and a knot of people strolled down the sidewalks, the last of the evening crowd. We would not be lured to the warmth and the crowds, however; a darker finger beckoned and we followed it, through a maze of narrow country lanes, down a cowpath lined with hedgerows, and finally over a post-and-rail fence and through a field of tall grass beyond which the Screaming Woods reared up like a creature sniffing the air.

Around us in the field, I could see the evidence of recent tourist visits. Beer cans, fast food wrappers, and other refuse littered the field through which we approached the wood. Several official signs had been posted on fenceposts and trees: "NO TRESPASSING IN DERING WOODS AFTER DARK. VIOLATORS WILL BE FINED."

A narrow, well-trod path snaked off through the trees. At first, I felt sure we were going to head down it, but Abigail turned at the treeline and continued along the edge of the wood. When she realized the rest of us were hesitating, she turned around and waved us onward. "Paths are not for such as we," she said in a quiet voice that nonetheless carried through the field. "We do not plan to tread where others have trod."

"Of course not," I muttered as we turned to follow her. "Because paths would lead people safely through the wood, and we aren't trying to get safely through the wood, are we? We're going to hurl ourselves right at the terrifying epicenter and hope a bit of tea and a bunch of metal junk will save us."

Annabelle gave a nervous peal of laughter. "At least your bit of junk shoots bullets," she said. "Mine will just act as a cute accessory while an Elemental destroys my sanity."

I couldn't be sure what Abigail was looking for, or how she knew when she found it, but she stopped suddenly at a clump of trees that looked exactly like every other clump of trees and said, "Ah. Here it is. This is the way. Hurry along, now. Keep up, keep up."

There was no logical reason a woman so old and so bent and so tiny should be so very adept at moving through dense forest; and yet, within minutes, all of us were panting to keep up. Even Finn seemed to be struggling. Ileana, who had spent her entire life maneuvering through the forest, was nonetheless used to her own familiar haunts in her own grove, and therefore her life as a Traveler did not provide her with as much of an advantage as one might expect in this strange and unfamiliar territory. Catriona kept lagging behind to wait for Lucida, who lacked the stamina for this kind of hike after years of malnutrition and lack of physical activity while locked away in the *príosún*. Both Annabelle and I fared better on this trip through the forest than we had in the Traveler grove, but that was an exceedingly low bar, given that we had been occupying each other's bodies at the time. When Abigail stopped to rest about thirty minutes later, every single one of us sank to the ground in relief, panting and pulling bits of leaf and twig and briar from our clothes. Finn passed a canteen of water around, from which we all drank gratefully except for Abigail, who waved it away as though she'd never seen such a thing and found its very existence absurd.

"Aye, there it is," Abigail said at last, clapping her hands delightedly and pointing up over her head. Hanging high in one of the trees was a collection of silverware, each individual piece strung up with a bit of ribbon. "We're headed the right way. You must leave your things here, now."

"What things?" I asked.

"Your bags, anything in your pockets. Go on, empty 'em out. Leave it all here under the tree. You'll be able to retrieve 'em on yer way out."

Catriona looked horrified. "You want me to leave my phone and my car keys and all of my ID under a tree we may never find again in a forest crawling with drunken wanker tourists?"

Abigail considered this. "Are the keys shiny?"

Catriona blinked. "I... suppose so."

"Then yeh can bring 'em along, but you'll have to offer 'em as tribute, so if you want to keep 'em for yerself, I suggest leavin' 'em right there."

"But why—"

"When you come to see the Keeper, you come as you are. You don't bring the outside world in. She hasn't no use fer it, because the outside world hasn't no use fer 'er, see? It frightens 'er, and fear is what the Elementals feed upon. You bring yer tribute and yer business, an' that's all. Understand?"

We didn't understand at all, but I didn't think any further explanation from Abigail was going to help illuminate things. Indeed, her vague explanations only made me more uneasy as I emptied my pockets and set my backpack carefully down on the ground, tucking it along with everyone else's belongings into a bush in an effort to mask them from view. Finn looked particularly displeased. I knew his pack contained a lot of supplies that would help us if we got lost or hurt in here.

Abigail looked us all over, forcing us to turn out our pockets, before continuing on through the trees, which seemed to be growing older and more prehistoric looking the further into the woods we ventured. There was no longer any sky to be seen above us, and no grass below: all was soft, mossy darkness. Abigail's lantern swung like a ship on a tempest-tossed sea in front of us, sending soft yellow beams of light back and forth across our path, casting and throwing long, distorted shadows all around us. The silence around us was oppressive, like a living thing forcing its weight down upon us. The temperature dropped steadily, and I knew from the unnatural chill that it was something more than the absence of the sun sending shivers up my spine and into my hair.

I looked over at Finn, whose face had gone suddenly very tense. He returned my look and nodded. The silence. The cold. He could feel them, too.

The Elementals.

I glanced around the rest of our group. I wasn't sure that any of the rest of them would come to the same realization as we had. After all, none of them had had the same up close and personal experiences with an Elemental that Finn and I had had. But though Annabelle shivered, and Ileana shuddered, and Catriona and Lucida trudged forward watching their breath rise in puffs like tiny cumulous clouds, I was forced to conclude that none of them had a clue what we were walking into.

Here and there in the trees above our heads, I began to see little flickers of light. At first, it looked as though we'd come across a swarm of fireflies, but then I realized that the light was simply being reflected from Abigail's lantern by a collection of objects hung high in the trees, each of them made of metal or glass or something else that could catch the light.

"A bit of shine," I whispered to myself, recalling Abigail's words when we pulled our chosen objects out of her sack. That must mean we were approaching the place where the Keeper lived.

"Castings," Finn whispered suddenly. "Protective Castings. Look." He threw out an arm to stop me and pointed first at the trunks of the trees, and then at the ground. Runes had been carved crudely into the wood over and over again, huge chunks of bark worn and torn away from the trunks. And on the ground, the shape of an enormous summoning circle was just visible, created from various sized stones arranged upon the mossy earth. In the center of the circle, a knot of three trees grew together, entwined like lovers, and in the shadows of their embrace, a strange dwelling seemed to have sprung up from the roots. Whether it had been built or simply dug out of the ground, it was impossible to tell. Its structure was covered over with moss and lichen and creeping plants. A grey, weathered wooden door, no taller than my shoulder, was set into the face of it. And all around it, shiny objects hung from branches and roots, strung between them on wires or else tied on with strings. It was like stumbling upon the world's most terrifying Christmas tree.

"Glad to see the Blair Witch is still doing her thing," I muttered.

"What are you on about?" Finn asked, frowning.

"Never mind. It's not important," I replied.

At that moment, Abigail raised her hand and we all stopped in our tracks. She hung her lantern upon a claw-like, low-hanging branch and turned to us.

"You must make yer offerings now," she said, reaching into her apron and pulling out a fistful of black ribbons. "Take out yer shine and tie it onto the wire there."

"What wire?" Catriona asked.

But Ileana was already pulling a length of ribbon from Abigail's fist and stepping forward. Barely visible in the gloom, a long rusty wire had been strung up between two tree trunks, like a clothesline, just before the border of the summoning circle. Dozens and dozens of strings and ribbons and ropes dangled from it, empty. It was amongst these that Ileana tied her tribute, the silver bracelet, set with sparkling green and blue gemstones. Then she stepped back, watching it swing gently back and forth, catching the lantern light. Following her lead, each of us stepped forward in turn, tying our gifts to the rusty wire with one of Abigail's black ribbons. Then we all backed away, watching the objects glitter and sway in the frozen breath of a breeze now sweeping through the forest.

For a few long, agonizing seconds, nothing at all happened. And then—

"The house! Someone's coming out of the house!" Annabelle announced in a terrified squeak of a voice.

She was right. The door of the little hovel was slowly opening with a long, grating squeak. As we all watched, not a single one of us breathing, a face peeked around the doorframe. It was impossible to make out any more than the shape of it, hidden in a tangle of long, stringy dark hair. It froze and looked at us for what felt like an eternity, and then it withdrew, pushing the door the rest of the way open, and emerging into the moonlight.

I couldn't draw enough breath to scream—the sound that came out of me was no more than a strangled gasp. The figure that emerged from the door was no larger than a small child, clad in a long grey nightdress, with bare, dirty feet and pale, skinny arms. She did not walk; she moved in a kind of crouch, pushing her palms against the ground to propel herself forward, her long, filthy hair swinging in front of her face, masking her features. She crept forward a few feet, face still fixed in our direction, and then stopped. Then, from behind her, a second figure emerged from the hovel, ducking its head and shoulders to fit through the door. This figure was the size of a small adult, also dressed in a shapeless grey garment, something like a nightdress. It was slightly stooped, and its head was covered in a brown bonnet. As it stepped more fully into the moonlight beside the first figure, it raised its head and revealed the rounded figure and features of an old woman.

Both figures held statue-still, waiting, it seemed, for us to make the first move. I don't think I could have moved or spoken even if I'd wanted to, and nearly everyone else around me seemed similarly paralyzed with fear. Abigail, thankfully, tottered forward and raised a hand in greeting, and then gestured to the objects we had hung upon the wire.

"A tribute from these Durupinen visitors to the Keeper of the Elementals, with whom they should like to speak," she called out in her croaky voice, making us all jump at the broken stillness.

The two figures did not reply. They did not confer. But then, suddenly, the smaller one reached out a hand, grasped the larger one's arm, and swung herself, monkey-like, onto the woman's back. The woman stepped forward and said, in a soft, almost childlike voice, "The Keeper will inspect your gifts."

"What the hell is going on?" Catriona breathed beside me. "The child can't be the Keeper, can she?"

"I guess she must be," I replied, watching in fascinated horror as the woman now came forward, picking her way carefully between the tree roots, the Keeper clinging to her back, one arm wrapped around her neck, the other hand wound through her grey tangle of hair. As they came closer, I could not help but back away, so instinctive was my revulsion. The woman reached the place where the wire was strung and pulled a pair of scissors from somewhere in her garments. The Keeper leaned forward on the woman's back, reaching out to examine each tribute in turn, her face still completely hidden by her hair, though I thought I glimpsed a twinkle in her eyes as she raised her chin. Her hands were strange for a child—veiny and large-knuckled. She turned Ileana's bracelet back and forth, watching how it caught the light. She let out a high, silvery giggle and nodded. The woman reached out and cut the bracelet off the wire, letting it drop into her hand and stowing it in a kind of pouch she had tied around her waist. They repeated the process with each offering until they came to mine. The Keeper lifted the tiny revolver into her hands, turning it over and over. Then she grasped it in one hand and lifted it to point directly at my face. Finn, panicking, jumped in front of me.

"Bang," the Keeper whispered. Then she laughed her silvery laugh again and motioned for the woman to cut the revolver down.

The woman did so, tucking it away and stowing the scissors as well. Then, she reached to the other side of her belt, lifting a small black bag I recognized instantly as a Casting bag. She turned in a circle, dropping stones around her and muttering words I could not make out, but that had the familiar lilt of Gaelic. A shiver seemed to run through the air around us as a Casting lifted. It was, we knew, the Casting equivalent of unlocking the door to let someone in.

Abigail nodded in satisfaction and turned to the rest of us. "I present to you Lira Blackwell, Keeper of the Elementals and her sister Ms. Margaret Blackwell."

Annabelle threw me a glance that reflected my own question back to me. How could this old woman and this child possibly be sisters?

"Lira, I present to you Catriona Harrington and Lucida Worthington of the Clan Soillseach, Annabelle Rabinski, Dormant of the Traveler Clan Boswell, Caomhnóir Finn Carey of the Clan Gonachd, Jessica Ballard of the Clan Sassanaigh, and Ileana Lovell, High Priestess of the Traveler Clans. They come seeking your counsel, if you will give it."

Lira leaned in and pressed her face against Margaret's ear, whispering. Margaret spoke her sister's words aloud, acting almost as interpreter. "You have come to see me before, High Priestess."

Ileana stepped forward. "Yes. You were kind enough to assist us in our hour of need."

Lira whispered again. "And did it work? The summoning of the Elemental you requested?"

Ileana shifted from foot to foot. "Yes. We were able to summon it. Many thanks for the knowledge you bestowed upon us."

"And did it solve your problem with the Walker?" Margaret asked Lira's question in her strangely high voice.

Ileana hesitated. "No," she said at last. "No, we were not able to contain her by means of the Elemental. We had to resort to other... methods."

I rounded on Ileana. "You tried to imprison Irina with an Elemental?" I asked in a voice that was practically a growl.

"Many years ago," Ileana said, and even she, who never faltered in her air of superiority, sounded ashamed. "It was a practice used for centuries in Durupinen *príosúns*."

"A practice that was abandoned because it was barbaric," I snapped back.

"Do we think maybe we could save this argument for another time and try to focus on why we're here?" Catriona muttered to me out of the corner of her mouth.

I turned to give her a piece of my mind as well, but Finn placed a hand on my arm and shook his head minutely. I contented myself with shooting a withering look at Catriona, and thereafter attempted to gain control of myself again with slow, deep breaths. I couldn't lose it now, not when so much rested on getting my message to Lira. There would be time to drag Ileana over the coals later, and drag her I would.

Lira had turned her attention to me now. Her dark eyes glinted at me through the curtain of crow-black hair that still hung before her face. Though her stare frightened me with its intensity, I found it impossible to look away once caught in its beam.

"And this one. You are the reason, aren't you? The reason the others are here." Lira's words came from Margaret's mouth in that saccharine voice.

I tried to reply, but no sound would come out. I cleared my throat and tried again. "Yes. I am the one who really needs to see you. My... my friends offered to accompany me."

"Friends?" It was Lira who whispered the word aloud, now, cocking her head so far to the side that her ear rested upon her shoulder. "What a strange word. What does it mean?"

I opened my mouth and closed it again. "Uh... friends are people you like. People you do things for and who do things for you."

Lira straightened her head and, leaning in toward her sister's ear, whispered once more.

"I see. The Elementals are my friends, then," Margaret said.

I swallowed spastically. "Sure," I said weakly. "If... if you say so." I couldn't think of anything more horrifying than looking at a creature like an Elemental—a being created from and nourished by pure human fear—and calling it a friend. But of course, I wasn't about to tell Lira that. I wasn't going to say anything more to her than I absolutely had to.

"The Elementals have tasted of your fear before," Lira said through her sister.

"Yes, at Fairhaven," I replied, and then could not help asking, "How do you know that?"

Lira gave that same high musical giggle again and delivered her reply through her sister. "They are all connected, the Elementals. They crave you. Your twin as well. Once they develop a taste for your fear, they long for it again."

"Bloody hell," Lucida said under her breath. Her eyes were wide and horrified, but she did not _seem_ able to look away from the bizarre spectacle of codependence that was Lira and Margaret Blackwell.

"What do you want of me, Jessica Ballard of Clan Sassanaigh, Harbinger of the Prophecy, True Northern Walker, Muse and Seer? Why do you seek me in the heart of this wood?"

I glanced at Finn, unnerved. How did she know so much about me, things I hadn't even told the others standing alongside me? The longer I stayed in her presence, the more deeply I feared her, the more desperately I wanted to turn and flee. I swallowed all of this, though. Too much was at stake, and I'd come this far.

"I have a message for you. From Agnes Isherwood."

"And what is this message from one who lived so long ago?" Lira asked in Margaret's voice.

"The Sentinels have begun their watch."

Lira froze, becoming at once like a porcelain doll her sister was holding rather than a living person. Margaret, sensing her sister's tension, might suddenly have been carved of marble. For several long moments, no one spoke. No one moved. Everyone simply waited, breath held, to see how Lira would respond to the words I had uttered. I had never in all my life been enveloped in such an all-encompassing, all-consuming stillness. It felt unbreakable.

But break it did, when Lira swung suddenly down from her sister's shoulder and landed with catlike agility upon the ground. Every one of us jumped in shock. Catriona actually screamed. Lira scrambled forward across the mossy carpet of the forest floor until she crouched right before me.

"You will come with me, Jessica Ballard. I have something to give you," she whispered.

"I... all right," I said, stepping forward. Finn, all defensive instincts heightened, stepped forward at the same moment.

"No!" Lira whispered, and though the word was quiet, its intensity was shocking. "She must come alone."

Finn's hands retracted into tight fists. "Why must she go alone?" he asked, his voice as taut as a bowstring.

"Only the Messenger can receive it. I must give it to her, and her alone. It is my sacred duty," Lira hissed.

"Receive what?" Finn asked.

"Her and her alone," Lira repeated.

"And where are you taking her, exactly?" Finn asked, still not backing down.

Lira did not speak, but pointed to the sagging little hovel in the tree roots. She wanted me to follow her into her home. I hesitated. When Ileana heard my message, she knew there was something—an object that she needed to retrieve. It hung around her neck now—the huge iron key, hidden for centuries inside the throne of the Traveler High Priestess. Wasn't it likely that the Keeper, too, had something—some relic or sacred ancestral object—that only the hearing of Agnes' message would compel her to reveal? For reassurance, I looked not to Finn, but to Ileana. She looked as pale and anxious as everyone else, but when I caught her eye, she nodded grimly, and that nod felt like the confirmation I needed.

"Very well, Lira," I said, and I was shocked to hear that my voice was quite steady. "I'll go with you. Please lead the way."

"Jess—" Finn began, his voice full of trepidation. But I held up a hand, and he fell silent at once, dropping his eyes to the ground. He knew. He knew I had to follow her, however much we both hated the very thought.

I looked toward the others, giving them a nod, hoping to reassure them, anything to wipe the identical looks of horror from their faces. Even Abigail, who had displayed nothing but cheerful confidence since we'd entered the wood, shifted nervously from foot to foot, mouth opening and closing as though she both longed to interject and yet had no idea what to say. Seeing her look so unsure sapped the last of my confidence, and it was with my heart in my throat that I took the first steps toward Lira, shuffling uneasily forward until I stood right beside her.

Without warning, she reached out, snatched a handful of my jacket, and swung herself in a single movement up onto my back. I could only stand there, absolutely paralyzed with shock, as her skeletally thin arm hooked around my neck, as her bare toes dug into my back, clawing for purchase. Everyone behind me shouted. I have no idea how Finn stopped himself from rushing forward and tackling Lira right off me, but somehow, he refrained. I stood motionless for a moment as the girl settled herself, swallowing my revulsion at the sensation of her breath against my ear, her matted hair against my cheek.

Margaret looked as though she might faint at the sight of her sister clinging to another human being in this way. Her expression was that of someone who had been utterly betrayed. She sank to her knees on the ground and watched, wordlessly, a marionette with her strings cut, as Lira and I set off in the direction of the hovel.

I moved my way carefully through the minefield of protruding tree roots, rotting stumps, and rusting bits of "shine" that had fallen to the ground. When we reached the door, to my intense relief, Lira swung off my back to the ground and pushed the door inward. All was rank, impenetrable darkness in the room beyond.

I stood in the doorway, unable to force myself to move forward until I had some inkling of what lay within. Then, from somewhere inside, a candle guttered to life, illuminating just enough of the interior to allow me to set foot inside. A single chamber lay within, hollowed out of the very earth and smoothed over with some kind of primitive plaster-like substance that was chipping away to dust. The floor was spread with a number of rotted blankets and roughly woven rugs. A black, round-bellied stove squatted in one corner, the plaster around it blackened with soot, its crooked pipe disappearing through the ceiling. A crate of dented metal plates and mugs stood beside it, along with baskets of dried berries, mushrooms, and what I was pretty sure was a skinned squirrel hanging by its tail. A squalid straw mattress and a nest of rotted wool blankets took up most of the space on the other side of the door. I could barely imagine spending a night in such a wretched place, let alone imagine someone living here for their entire life—and a child of all people. It was beyond comprehension. My insides still hollow and aching with fear, I ducked my head under the lintel, took several steps inside at a crouch, and knelt upon one of the fetid rugs nearest the door. I did not close it behind me.

Lira turned to face me, and I quickly pressed my hand to my mouth to stifle my cry of shock. With the candle held just below her chin, her features were at last illuminated properly, and what I saw at once fascinated and repulsed me. Lira was not a little girl at all. She was an old woman, her cheeks hollowed with age, her skin a relief map of deep wrinkles, veins, and age spots. Her wide eyes had a cloudy quality to them, like the eyes of an old dog, and her hair was actually a dark grey, not black, as the moonlight had painted it. Her mouth, as she opened it to speak, contained not a single tooth.

"Do you know from whence the Elementals came?" she whispered in a voice dry and cracked as chalk.

I shook my head, my hand still clamped over my mouth, my voice still unable to penetrate the pall of my horror.

"Once the doors were always open, you see," Lira said, her eyes on her candle, watching it dance with a childlike fascination. "Spirits Crossed freely. It was as it should be."

"I know," I said, finding my voice at last. "Agnes told me. The Gateways belonged to the Geatgrimas. But how did you know that? The Durupinen have always kept that a secret."

"I did not learn it from the Durupinen," Lira said, shaking her head. "I learned it from the Elementals. When I was young they came to me. I could wish for them to find me, and they would. I could summon them. And I could send them away. I was immune to their power. They could not hurt me, as they had hurt so many others. They were my companions. And they whispered to me. They told me things."

"Why... why couldn't they hurt you? Why didn't they try to attack you, to feed on your fears, like they do everyone else?"

Lira tapped on her chest. "In here. They can't get in. Like my mother before me. And her mother before her. They do our bidding but cannot harm us. This is how we came to be the Keepers."

I nodded, pretending to understand.

"The Elementals are crimeborn," Lira went on, and her voice became soft, almost musical. "Our crime, the crime of taking the Gateways into ourselves. It spawned them."

"How?" I murmured.

"Tore at the fabrics between the worlds, we did. All the fear and uncertainty of death, trapped in the Aether. It crystallized. It swelled. The Elementals were born of it as the Geatgrimas sealed up forever, thrusting them forth into the world, the evidence of our crime."

"We created them," I said, understanding at last. "The sealing of the Geatgrimas created them."

Lira nodded. "And once made, they had to be controlled. For years we held them trapped, used them as weapons born of our new power. But they grew stronger, more difficult to control. And so the Keepers were called upon to gather them."

"Gather them? How?"

"We sing to them. They cannot resist the song. They come and they go as the song commands."

I gasped. "You can Call them. You're a Caller. A Caller of Elementals."

Lira cocked her head to the side again. It was clear she didn't know the term, but it didn't matter.

"But there's an Elemental at Fairhaven," I told her. "Why wasn't that one gathered?"

"A gift. A gift for the High Priestess," Lira said.

"A *gift*? Who the hell wants a gift like that?" I exclaimed.

"Useful, it is," Lira replied, almost indignantly, as though I had offended her. "Powerful."

"Ah, I see," I answered, my insides boiling. Having an Elemental must have been a forbidding thing, a way to scare your enemies and shore up your grasp on your territory. Sort of the Durupinen version of a weapon of war. It sounded like exactly the kind of thing our Council, drunk with their own power, in the heyday of Northern dominance, might have prized above all else, even if they later abandoned it.

"Now you come to me, Jessica Ballard, and speak the words no Keeper has ever heard before," Lira said, and she shifted forward until she was uncomfortably close to me. I could not get away from her without backing right out the door again. "Words I have been warned of."

"Warned? By who?" I asked.

"My mother. My grandmother. The Elementals themselves."

"Did—did your mother or your grandmother tell you what to do, if you ever heard these words?" I prompted. All of this information about the Elementals was fascinating, but I wanted nothing more than to get out of this rotting corpse of a house as quickly as possible.

"Oh, yes," Lira said. "I'm to give you this."

And she crawled to the back of her hovel, where a thick and ancient expanse of tree trunk was visible beneath the thin spackling of plaster. With filthy, clawlike fingernails, Lira began to scratch and dig away at the plaster, pulling crumbling hunks of it away in her hands like a burrowing rodent until she reached a knothole sunken in the face of the trunk. Slowly, she reached her hand inside the hollowed out knot and pulled from its depths a key, identical to the one that now hung around Ileana's neck. She held it up, transfixed for a moment at the way the light from the candle flinted off the metal, making it look as though it was alive with tiny golden sparks.

"A bit of shine for you, Jessica Ballard," Lira whispered, holding it out into the space between us. But just as I gathered the courage to reach for it, she pulled it back again, clutching it protectively against her sunken chest. "What will you do with it?"

"I don't know yet," I said, feeling it was best to be honest. "I'll bring it with me to the High Priestess of the International High Council. She is the last one to whom I'm supposed to deliver the message."

"And then?"

"And then I'm going to save my friend, I hope. Restore the Gateways to the Geatgrimas, where they rightfully belong, before it's too late."

Lira closed her eyes. She swayed. For a moment, I wondered if she might pass out. But then her eyes snapped open again and she looked down sharply, as though she thought that the key might have disappeared from her grasp while her eyes were shut. Then she glared at me, a breathtaking ferocity newly kindled in her eyes.

"And you are sure, are you, that you want to risk such a thing?" Lira hissed at me.

"I... I'm risking much more, I think, by doing nothing," I said, my sense of unease growing.

"And what if you are wrong?" Lira asked.

"I don't think I am," I said. "I..."

"Jess."

I jumped, turning on the spot. The voice? Where had it come from? Not from Lira, who was sitting there staring at me, her mouth shut.

"Jessica."

I forgot how to breathe. That voice. I knew that voice. That voice that sang to me. That comforted me. That drove me crazy and spoke more love to me than any other voice in my life. Where was it coming from? What was happening?

"Out here, Jessica."

I turned, following the sound of the voice out of the hovel and around the back side of the clump of trees. A low mist hung around the clearing, curling around me, obscuring everything further than a few feet away. Then I heard it again.

"There you are, kiddo. Long time, no see."

Everything stopped. My mother. The spirit of my mother stood there, cloaked in mist, a wide, joyous smile on her face.

ARTIFICE

THAT FACE—the face I'd longed to see more than any other. How was it possible it was there, beaming at me?

"Mom?" I choked out.

Her smile grew wider. "Don't be afraid, sweetie. It's all right."

"But... I don't understand. You... you can't be here. You Crossed. I saw you, in the Aether. What—what are you doing here?" I couldn't tear my eyes from her, couldn't bear to look away.

"When the Gateway was reversed, the Aether became unstable. Some of us were drawn out."

I shook my head. "No. No, that doesn't make sense. That can't happen, it's—"

My mother laughed, and the sound of it squeezed my heart like a vice. She took several steps toward me. I might have been able to touch her, if I reached out my hand.

"Don't tell me you still believe in impossible things after all you've seen and done, kiddo."

"I... I don't know," I whispered. The sight of her was filling up every aching, empty place where she used to be, those places that nothing and no one else could ever fill.

"Jess, you must be careful," my mother went on, and her smile faded. "I'm not just here to see you, but to warn you."

"Warn me? About what?"

"Don't go to the International High Council. You can't understand the danger you're putting yourself in. That you're putting everyone in!"

"What kind of danger? What are you talking about?"

"Please, darling. Forget what Agnes told you. Forget all of it."

"Mom, I can't just forget it. And I still don't understand. If you've been here since the Gateway reversed, where have you been? Why haven't I seen you?"

"We didn't want to interfere, sweetheart. We didn't want to disrupt the life you've built for yourself."

"Who's... who's we?"

And from the mist around her, other figures were stepping forward, vaguely recognizable: Pierce. Carrick. Evan. Bertie.

"I... don't understand..." I whispered, my heart in my throat, my eyes filling with tears.

"Come here, kiddo. Come to me." My mother held out her arms, and the space within them was the most beautiful, most inviting thing I'd ever seen in my life. I was walking toward her before I even knew what I was doing.

Her arms enclosed around me, and then seemed to lengthen, like tendrils...

Wrapping. Flickering. Tasting.

And then the pain began. Pain so blinding, so intense that I didn't know where I was, didn't know who I was. All I knew was that I wanted it to end, even if that meant my life ended with it.

The sound of my own screams filled my ears, along with the ecstatic moans of the creature now gorging itself on every fear, every doubt, every negative emotion and terrible memory I'd ever locked away in the deepest corners of myself. It found each and every one of them, exposing them, ripping away the scar tissue and sucking them dry. Their ecstatic voices rose in a chorus.

Such fear. Such despair. Such a feast. We've been hungry for so long. So long...

Through a haze of pain, even as I called out for help, I could see Lira crouching on the ground, watching it all happen. There was an almost feral glee upon her face, as she watched her beloved charges slowly destroy me. I knew in that moment what I ought to have known the moment I laid eyes on her: there was nothing she wouldn't do to protect the creatures she was sworn to keep, even if it meant the destruction of the entire Durupinen world. If all that remained when it all went to hell was her and her Elementals, well... that was all that really mattered, wasn't it?

Oh glorious, glorious. It has known so much pain. So much delicious pain. It deepens, even as we feed.

Why was no one coming to help me? Where was Finn? Where were the others? Was I even screaming aloud, or was the screaming only inside my own head? I didn't know, and I was losing the will to care. I just wanted it to be over, for the Elementals to stop playing with their food and just end it already. What sweet relief it would be, to not feel anything anymore. This thought, as the Elementals got a taste of it, sent them into an even deeper frenzy of bliss. But even in the midst of the torture, at this lowest moment, a small bubble of a thought—where had it come from?—rose to the surface and burst.

At least I'd been able to see my mother one more time.

And then, as suddenly as it started, it was over. A scream that was not my own echoed inside my head, and then seemed to be sucked from my head to echo in the open air. The tendrils that had so tightly bound me were loosening and falling away. The pain was receding from every cell, my fears and guilt and sadness were dragging themselves, bruised and battered, back to the boxes I kept them locked away in. I opened my eyes and found myself on my hands and knees on the forest floor, panting and sobbing, but wholly unhurt.

"Jess!"

It was Finn's voice that came to me now, his arms that lifted me from the ground and into his embrace.

"Love, speak to me! Are you all right?"

"I'm okay," I gasped between the sobs that would not let go.

"Everything's all right now, I've expelled them. They're gone. Are you still in pain?"

"No, I'm not," I managed to reply. "I... I just..." But the tears continued to overwhelm my ability to speak through them. It took me several more minutes to calm down enough to pull my face off Finn's shoulder and look around me.

The mist had lifted from the clearing. The Elementals—for that is what they had been, not spirits of those I'd lost, just Elementals playing upon my weaknesses—were nowhere to be seen. Abigail stood near the entrance to the hovel, both looking pale and shocked. Ileana and Annabelle had pulled Margaret's arms behind her back and held the woman pinned against a tree trunk as she struggled to get to her sister. Lira was fighting and flailing like a possessed thing against the grip of Catriona and Lucida, who had, it appeared, tackled her to the ground. It now took both of them to keep her restrained as she kicked and shrieked a stream of incomprehensible ramblings. I tore my eyes from her struggle to look at Finn again, who was looking me over as though expecting to find some wound that needed staunching, something he could bandage or fix.

"I don't understand," I said, my breathing still hitched and uneven. "What happened?"

"Lira must have summoned the Elementals. It was a trap," Finn said. "They lured you out of the shack and attacked you. We didn't know what was happening until you started screaming, and by that time, they'd already latched onto you."

"But the Casting Abigail put on us—I thought we were supposed to be protected from the Elementals!" I said, trying to keep the accusation out of my voice, but throwing a sharp glare at Abigail all the same.

Finn grimaced and lifted my hair from the back of my neck. "The rune is gone—wiped away. Lira must have done it when she crawled up onto your back."

I reached around to feel the place where the rune had been, remembering the shivers up my spine as Lira had twisted her fingers into my hair and wrapped her arms around my neck.

"But how did she do it? How did she summon them without you knowing? There's a whole Casting that must be performed, just as Peyton did when she left you to the mercy of the Fairhaven Elemental."

"Lira doesn't need a Casting," I told him. "She's a Caller. A Caller of Elementals, not spirits. Her clan has had the gift for generations. That's why she's the Keeper."

"She Called them?" Finn asked, looking horrified. "But... why? What happened in there?"

"I don't know," I said, trying to think back past the pain to the conversation we'd had. "We were talking. She told me about how the Elementals came to be—that they were spawned from the moment the Gateways were stripped from the Geatgrimas—formed from the fear and doubt that's trapped in the Aether itself. And then she took out a key to give to me—like the one Ileana's got—but then she asked me... she asked me what I would do if she gave it to me."

"And what did you say?"

"That I was going to try to save my friend and restore the Gateways. And then I heard a voice and... oh my God."

"What? What is it?"

The realization had just hit me. I looked at Lira, still writhing on the ground, and understood. I turned from Finn and started walking toward the place where Catriona and Lucida were struggling to restrain her.

"Jess, be careful! Don't get too close! She may attack again!" Finn hissed, jogging along after me.

"It's okay, I just want to ask her something," I said. As I drew nearer, I expected Lira's thrashing to grow wilder, but instead, she seemed to calm with every step I took. By the time I was close enough to speak to her, she had gone limp in Catriona and Lucida's arms. Margaret, too, had stopped struggling and slumped down against the tree, crying quietly and mumbling her sister's name over and over again.

Lira looked up at me, her sunken chest heaving, pure loathing in her expression. I ought to have hated her for what she had just done to me, but I couldn't. I felt nothing but pity in my heart for her and the empty, isolated existence she led.

"What happens to the Elementals if the Gateways are restored to the Geatgrimas?" I asked her.

Lira's face twitched, and her eyes filled with tears. "They return. They return from whence they came."

"Are you sure of that?" I asked. "Or are you only afraid they will?"

Lira did not reply. Her lip quivered.

"You thought that if you let me go with the key, that I would take them away from you?" I asked.

Lira nodded, tears running down the deep crags in her face.

"I told you I was going to try to save my friend. You were just trying to do the same, weren't you? You were trying to save your friends."

Lira curled herself into a fetal position and completely broke down, all the fight gone out of her. Feeling slightly sickened with myself, I reached down and pulled the ancient key out of Lira's clasped hands. She gave it up to me without a hint of further resistance.

"I'm sorry," I told her. "But we both know I'm meant to have this, and I have to take it with me. I wish there was another way."

Now that it was clear that Lira was beyond attacking anyone else, Lucida and Catriona removed their restraining hands and stepped back from her, both panting with the enormous effort it had taken to restrain such an old creature. As soon as they moved out of the way, Margaret came hurrying <u>over</u> to Lira, bending over her and shielding her with her body as though expecting an aerial attack. She began shushing and singing softly to her sister, rocking and crying in tandem with her.

"Let's leave them," I said to the rest of the group, who were all standing around looking shell-shocked. "There's nothing else we can do for her. We've caused enough damage."

I was surprised to hear the authority in my voice, and even more surprised when no one questioned me, but turned their backs on the squalid little hovel and its traumatized residents and set back off through the woods. We walked in silence for several minutes, Abigail taking the lead, before anyone finally found their voice.

"She was old," Catriona said, her voice full of shock and revulsion. "I... I thought she was a child until we had to restrain her."

"So did I," I admitted. "But then she lit the candle inside the house and I realized the truth."

"What happened in there, Jess? Why did she attack you with the Elementals? What did you say to her?"

"She realized that if I delivered my message to the High Priestess of the International High Council, that would likely be the end of the Elementals," I said. Now that my shock was wearing off, I was shaking like a leaf. I clenched my fists to stop the trembling in my hands.

"How does she figure that?" Annabelle asked.

"I'm not sure. It had something to do with the origins of the Elementals. But my words from Agnes were a trigger for her. She's spent her entire life with them. She has nothing else. She saw me as someone who wanted to take away her purpose and her calling." Which, I realized, was how even my own sister had felt at first; and was likely how many other, very important Durupinen would feel as well. Would they listen, or choose to silence me? This message I was carrying was more dangerous than I knew.

"And why... Jess, why in the world would you let those monsters come anywhere near you? Why didn't you run?"

"Because," and I was ashamed, although I knew Finn would never fault me for what I had done, "because it pretended to be my mother."

"It... *what?!*" Finn's expression was devastated.

"I know it was stupid, but I couldn't help it. It... it took the form of my mother and told me she _had_ come to warn me not to go to the High Council. Then others appeared, in the forms of other people I've lost—Carrick, Pierce—and I was just too confused and emotional to make a rational decision. I didn't realize it was a trick until it was too late. I'm sorry."

"Love, what in the world are you apologizing to me for?" Finn asked, exasperated. "Surely you don't think you owe me or anyone else an apology for being subjected to something like that? The Elementals played on your deepest pain and twisted it to their advantage. Anyone would have been vulnerable."

"I was such an idiot," I said, hot tears springing into my eyes and rolling down my cheeks before I could stop them. "I knew my mother had Crossed. I knew that. And the others, too. But I couldn't stop myself from hoping, just for a moment—"

"You can't blame yourself, Jess."

"Watch me," I grumbled.

"That's not fair to yourself, love."

"How the hell did those Elementals know how to get to me, anyway?" I asked, the question bursting from me suddenly, like a projectile. "How did they know what form to take? How did they know what to say?"

"All Elementals were born of the same darkness," Finn said. "They're all connected to each other. Once the Elemental at Fairhaven fed itself on your pain and fears, all the Elementals had a taste of it. They knew your weaknesses because they'd tasted them before."

Every bit of the aching longing and sadness that had filled me at the sight of my mother and the others had drained away now, and the space had been filled with gnawing anger and guilt. I'd set myself up as an easy target. Every time I opened myself up to being vulnerable – to missing someone, to loving someone, to letting someone in—life turned around and sucker-punched me right in the face. It was enough to make the whole hermit-in-the-woods lifestyle look appealing.

Finn reached out and took my hand. I had a momentary impulse to pull it from him, but the impulse melted away as he squeezed my fingers gently. I looked up to see him looking at me with an expression that took my breath away, and I knew that he would always love me in these moments I couldn't love myself. I interlaced my fingers with his instead, locking his hand in place. My other hand I kept tightly wrapped around the key that I had taken from Lira.

The walk out of the woods went much more quickly than the walk in. Before I knew it, we had arrived back at the clump of bushes where we had stashed our belongings. Everything was still there, just as we had left it, with no signs that it had been disturbed. It was with obvious relief that Finn re-armed himself and slung his readiness pack over his shoulder. We saw not a single hint that anyone other than ourselves had ventured into the woods that night—no freshly abandoned campsites or still smoking fires, no fresh tracks in the muddy path that we rejoined and led us out of the woods and back out into the adjoining field. Perhaps the ordinance the village had put in place was indeed working—or perhaps the sounds of my own screams had kept the thrillseekers at bay. If anyone nearby had doubted the Screaming Woods were aptly named, they would have no doubt now, and it was with distinct relief that I left them at my back, hoping I would never have to enter them again. From the looks on the faces of my companions, I could tell that the feeling was mutual.

"So, what do we do now?" Annabelle asked. "What's our next move?"

I faltered as six pairs of eyes all turned expectantly toward me. I tried to wrangle my scattered thoughts into a concrete plan of action, but my exhausted brain wouldn't cooperate. I sighed. "We sleep. I don't think we can formulate next steps without getting some rest first—at least, I don't think *I* can." Now that the adrenaline was wearing off, I was feeling more and more like I was mentally and physically made of gelatin.

"Yeh've been through an ordeal that few have lived to tell about, being attacked by them Elementals," Abigail said sagely, her ancient head bobbing up and down on her spindly neck. "Abigail has got just the remedy for that. Just leave it to me, lass."

We followed Abigail back around the outskirts of the village, now silent and still in the last hour or two before dawn. Back inside the Milkweed Teahouse, she set to work, and within a few minutes had brewed up an herbal tea of sorts that smelled horrible and tasted even worse.

"Once the Elementals get into yer mind like they do, it can be a right struggle to pry them out <u>again</u>," she explained, thrusting the cup at me. "And that can make for a devil of a nightmare when yeh close yer eyes. Get that straight down yer gullet, now, and it'll give yeh a bit of peace while yer dreamin'."

I gave the tea a suspicious look, but honestly, after what the Elementals had put me through, I'd try almost anything to put it behind me, including drinking what looked and smelled like rotting produce. I threw my head back and downed the tea in three large gulps, feeling it scald my throat all the way down and sear the insides of my nostrils with its pungent, spicy fumes. I coughed and sputtered a little, but succeeded in not spraying tea all over the room.

Everyone else stood around awkwardly for a few moments, wondering if they were going to be forced to withstand the tea as well, but when it became clear that I was to be its only victim, we all turned and started for the stairs. Only Ileana remained behind, settling herself in a chair by the fire and pulling a book from the nearby shelf. She nodded her head at me, and I couldn't be sure if the gesture was meant to reassure me that she would watch over things while we slept, or to shame me for succumbing to such a human weakness as sleep. I decided I didn't have the emotional bandwidth to care. Each step up the staircase was more difficult than the last.

I lay in the darkness with Finn beside me, the full weight of what had happened that night pressing down upon me like weights. My thoughts inside my brain felt like rocks in a clothes dryer, clunking loudly and painfully around inside my skull. Thankfully, I did not have to open the connection and add even more chaos—while I washed up in the bathroom, Finn had texted Hannah to fill her in on everything that had happened in the Screaming Woods, and asked her to hold off on trying to contact me so that I could get some rest. I had no idea if he had told her about the Elementals taking the shape of our mother. I hoped he hadn't, just to spare me a bit of humiliation and an unwelcome dose of pity.

I knew where I needed to go next, and who I needed to try to see, but now I was scared. Agnes had said that there were only three people who would understand the message about the Sentinels. So far, I had delivered my message to two of them. The first had me arrested and imprisoned, though admittedly not because of the content of my message. The second had attacked me with Elementals, and this time, the ferocity of the response was directly related to the words I had delivered to her. Now there was one person left to whom I needed to speak Agnes' words, and that person just happened to be the single most powerful figure in all of the Durupinen world. Her response would be proportionate to her power, no doubt; she could either make sure that every Durupinen in the world knew the urgency of Agnes' warning, or she could bury it—and me—so deeply that it would take another handful of centuries for us to resurface. What if the High Priestess of the International High Council didn't like what I had to say? What if she, like Lira, thought that the restoring of the Gateways to the Geatgrimas would render her irrelevant? That seemed like a pretty good reason to render me irrelevant.

I took a deep breath and let it out very slowly, trying to calm my frantically beating heart. Beside me, Finn shifted in the bed. "You all right, love?"

"Yeah. I will be. I'm just... processing."

"Do you want to talk about it?"

"I don't even want to think about it. I just want to be asleep."

"Is that your way of telling me to bugger off?" he half-laughed.

"No, no," I said quickly. "In fact, get over here." I rolled over into the curve of his body and pulled his arm over my torso, like I was buckling myself in against the mental onslaught. "There. Much better."

Finn buried his face in my hair and I focused on breathing along with him. And then, all at once, everything felt heavy.

The darkness pressing in upon us felt heavy.

Lira's key, clutched to my chest, felt heavy.

The thoughts swirling in my head felt heavy.

My eyelids felt heavy...

And finally, sleep took me.

THE WARNING

S UDDENLY I WAS AWAKE, but somehow, some protective instinct was keeping my eyes from opening. A creeping feeling was inching its way up my spine like an insect, and the hairs on my arms stood at attention. The air around me had dropped at least thirty degrees. Goosebumps had erupted all over my body, and I was shivering.

A spirit. There was a spirit in the room.

Even with this realization, I did not yet open my eyes. Instead, I fumbled around with my numb fingers until I found Finn's hand and squeezed it. He snorted and snuffled in his sleep but did not wake. I swore under my breath. I had no idea if the Milkweed Tavern was Warded or not—it seemed ridiculous that it wouldn't be, but then again, Abigail was a bit eccentric. A brushing sound and a sudden expulsion of cool air against my cheek made me freeze, and I knew that when I opened my eyes, the spirit, whoever it was, would be face to face with me.

Steeling myself, reminding myself that this was something I did every day and probably would do for the rest of my life, I opened my eyes, prepared to calmly confront my nighttime visitor. Instead, I let out a shout of relieved laughter.

"Annabelle, what the hell!" I cried. "You scared the crap out of me!"

Annabelle stepped quickly back from the edge of the bed, retreating from the light as I switched on the bedside lamp.

"What are you doing? Is everything okay? You could have just knocked, you know. That would have had less chance of giving me a heart attack."

Annabelle gave an odd sort of shrug, but didn't reply.

"Why the hell is it so cold in here?" I asked, looking around hopelessly for something as modern as a thermostat. "Do you feel that?"

Annabelle nodded, arms wrapped around herself.

"I think there must be a spirit lurking around. I'm not sure this place is even Warded. Is that what woke you up?"

Annabelle shrugged again. I looked more closely at her. Something was… off.

"Annabelle? Are you okay?"

She didn't reply. She just kept staring at me with strange, wide eyes that somehow weren't her own.

"Annabelle?" A horrible thought crossed my mind, but I quashed it at once. She wasn't a ghost, that much was clear. I'd made that mistake once before, and I wasn't going to make it again. She wasn't Walking either. Her form was solid. Her feet made the floorboards squeak. She cast a shadow on the wall behind her. But if she wasn't a ghost…

"Annabelle? Can you speak to me?"

Annabelle just stared for several long seconds. Then she gave an odd shudder and shook her head.

Another thought occurred to me, a thought which shaped my next question as it fell from my lips. "Am… am I speaking to Annabelle right now?"

Another pause. Another violent shudder. Another shake of the head.

The sound of my voice had roused Finn. He sat up behind me, blinking around in confusion.

"Jess, what's going on? Annabelle? Is everything all right?" he mumbled, dragging his hand over his face.

"I… no, I don't think everything is all right," I muttered to him, and felt his body tense at the words. "She's… something's happened to her. A spirit maybe? A Habitation?"

"A Habitation?" Finn asked, alarmed. "But how—?"

"I don't know how. But… I know this isn't Annabelle, so what else could it be?"

I'd had my fair share of experiences with Habitation. A spirit had forcefully Habitated with me once, before I even knew I was a Durupinen—the experience had been torture. Since then, I'd willingly allowed Milo to Habitate within my body. It had been an undoubtedly strange experience—unpleasantly crowded both mentally and physically. But in both cases, I had retained a firm grip on my faculties. I knew who I was, and what was happening, and at no point did I feel that I had lost control over my own body. But Annabelle was not a Durupinen, and I knew from all the studying I'd done as an Apprentice at Fairhaven that non-Durupinen bodies could be taken over in ways that rendered them incapable of resisting the will of the Habitating spirit. In other words, when the average person was taken over by a spirit, they became, in essence, a puppet. I watched as Annabelle's body twitched spastically. She may not have been in full control of her physical form, but she was putting up a damn good fight. It seemed there was just enough Durupinen blood in her to allow for that struggle.

I stood up slowly and took a step toward her. Finn reached out and grabbed my arm, but I shook him off. "Just give me a second," I murmured to him. I felt his grip slacken, and though I could practically feel the tension rolling off him in waves, he did not try to stop me again.

I stepped forward very carefully, muscles tensed, ready to jump back at the slightest sign of hostility. "Do you need to talk to me?" I asked the figure cowering in the shadows.

A shudder. A nod.

"It's all right. What do you need to tell me? I'm listening."

I reached a hand out to her, and it was as though it was the key needed to unlock a door. Annabelle leapt forward, grabbed my hand in both of hers, and began shrieking at the top of her lungs. But though the words were pouring from her like water from a fountain, I couldn't understand a single one: she was shouting in rapid Romanian.

"I... I'm sorry, I can't understand you!" I cried, trying to make myself heard over the steady stream of pleading wails. "English? Do you speak any English?"

It did not even seem as though the spirit heard my question. The Romanian monologue bubbled forth uninterrupted, increasing in intensity with every passing second as it became clear that I could not make sense of what the spirit was trying to say. And then, suddenly, a lightbulb went on, and I could have smacked myself for not thinking of it instantly. I couldn't understand this spirit, but there was someone in this house who could.

"Finn, go get Ileana. Now, now, we need her to translate!" I cried.

Finn leapt from the bed, threw our door open, and dashed from the room. Annabelle—or whoever she was—paid not the slightest attention to him as he flew past. Now that she had my attention, she seemed not to care about anything in the world except willing me to understand what she was _saying_. But no amount of pleading and hand wringing could translate her words into something I could comprehend.

"I'm sorry," I kept saying, over and over again. "I'm sorry, I don't know what you're saying. Just hang on. Hang on and someone will be here to help us."

Annabelle was crying now, tears streaming down her face, her whole body shaking not only with the struggle to maintain control over it, but with the emotional upheaval of the being who had hijacked it. Several times I wondered if she would be successful in forcing the spirit out—her eyes rolled back in her head and the pleas tumbling from her mouth took on a stilted, garbled quality, as though other words were trying to break through.

"Annabelle, if you can hear me, I know this is terrifying, but don't fight it. Whoever this spirit is, they're using you to deliver a message. Let them deliver it! The faster they do, the faster they'll let you go!"

The commotion sent Catriona and Lucida barreling out into the hallway in frightened, sleepy confusion. "What the bloody hell is going on?" Catriona shouted over Annabelle's continued pleas. She hesitated in the doorway, clearly unsure if she should intervene to pull the two of us apart.

"She's possessed, Cat!" I shouted over the Romanian wailing. "She's possessed, and I can't understand what she's—"

At that moment, Finn returned with Ileana, whose disoriented expression told me that she, too, had finally succumbed to her exhaustion. She stared at Annabelle and me for several seconds in utter bewilderment before springing into action.

"The dialect is antiquated," Ileana said, snapping into a calm, businesslike tone, in stark contrast to Annabelle's unhinged raving. "She's... she's apologizing for something... she's sorry... she's sorry she told... she's *got* to slow down."

"Tell her, then!" I yelled. "Tell her to slow down!"

Ileana began replying in Romanian. Annabelle cowered away from her at first, as though she was terrified to speak to anyone but me. I watched a kind of light come into her strange, dark, dilated eyes as Ileana's words at last broke through. Annabelle gave a cry of relief. One hand shot out and snatched at Ileana's hand, and the other reached out and grabbed mine. Now, having created a kind of conduit between us, she took a deep, gasping breath, and tried again, speaking more slowly this time.

"I'm sorry," Ileana said, translating directly now. "I am so sorry. I have done wrong."

"It's okay," I told her. "Just tell me what's wrong."

"I told them. I told them everything. But they promised. They promised to let me go. And it has been so long... so, so long since I have been free... they promised..."

"Who are you talking about? Who did you tell?"

Ileana had trouble with the translation. "The dead... no, the death raisers?"

"Dead? You mean the spirits? You told the spirits?"

Annabelle shook her head violently and repeated her words.

Ileana gasped. "Necromancers. She means the Necromancers."

My heart, already pounding, started hurling itself against my ribcage. "You told the Necromancers what? What did you tell them?" I asked, trying to keep the terror out of my voice.

"The keys. I told them about the keys. They are coming for the keys."

I looked at Ileana, whose face bore the same horror I could feel in my own expression. Ileana raised a hand to her bosom and pulled the long, golden chain upward until the large iron key was revealed dangling from the bottom of it. My hand, as well, went immediately to the key nested in my sweatshirt pocket. We looked at each other, and in that moment, I knew that, for perhaps the first time in our lives, we were on exactly the same page.

"What did you mean when you said that the Necromancers promised to free you?" I asked. "Free you from what?"

Annabelle watched with a tortured expression while Ileana translated the question, and then threw her head back and gave a long, guttural moan so full of pain that I felt dizzy and ill at the sound of it. Then she leaned toward me, scrabbling with her fingers to gain a hold on my sweatshirt and pulling me close to her so that our faces were nearly touching. Her breath was like ice as she gave her tremulous answer.

"Locked away. Locked away and forgotten, all for the crime of knowing the truth," Ileana translated.

And it clicked. Finn gave a sharp intake of breath, and I knew that he had just had the same epiphany that I'd had.

"You're the Tansy Hag," I whispered. "You were the Traveler woman who helped Agnes Isherwood learn to Rift so that she could find me. They locked you away so that you could never tell anyone what the Durupinen had done to the Geatgrimas."

"It was my only trespass. Knowing too much."

"And the Necromancers offered you freedom if you told them the truth. So, now they know. They know that we're raising the alarm, and gathering the keys."

"Yes. Forgive me. I have been in agony for so long. Get to the last key before they do. It is your only chance. Forgive... me... please..."

With a violent, jerking motion, the Tansy Hag first released me, and then released Annabelle. Annabelle's entire body went rigid, then her back arched, and her mouth opened in a scream, and the Tansy Hag rode the tremors of that scream out into the open air above our heads. I barely had a moment to get a glimpse of her wrinkled face, sunken and eloquent with sorrow, before she shot through the wall like a bullet out of a gun and disappeared into the night.

Annabelle crumpled, but Ileana and I managed to catch her before she hit the ground.

"What happened? Did you expel her?" I asked Finn.

"No! The space is Warded after all. As soon as she left Annabelle's body, the room expelled her for me!" Finn bounded at once from the room. I knew without his saying that he was heading outside to see if he could find the Tansy Hag.

Annabelle was beginning to stir, moaning softly and struggling into a sitting position on the floor. She blinked around at all of us, clearly still disoriented.

"She... is she gone?" she mumbled at last.

"Yes," I told her. Catriona hurried forward and together we managed to lift Annabelle from the floor and settle her onto the bed. Ileana, now that the Tansy Hag had vanished, collapsed into the nearby chair, a shaking hand pressed over her eyes.

"Does anyone want to explain what the buggery bollocks is going on?" Lucida asked, sounding breathless.

"I'm not sure any of us can, quite yet," I replied before turning back to Annabelle, whose face was chalky white. "Can someone get her some water?"

Lucida hurried over to the washstand and poured a glass of water from the porcelain pitcher, and then leaned across the bed to hand it to me. Annabelle reached for it, but I doubted she had the strength to hold the glass, and so I sat her up and held the glass to her mouth. She did not protest, but drank greedily, rivulets of water dripping down her chin. When she had drained the glass, she flopped back against the pillows with a groan.

"Are you okay, Annabelle?" I asked, half expecting the Tansy Hag's cracked old voice to reply.

"I am," Annabelle replied, her voice tremulous but very much her own. "I... what happened?"

"You were possessed by the Tansy Hag," I told her. "We're not really sure how. What's the last thing you remember?"

Annabelle furrowed her brow, then clutched her hands to either side of her head, as though just the act of trying to recall a memory was agonizing. "Uh... I couldn't sleep. I went outside to have a cigarette," she began.

"A cigarette? I didn't think you smoked," I said, frowning.

"I don't, much," Annabelle said. "But David was taking cigarette breaks constantly when we worked together. I would always follow him outside—we had some of our best talks standing against the outside of a building under a haze of his cigarette smoke. So, when I'm feeling particularly anxious, sometimes I'll go outside and light one, just to smell it and watch it burn."

I swallowed back a violent urge to burst into tears. I didn't know if Annabelle saw that one of the Elementals had taken on the appearance of Pierce, and I didn't want to ask. Instead, I plowed forward with my questions. "And then what happened?"

"I thought I sensed a spirit presence nearby, but it was... odd. It felt almost like the feeling I had when those Elementals came into the clearing."

I looked sharply at Ileana. "Are we being tricked again? Could Lira have sent that Elemental to impersonate the Tansy Hag, like it impersonated my mother?"

But Ileana was already shaking her head before I finished my question. "When a spirit is that ancient, the link to the living human being degrades over time. It feels less and less human, and more like a purely spirit form. And an Elemental cannot Habitate, as a true spirit can. It could feed on her, certainly, but it could not have possessed her like that."

I turned back to Annabelle, reassured. "And after that?"

"After that, it's a blur," Annabelle said. "I had brief moments when I could see and hear where I was, but mostly it was just… just blinding pain and darkness. And then it was over." She looked up at me, frowning. "You're telling me the Tansy Hag was actually possessing me?"

"Yes, it appears so," I said.

"But you said she was incarcerated in the deepest levels of that Durupinen prison for hundreds of years, right? So, how did she get out?"

"That's a really good question," I said before throwing a sharp glance at Catriona, who was looking nothing short of disturbed.

"I'm on it," she said, and jogged out of the room.

As succinctly as I could, I filled Annabelle in on what the Tansy Hag had said while she was in control of Annabelle's body. By the time I had finished, Annabelle was looking terrified, and Ileana had begun pacing the room like a caged jungle cat.

"If the Necromancers are after those keys, that means they could be on their way here right now, doesn't it?" Annabelle asked. She kept her voice calm, but there was a definite spark of panic in her eyes.

"Yes, I suppose it might," I admitted. I turned to Ileana. "It also means that the Traveler camp is in danger."

Ileana nodded. "I must return as soon as possible."

"Ileana, it would be insanity to go back there now," I said.

"I cannot abandon my people, my blood. If they are going to face an enemy, I must face it with them. It is my duty to protect our clans," she said, drawing herself up proudly.

"Yes, but the best way to protect them is to get as far from the camp as possible!" I cried. "Listen, if the Necromancers know about these keys, then they likely know who has been charged with keeping them secret. They'll be looking for you, Ileana. And if you've left the camp, then there's no reason for the Necromancers to linger there. Draw them away, and you'll save lives."

Ileana stared blankly at me for a moment as these words sunk in. Then, suddenly, she gave a grunt and a nod. "There is some sense in what you say. Very well then, I will not return to the camp. But I must get word to them at once. They must fortify themselves against attack."

"But how will you..."

Ileana crossed to the bedroom's only window and opened it as wide as it would go. Then she stuck her entire head and shoulders out into the cold night air and began cawing loudly.

"What the bloody blazes...?" Lucida muttered.

But before any of us could question this odd behavior further, an answering "caw" echoed out in the alleyway, and Ileana pulled herself back in through the window just in time for her large, black raven to soar through it. As we all shrieked and threw our arms protectively up over our heads, the raven soared once around the room and came to rest on Ileana's shoulder. She clicked her tongue affectionately at the bird and stroked the glossy feathers on its breast.

"Where the hell did that thing come from?" I asked, still breathless.

"My sweeting is never far from me," Ileana chirped, more to the bird than to me, and produced a sunflower seed from her pocket, along with a scrap of paper, a ribbon, and the stub of a pencil. The raven snapped up the seed and then sat glaring down at his mistress as she hastily wrote out a note. She then tied it to the bird's leg as he ruffled his feathers impatiently, and returned to the window. With one last ear-splitting caw, the bird took off into the rosy pre-dawn sky.

"You're going to warn the other Travelers by messenger raven?" I asked weakly.

Ileana glared at me, as though daring me to suggest there might be a faster or more effective means of modern communication than a note tied to a bird's leg. I decided I didn't have the strength to get into yet another argument with her.

"What did you tell them?" I asked instead.

"To ready the camp for a fight, and to fortify the borders," Ileana said, eyes still on the sky, determined to track the raven for as far as she could still make out his inky shape against the dawn.

"Why not tell them to pull up stakes and get the hell out of there?" Lucida asked.

"There is not enough time," Ileana said. "They cannot make a clean getaway. The Necromancers will track them, and if they are ambushed on the road, they will be decimated. Besides, they will not leave the child behind, <u>not</u> while she is in the thrall of the Geatgrima. She must be protected. The Travelers will stand their ground and fight."

She spoke with the full authority of her High Priestess status, and it was clear she would not be dissuaded. Lucida gave every appearance of continuing to argue the point, but I raised my eyebrows and shook my head at her, and she let it go. We had enough to worry about keeping ourselves safe now without picking this fight.

Finn came back into the room, panting slightly. "All is quiet outside. No sign of the Tansy Hag, nor of the Necromancers, if they are indeed on the way. But we cannot stay here, that much is clear from the Tansy Hag's warning. If they know the locations of these keys, they must surely be on their way. Can I assume that was your bird carrying that message, High Priestess?" Finn asked.

Ileana gave a haughty nod of the head. "He will warn the Travelers of the oncoming attack from the Necromancers."

"Would you like me to send reinforcements from the Northern Clans to assist your Guardians?" Finn asked. "My men would be glad to lend their services."

Ileana raised her chin defiantly, and Finn hastily added, "I do not mean it as an insult to the skills of your own men. I merely wish to be of assistance, if you require it."

Ileana inclined her head. "Thank you, Caomhnóir Carey. I shall consider the matter."

I turned to Finn. "Won't sending a Caomhnóir contingent to defend the Traveler camp blow our cover? The leadership at Fairhaven will have to be told why the Travelers require protection, and then they'll know everything."

Finn nodded. "We've reached an impasse, Jess. If we keep it a secret any longer, we put everyone at risk. The Necromancers will surely descend on Fairhaven if they think there's any chance you're there. The castle must be fortified as well, and all members of the Northern Clans put on high alert."

Catriona entered the room, looking pale. She held her phone in her hand. "I missed a call while we were all sleeping. It was from Elin. But she left me a voicemail." She stared down at the phone as though it had betrayed her in some way.

"Well? What did it say?" Lucida asked.

"It's about the *príosún*. Don't worry, they haven't gotten wind that your transfer was actually a breakout—not yet, anyway," she added quickly, for Lucida had started toward her cousin in alarm.

"What happened?" I asked.

"There was a disturbance in the cellblocks. Two disturbances, actually. The first was in the cellblock where you were being held, Lucida."

A muscle started jumping in Lucida's jaw. "Yeah? What kind of disturbance."

"A Necromancer prisoner overpowered a Caomhnóir guard and was apprehended trying to break into your old cell," Catriona said.

Lucida swallowed convulsively. "I knew it. I knew I wasn't safe there."

Catriona nodded solemnly. "It would appear you were bang on about that. The Necromancer was captured and returned to his own cell, but he will not explain why he attempted to enter your cell, nor on whose orders he was acting. Elin couldn't get a straight answer about why he was out of his cell in the first place. It's all very suspect."

"And what was the second disturbance?" I prompted.

"The second disturbance took place in the deepest levels of the *príosún*, in a cellblock reserved for spirits alone," Catriona began, but I'd already clapped my hand over my mouth.

"The Tansy Hag," I whispered. "She's gone, isn't she?"

"Gone," Catriona confirmed. "And no one can understand quite how it was done. The Castings all appear to be intact, and yet she's simply not there anymore."

I remembered the helpless horror that permeated that cellblock. The spirits who had dwelled there did not have locks upon their doors—in fact, many of their cells had had no doors at all, no physical barriers to prevent them from simply floating out. No, it had been Castings—Durupinen magic—that had kept those most ancient and dangerous of prisoners confined in their solitude and despair. A single Necromancer—or Caomhnóir working for the Necromancers—could have released the Tansy Hag easily and virtually silently, if only he knew how to undo the Castings under which she was imprisoned. After so many centuries of being locked away and forgotten, who wouldn't have traded what she knew for freedom at last?

"They're going to be looking <u>for</u> you, Cat," I said. "They're going to want you there, investigating the situation. And when they can't find you—"

Catriona nodded. "Yeah. My clock's just about wound down on this adventure, I think."

"Mine as well," Lucida said. "We ought to scarper now, before we bring the Council down on all of your heads."

"Oh, come off it," Finn scoffed. "The Council is coming down on our heads anyway. This whole operation is about to be blown wide open. It's no good splitting up now. They'll know, if they don't already, that we've been working together. The damage is done."

"Finn is right," I said. "Our best bet now is to get to Havre des Gardiennes and throw ourselves on the mercy of the High Priestess. Once she realizes why we've come to see her, and what we've risked to get there, surely the rules we've had to break along the way will be forgiven?"

Catriona bit her lip. "I'm not too sure about that bit, Jess. She's a very powerful woman and she is not known for her leniency or her mercy."

"The integrity of the Gateways hangs in the balance here," I pointed out. "I don't think past measures of leniency really apply, do you?"

Finn and Catriona shared a look full of misgivings. It was clear they were both in full professional mode now, Caomhnóir and Tracker, weighing all of the rules and regulations, the relative safety of possible solutions and the likelihood of possible outcomes. I slammed my hand down on the table.

"We don't have time for this!" I shouted. "The Necromancers could be on their way right now! Whether we like it or not, everyone in the Durupinen world is about to find out what we're doing. We can't hide it anymore! It's bigger than all of us now. We've got to put everything we know in front of the High Priestess and let the chips fall where they may, and we have to do it fast, because the Necromancers would like nothing better than to stop us."

"And what do we say about showing up at the gates of Havre des Gardiennes with a convicted traitor and the woman who broke her out of prison?" Annabelle said, glaring at the two of them.

"We tell them the truth," I said, giving Annabelle a warning look. "Lucida is our witness to the fact that the Necromancers know both about the Tansy Hag and _the_ secret she was imprisoned for harboring. Catriona broke Lucida out to foil a Necromancer plot to murder her before she could tell the International High Council what she knew. It's all been done to preserve the truth and make sure that Agnes' message was delivered to the High Priestess."

Finn frowned, but nodded. Catriona looked at Lucida, who shrugged reluctantly and said, "Yeah, all right. It's as fair a shake as we'll get, I think."

"Good. We can sort out the details on the way," I said, "but we need to get out of here as quickly as we can. Finn, where do we go next? What's our next stop?"

"London," Finn said. "We catch the Chunnel to Paris and from there it's by car and then by foot into the Auvergne mountains."

"I'm no mountain climber, Finn," I said warily.

"You don't need to be. The Castle is set in a valley, not on a mountaintop. But for the last few miles there is no road," Finn said.

"Couldn't we just get one of the helicopters from the Northern Clans and, like, land at the front door? It would be a hell of a lot faster," I suggested hopefully. It was a mark of the direness of the situation that I was volunteering to be airborne.

Finn shook his head. "To do that, we'd need to go back to Fairhaven, and that would mean a mountain of red tape, even if the Council did agree to let us go without days and days of questioning. I think it's best to go first and ask forgiveness later, frankly."

"No, you're right. But," I looked around, spotting a roadblock. "If we're going to France, we all need passports! How the hell are we going to pull that off without Durupinen connections?"

"I've got mine. And I've brought yours with me," Finn said, reaching into his bag and pulling both documents out to show me.

"I've got mine, too," Annabelle said. "I needed it to get to England, remember?"

"I've got ours as well," Catriona said, referencing Lucida and herself. "I wasn't sure if we might need to disappear, now that we're on the run, so I made sure to bring them along."

I looked over at Ileana, who, to my intense shock, pulled a passport from somewhere amongst her shawls and scarves and held it up with a satisfied smile. "You needn't look so shocked, Northern Girl," she said smugly. "The modern world hasn't completely bypassed the Traveler Clans. We are nomads, after all, and that kind of life comes with certain hassles that even we must abide by."

I laughed in shock, and then stood up. "Well, then. We haven't got any time to waste. Gather your things quickly and let's get out of here."

THE KNIFE'S EDGE

AS DESPERATE AS I WAS to get out the door, there were certain preparations that needed to be made. Ileana spoke with Abigail, who set out immediately for the Screaming Woods to alert Lira and Margaret to the possibility of the Necromancers coming in search of the key.

"Couldn't she convince them to leave the woods and go into hiding somewhere?" I asked Ileana as we watched Abigail hobble out into the early morning sunlight.

Ileana cackled. "Leave that forest? They'd sooner step out of their own skin. But I promise you, they can defend themselves more completely with the aid of the Elementals than any of us could defend them out here, even if we had an army of Guardians at our disposal."

I shuddered as I remembered the pain of the Elemental assault. It was true. The Necromancers attacked the Keeper of the Elementals at their own peril.

At Ileana's suggestion, we armed ourselves with as many Casting supplies as we could gather from the Milkweed Teahouse. We created a Casting bag for Annabelle, who, not being a full Durupinen, had never owned one, and another for Lucida, who had not been permitted one since she had been imprisoned. It was with a look of intense relief that she fastened it around her waist, as though she had long felt naked and vulnerable without it. The rest of us supplemented our basic supplies of herbs, stones, and candles from Abigail's stock, and helped ourselves to some of the rarer elements she had on hand, given the completely unpredictable nature of the journey ahead. Then, when the cars were packed up with all our belongings and Finn was on the phone arranging our travel, I opened the connection at last with Milo and Hannah so that I could fill them in on what had been happening. I hardly expected when I had finished unloading the full horror of what we had encountered in Pluckley, that they would have news that could match mine for its capacity to horrify.

"Jess, there are some things we've got to tell you, too, and it's... it's bad," Hannah said.

"I'm running out of headspace for bad news here, Hannah," I replied, the tension in my head cresting and breaking in a throb of pain. "Please don't tell me this has to do with Marion. She hasn't convinced the clans to hold the vote of no confidence, has she?"

"No, not yet, thank goodness," Hannah replied.

"Only because she's still trying to nail down enough votes in her favor," Milo added, his tone full of venom. "She wouldn't dare try to hold the vote unless she was absolutely sure she was going to win. Judging by the way Siobhán is skulking around the place with her tail between her legs, I'd say Marion's already got her vote in her back pocket."

"Do you think she'll be able to get enough votes? It's just so hard to believe that anyone around that castle would want to be involved with her after what she's done."

"The longer Celeste waits to go to the International High Council, the better chance Marion will have. People are starting to panic. They're starting to think that Celeste is incapable of making a decision," Hannah said.

"And what do you think?" I asked.

"I'm starting to wonder if they're right," Hannah replied. "She's certainly stalling, at this point. But she might have to make a decision now, that's what I'm getting at. A woman arrived at the castle late last night. She came down from Wales and would not be turned away at the gates. She said she needed the Council's help, that she had nowhere else to turn. The Caomhnóir took her straight to the Council—we were in emergency session again—and she told us... well, she told us..."

"Just spit it out, Hannah," I urged.

But Hannah didn't seem to be able to bring herself to say the words, so Milo finished for her. "Another Sentinel. There's been another Sentinel reported."

My breath caught in my throat. It wasn't as though I hadn't been expecting this to happen. If I was being honest, I'd been expecting it ever since finding Naomi at the ruins of the Geatgrima in the Traveler grove. But it was still a blow to realize that it was happening so quickly now.

"There are bound to be others," I said when the shock allowed me to speak at last. "You know there must be others we haven't heard about yet, perhaps even being reported to other Councils in other parts of the world."

"That's what we were thinking, too," Hannah said, "which is why I think it's time for Celeste to go to the International High Council and tell them what's happening here. Between the appearance of another Sentinel and Marion gunning for her position, time has run out."

"I think you're right," I said.

I felt both Hannah's and Milo's surprise zing through the connection.

"Are you serious?" Hannah asked.

"I was sure you were going to fight us tooth and nail on that one," Milo replied.

"A day ago, I would have," I agreed. "But everything's changed. The Necromancers know about the keys. They know I have them, or at least that I'm searching for them, which means we've run out of time. We've got to beat them to the safety of Havre des Gardiennes, and hope Agnes' message falls on friendly ears."

"What if it doesn't, Jess?" Hannah asked. The question floated through my head, quivering with fear.

"I don't know."

"We're coming," Milo said at once. "We're coming with you."

"No, you're not," I said. "The Necromancers are going to target anywhere they think I might be, and the safest and best protected place by far is Fairhaven. You have to stay there. The Caomhnóir will keep you safe. Everyone traveling with me is in terrible danger. I'm carrying enough guilt on that score without adding the two of you to that list."

"Jess, we can't let you go on your own," Hannah argued.

"I'm not on my own," I cut in. "I've got Finn. I've got Cat, who is probably the savviest and fiercest Tracker the Durupinen have. I've got Lucida, which, oddly enough, is somewhat comforting, given her skill set. And I've got Ileana, who hates me, it's true, but carries with her the authority of her High Priestesshood, which has to count for something in the eyes of the International High Council."

"Jess, we can't just sit here and do nothing while you—" Milo began.

"I'm not asking you to do <u>nothing</u>. Do everything you can to convince Celeste to come to Havre des Gardiennes and tell the International High Council everything. If she does that, I'll have the full might of the Northern Clans in my corner, too."

"Jess, I don't like this at all," Hannah said, and her fear sang like a chorus inside my skull.

"I don't like it either," I admitted. "But we're out of options. This is the only way forward if we're going to help Savvy and the others. We can't wait around for the Necromancers to get the upper hand. The entire spirit world is counting on us."

"So, as usual, no pressure," Milo snorted.

"Correct. It's all totally chill and low key," I confirmed.

"Well, I'm not waiting around," Hannah said. "I'm going to Celeste's office right now. I'll sit outside it all day if I have to. I'll let you know if I make any progress convincing her to go to Havre des Gardiennes."

"Thanks, you two," I said. "This will all be over soon."

"That's what I'm afraid of," Hannah said, and pulled out of the connection.

"Take care of her, Milo," I said, before Milo had a chance to slip out after her.

"I always do, sweetness," he replied, and I felt his energy cut out as the door to the connection slammed shut between us. My head felt strangely empty without it. It was almost enough to make me take back what I said about them coming to meet us at Havre des Gardiennes—almost, but not quite. There was precious little I could do to protect anyone from the fallout from this nightmare of a situation, but damn it, I could do this. I could do the unselfish thing for once and choose their safety over my own desire to have them by my side as I faced this uncertainty.

"Jess! We've got to go!" Finn called. "We haven't a moment to lose here. Are you ready?"

"Yeah," I said, feeling my brain probe longingly at the closed connection, aching for it to open again. "Yeah, I'm ready."

I arrived in the alleyway outside of the Milkweed Teahouse to find our group split between the two vehicles; Lucida, Catriona, and Ileana sat in Catriona's running car, all three faces staring out the windshield, all three expressions tense and anxious. Finn and Annabelle waited for me in Finn's vehicle, the passenger side door open to receive me. Finn was <u>scanning</u> the surrounding area so quickly and constantly, he would have looked comical but for the deadly serious look on his face. I broke into a jog and hopped into the car, closing the door behind me.

"All still clear," Finn said, though I could tell from his tone that he didn't trust his own assessment of the situation. "I've been able to use a Durupinen connection to book the Chunnel tickets and arrange the transfers once we arrive in Paris. There will be a Caomhnóir vehicle waiting for us at the station that we can take down to Auvergne."

"How long will it take us to get there?" I asked.

"About five and a half hours," Finn said through clenched teeth, and it couldn't be clearer that the length of the trip out on the open road had him on edge. "And then another hour or so on foot through the lower foothills of the mountains to Havre des Gardiennes. That's the portion of the journey that worries me most."

"Why?" I asked.

"They won't just let us walk in the front doors. We'll need to send a formal request for an audience with the High Priestess, and they won't admit us even within the grounds of the fortress until the request has been approved, if indeed it is approved. And while we wait, which could be for hours, we will be completely exposed, utterly vulnerable."

"Do you expect the borders of the fortress grounds to be crawling with Necromancers?" Annabelle asked, eyebrows raised. "Surely the Caomhnóir that guard Havre des Gardiennes will have the security of the area well in hand."

"Let us hope so," Finn said. "There is one thing of which I am completely sure, however; the Caomhnóir of Havre des Gardiennes will not sacrifice even a modicum of the fortress' security to keep the likes of us safe. While we await word from the High Priestess, we fend for ourselves."

"That sounds kind of counter-intuitive," I said, frowning. "When have you ever known a Caomhnóir to leave a Durupinen in peril for any reason, even if she was not his direct charge?"

"Havre des Gardiennes is different," Finn insisted. "There is no greater duty than protecting the High Priestess and her inner circle. Every decision they make will be with that objective in mind. Every outsider is a potential threat, even other Durupinen. No one will take our trustworthiness for granted. We will be treated, if not with hostility, then at the very least with a healthy dose of suspicion."

"Do you know anything at all about the High Priestess herself?" I asked. In all the time since Agnes had charged me with delivering her message, I had not until this very moment thought of the High Priestess as a living, breathing individual. In my head, when I'd pictured the eventuality of meeting with her, she was nothing more than a looming, faceless figure upon a throne, an eventuality cloaked in doubt. I was far too worried about how I would reach the moment of meeting her to wonder what the actual meeting might be like. But now that I'd delivered my message to both Ileana and Lira, my curiosity about the woman herself had finally been piqued.

"Simone de Chastenay," Finn said, and the name fell from his tongue with a certain reverence. "She has been the High Priestess of the International High Council for nearly fifty years."

"Fifty years!" I cried. "So, she's either really old, or she became High Priestess when she was really young."

"The former, I believe," Finn said. "I don't know a great deal about her, other than the fact that her reign has been marked with an almost medieval adherence to tradition and ceremony. She revived a number of antiquated practices throughout the Durupinen world including, for example, the Sanctity Line."

I groaned. The Sanctity Line was, quite literally, a physical divide in spaces occupied by both Durupinen and Caomhnóir, which dictated that the sexes not interact in any physical way, even in so innocuous a manner as sitting in desks beside each other. It had been one of the very first things I noticed when I began my training as an Apprentice Durupinen, for it had adorned the floor of every classroom, and little had chafed my feminist sensibilities quite so directly as that ludicrous marking upon the ground.

"So, she's not exactly progressive, is that what you're getting at?" I asked innocently. "Like, should we maybe not make out in front of her?"

Annabelle snorted with nervous laughter from the back seat, but Finn was too highly strung to crack a smile, so I quickly dispensed with the wisecracks and put my serious face back on. "Anything else?"

"She's allowed a great deal of autonomy in local matters over the years, but this was primarily because she had seen to it that the reigning High Priestesses were nearly as traditional and strict as she was. From what I can gather from the members of the Council, she relishes the opportunity to put her foot down and quash insubordination. She is not meant to weigh in on expressly regional matters, but when she does, her opinion is never ignored. The other High Priestesses have a long and storied history of trying to avoid her involvement, which I imagine is why Celeste is doing just that as we speak. Simone's clan is extraordinarily wealthy, though I do not know how much of that wealth is a direct result of her position and how much is simply old money. She has royal blood—and I mean non-Durupinen royalty. I do not expect we will find her either accommodating or easily persuaded."

"Awesome," I replied dryly. Sarcasm was always the perfect disguise for blind terror, right?

The entire ride to London, I waited for Hannah to pop back into the connection with word of Celeste's reaction to the news that we'd been lying to her by omission for the last few days, but the connection stayed frustratingly closed. Not even Milo popped in to distract me, which left me with altogether too much time on my hands to worry about what was going to happen when we reached Havre des Gardiennes. The only person who seemed even more nervous than me was Lucida, who actually jumped out of the car at the first gas station we stopped at and violently vomited all over the pavement.

"Is she all right?" I asked Catriona as she fiddled with the gas pump.

Catriona glanced over at Lucida, who was now wiping her mouth with a shaking hand and walking unsteadily back to the car. "She's a piece of raw meat on legs walking into the lion's den. Of course she's not all right."

"What do you—?"

"Oh, come off it, Jess. She's a traitor. A jolly good percentage of the Northern Clans would have gladly seen her hanged and thrown confetti at the scaffold for what she did six years ago. Havre des Gardiennes is full of the most powerful Durupinen in the world, women who would have dearly loved to tie the noose themselves. She's terrified."

"Why didn't they?" I asked, the thought occurring to me for the first time. "Why didn't they execute her for what she did? Surely there can't be any greater crime?"

"The Durupinen do not employ the death penalty under any circumstances," Catriona said, raising her eyebrows and looking at me in apparent surprise. "Surely you know that?"

I shrugged. "I never thought to ask," I said, a bit defensively.

Catriona shook her head solemnly. "If centuries of guiding the passage from the land of the living to the land of the dead has taught us one thing, it is that it is never up to us to decide what moment is appropriate to end a person's life. That decision is and has always been the universe's mandate to make and carry out, not our own. It is the reason the Caomhnóir do not carry firearms, and the reason our *príosúns* are full of dangerous traitors, criminals, and enemies who will never be released."

"But now Lucida is out," I said.

"Yes. And I doubt very much that the International High Council will care much for her presence within their walls, particularly when she arrives without guards or shackles or invitation."

I looked back at Lucida's figure in the car, her forehead pressed to the glass of the window, her eyes closed, her expression pained. "She doesn't have to come," I said. "She knows that."

"She knows no such bloody thing," Catriona said stiffly, looking indignant as she snapped the gas cap shut. "Lucida's had precious little opportunity for redemption, and for all she swears she doesn't regret what she did, I know her better than that. I know she'd rather die than miss the opportunity to tip the scales just a fraction in her direction."

I shrugged. "It's her choice. I just hope she knows what she's doing."

Catriona raised a single eyebrow at me. "Do any of us, really? Each one of us is throwing ourselves on a mercy we're not sure will be there to catch us."

"Touché."

The rest of the ride to London was uneventful, unless you counted Finn intentionally taking three wrong exits to "lose" people who weren't actually following us and jerking his head back to look in the rearview mirror so many times that he cricked his neck. By the time we had arrived at St. Pancras Station to board the Eurostar, Finn's anxiety was ratcheted up so high that he was even giving the conductor who took our tickets a sideways look, as though sure the man would peel off his entire face like a villain in a spy movie to reveal Charlie Wright hiding beneath the skin of a decidedly plump middle-aged gentleman. It was with a definite sense of relief that we all settled into our seats, and once Finn had done a sweep of the train car to determine it was safe, he settled into a seat at the far end, where he could keep an eye on both doors, and finally seemed to relax just a bit.

Under any other circumstances, I would have found my first journey to Paris to be exciting—after all, what could be more fascinating for an art history major and museum nerd than to arrive in one of the most storied and artistically rich cities in the modern world? The thought of the Mona Lisa smiling away cryptically in the Louvre alone should have left me breathless with anticipation. But these were not such circumstances. There would be no time for ambling strolls through cultural landmarks or sipping coffee in charming outdoor cafes. There would be no stereotypical tourist selfies in front of the Eiffel Tower. The ride through the Chunnel was a blur. I jerked in and out of an uneasy, nightmare-filled doze, each time staring around half-panicked for several seconds before remembering where I was going and why I was going there. Beside me, Annabelle looked as though she'd forgotten how to close her eyes altogether, instead gazing out of the window with a blank stare. Ileana, for all her bluster about Travelers keeping up with modern customs of travel, looked vaguely horrified to find herself speeding along under the English Channel, her expression making it clear that she'd rather be almost anywhere than where she was. Lucida had fallen into a deep sleep with her forehead pressed to the cool glass, still looking ill. And Catriona, much like Finn, had chosen to distract herself by gazing suspiciously at every passenger with whom we shared the train car and imagining each of them to be a Necromancer lying in wait to ambush us the moment one of us rose to use the bathroom. In fact, the one time I tried to do just that, she found an excuse to follow me, lingering around outside the door until I had finished, and ignoring my demands for an explanation as to why I wasn't allowed to pee by myself.

When we pulled at last into the great vaulted interior of the Gare du Nord station in the heart of Paris, I felt my anxiety kick into high gear once again.

"Stick closely together and follow me," Finn said tersely as we all stood up and joined the queue to exit the train. "Don't speak to anyone, even if they approach you. The less attention we draw to ourselves, the better." He threw a frustrated, regretful look at Ileana, the lone member of our party who looked much more like a lost carnival performer than a run-of-the-mill tourist. She was not paying him the slightest attention.

A sleek, black SUV was waiting for us, parked in the shadow of the Gare du Nord's gothic exterior. The late afternoon sun sparkled off the arches of the stone and glass façade of the building. The car had attracted a certain amount of attention from nearby pedestrians, who likely thought the vehicle belonged to a celebrity or another wealthy and important person; their heads turned curiously as they walked by. A stony-faced man with aviator sunglasses sat in the driver's seat. As soon as Finn approached and knocked upon the glass, the man stepped out of the car, shut the driver's side door and, without so much as a glance at us, slipped into a waiting taxi and sped away. Finn pulled the door open again and gestured for the rest of us to enter the car, and we all hurriedly obliged his silent request.

Our car slipped the outer limits of the city just as the sun was slipping through the cradled fingers of the horizon. The buildings and neighborhoods gave way gradually to open fields and lush green hills, and the rosy glow of sunset deepened to a velvety violet twilight, punctuated here and there with the faint glimmer of an early star. The moon that rose to preside over the French countryside was huge and round, a cherub-cheeked orb that leeched the color from the landscape as it illuminated our way like a great spotlight into the foothills of the Auvergne Mountains.

We did not approach through the national park, which would have been the traditional route for tourists, but instead slipped unseen into the green rolling hills by a little-used road hardly wide enough to be called a road at all. After a few miles, we reached a barrier and a sign which read, when translated into English, "Road washed out. High flooding. Seek alternate route."

"Shit," I said, once my spotty recollection of high school French made sense of the sign. "We'll have to go back. We can't get through this way."

Finn, however, merely chuckled and rode around the barrier.

"What are you doing?" I asked him. "Didn't you see the sign?"

"That sign is not for us," he replied, steering the car back onto the road on the far side of the barrier and resuming our drive.

"What do you mean, it's not for us?" I asked. "Is this one of those James Bond cars that converts into a boat or something?" Not that I would have been all that surprised, given my experience with the breadth of Durupinen resources.

"I mean that barrier has been placed there to stop random tourists and hikers from stumbling upon Havre des Gardiennes. We'll come across several other such deterrents along our way, I expect."

"But surely the French authorities know the castle is there," I replied. "You can't actually hide a castle, not in this day and age."

"Of course you can't," Finn said. "Just as with Fairhaven, the true nature of the castle has been concealed, and a great deal of money has been spent to ensure it remains a secret. And as for those persistent enough in their recklessness to venture beyond the barriers and roadblocks, they are turned away before they can get even a passing look at the place. The Caomhnóir who patrol the forests surrounding the base of the mountain wear the garb of mountain rescue and park rangers, not traditional Guardian attire. Trespassers are escorted away, by force, if necessary, to ensure that Havre des Gardiennes remains in seclusion from the outside world."

I shook my head in wonder. It still boggled my mind sometimes, even after all these years, what the power, influence, and great wealth of the Durupinen could accomplish.

At last, the road upon which we had been traveling narrowed to nothing more than a rutted path overgrown with weeds, and then disappeared altogether into the tall grass. Finn threw the car into park and killed the engine. "This is where we get out," he announced.

"How do you know?" I asked him, blinking around into the gathering darkness.

In answer, Finn pointed to a nearby tree. About five feet up on the trunk, carved deeply into the wood, was a large, distinct triskele. "Now, that *is* meant for us," he said, smiling slightly. "A symbol to allow for fellow Durupinen and Caomhnóir to continue on the path toward the castle unimpeded. We'll reach the outpost soon—it's about a mile further along. That's where we'll declare ourselves and make our formal request for an audience with the High Priestess."

"You mean we need to walk from here?" Catriona asked, a shrill edge to her voice. It was clear she didn't like the idea at all.

"It's the only way in," Finn said. "Unless you're here on official business for your clans, and then you get the red carpet treatment—chopper, direct castle access, the lot."

"You've never been here before?" I asked Catriona in surprise. "I thought surely, as a Council member…"

She shook her head. "I've never had cause, thank God. There's never been a full gathering of the Councils in my tenure as a member. Even after the Prophecy came to pass, only the High Priestesses of the various regions were summoned to Havre des Gardiennes." She took a couple of steps closer to Finn and lowered her voice, though not quietly enough that I couldn't still make out her words. "Finn, I don't like this one jot. Do you really think we ought to be on foot, in the dark, knowing the Necromancers are on the hunt for us?"

"I don't like it either, much," Finn said. "But you've been monitoring things as closely as I have. Have you yet to discover a hint that we're being tracked?"

"No," Catriona admitted grudgingly.

"Nor have I," Finn said. "It seems, at this moment anyway, that we're ahead of them. But if we wait things out in the car until it's light, it's likely they'll have caught up with us, and then we'll be without cover."

Catriona chewed the inside of her cheek, but she didn't argue.

"I think our best bet is to make for the safety of Havre des Gardiennes as quickly as possible. Once we're at the gates, we're home free."

Catriona crossed her arms, brows furrowed, clearly trying to come up with a counterargument. When she came up empty, she simply nodded and waved for the rest of us to follow.

Annabelle gave a long sigh. "I think I've had enough walking through dodgy forests to last me the rest of my life," she said, with just a twitch of a smile.

"Me too," I agreed.

We trudged along in silence after that, everyone too tense and too intent on not tripping in the dark to have any energy left for conversation. Finn paused every once in a while to consult his compass, just to double-check that we were on the right path. Luckily for all of us, the route through this particular forest was far easier to traverse than the others we'd ventured down in recent days. A wide dirt path wound gently through the trees, free from rocks, tree roots, and low growing shrubbery and ground cover that would surely have tripped us up. The mile's walk, all things considered, was an easy one. Before I'd even thought to ask how much further we had to go, a small wooden building, rather like a shed or an oversized outhouse, appeared out of the gloom ahead of us. A dull orange glow shone out from one large, square window.

"There it is," Finn said, and I could hear the clear relief in his voice. "There's the Guardian outpost."

"Thank God," Catriona said.

Lucida smirked at her. "There you are then. All that doom and gloom for nothing."

When we had come within about twenty yards of the building, Finn held up a hand for all of us to stop. He cleared his throat and called out, "Finn Carey, Caomhnóir for the Northern Clans, declaring his presence and requesting to approach the outpost."

There was no reply. No face peered out from the window. The door remained closed.

Finn shifted restlessly from one foot to the other. "Hello? We wish to make a petition for entrance."

Still no answer. Ileana cleared her throat. Annabelle's breathing had quickened. The quiet of the woods suddenly felt oppressive—unnatural.

"What's going on?" I asked at last, as the tension became unbearable.

"I don't know," Finn replied, and his voice was sharp. "This outpost is meant to be manned at all times."

"Something's wrong," Catriona said. "Let's get back to the car."

"But you said this is the only way in," I said. "How the hell are we supposed to get in if not through here?"

"Can't we just keep going?" Annabelle asked. "I mean, if there's no one here..."

"Not unless you want to be killed or arrested on the spot by the first patrol to spy you approaching the gates," Catriona snapped at her. "They brook no trespass here."

"So, what do we do now, then?" Lucida asked. "Do you reckon we should wait a bit, see if someone comes back?"

"I'm going to check the outpost building itself," Finn said. "Wait here."

"Wait here?! Finn, we're not going to let you just—"

"Wait here," Finn repeated, more forcefully this time, and began to walk toward the outpost building, continuing to loudly announce his presence as he did so. He walked slowly around the entire outside of the building first, peering in the window and examining the door handle carefully before knocking upon the door. He knocked three times before, at last, trying the knob. The building was locked. He turned back to us, shaking his head.

"I can't make sense of it. Perhaps we ought to head back and—"

"Finn on your left!" Catriona screamed out.

A dark shape came running out from behind a tree at Finn and hurled itself at him, but Finn was quicker. He caught the figure by the arm, swinging him over his back and slamming him to the ground. I started forward, determined to help him, but other figures were detaching themselves from the shadows now, men in black hooded cloaks, faces masked. Before I could so much as cry out, one of them was bearing down on me, a flash of silver in one hand, the other hand reaching out toward me.

Someone barreled into my shoulder, shoving me out of the man's path. I hit the ground hard and tried to roll away but the two figures, locked in a struggle now, became tangled up in my legs and fell on top of me. All the breath knocked from my body, I struck out hard with my arms and feet, hearing a grunt as my elbow connected with something that made a crunching sound. My attacker and whoever was fighting with him rolled away, and I scrambled to my feet just in time to run smack into Annabelle who screamed and flailed her fists at me until she realized who I was and then gripped my arm, pulling me down to the ground again and dragging me around the back side of a tree just as another attacker shot past us. Suddenly the path was full of renewed shouting. More voices had joined the fray, and with a thrill of relief, I saw that the newcomers were Caomhnóir, bearing the crest of Havre des Gardiennes on their chests.

Flashlight beams were swinging wildly. It was impossible to make sense of the chaos around me. One of the beams of light hit Annabelle and me full in the <u>face</u>, and a voice cried out. "She's there!" Annabelle and I made a mad scramble to our feet, but before the man had taken two steps, one of the Caomhnóir had tackled him to the ground. A thump and a crack, and the man moved no more. His flashlight lay in the dirt, still flooding our hiding place with light.

Annabelle looked at me and horror broke over her face. "Jess, you're hurt!"

"What? No, I'm not!" I said.

"Jess, yes you are! You're covered in blood!"

I looked down and saw that she was quite right. The entire front of my sweater was smeared in blood. I groped my chest and abdomen with frantic hands, but could find no wound.

"It's okay," I gasped. "It's okay, I... I don't think it's mine."

The various scrabbles and fights had been fought out. Bodies lay slumped all over the ground, and figures were running from one to the other, bending over them, binding hands, removing weapons. Heart in my throat, I stared around for Finn and the others.

"Jess!" His voice rang out and I saw him sprinting toward me, leaping over bodies, his face terrified.

"It's okay, Finn! I'm not hurt!" I cried, realizing he, too, must be panicking over the sight of the blood. "The blood's not mine."

"Oh, thank you, God," he breathed, a hitch in his voice as he folded me into his arms.

"Are you okay?" I asked him, searching his face and body for any signs of injury.

He seemed scarcely to know, as though it had not occurred to him to make that kind of assessment. He stared down at himself in a kind of surprise and said, "I... yes, I am." Then he pulled back from me, looking around for the rest of our group. "Annabelle?"

"I'm all right," she said dazedly, wrapping her arms around herself to stop the shaking. "And I can see Ileana over there."

The Traveler High Priestess sat with her back pressed to a tree, slapping away the attentions of a Caomhnóir who was trying to examine a long, jagged cut on her forearm. A great purple bruise was already rising on her cheekbone just below her right eye.

"What about the others, Finn?" I asked breathlessly.

"I don't—"

But a gut-wrenching cry pierced the night, cutting off his words with the sheer force of its pain. We all turned toward the source of the sound and saw Catriona crouched on the ground, head bent, shoulders shaking.

I don't remember walking—my legs felt numb—and yet I moved forward, drawn to the place where she knelt, at once needing to know and wishing never to know what had elicited such a sound from Catriona Harrington, the woman who was always all right.

Catriona had Lucida cradled in her arms, rocking back and forth, sobbing with a ferocity that surely hallowed the ground beneath them. Lucida's eyes stared up into the starry night, wide and empty, the hilt of a dagger protruding from her scarlet-drenched chest. It was with a detached kind of shock that my eyes traveled from the blood on her body to the blood on my own, and the realization felt like a second stab of a knife.

I was covered in Lucida's blood. She was the one who had thrown herself between me and my attacker.

She had died to save me.

It was too much. Too much to feel. Too much to absorb. The scene around me flickered, blurred, and went out.

AN AUDIENCE

I AWOKE SECONDS LATER to a cacophony of angry shouting.

"What the bloody hell were Necromancers doing undetected so close to your gates?"

"We may well ask you the same question!"

"It's not our responsibility to patrol these woods!"

"And yet it seems likely you unwittingly drew them here!"

"They were lying in wait! It was an ambush! Where in the world were your guards? Why was your outpost empty?"

My head swam, and I was surprised to see that I was on my feet, though unsteadily. Finn was beside me on one side, Annabelle on the other, and they seemed to be trying to support me while Finn continued to argue furiously with the Caomhnóir. Catriona still knelt on the ground nearby, oblivious to everything but the absence of Lucida and the weight of her own grief.

"We have to get up to the castle. There could be more of them. The grounds must be searched and secured," one of the Caomhnóir said, stepping in and raising a hand to signal an end to the argument. His face was badly scarred, and his vest was torn and blood-stained. "You will follow us there, without delay. Once inside, we will inform the High Priestess of what has transpired, and of your arrival."

Finn gave every indication of objecting, but he swallowed his anger and gave one curt nod. "I agree. We should get under cover as quickly as possible."

But Catriona wouldn't stand. She just continued to cry stormily, rocking back and forth, her face now buried in Lucida's mass of dark curls. Softly, Annabelle began to talk to her as I, trying desperately not to look at Lucida, worked to gently pry her fingers, one by one, from her cousin's body. At last, her hands came free, and she flung them up over her face in despair, smearing blood across her cheeks, her tears cutting crooked pink tracks through it. We pulled her unsteadily to her feet and began to shuffle her slowly toward the group of Caomhnóir. Suddenly she stopped, raised her face from her hands and glared at the men so fiercely that she looked quite terrifying.

"You will not leave her here alone," she said, and it wasn't a question. She said it again, and this time each word was a threat. "You. Will. Not. Leave. Her. Here. Alone."

A Caomhnóir stepped forward from the group. He looked to be barely older than a Novitiate, but his voice when he spoke was deep and sincere.

"I give you my word. She will not be left alone."

Catriona's face spasmed, and she managed to nod in acknowledgment of the man's gesture before finally moving her feet of her own free will. Taking her steps as a signal that we were, in fact, ready to leave, the Caomhnóir fanned out, forming a protective barrier around our group as we left the clearing.

The sight of Havre des Gardiennes, tucked like a dragon-guarded figment of a fairytale amongst the rocky peaks of the mountain with the moon hanging in the sky above it, ought to have taken my breath away. Instead, I barely registered any emotion at all, except perhaps a weary frustration at how many steps we would be forced to climb before we could finally enter the place and sit down to rest. The gates were set into a long stone wall that seemed to stretch for miles, beyond which the castle rose, pearly white against the verdant green and stormy grey of the mountain itself.

The room into which we were ushered was little more than a huge, round high-ceilinged stone tower, bare but for a wooden bench that ran around the entire perimeter of the space. The walls rose up into shadowed obscurity, crisscrossed with heavy beams, arcing away into echoing darkness. We were stripped of everything we carried—our Casting bags, our supplies, Finn's weapons, everything we had brought along for the journey. Then we were roughly patted down in a humiliating fashion and told to sit.

"Wait here," the scarred Caomhnóir said curtly and, without another word, disappeared through the door at the opposite end of the room from where we had entered.

Catriona had been comparably quiet on the walk to the castle; but now, with every mental and physical resource depleted, she sank to the floor, sobbing inconsolably. Annabelle, who had been helping to support Catriona as she staggered into the fortress, sank to the ground with her, looking slightly bewildered to find herself beneath a hysterical woman, and yet fell naturally into the role of comforter, stroking her back and whispering consoling platitudes into the golden tangles of her hair. Both of them were now spattered with Lucida's blood.

"What are they going to do with her?" Catriona kept sobbing. "What have they done with her? Where will they take her?"

"The Caomhnóir are protectors," Annabelle was murmuring. "They will protect her still, you'll see. They won't leave her. You heard them, they gave you their word."

Ileana was clearly deeply shaken as well. Her arm was bleeding, but she wouldn't let anyone touch it or look at it. She simply swaddled it like a baby in her many shawls and scarves and cradled it gingerly against her chest. Her expression was one of shock, as though she simply couldn't believe that a woman of her stature and position within her own clans could be so casually abandoned to wait and bleed like some kind of criminal. But it became clear as we all waited—shaken, injured, devastated—that we were being quarantined like animals so that our threat could be assessed, our story checked out, our value weighed against any risk we might pose.

"What's happening?" Annabelle asked after what felt like an eternity. "What's taking so long?"

"The Caomhnóir will be conducting a sweep of the area," Finn said, pacing in frustration. "They'll have to be sure the Necromancers have retreated, and they'll need to send men after them to ensure they don't escape. They'll have to be captured and contained. Then the International High Council will have to decide if we are more trouble than we're worth."

"What do you mean, more trouble than we're worth?" I cried. "We've done nothing but been victimized on the very grounds they were supposed to be protecting!"

"Yes, but as we are the clear targets, that means we've drawn the danger toward them. That makes us a liability, and that must be weighed against our worth if they are to protect us."

"Our worth?" Ileana spat, looking frankly dangerous. "Our *worth*? How dare they!"

"They shouldn't have been able to get so close," Catriona mumbled, her words barely distinguishable through her tears. "What the hell were Necromancers doing unchecked so close to the fortress? Why was the outpost deserted when it ought to have been manned?"

"Maybe the Necromancers got to the guards and attacked them as well?" I suggested.

Catriona shook her head. "That whole border area ought to have been impenetrable. We should have been safe if we'd made it that far."

"She's right," Finn muttered, so quietly that only I could hear him. "Something very strange happened out there."

"Strange how?" I asked. "Strange like you think the Caomhnóir might have known about it?"

"I'm not sure yet," Finn said.

"So, can we even trust them?" I asked. "Are we just sitting ducks now?"

"If we are, there's not a blasted thing we can do about it," Finn replied, his expression grim.

For nearly an hour we paced and waited, tense with frustration and fear, jumping at every sound that echoed endlessly through the enormous, empty chamber, utterly unable to tell from which of the dozen doors the sounds had originated. At last, one of the doors swung open and a woman entered, flanked by two guards. She was tiny, both in stature and in manner, a woman who seemed to shrink in upon herself, as though she was constantly trying to take up as little space as possible wherever she happened to be. Her face was delicate looking, almost frail, and yet completely unlined. It was impossible to tell how old she was—she moved like an older woman, and yet her features gave off the glow of youth. Her wispy blonde hair was pulled back in a braid that fell all the way down past her waist, and she was dressed in a long, pale blue silk gown that trailed on the floor behind her like a rippling stream. Even her voice, when she spoke at last, was insubstantial, a breathless tinkling bell of a voice.

"Greetings to you, visitors," she said, and she opened her arms wide in a forced gesture of welcome before swiftly pulling them in against her chest again. "Welcome to Havre des Gardiennes."

"Welcome?!" Catriona cried out from where she was still struggling to her feet. "What kind of a welcome do you call this? We've been locked up in here for hours without a scrap of news!"

The woman shrank away from Catriona's words as though they

were projectiles being flung at her. She did not reply, but instead waited meekly for the silence before continuing on with her prepared words. "My name is Marguerite de Chastenay. My sister, the High Priestess of the International High Council, has sent me to you on her behalf. I regret that there is no one else from the High Council to receive you, as the Council is not currently in session."

Catriona showed every indication of a further outburst, but Annabelle lay a restraining hand on her upper arm, and this seemed enough to coax her into a grudging silence.

"Simone was most aggrieved to hear of the attack you endured near our outpost, and sends her sympathies for the loss of your companion. She requests that you make known to me the nature of your visit, so that she may prepare to receive you," Marguerite went on in her bird's wing flutter of a voice, sounding for all the world as though these were lines she had memorized and rehearsed for the sole purpose of coming here to deliver them to us. Her tiny hands twisted within each other, and her eyes barely left the floor. This was the sister of the High Priestess? This was one of the legendary women of the Clan de Chastenay? She was so... *diminished*. How could a woman of such consequence seem so completely inconsequential?

It was Ileana who took charge now, stepping forward and mustering what authority she could while still so disheveled from the ambush. "I am Ileana Lovell, High Priestess of the Traveler Clans. I have come a long way to seek an audience with the High Priestess. Never in my life would I have believed that I would be abandoned here, without medical attention or refreshment, for hours on end, like some common criminal. I demand an explanation as to why we have been treated in this manner."

Marguerite looked positively terrified to respond to a demand for an explanation that she had not been expressly prepared to deliver. She cleared her throat several times before replying. "I... I am sure that my sister will be able to explain everything to you most clearly. Our Caomhnóir have spent the last several hours doing extensive sweeps of the grounds to ensure the castle and all within it are safe. My sister would hold no audiences nor leave her chambers until the Guardians could guarantee her complete safety."

"And what of our safety?" Catriona asked, her voice breaking once again.

Marguerite made a movement that might have been a shrug before replying, "My sister always proceeds with utmost caution and makes decisions with great care. I am sure, if you have been neglected, it was for very good reason."

I stepped forward now, gathering what fortitude I had left. "Ms. de Chastenay, my name is Jessica Ballard of the Clan Sassanaigh. Along with Ileana, I've brought with me my Caomhnóir Finn Carey; Catriona Harrington, Lead Tracker of the Northern Clans; and Annabelle Rabinski, Dormant of the Traveler Clan Boswell. They have all been instrumental in helping me to reach the gates of Havre des Gardiennes. I've come to see your sister the High Priestess, to request an audience with her, so that I might pass along a very important message."

Marguerite's eyes widened like marbles and she let out a gasp. "You are the Walker. The Walker of the great Prophecy."

I cringed internally, but knew there was little point in denying it. "Yes, I am."

"And what message do you carry for my sister?" Marguerite asked, her delicate features wrinkling with mild curiosity.

"I am deeply sorry, but I cannot say. The message must be conveyed directly to the High Priestess, and as soon as possible. Time is running out."

"Time for what?" Marguerite asked, her pale blue eyes widening in alarm. Then she shook her head, like she was shaking off a fly, and dropped her gaze to the floor again. "But, of course. How foolish of me. You cannot reveal this either, can you?"

I shook my head. "No, I can't. I'm sorry."

Marguerite tapped her finger thoughtfully on her chin. "I do not know if my sister will consent to see you without understanding the exact nature of your visit. She is very particular about who she will agree to devote her time to."

Catriona stepped forward. "Perhaps you could tell her this message is what brought Necromancers out of the shadows and to the very gates of her castle. Perhaps you can tell her that my cousin has just died in the quest to deliver it. That might just convince her of its urgency," she said, and though I could hear the effort she was making to keep herself calm, her voice was trembling violently.

Marguerite seemed to consider this, nodding thoughtfully. "Yes. Yes, you'd better come with me. I will bring you up to her audience chambers at once. You may have longer to wait once you are there, but you will be more comfortable. If you would please follow me."

Marguerite turned toward the door through which she had entered a few minutes earlier, and we all crossed the room to follow her. Her two hulking Caomhnóir, who had said not a word since entering with her, now walked behind her, maintaining a barrier of safety between her and us, never allowing us to walk too close to her. Marguerite led us through a long stone tunnel and up a winding staircase into a wide, airy, white marble hallway on the upper level, our way lit by torches and great glowing chandeliers set into the smooth glossy ceilings. There was nothing upon the walls—no tapestries or sculptures or great works of art—just section after section of flawless white marble interspersed with high arched windows through which the mountaintops lay basking in a swath of silvery moonlight. The hallway gave way to a great hall, carved from floor to ceiling in white marble, supported by great curved pillars and lit with dozens of round sunken pits of fire. It felt like something out of a vision of fairyland or some far-off fantasy realm, a place where elves or angels surely dwelt, and even in my fear and anxiety about what was to come, I took a moment to appreciate the unearthly splendor of it all. Havre des Gardiennes was as removed from the real world as a dream. But for all its ethereal beauty there was something remote about it—cold and distant and sterile in its perfection.

We came to a stop in front of a pair of enormous arched doors made of blonde wood and carved elaborately with vines and leaves and flowers. Marguerite gave a gentle nod, and the Caomhnóir stepped forward to push them open so that we could pass through. The chamber beyond was smaller than I expected, given the sheer magnitude of the doors. A thronelike chair stood in the corner on a pedestal, beside the yawning mouth of an enormous fireplace in which a fire crackled and popped. Marguerite gestured to several white-cushioned benches with carved golden legs. "I invite you all to wait here while I inform my sister of your intentions. Please do make yourselves comfortable. I will have some tea and sandwiches brought up for you." With that, Marguerite continued through a second, smaller set of doors and disappeared.

Ileana sank down onto the bench, wincing as she adjusted her arm. Annabelle perched uneasily beside her. Catriona remained on her feet, hovering near the door, her face tense and drawn. Finn, too, seemed incapable of sitting, but chose instead to pace the floor, scrutinizing all the details of the room as though he would shortly be tested upon them. I considered for a brief moment taking the seat on Annabelle's other side, but thought better of it. After all we had been through that night, I was so emotionally and physically drained that if I dared to sit down, I may not have the strength to get back up.

Finn stopped his pacing long enough to give my hands a quick squeeze. "You all right?" he whispered.

I shrugged. "I don't really know. I just want to get this over with."

He nodded solemnly. "I know what you mean. Let's just have done with it and bugger the consequences, right?"

"Something like that, yeah," I said.

Two servants entered, each bearing a tray. Even Ileana, who looked down her nose at the offerings as though it was too little too late, was not too proud to snatch a sandwich off the tray and cram it hungrily into her mouth.

The tray and teapot were empty and the fire had burned nearly down to embers when the door swung open again, and Marguerite's face peered out from around it. "Jessica, my sister has agreed that she will see you," she said, beckoning me forward.

I heaved a sigh of relief. I heard Ileana mutter, "Thank God." Everyone else stood up and we proceeded toward the door together, but Marguerite, looking alarmed, stepped back into the room and closed the door behind her, blocking our path.

"You misunderstand me," she said, flapping her hands nervously at us. "She wants to see Jessica alone. The rest of you are to remain where you are."

Finn's entire body stiffened beside me. "Why? Why will she not permit the rest of us to accompany Jess, when we have accompanied her on the entire journey to get here?"

"It is not our place to question the decisions of the High Priestess," Marguerite said in a sing-song voice, as though she was reciting a rhyme she had known from childhood. "She will have her reasons, and they will be wise in their origins and just in their application."

Finn looked at me. "What do you think? You don't have to go in there alone."

"I think I do," I said. "Turning back isn't an option. I have to speak to her, Finn, and if this is the only way she will agree to see me, then this is what I have to do. It will be fine."

Ileana stepped up beside me, looking defiant. "You have told the High Priestess that I am here, and she still wishes to see only this child?"

I bristled at being called a child but, uncharacteristically, managed to keep my mouth shut about it. Now was not the time to start a petty argument.

Marguerite gave an apologetic shrug of her narrow shoulders. "I have explained who has arrived in your party. She wishes to see Jessica alone."

Ileana narrowed her eyes at Marguerite, who shrank back from her, and then turned to me. "Here. You'd better take this," she said, fishing around inside her blouse and extricating the key on the golden chain from within her many shawls. She pulled it over her head and draped it around my neck instead. "You'll need it to prove to her that what you say is true."

I nodded. "Thank you, Ileana. Thank you for coming this far with me."

She did not reply—perhaps it was too much for her to admit the importance of what we had done together even in the face of our intense dislike for each other. Instead, she flared her nostrils at me and gave a single, fierce nod before stepping back and gesturing toward the door, as though suddenly wondering what the hell I was waiting for.

She had a point. What the hell was I waiting for? Agnes' words echoed in my head.

"Have faith."

"Faith?!" I had asked her. *"What have I got left to have faith in?"*

"Yourself," she had answered. *"It's all we ever have, in the end."*

I stepped forward and forced my face into what I hoped would pass for a calm, determined expression. "Very well. Lead on, please, Marguerite."

The room was as high as a church and as cold as a tomb. White marble rose in smooth, flawless curves all around me, encircling me, arching high to a domed ceiling with a single circular window set in its top, so that the stars could wink down through it. There were no ornaments. No trinkets. No piles of riches or furs or jewels, as one might expect such a wealthy and powerful figure to surround herself with. There was only a white marble chair on a white marble pedestal in a white marble room. Two Caomhnóir stood on either side of the throne, dressed from head to toe in a uniform of white linen and carrying swords and knives with ivory handles. A young woman in a white linen robe was kneeling in front of the fire, watching the flames intently and immediately sweeping any speck of ash or ember back into the heart of the fire, lest they mar the flawlessly clean floor in front of the hearth. And there, upon the throne, looking like a creature dropped out of a celestial fever dream, was Simone de Chastenay, High Priestess of the International High Council.

At first, it felt as though there must be something wrong with my eyes—perhaps I was dazzled by the gleam of marble and the glint of firelight, but the woman seemed to have an unearthly glow about her, as though she was lit from within. Her features were flawless—wide blue eyes, rose-kissed cheeks, full lips, cascades of golden hair, creamy skin without a hint of blemish, freckle, or imperfection. Her slender hands rested delicately in her silk-clad lap, and the folds of her ivory-colored gown spilled down around her like drifts of freshly fallen snow.

Something was very wrong. She looked no older than me. She had been High Priestess for fifty years.

"Am I truly meeting the infamous Jessica Ballard at last?" Simone de Chastenay asked in a voice like birdsong. "Tales of your exploits in the North have traveled as far as Havre des Gardiennes, as I'm sure you must have guessed."

"I'm very pleased to meet you, High Priestess," I replied, unsure what kind of deference to show—should I bow? I wasn't sure I was coordinated enough to curtsey. I settled on a respectful inclination of the head. "And I'm sorry to hear that my reputation precedes me. I assure you, I'd much prefer obscurity to notoriety."

Simone's face curved into the suggestion of a smile. "Indeed? In this, the two of us are different, I suppose. I have always enjoyed the spotlight, as it were."

I tried to smile back, but my face didn't want to cooperate. "It agrees with you," I said, though I had not meant to say it out loud.

Simone did not grow angry, however. On the contrary, my candor made her smile still more broadly, revealing rows of perfect, white teeth. "I welcome you to Havre des Gardiennes. Has my sister seen to it that you have all that you require?" She made a limp gesture in Marguerite's direction, though she did not look at her. Marguerite, who had seemed to diminish even further when entering her sister's incandescent presence, blushed and bowed so low to the ground that her long braid dragged upon the floor in her eagerness to show deference.

"Yes, thank you," I said. "She has been very... hospitable." Now didn't seem like the right moment to complain about how long we were detained before Marguerite finally came to greet us. I didn't want to question the way things were done at Havre des Gardiennes so early in our meeting, and anyway, it seemed unlikely that any of that was Marguerite's fault.

"I was very distressed to hear of the attack you endured at our outpost. I understand a member of your party was killed?" Simone went on, her mouth pulled into a neat little bow of concern that did not quite reach her eyes.

"Yes," I said, fighting against the audible tremor in my voice. "Yes, she was."

"My guards inform me that she was one Lucida Worthington, the woman who betrayed the Northern Clans and your own sister to the Necromancers during the time of the Prophecy. I must confess she seems an odd travel companion, let alone a woman over whom you might shed tears."

I felt myself stiffen. "It's complicated," I said. "But just because she made mistakes in her life doesn't mean I'm happy to see her die. She died saving my life."

"Mistakes is putting it rather mildly, in my opinion," Simone said, in a tone that suggested her opinion was nothing to be trifled with. "But I grant you, the circumstances that bind people's lives together are often complicated. It was my understanding, though, that Lucida Worthington had been locked away in Skye Príosún for her transgressions against the sisterhood."

"Her cousin had her... removed," I replied, my heart thumping madly. "She was in danger there."

Simone arched one perfectly curved eyebrow. "In danger? From whom?"

"The Necromancers. They've made several attempts on her life in recent weeks."

"And yet the Necromancers found her here, hundreds of miles from the *príosún*. It seems she ought to have stayed where she was." Simone let out a tinkling laugh—musical and yet, somehow, cold. The sound of it sent a shiver up my back, especially when it was echoed from my other side by Marguerite.

I said nothing, but I did not indulge the laughter with even a hint of a smile.

"You have traveled a long way and endured much to seek an audience with me. You left yourself exposed to danger by taking the open route. Why did you not seek the help of your own High Priestess at Fairhaven to secure safe passage to my gates?" Simone asked.

"I did not tell my High Priestess that I was coming. I told no one outside of my own close group of confidantes," I said.

"And what would possess you to keep a journey of this nature from your High Priestess?" Simone asked.

"Because the message I have been tasked with delivering is not for her ears. It is for yours," I replied.

Simone gave a look of mild surprise, which I was sure must be artifice, as Marguerite had surely told her that I had come with a message. "A message for me? From whom? Who would presume to task you with a message for me who would not come before me themselves?"

"The message is from Agnes Isherwood," I said. "And I should imagine that the reason she could not deliver it herself is abundantly clear."

Simone's lovely face went very still, and for a moment she appeared to be carved of the very same marble that surrounded her. Then she gave me a small, tight smile and said, "Very well, Jessica Ballard. What is this message?"

I took a deep breath. This was it.

"The Sentinels have begun their watch."

The effect was chilling. The very air in the room seemed to stop circulating, the fire to stop crackling. Even Marguerite, still sunk into a perpetual half-bow, seemed to cease to exist. In that moment, there was only Simone and me and the great, devastating truth that hung in the space between us.

Simone's lips barely moved when at last she managed to whisper. "Tell me how you know this."

And it all came spilling out. "I found a message hidden in an ancient tapestry of Agnes Isherwood at Fairhaven. It had been woven right into the fabric itself. You would never believe me if I told you how it got there, so suffice it to say that it was left for me, and I found it. I realized that the message was a catalog number, of the kind used at Skye Príosún. I followed it back to the Catacomb Archives there, where a hidden panel within a drawer revealed both a sketch of my likeness, and the instructions I needed to go Rifting."

"Rifting?" Simone said, the sharpness of her tone causing her sister to shrink back in alarm, lest that sharpness be directed at her. "You refer to the antiquated Traveler practice of communing with the spirit world?"

"Yes," I confirmed, nodding. "I had done it once before, when I was staying in the Traveler camp. And while I was at Skye Príosún, I learned that the Travelers were deeply connected to the mystery through the existence of the Tansy Hag."

A spasm of something shot across Simone's flawless features—was it fear? "The Tansy Hag?"

"Yes," I said, intrigued that she had not even balked at the mention of so obscure a name. "She has been imprisoned there for centuries. It was Lucida Worthington who convinced me I must go to see her. It was the mark of the Tansy Hag that a Necromancer had broken into her cell to carve into the flesh on her back. An ancient mark, so obscure, so relegated to Durupinen fairy tales, that even the most knowledgeable of Scribes was ignorant of its existence. It was the Tansy Hag who explained to me what I must do in order to understand the clues left behind for me by Agnes Isherwood. She told me that I must Rift, and that when I did, I must look for and go through a second door."

"I do not follow," Simone said, holding up a hand meant to slow the progress of my story.

It felt strange to be explaining an aspect of Durupinen culture to the most powerful Durupinen in the world, but I did my best. "When one enters the Rift, there is always a door, and that door is always ajar. That door exists so that the Rifter can exit the Rift at any point she chooses. But the Tansy Hag told me that there would be a second door—a deeper door, and that I was to go through it if I wanted to understand the clues that Agnes had left behind for me. And so, when I arrived back at Fairhaven, a Traveler friend helped me prepare the herbs and artwork, and I Rifted."

"And did you find this... this second door of which the Tansy Hag spoke?" Simone asked, rather breathlessly. For all her imperial aloofness, I could tell that she was hanging on my every word. Her hands were tense upon the arms of her throne. Marguerite looked enraptured as well, though whether she truly felt that way or whether she was simply emulating her sister, was impossible to tell.

"I did," I replied. "Agnes Isherwood had created it, hundreds of years ago, so that she might warn us all of the danger that was to come, and she was waiting for me on the other side of it. She told me to deliver her message to three people: the High Priestess of the Traveler Clans, the Keeper of the Elementals, and the High Priestess of the International High Council. She told me it was the only way to save the Gateways."

"And did she illuminate to you further on what she meant by 'save the Gateways?'" Simone asked.

"She... she did," I replied, hesitating now. How much did the High Priestess know? What did Agnes' words mean to her? "She told me that hundreds of years ago, during her time, the Gateways were contained not within the bloodlines of the Durupinen, but within the Geatgrimas themselves. They were the true Gateways: actual physical landmarks located around the world. When the Necromancers waged a great battle to gain control over the Gateways, the Durupinen worried that they would not be able to hold them, and so they... they created a Casting that would remove the Gateways from the Geatgrimas and conceal them within the bloodlines of the Durupinen themselves."

Simone's face was completely unreadable as she listened to what Agnes had explained to me. I could discern nothing of her reaction. Marguerite, however, had risen up out of her groveling posture and was staring back and forth between her sister and myself as though she could hardly believe what she was hearing. "Simone, that's... that can't possibly be true, what the girl says. Tell her she is mistaken, sister."

But Simone did not contradict me. She simply continued to gaze at me, appraising me. As her silence stretched on, I blurted out the rest of my story.

"Agnes also told me that she feared they had made

the Geatgrimas unstable, and that one day, they would collapse altogether. She told me that I must deliver her message before it was too late, but she... the Rift sort of chucked me out before I could ask her what her message meant."

"And have you delivered it to all three of the intended recipients, as you promised?" Simone asked me.

"Yes," I told her. "Ileana Lovell, the High Priestess of the Traveler Clans is here with me. She wanted to accompany me on the rest of the journey because she thought it might be dangerous, which has turned out to be an accurate prediction. I went to see Lira Blackwell as well, the Keeper of the Elementals who lives in the Dering Woods. She was... less than happy to hear the message."

Simone gave a grim smile. "And if you have delivered the message as you say, then each of these women ought to have given something to you—a relic hidden away for the very moment when they heard the words that you spoke to them."

"Yes," I said, my pulse quickening now. I reached down and pulled the two chains from around my neck, holding the keys aloft in the space between us. For a moment we all just stood there watching them swing gently on the ends of their chains, glinting as they reflected the firelight.

Simone leaned forward and held out a hand. I dropped the two keys into her palm. As I did so, my finger brushed against her skin, which was icy cold.

"I never thought the day would come when I would see these keys for myself," Simone said with a sort of sigh. "I'm not sure I even believed they existed. Or perhaps I merely hoped that they did not." She rose from her throne in a fluid, graceful movement and beckoned me forward. "Come with me, Jessica Ballard. I have something I must show you."

ALLIANCES

S IMONE SWEPT DOWN off her pedestal and strode gracefully across the room. Marguerite roused herself from her shock in time to scurry along behind her sister, gathering up the frothy lace edges of the train in her hands, like a perpetual bridesmaid. The girl in the fireplace sunk down so low as her mistress passed that her nose brushed the soot in the hearth. I followed behind Marguerite, who continuously stole frightened glances at me as we followed Simone through another set of doors, and then another.

Simone's chambers seemed to go on forever. From the chamber where we had our meeting, we passed through a chamber that seemed to serve as a kind of office, with a white marble desk, a collection of porcelain ink bottles and fluffy white quills. Beyond this chamber was a private library, where all of the books had been bound in ivory or pale gold-gilded leather and shelved from floor to ceiling. A single white chaise lounge stood in the center of the room upon a round white fur rug with a white marble-topped table just beside it. A book lay open upon the table, waiting patiently to be taken up again. Beyond the library was a room full of nothing but maps and globes, hung on the walls, reposing on shelves, and spread out upon great drafting tables. The largest globe I had ever seen hung suspended from the ceiling in the center of the room and turned very slowly on a heavy golden chain that ran through its center. As we passed through, I heard a fluttering of restless wings, and looked up to see hundreds of pure white doves nested in the rafters above our heads. The next room looked like a kind of museum showroom, with case after glass case of spectacular jewelry, crowns, swords, and armor on display. Though we did not pause long enough to examine the treasures closely, I spotted several triskeles worked into the metal and inlaid in precious gems.

It was in this room that we turned and entered a second, less imposing door on the lefthand wall. It led to a second chamber much like the one we had just left, only the relics on display were much less spectacular and showy. The cases in this room contained not fabulous jewels, but old books, scrolls, and documents, all carefully preserved under glass, protected from prying hands and the destructive effects of air and dust. Within this room, along the wall, there were several rows of black metal safes, each with a numbered combination lock upon it. It was along this wall that Simone stopped at last. Marguerite, panting from the pace of our excursion, smoothed her sister's train carefully out on the floor around her, and then quickly backed away into the nearest corner in an attempt to make herself disappear as much as possible. Simone spared not a glance for her, but kept her eyes fixed most firmly upon mine.

"You stand, Jessica Ballard, amongst the most treasured relics of the Durupinen world," Simone said, flicking a hand casually up in the air to reference the many priceless items around us. "Many of them have never been seen by any Durupinen who was not a High Priestess herself—or the shadow of one," she added, with a smirk toward her sister. "Every one of these relics has its own special place in the history of our sisterhood, except for one, whose moment it was said, was still to come."

Simone turned to the smallest of the safes and turned the dial once, twice, three times, and then with a click and a whooshing of air, the door swung open. She pulled from its depths a bundle of faded purple velvet, which she cradled carefully in her hands for a moment before unfolding it to reveal a third iron key.

Marguerite muttered a soft oath in French as Simone held it up on its fine golden chain and then, pulling the other two from the pocket of her gown, let all three of them dangle in front of us, clinking lightly together, like wind chimes.

"The Three Keys of the Reckoning," she whispered. "Together again for the very first time, perhaps, since they were forged."

"The… the three keys of the *what*, now?" I asked faintly.

"The Reckoning. I gather Agnes did not go so far in her explanations to you as to explain the Reckoning."

"She… I… no, she didn't have the chance," I whispered. For some reason, the sight of the three keys dangling back and forth made me feel dizzy, as though they were hypnotizing me. Then I realized I'd nearly stopped breathing and took a deep breath.

"Everything Agnes told you about the history of the Gateways is true," Simone said, in a tone that seemed to suggest that it cost her something quite precious to admit it. "The Durupinen have always been tied to the spirit world. We were shepherdesses once, guiding and coaxing the spirits in our charge to the Geatgrimas, where they could Cross of their own free will. Our ability to see and sense them was innate in our blood; the Gateways themselves were not."

Marguerite was making a soft animal sound in the corner—it might have been stifled sobbing. But Simone ignored it, all her attention now on the keys in her hands.

"We acted for the right reasons. We sought only to protect, not to empower or enrich ourselves. When the Casting was performed that made us the Gatekeepers, a counter-Casting was also created, a counter-Casting that would reverse the process and return the Gateways to their rightful places in the world once again. One could not exist without the other; they were the light and the darkness, the yin and the yang, the two sides of the scale that would hold the two worlds in balance. And only in the timely performing of the counter-Casting could the delicate trust that existed between the Durupinen and the spirit world remain intact. That moment when the counter-Casting was to be performed became known as the Reckoning."

"But it wasn't performed," I said. "It was all but forgotten."

"For a long time, our foremothers did not believe it safe to attempt to return the Gateways to the Geatgrimas. For many centuries after we internalized the gift, they feared the Geatgrimas would fall into Necromancer hands. And so, we built ourselves up as powerfully as we dared. We grew our armies, nurtured our prestige, and consolidated our power and influence around the world. We became, over time, a force to be reckoned with; and when the Necromancers next dared to try their strength, they were all but wiped from the face of the earth. The Geatgrimas were safe."

"But the Gateways were not returned to them," I said.

"No, they were not," Simone replied. "Becoming the mistresses of so much power took its toll on us. We became drunk with it. Why, we asked ourselves, should we not hold on to the Gateways a little while longer? Where could they possibly be safer than within the blood of the most powerful organization on the earth? Who could better protect them, better defend them? And if we used them to our benefit, was that not our right? Our privilege? If we siphoned off a bit of energy here or there to sustain us in our fight, had we not earned it, after everything we had sacrificed for the spirit world?"

I suppressed a shiver, for at last my overwrought brain understood why the woman now standing before me looked so utterly unworldly, so unnaturally flawless. It was a result of Leeching, the practice of using the energy of a Crossing spirit and taking it into oneself, to make oneself appear younger, more beautiful, or even to heal a wound or illness. The practice had been rampant in the upper levels of the Northern Clans when I'd first arrived at Fairhaven, and it wasn't banned until the reversal of the Gateways revealed many weakened spirits trapped in the Aether, lacking the energy they needed to Cross fully because it had been sucked from them, like blood from a vampire's victims. But here at Havre des Gardiennes, it seemed Leeching was still very much practiced, and nowhere more so than by the woman in front of me, an unchanged vision of youthful perfection for the more than fifty years of her reign.

Simone smiled cryptically, as though she knew exactly the realization that had come over me. "We buried the truth about the origins of the Gateways, at first to protect them, but as the years went by, we buried them deeper to protect ourselves. Now only a very small, tightly controlled number of us even know that our gift was not ours at all—a number you and your companions have now joined." Vaguely in my peripheral vision, I saw that Marguerite had sunk to her knees, brought to them, no doubt, by the weight of the knowledge that she had only just, at that very moment, discovered.

"And now the scales we meant to keep in balance have tipped so far that we are very nearly too late to right them again. And now, our last defense, our failsafe, the Sentinels have risen." She looked at me, tilting her head to the side like an inquisitive child. "Do you know, I wonder, what the Sentinels are?"

"I... have some idea," I said. "There is a second part of the story that I haven't told you yet, about the Geatgrima at Fairhaven. You see—"

But Simone waved a hand dismissively at me. "A Durupinen has entered into a connection with the Geatgrima there."

My jaw dropped. "Yes. How did you—"

"It is happening everywhere. Celeste may not have chosen to come to me at first, but others have, from other clans all over the world. At nearly every Geatgrima around the globe, a Sentinel has now risen. In fact, I believe one _of the_ only Geatgrimas in the world that still stands without a Sentinel is the one at the heart of Havre des Gardiennes."

I stood transfixed for a moment at the mental image of women like Savvy trapped all over the world, pinpoints of light on a globe spinning terribly out of control, the points of light blurring, connecting, and finally...

"What's happening to them? What are the Sentinels, really?"

"We had to make sure that we had a way to keep the Geatgrimas open if ever the day came that they grew so unstable that they were in danger of collapse. And so the Casting that created our gift also created the Sentinels. When the time came, when the Geatgrimas were at imminent risk of closing forever and taking the Gateways with them, the Sentinels would be called to use their gifts, to keep the Geatgrimas stable until we could complete the counter-Casting to return the Gateways to their rightful place."

"So, what you're saying is that Savvy—that's my friend at Fairhaven—and the other Sentinels are using their Gateways to keep the Geatgrimas open?"

"Yes," Simone replied. "Their Gateways are circulating like lifeblood between themselves and the Geatgrimas, feeding the Geatgrimas, keeping them alive, in a sense."

"And so, what will happen to them—the Sentinels—when the counter-Casting is performed?" I asked, tears springing into my eyes. "Will... will Savvy and the others be all right?"

"The counter-Casting was designed to protect the Sentinels," Simone said. "If it were to be performed, the Sentinels would survive."

"Oh, thank God," I gasped, dropping my face into my hands and taking several long, cleansing breaths to calm myself. *She'll be all right,* I kept telling myself. *She'll be all right.*

But then, another thought burst to life in my head. I raised my head from my shaking hands and looked Simone in the eyes.

"You said 'if.'"

She frowned at me. "Pardon?"

"You didn't say 'when' the counter-Casting is performed. You said 'if.' Why did you say 'if?'" I repeated.

Simone smiled at me, a sad, pitying sort of smile. "Oh, Jessica. I really ought not to be surprised. After all, you were not raised in the Durupinen world. And despite your time among us, I fear you do not really understand it at all, do you?"

"I… guess I don't," I said, trying to keep my voice calm. "Perhaps you would be so kind as to enlighten me, High Priestess."

"Look around you, Jessica," Simone sighed, gazing around enraptured at her marble halls, at her vault of treasures. "Look at all we, the great sisterhood of the Durupinen have built—all we have achieved. What do we stand to gain if we give up that which has enabled us to attain such heights? What profit do we gain to face this Reckoning that has come upon us?"

"I… was not under the impression that it was about gain or profit," I said through tightly clenched teeth. "I was taught that our gift was about serving and protecting those who could not protect themselves."

"And a noble sentiment it is, too," Simone said with a patronizing smile. "I do find it endearing, truly, to see the way our Apprentices soak up the rhetoric in those early school days, before the realities of our duties overtake their lives. We have sacrificed, have we not? We have struggled and fought and defended, have we not? We have earned the gift that runs now within our blood. Every drop of it, we have earned, and we would be foolish not to reap our reward for all we have done."

"And what is our reward?" I asked, my voice rising now. "Leeching the life out of spirits who trust us with their safe passage? Sacrificing them for our own vanity? Is that what you think we're owed?"

"Oh, my sweeting, you don't honestly think this to be about mere vanity?" Simone asked, and her tone was truly disgusted even as she stood there, shining like a beacon of almost indescribable beauty. "Vanity is easily satisfied. You neglect to connect beauty and youth to their true source: health. Vitality. *Life.*"

"Life? You mean, like… what, immortality?" I asked, incredulous.

Simone shrugged, looking unconcerned. "I'm not sure if any person really wants to live forever. But to choose the manner and time of one's death? To have that level of control—that level of power over the mechanisms of life and death? Who would not desire such a choice in forging one's own destiny—in shaping her legacy?"

I took an unconscious step back from her, wanting nothing more than to put all the distance I could between myself and the gleam in her eye, which looked a little less like beauty now and a little more like madness. "The only people I've ever heard spouting rhetoric like that were not Durupinen at all. They were Necromancers."

Simone laughed lightly—the sound was like a shard of ice right through my heart. "It is most amusing, isn't it, that hundreds of years of trying to protect the Gateways from the Necromancers could result in ascribing to their very philosophies? I promise you the irony is not lost on me, Jessica. I would never have believed, even a few short years ago, that a Necromancer and I, of all people, would have anything in common. It was, to be sure, a true surprise to find ourselves very much on the same page, was it not, Mr. Wright?"

"Indeed, it was, High Priestess," came a familiar voice from behind me—a voice I knew but had hoped never to hear again. I spun on the spot, every defensive impulse heightened.

Charlie Wright walked out of the shadows, a satisfied smile upon his face.

§

"Hello, Jessica. I was hoping I might have the chance to see you here," Charlie said pleasantly.

I felt as though all the air had been sucked from the room, as though the very walls were caving in around me. He couldn't be here, walking so casually toward me, within the most hallowed walls of the Durupinen world. It just couldn't be true. Not taking my eyes off him, I threw my next words back over my shoulder at Simone. "What the hell is he doing here?"

"But of course, there is no need to introduce you, is there?" Simone said. "It is my understanding that you two are already acquainted."

"If by acquainted you mean he drugged me, tied me up, and attempted to torture me, then yes, we're acquainted," I snapped. "And you haven't answered my question. What is a Necromancer doing at Havre des Gardiennes?"

"Simone, you... you haven't... this man is not a Necromancer, is he?" came Marguerite's weak bleating from her corner, where she still knelt upon the ground, watching the scene play out in front of her like a woman unable to wake from a nightmare.

"Silence, Marguerite. Sister knows best, *ma petite*," Simone said with a tight smile; and Marguerite, rather than displaying resentment at being told, in essence, to shut the hell up, looked nothing short of blissful to be directly addressed by her sister in this manner. She bowed her head again and resumed an expression of sycophantic attentiveness.

Simone turned back to me and answered at last. "A few months ago, when the coup was discovered at Skye Príosún, I demanded the masterminds behind the plot be brought before me. I wished to mete out justice personally."

"But Charlie wasn't captured in the coup at Skye," I cut in. "He escaped."

"And so imagine my surprise when he arrived at the gates of Havre des Gardiennes to turn himself in," Simone said with an amused smile. "I thought him a fool, and was determined to make an example of him, but when Mr. Wright and I came face to face, he made a proposal that intrigued me. Rather than beg for his life or his freedom, as his pathetic co-conspirators chose to do, he offered me information. Information, he said, that I needed to possess if I hoped to maintain my position and my power. 'What threat are you to me anymore, Necromancer?' I asked him. 'Your life is in my hands.' 'Yes,' he replied, 'But the Necromancers are no longer the threat you should fear. It is from within your own ranks that the serpent has sprung.'"

I was still staring at Charlie, unable to look away, every muscle tensed, every sense working overtime, trying frantically to work out how I would get out of this room alive.

"I had her ear, then, and she heard me out," Charlie said. "I told her how I learned in Skye Príosún of a spirit called the Tansy Hag, a spirit who held the key to the origins of the Durupinen's power. It was a core belief of the Necromancers that the Durupinen's control of the Gateways was a coup—an abomination in the natural order of things. And here in the depths of their mightiest fortress, it was said, was a spirit who could prove it. By the time I had arrived, the mission to subvert the Caomhnóir and turn them was already well underway. It was almost too easy to find a Caomhnóir who would be willing to take me to the remotest of the spirit cellblocks to visit the creature, and to begin to probe her for what she knew. She remained tight-lipped at first, but the symbol she had scrawled all over her cell gave us our first hints about who she might be and what she may know, if only we could convince her to speak. And then, deep in the Catacomb Archives, we found some of our own ancient documents, stolen many centuries ago when our Brotherhood was first forced underground. There, we discovered our own accounts of how the Durupinen had stolen their gift."

He smiled a gloating smile at me, as though I had personally left the documents for him to find. My hand twitched with the urge to reach out and slap him as hard as I could. I clenched my fist to fight against the impulse.

"It was my intention to bargain with the Tansy Hag, to trade her freedom for what she knew; but, most inconveniently, our operation at Skye was uncovered and we were forced to flee before such a bargain could be struck. I do believe you were rather instrumental in that little—ah—hiccup in my plans, weren't you, Jessica?"

"I do what I can," I said with a brave attempt at airiness. "I've got to make you work for it, after all, Charlie."

Charlie laughed, a hearty sound that nevertheless lacked any hint of warmth or real humor. "After that, we had to do some damage control. Some of us had gotten ahead of ourselves, overplayed our hands and said too much. One of my men, overcome with excitement over our impending victory, had foolishly bragged to the Durupinen traitor about what we knew. We made it a priority to have her dispatched before she was able to reveal too much. She turned out to be much more of a liability than we had anticipated, and several attempts to deal with her were unsuccessful." He shrugged and gave a theatrical sigh. "Ah, well. Better late than never I suppose."

"Her name is Lucida Worthington," I hissed through tightly gritted teeth.

"*Was* Lucida Worthington," he corrected, a savage note of pleasure in his voice. "Once we were able, through both prisoners and guards, to reinfiltrate the prison, we learned that we were not the only ones on the quest for information from the Tansy Hag. Miss Ballard yet again had insinuated herself most inconveniently into our plans, forcing us to take action much sooner than anticipated. We garnered what information we could from the Tansy Hag in exchange for her freedom. We were now racing, it seemed, toward the same goal, Jessica: to reach the gates of Havre des Gardiennes with the Keys of the Reckoning in hand."

I turned back to look at Simone, the keys still swinging in her hand. What would happen, I wondered, if I simply lunged at her and snatched them back. But then what? What did I do with them? What did they open? I'd be dead at the hand of a Caomhnóir before I could find my way out of Simone's labyrinth of chambers.

"Not knowing how far you'd gotten, the Necromancers spread out," Charlie went on. "We set out for the Traveler camp, the Dering Woods, and Havre des Gardiennes all at once. Only here did we manage to beat you to the punch."

I longed to ask, but could not bear to ask, what had happened at the Traveler camp and the Dering Woods. Whatever havoc the Necromancers had wreaked there, whatever violence they had rained down upon those we had left behind, it was my fault. All my fault.

"And you listened to this man?" I asked Simone venomously. "This man, who has tortured your fellow Durupinen and fought to undermine everything we stand for? What could he possibly have to say that would merit your attention?"

Charlie clicked his tongue disapprovingly. "Jessica, I think you might be a bit prejudiced to think ill of me," he said, smirking at the shock and anger that broke over my features. "We've had our disagreements, certainly. I, for one, will never forget the memento of our last encounter." He reached up and lightly brushed the top of his left ear with his fingertips, where I had torn away the top edge with my teeth. The memory made me cringe. "But the High Priestess has proven to be far more reasonable. She does not allow her passion to rule, but takes a far more practical approach."

"Practical?" I said, laughing hollowly. "There's a word for selfish I've never heard before."

"Don't be a fool, child," Simone snapped, and for the first time, her calm and ethereal voice was tinged with anger. The effect was unsettling. "What profits us to throw away everything we have built? One does not allow a great empire to simply slip through her fingers like sand through an hourglass."

"Don't use metaphors you don't understand!" I cried, feeling hatred for the woman rise like a tide within me. "Time means nothing to you. You've stopped time out of fear and vanity, and would watch the world burn if only the flames would warm your hands. How dare you speak of <u>profit</u> and empires when your very own sisters' lives hang in the balance at Geatgrimas all over the world, and the spirits you are supposed to protect could be trapped forever."

"The Sentinels make a worthy sacrifice," Simone said callously. "They have willingly devoted their lives to the protection of the Gateways. Their role now is the ultimate fulfillment of that destiny—an honor and a privilege. They will be revered from this day onward."

"They don't want to be revered, they want to be freed!" I shouted.

"And they shall be, someday," Simone said. "The Necromancers have spent centuries studying the mechanism of the Gateways. They have experimented and pushed the boundaries of what we can be capable of in our manipulation of the spirit world. We were foolish to demonize their work. With their help, we will be able to use the Gateways in ways we never dreamed possible."

"You're mad," I whispered. "What have you done? What have you promised them?"

But it was Charlie who answered. "A partnership of sorts. We will lend our men and the full force of our knowledge to the High Priestess as she exerts her authority over the world's Gateways. We will help to quell resistance wherever she meets it. We will bring the full network of Geatgrimas under her control, so that she has full reign over their powers and possibilities."

"And why would you make such an offer to her?" I asked. "What do you get in return?"

"What we have always desired," Charlie replied, a mad glint in his eyes. "Equal access to the mysteries of the spirit world. A Gateway of our very own and the freedom to control it."

I could hear myself gasping, but the air did not seem to be reaching my lungs. "You can't do this," I wanted to shout, but the words came out in a breathless cry. "You'll never get away with it. The rest of the Durupinen will never agree to this. They've devoted their lives to the spirit world, and they won't stand by while you destroy it. The Caomhnóir will never—"

"The Caomhnóir at Havre des Gardiennes are the finest skilled fighters in the world," Simone said with a smug confidence. "They would run themselves through with a sword without hesitation if I commanded it of them."

"If you doubt where their loyalties lie, I suggest you ask yourself why it was so easy for my men to ambush you at the outpost," Charlie said brightly. "Ask yourself why the most highly trained soldiers in the world simply walked away from their guard post, leaving it vulnerable to infiltration and attack."

I felt my heart sinking. Finn and Catriona had both been suspicious about the whereabouts of the guards. They had known immediately that something was very wrong.

"The Northern Clans will fight," I said fiercely. "And the other clans, too."

"If they are foolish enough to do so, they shall be decimated," Simone said in an almost bored voice. "The Necromancers have already deeply damaged the Caomhnóir fighting ranks with their infiltration at Skye Príosún. The other High Priestesses will see reason, I have no doubt, when they see themselves outflanked. After all, many of them have grown accustomed to the power and privilege they enjoy."

"We saw firsthand at Fairhaven what that kind of power and privilege could do," I said, fighting my mounting fear and digging deep for a confidence I did not feel. "Finvarra and the others, they used to be like you—but when they saw what it had done, the damage they had caused, they recommitted themselves to their true duty. They will never go back."

"And where is my dear friend Finvarra?" Simone asked, in tones of mock curiosity. "Oh, that's right. She's dead, so full of foolish nobility that she lacked the courage even to save herself from the ravages of human frailty. So weak I cannot even pity her."

"It is not a weakness to face death," I hissed. "You are the coward. You and every Necromancer who follows you."

"Give it a bit of time, Jess Ballard, and we'll see just how much courage you have," Charlie said, stepping forward so that he was standing offensively close to me. Every defensive impulse I had was screaming at me, but I did not move. "I will take immense pleasure in walking through the gates of Fairhaven and taking that Geatgrima for my own. I can only imagine Neil Caddigan would be proud of his protégé, wouldn't you? Just a few short years of following in his footsteps and I've achieved what he could only dream of."

"I'm not sure if people can feel pride while they're busy burning in hell," I replied smoothly. "You'll have to ask him when you get there."

Charlie smiled. "You really are most amusing, aren't you?"

"And you're not worth the effort it would cost me to spit in your face."

A sudden ringing of a bell behind me made me jump away and I turned to see Simone replacing a small gold handbell on a table. "I think it's time you made your acquaintance with our dungeons, Miss Ballard. I've grown weary of your recalcitrance, and anyway, you've outlived your usefulness, though I thank you for bringing me the keys." She dangled the keys toward my face for a moment before turning and placing all three of them in the safe behind her and snapping the door shut.

A moment later, the door through which we had entered swung open and two Caomhnóir entered, snapping to attention and looking to Simone for instruction.

"Escort Miss Ballard to the cell we have reserved for her in the dungeons," Simone said with an ingratiating smile, as though she was instructing them to invite me to high tea. "I take it you've already seen to it that her companions are comfortably settled into similar quarters?"

"Yes, High Priestess," the taller of the Caomhnóir replied. They both marched forward at once, and before I could even cry out, they had seized me by the arms and began dragging me toward the door.

"This is where I bid you *adieu*, Miss Ballard. And thank you again, for your message. Agnes Isherwood chose her messenger well. You've been most helpful." And she patted a hand against the door of the safe.

I cursed and struggled fruitlessly against the powerful grip of the Caomhnóir as they pulled me effortlessly over the threshold. From the far corner, I could hear Marguerite's confused whimpering, like a trapped and frightened animal. The very last thing I saw before the door slammed shut was the satisfied smile breaking like a sunrise over Charlie Wright's face, and the triumphant gleam behind his wire-rimmed spectacles.

LION AND LAMB

TO GIVE MYSELF CREDIT, I did not go quietly. Even though I knew it was absolutely no use whatsoever, I fought with every ounce of fire I had, and after my encounter with Charlie, I was basically a human inferno. My unlucky captors had to endure biting, scratching, kicking, flailing, and elbow jabbing as they hauled me, like a thing possessed, to the depths of the dungeons. I shouted all the way, too, screaming about the High Priestess' betrayal until my throat was hoarse and raw. And though we passed several living and many dead inhabitants of the castle, not a single one of them spared me even a passing glance. It was as though I did not exist, as though my struggle, rather than earning their attention, had created a barrier between us that could not be breached. By the time the Caomhnóir hurled me unceremoniously into the cell and slammed the door behind me, it was with a distinct grunt of relief to finally be rid of me.

I paced the room in an aimless sort of panic, taking in the runes, the bars, the chains on the wall, all without really seeing them at all, already sure I would find no means of escape. My mind was racing out of control, terrified of what Simone and Charlie might be planning, what wheels had already been set in motion, just in the time it had taken me to reach this godforsaken cell. I sank to my knees, every bit of fight finally draining from me, leaving me a sobbing heap upon the filthy stone floor.

"I'm sorry," I whimpered over and over again, my face pressed against the cold, damp rock. "I'm sorry, Agnes. I did everything I could. I'm sorry. I'm sorry."

"Okay, we get it, you're sorry, but now is not the time to go to pieces. Pull yourself together, sweetness."

My head shot up at the sound of the voice. I blinked away the blinding film of tears to see Milo strolling casually through the wall of the cell. He looked exhausted and worried, but his face broke into a wide grin.

"Milo!" I gasped and flung myself forward onto him, enveloping myself in the shivery comfort of his spectral embrace. If I'd gone to pieces before, it was nothing to what I did now. He didn't tease me anymore, just shushed me and stroked my hair with the whisper of his touch until I cried myself out.

"There now," he said, pulling back to look me in the face. "Are we functioning now?"

"I have never been so glad to see anyone in my entire life as I am to see you right now," I laughed in a shaky voice.

"Oh, I am SO going to hold that over your head for eternity," he said with a wink before his face fell back into lines of seriousness.

"I don't understand. What are you doing here? How did you get in?"

"I came with Hannah and Celeste. They're here, Jess, they're in the castle."

"What?!" I cried. "But why didn't she tell me? I kept trying to open the connection but she'd closed it and I couldn't get through."

"She was blocking you on purpose," Milo said. "She knew you'd flip out if you knew she was on her way, so she didn't want to tip you off. Seems like it was a pretty stupid plan in retrospect."

"You're damn right it was a stupid plan, but never mind that now. What are they doing here?"

"Hannah did what you asked her to do. She went to Celeste and told her everything," Milo said.

"Oh, God," I said, putting my hand over my mouth. "How... how did she take it?"

"How would you take it?" Milo asked, raising an amused eyebrow.

"She was pissed, huh?" I asked, feeling the mounting guilt that I'd left Hannah holding the bag.

"She was furious," Milo said. "But to be honest, she didn't have much time to go on about it, because she was immediately making arrangements to come here. Hannah threatened to set out on her own if Celeste didn't bring her along, so she agreed. They got here even before you did, since they came by helicopter. They brought Seamus and Kiernan for security and, since I wasn't about to let Hannah out of my sight, I tagged along as well."

"But what happened when they got here? Why aren't you with them now? And how did you find me?"

"Whoa there, sweetness, one question at a time. Let a girl get a word in," Milo said, flapping his hands to silence me. "As soon as we got within range of the castle's Castings, something really strange happened. I started to feel a pull, like a magnet toward the place, and the closer we flew, the stronger it got. And then suddenly, as we approached the landing pad up on the mountaintop, I was just... *yanked*... right out of the helicopter and through the walls of the castle."

"What the hell?" I muttered. "Has anything like that ever happened to you before?"

Milo shook his head, and I could tell he was shaken. "This place is like a giant spirit magnet. You can't will yourself out of its influence. If I weren't Bound to you and Hannah, I honestly think I might be trapped here."

"What reason would Havre des Gardiennes have to draw in spirits against their will? Surely enough spirits are drawn here on their own, by the sheer spiritual connection of the place."

"That's what I thought, too. It was unnerving. But then I started interacting with the other spirits around this place and I think I might have figured it out. Have you met any of the spirits here?"

"Not really," I said. "I haven't talked to any of them. But we noticed they seemed very... I'm not sure what the right word is..."

"Zombie-like?" Milo suggested grimly. "Like, the walking dead... literally?"

"Yeah," I said. "I'd say that's a pretty apt description."

Milo gave a shiver. "Jess, I think there's something wrong with them. They don't respond when I try to speak to them. They just sort of... drift aimlessly around. Aimlessly isn't even the right word—it's like they're on tracks, and they're just following a predetermined pattern over and over again. I watched one spirit—she looked like she might have been a maid when she was alive—who walked up and down this one hallway, dusting the same three portraits over and over again. It was like she was stuck on a loop."

"You mean like Blind Summoners?" I asked. I shuddered to remember these spirits that the Necromancers had created, their very essences dragged from their bodies and captured in flame, so that they were merely empty spirit shells, ready to be controlled and ordered around.

"I guess so, yeah," Milo said. He gave a delicate shiver. "Anyway, none of them were any help figuring out why I was literally sucked into the place, so I went off in search of Hannah and the others."

"Did you find them?"

"Sure did! Opened the connection right up—you can't imagine how relieved I was to discover it still worked. Hannah described her surroundings, and I just kept searching until I found a Warded room I could enter, and there they were. Celeste was in a real huff. Seamus and Kiernan had been taken away by the other Caomhnóir upon arrival for a 'security search' and never came back. Then I guess Celeste and Hannah had been told the High Priestess would be right with them, and then the Caomhnóir just locked them in that room. Celeste was going on and on about how she had never been treated like this in all the times she'd come here, that something wasn't right."

"Yeah, Ileana mentioned something to that effect, too. So, then what happened?"

"Hannah suggested I try to find you. She thought you might be locked away somewhere, too."

"And how *did* you find me?" I asked. "*I* don't even know where I am right now."

Milo chuckled. "It wasn't exactly difficult. Not two minutes after Hannah sent me to find you, you started screaming like a lunatic. I just followed the dulcet sounds of your hysteria and kept myself out of sight until the guards left. And of course, they haven't invented the Casting that can keep me out if one of my girls is around, so I just floated on in."

"Well, like I said, I'm glad to see you, but unless you can float both of us on out of here, I'm no better off than I was doing the whole shrieking pointlessly thing," I said.

Milo's smile slipped from his face. "Yeah, I have to admit, I haven't figured that part out yet."

"We need to find the others," I said. "Finn, Annabelle, Catriona, and Ileana. I was separated from them when Simone agreed to see me, and I have no idea what happened to them."

"Isn't Lucida with you, too?" Milo asked.

I stiffened. "She's dead. The Necromancers ambushed us as we were approaching the outpost. They killed her. She was... trying to protect me."

"Oh, shit," Milo whispered. "I... I don't know what to..."

"Neither do I," I said shortly, cutting off the avenue for a conversation I was not ready to have. "So, the others... do you think you could find them?"

"I can try," Milo said. "Spirits seem to be able to wander this place pretty freely. If I just stay pale and despondent-looking, I should blend right in. Do you want me to search the dungeon, or... hang on, you haven't even told me what happened with the High Priestess. Did you get to deliver your message? What the hell are you doing down in the dungeon anyway?"

As quickly as I could, I explained to Milo what had transpired in my audience with Simone. By the time I had finished, Milo's hands were so tightly wrapped around his face in horror that his next words were barely distinguishable. "She's working with the Necromancers?! The most powerful Durupinen in the world is working with the Necromancers?"

"Yes," I said, relieved to share the burden of this gut-wrenching knowledge with at least one other person before the weight of it crushed me. "And she doesn't care what or who she destroys as long as she maintains her position and her ability to Leech her way to immortality. She's sold us all out, Milo."

"What do you think she's going to do to Celeste and Hannah?" Milo asked, still peeking at me from between his own fingers.

"I don't know," I said. "Probably just keep them locked up where they are, so they can't alert anyone to what's happening. Unless of course, she decides to just do away with pretense and drag them down here to the dungeons. She may even try to persuade Celeste—to get her on her side. After all, the fewer clans she has to subdue, the better."

Milo shook his head. "Celeste has made some poor decisions recently, but there's no way in hell she'd ever agree to sell out the Northern Clans to the Necromancers."

"I agree, which is why we've got to warn Celeste and Hannah about what's happening," I said.

"Okay, well should I try to find Finn and the others first? Or go back to Hannah and Celeste? And once I find everyone, how the hell are we going to get out of here?"

As though in direct answer to his question, a grating squeal sounded from the hallway, and the door to my cell slid partway open. A face, pale and terrified, appeared in the gap.

"Marguerite!" I cried.

Marguerite's eyes widened in fear, and she put her finger up to her lips in a plea for silence. Then she struggled against the door, forcing it a few inches wider so that she could slip inside. A large ring of keys was clutched tightly in her hand, and her chest was rising and falling rapidly.

"Um, who is this, exactly?" Milo asked, backing away from Marguerite in alarm.

"This is Marguerite de Chastenay, Simone's sister," I replied hastily before turning back to Marguerite. "What are you doing here? What's going on?"

Marguerite's wide eyes filled with tears. She looked down at the cell keys in her hands and then at me before whispering. "I don't know. I... Oh, *mon Dieu*, I just don't know. I must be out of my mind." She turned in a circle on the spot, as though trying to decide whether she ought to just run right back out of the cell again, and slam the door shut behind her.

"No, please," I whispered, reaching out a hand toward her, but the movement made her flinch, so I hastily retracted it. "You... must have come down here for a reason. You've unlocked my cell. Please. Please talk to me."

She met my eyes, and I could see that hers were awash with tears and doubt. "My... my sister... the Necromancers... I never dreamed... never once would have believed it of her..."

"I know," I said, trying to sound sympathetic. "I was betrayed myself once. The Necromancers have always been able to manipulate people. It's one of the reasons they've survived for so many years."

"She... they must have lied to her... she must not be thinking clearly. My sister is a wise and judicious ruler," Marguerite said, flinging the words at me in a sudden burst of anger.

Somehow, I sincerely doubted this interpretation of events. Simone had seemed to know exactly what she was doing. But if nurturing this delusion of Simone's innocence was necessary to persuade Marguerite to help me, then so be it. "I'm sure you're right," I said soothingly. "My own sister was manipulated into working with them once. They are so persuasive, so unscrupulous. They would say anything, tell any lie."

"Yes," Marguerite muttered, nodding along. "Yes, they've tricked her. I'm sure that's it."

"There's still time," I said, though I had no idea if this was true. "We might still be able to stop her—I mean, stop the Necromancers. But you've got to let me out of here and help me find my friends."

"I know where your friends are being held," Marguerite said. "And I... oh..." she stopped, biting her lip, the tears in her eyes brimming over and spilling down her cheeks. "What have I done? I'm going to be in such trouble."

"What is it?" I asked her. "What is it you've done? I can help you. We'll figure it out together if you'll just tell me."

"I... I brought you these," Marguerite answered. And she reached into the pocket of her dress and pulled out the three Keys of the Reckoning.

I gasped. Even Milo, who had only moments before even learned of the existence of the keys, threw his hands up over his mouth as he realized what he was looking at. I took a very cautious step forward, hardly daring to believe my eyes.

"Marguerite... how did you get your hands on those?" I squeaked.

Marguerite shrugged. "It was very simple. I know the codes to the vaults. She often sends me to fetch things for her if she does not want to fetch them herself, but I have never opened one without her permission. After you were escorted out, I asked Simone to please explain what was happening."

"And did she?" I asked, when Marguerite did not go on.

Marguerite's face twisted strangely, as though she was fighting against feelings she had never felt before—or at the very least, had never allowed herself to acknowledge. "She... she told me to stop crying and go to my chambers. And to speak of this to no one. And then she left with the Necromancer and I was alone."

"I... I'm sorry she treated you that way, Marguerite," I said quietly.

Marguerite's head snapped up, a defiant gleam in her eye. "She is not herself. She is hoodwinked."

"Yes, of course," I said quickly.

"But I knew I must do something," Marguerite said. "I waited until I was sure she was gone. And then I took the keys from the safe. I… don't think my sister should have them. Not until she… until she comes back to her senses. Can… can you take them? I think you are meant to have them." She suddenly looked terrified at the thought of having the keys in her possession a moment longer and practically threw them at me. I fumbled awkwardly but managed to hang on to them, pulling all three chains around my neck and tucking them down the front of my sweater.

"Thank you, Marguerite," I said, gripping the keys gratefully through the fabric. "You've done the right thing, I promise."

Marguerite did not reply but wiped the tears from her face with the backs of her hands.

"Jess, we're wasting time," Milo said, floating up alongside me and speaking into my ear. "Do you think we can trust her to help find the others?"

"I don't think we've got a choice," I replied, and addressed Marguerite again. "Marguerite, we need your help."

"I don't know," Marguerite replied, wringing her hands now, her nerves clearly mounting.

"Please, I'm begging you. We've got to find my friends, the ones I came with. My sister and the High Priestess of the Northern Clans are here too, and they're being detained. Please, can you help me to get them out? There's no telling what the Necromancers will do to us if you don't help us."

Marguerite's face twisted in an agony of doubt. And then suddenly, she seemed to come to a decision. She took a deep breath, and said, "Very well. Follow me and keep very quiet."

The cellblock in which I had been imprisoned seemed completely deserted. I heard no moans or clinking from the other cells, no cries for mercy or freedom. And because there were no other prisoners, there were no other guards. We slipped from one cellblock up a staircase to a second without encountering a single person except for the occasional spirit, each of whom drifted past with the same empty, expressionless demeanor as the others we had encountered, taking as little notice of us as they did of each other.

Marguerite crept along until we reached the very last stretch of cells before the wall curved and disappeared up another flight of stairs. I could hear shifting and coughing in the cell closest to us, and stretched up onto my tiptoes to see Catriona sitting inside it.

"Cat!"

"Jess! Oh my God, how did you... what in the bollocking blazes is going on?" she cried, jumping to her feet at the sound of my voice.

"Jess?"

"Did you say Jess? Is Jess out there?"

The voices echoed from the other cells as Marguerite scurried around and opened them with her ring of keys. One by one, Catriona, Ileana, and Annabelle stumbled frantically from their cells, falling upon me in a torrent of questions.

"What happened to you?"

"The moment you were gone, the Caomhnóir arrived and arrested us!"

"No explanations! Just told us we had to come with them."

Finn was the last to be released. He opened his mouth, probably to ask me if I was okay, but instead, his eyes fell on Milo and he gasped.

"Milo! What are you doing here? Jess, how did you...?" He couldn't even finish his question. He was now staring at Marguerite in absolute bewilderment.

"We can answer all these questions when we get somewhere secure," I said. "Marguerite, is there such a place? Can you take us somewhere in the castle where we won't be discovered?"

Marguerite bit her lip and considered this a moment, then nodded. "My chambers. No one will look for you there," she said. "But we must move quickly."

"What about Hannah and Celeste?" Milo piped up. "We can't leave them locked up either."

Marguerite whimpered, as though she was already regretting her decision to help us. "Very well. You will go to my chambers and wait for me there. I will go release the others and bring them along with me as quickly as I can."

"But how will we find your chambers?" I asked. "None of us have ever..."

Marguerite raised a hand to cut me off. "I shall enlist one of the spirits to guide you there."

"The spirits?" Milo asked, looking doubtful. "Are you sure..."

But Marguerite was already hurrying toward the nearest staircase and beginning to climb it. She turned and waved frantically to us. "Come along! *Rapidement!* We could be discovered at any moment, don't you see, and then all will be lost!"

We all looked at each other before turning and following. Marguerite led us down what could only be described as a backroad route through the castle. None of the halls we traversed were like the wide marble ones we had walked through while on the way to my audience with Simone. They were narrow and dark, with obscure entrances through tapestries and behind portraits that swung outward on hinges like doors. Marguerite was like a little mouse who had burrowed into the walls and created her own secret labyrinth she could traverse safely without ever encountering a soul. Well, at least not a living soul.

After the third portrait we stepped through, we encountered the spirit of a young girl dressed in a maid's uniform. She couldn't have been more than eleven or twelve when she passed. Her cheeks and eyes were hollow and her arms thin as twigs. She was struggling under the weight of a spectral bucket.

"You, there, come here," Marguerite said, in an imperious tone that did not at all suit her. It was as though she was doing a poor impersonation of her sister. It worked, however; the spirit halted at once, staggered back toward her, eyes empty, expression vacant.

"Take these visitors to my quarters and do not tell anyone you have seen them," Marguerite said. "Take the servants' routes. Avoid all Guardians."

The girl did not reply or indeed acknowledge that she had even heard Marguerite's words, but turned at once and floated in the direction we had been traveling when we had come upon her.

Marguerite looked at us all in surprise that we were still standing there. "Go on, now! What are you waiting for?"

"What's wrong with her?" Milo cried, blurting out what the rest of us were thinking. "Why are all the spirits here so... empty?"

Marguerite looked genuinely puzzled. "They serve the High Priestess," she said.

"Yeah, Fairhaven has spirits that serve the High Priestess, too," he said. "But they aren't like... like *this*." He gestured to the girl, who had paused in her drifting down the hallway and was now completely stationary, waiting for us to follow. "Are... are they Blind Summoners, or something?"

Marguerite stared blankly at <u>him.</u> "Blind what?"

"Never mind," Milo muttered.

"I'm sorry, but you really must go. Make haste, please. I will endeavor to bring the others to you, if I can," Marguerite said, shooing us along until we were all trotting behind the spirit of the maid.

The girl, who surely had been familiar with the discreet servants' paths in her lifetime, continued through the obscure passages and narrow staircases, until, at last, we emerged at the top of a rickety wooden staircase. We climbed it in near-total darkness, then pulled aside a tapestry and found ourselves staring at a stretch of wall that contained two busts of beautiful women set in niches and, between them, a door.

The girl did not speak to us, or even acknowledge that she remembered we were there, but she came to a stop with her nose about an inch from the door and froze, as though waiting for further instruction.

"I... I think that must be Marguerite's room," I said when no one else spoke. "Let's just get in there quickly before we're discovered."

But Finn, clearly taking nothing for granted, would not simply allow us to enter the room. Signaling for us all to stand back, he approached the door and listened intently with his ear against the wood. Then he eased the door open and slipped past the ghost of the maid, and went inside. We all waited, breath held, until he poked his head back out and gave us the all-clear that it was safe to enter.

The chamber was not the same as the cold, peerless marble rooms down below. This room was warm and comfortable, with rich silks adorning the windows and a massive four-poster bed in the corner. Shelf upon shelf of books filled the walls, and there was a gold-framed oil painting hanging in pride of place over the fireplace: two little blonde-plaited girls in matching blue satin dresses, with white gloves and white buttoned boots, holding hands with each other and gazing imperiously out over the room. One held a book in her free hand; the other, a parasol.

The door safely shut behind us, Finn sank into the nearest chair, ran his shaking hands through his hair and said to me, "Okay, now can you please tell us what the bloody hell is going on?"

Everyone listened raptly as I explained, in as much detail as I could recall, my meeting with Simone, the unexpected arrival of

Charlie Wright, my reunion with Milo, and Marguerite's shocking decision to free us all. Aside from a violent torrent of expletives from Catriona when I explained about Charlie, no one spoke a word or interrupted me until I had talked myself out. A deeply uneasy silence followed the conclusion of my story. Ileana was the first to break it.

"If the High Priestess of the International High Council has fallen to the whims of the Necromancers, there is no hope for the rest of us to get out of this alive," she said. "This castle is the most secure of fortresses. There is no chance that we will escape the place. We are simply delaying the inevitable by waiting here."

"Well, sure, with *that* attitude," Milo muttered under his breath, so that only I could hear him. I couldn't help but trade a tiny smirk with him.

"I wouldn't say that just yet," Finn said. "After all, Marguerite has gotten us this far, hasn't she, and that should have been impossible. I'd written us off the moment we'd been locked up downstairs, if I'm honest, but here we are, free—at least for the moment. It is clear that Marguerite knows as much about this castle as anyone alive. We ought to take any help she can give us."

"She's also half-mad with adoration for her sister," Catriona said. "So, we must be careful about how we discuss Simone in her presence. If she thinks we've turned on Simone as much as the Necromancers, she'll be running for sister dearest before we can correct ourselves."

I nodded. "Cat has a point. Marguerite really believes her sister to be hoodwinked or under some kind of spell or something. We have to help support that delusion if we want to keep Marguerite on our side. We have to make it sound like we want to help her sister as much as anything else, even if what we really want to do is bitch-slap the Leeched beauty right off her face."

"We'll need to stay clear of the ghosts as well," Annabelle added. "It doesn't matter when they're just wandering around all empty, but once they get the orders to search for us, there will be no reasoning with them."

"And there's no doubt the whole lot of them will be used like an army once it's discovered we're gone," Finn agreed. He made a quick circuit of the room, checking all the doorways and windows.

"This room is thoroughly Warded, at any rate; so for the moment, I don't think we need to worry about spirits finding us."

"Also, it seems they follow orders from Marguerite, not just Simone," Catriona said. "But I can't imagine that anything Marguerite says can override what her sister may demand of them."

"Is that spirit she ordered to bring us here still just waiting outside the room?" I asked suddenly. "It would be a bit of a giveaway, don't you think, a spirit just standing out there staring at the door?"

Finn ran a hand through his hair again. "Blast it, you're right. Do you suppose there's any way to—"

He was halfway to the door when it burst open and Marguerite, Hannah, and Celeste hurried through it. Marguerite murmured something to the spirit still waiting outside, and we saw the girl vanish on the spot as Marguerite closed and bolted the door behind her. Hannah did not stop, but pelted straight across the room and threw herself at me, nearly knocking me flat.

"Oh, Jess, thank goodness, thank *goodness,* I thought I'd never... I thought you..." she couldn't complete the thought, her words swallowed up in a great heaving sob. I wrapped my arms around her and allowed myself a moment to bask in the completeness of being near her. Breathing in her scent was like the first breath of fresh air after being underwater. Finally, she pulled back and looked at me, placing her hands on my face like she was trying to memorize me with her fingertips. "I'm so sorry. I didn't dare use the connection. I was afraid that if you knew I was here, you would do something stupid and reckless to get to me."

I grinned at her. "Who, me? Making stupid and reckless decisions? You must have me confused with your other twin."

She gave a laugh that almost immediately became a sob and buried her face in my neck again. I looked up at Celeste, who had sunk down into a chair and was trying to catch her breath.

"Celeste, I'm sorry," I said at once. "I'm sorry I didn't tell you. Please understand that I was only trying to do what Agnes told me to do."

Celeste looked up at me, and though her expression was still harried and tense, she nodded. "I won't pretend that I'm happy about it," she said, "but I do understand. And, to be frank, I gave you no cause to trust me. It must have seemed that I was very eager to hang on to my power, the way I refused to bring the news of the Sentinel to Havre des Gardiennes."

"Well, yeah, kind of," I said with a sheepish shrug. "I just knew that the more important, the more invested a Durupinen was, the less likely they'd be to believe me or want to help. I couldn't be sure of anyone's response. I think Agnes knew that, and I think that's why they created the keys and kept them so secret."

"They were wise to do so," Celeste said. "Though, it seems they put too much trust in the highest among us. Is it true what Marguerite has told us, about the Necromancers?"

"Yes," I said, looking at Marguerite and nodding. "Simone has been... compromised. We don't know exactly what the Necromancers have said to her or done to her, but she took the keys and locked them away, and has chosen to ignore the warnings about the Reckoning."

Finn stepped forward, giving Celeste a meaningful look. "Marguerite loves her sister very much, and she is quite sure that Simone would never do such a thing unless she had been tricked or was under extreme duress. We quite agree, don't we?"

Celeste, thank God, was extremely quick on the uptake. She adopted a very solemn expression and nodded sympathetically at Marguerite. "Oh yes, certainly. Whatever the Necromancers have done to Simone, she cannot be held responsible for this terrible turn of events."

Marguerite looked at us all with tears in her eyes, nodding gratefully. "Yes, indeed. Her goodness and her wisdom shall not be impugned. She is without compare in her commitment to the spirit world. All she is and all she does is in service to our sacred gift."

We all made a show of agreeing with her, some of us more successfully than others—Ileana's face was stony as she nodded along, and Catriona looked like she would quite like to punch something, but these details slipped past Marguerite unnoticed.

"So, what do we do now?" Hannah asked, when Marguerite seemed sufficiently placated. "We can't just stay here. It's only a matter of time before it's discovered that we've escaped—they may already know."

"They will not look for you here," Marguerite said, sounding surer of this fact than anything I had heard her say since we'd arrived.

Finn looked skeptical. "Surely they will look for us everywhere," he said gently.

"Not in my chambers," Marguerite said. "They will not conceive of my helping you."

"Why not?" Catriona asked.

"Because I have never disobeyed my sister," Marguerite said, her mouth twitching with emotion. "She believes me incapable of it. They will not look for you here."

"But even if that's true, we can't stay here indefinitely," I said. "We'll have to leave at some point. And even if, by some miracle, we manage to get out of here, I still don't know what to do with these." I held up the three keys now hanging around my neck. "We can't restore the Gateways or save the Sentinels unless we figure it out, and Simone is the only one who knows."

"No, she's not. I know what you must do," Marguerite said, almost casually.

My mouth fell open. "You... you do?"

"Oh, yes. You must bring the keys to the Geatgrima," Marguerite said, so quietly that I wasn't even sure she had spoken at first. "The three Keys of the Reckoning must be brought to the Geatgrima at the heart of Havre des Gardiennes. There, they can be used to reveal the counter-Casting that will restore the Gateways to their rightful place," Marguerite said, sounding as though she was carefully reciting something she had memorized.

"How... how do you know that?" I asked breathlessly.

Marguerite wrung her hands anxiously, as though afraid she had already said too much. "Simone explained it to the Necromancer while I was still in the room. She told him that this was why the keys needed to be destroyed—that the Reckoning could never come to pass without them. She... she said they ought to thank you for gathering them together for her."

"Do you know what we're supposed to do with the keys if we get them to the Geatgrima?" I whispered.

"No. She did not elaborate further than that," Marguerite said.

I looked at Finn, whose mouth was hanging open. Everyone was just staring wordlessly at Marguerite, who was looking rather alarmed with herself now.

"Marguerite, can you... do you think there's any chance that you could get us to the Geatgrima safely, without being discovered?" I asked.

Marguerite looked terrified at the very thought. "Oh, I... I don't know..."

"It's the only way, Marguerite," I said, kneeling beside her and taking her hand—it was nearly as cold as her sister's. "If we don't find a way to bring about the Reckoning, your sister will remain in the Necromancers' clutches."

Celeste stood up. "I have known your sister for many years, Marguerite. She has been a great defender of the Durupinen. She has made many wise and judicious decisions that have upheld the great mission of our sisterhood. You know this."

"Yes," Marguerite said, tears springing into her eyes. "Yes, I do."

Celeste nodded sagely and went on, "She would not want this to be her legacy—her gift, meant to be a great light in the world, twisted to terrible darkness. You must help us, Marguerite. You must help us protect your sister and her reputation from this great travesty. Say you'll do it. Say you'll try. For Simone."

For a moment, it seemed that Marguerite's sorrow for her sister would consume her. And then, suddenly, whatever fount of courage she had discovered within herself to help us in the first place buoyed her yet again. She met Celeste's eye with a look of determination and nodded. "Yes. Yes, I will try to help you. For Simone."

"Thank you," Celeste said. "Thank you, Marguerite. And I know that your sister will thank you, too."

I gave Celeste a grateful smile and turned to the group at large. "Well, then. We need to figure out how we're going to do this."

"It's only the most secure and heavily guarded place in the Durupinen world, should be a cakewalk," Milo said with a slightly manic laugh.

Marguerite stared at him with a curious expression, as though she had never seen anything quite like him before—which, judging by the behavior of the spirits that haunted the halls of Havre des Gardiennes, she likely hadn't. I patted Marguerite's hand to regain her attention.

"We will defer to you, Marguerite. We are all strangers here. We do not know the castle or its defenses. Surely you know the safest route to the Geatgrima."

Marguerite brought her trembling hands to her face, cupping her cheeks and falling into deep consideration. "Yes," she said at last. "Yes, I believe I know a route we can take to the Geatgrima where we will meet no opposition from the Caomhnóir. But there will be spirits along the way, and they will surely have been ordered to search for you. I do not think we can avoid them."

"I may be able to help with that," Hannah said, speaking up for the first time. "I am a Caller, after all."

"Of course!" Milo cried, his face breaking into a relieved smile. "If Hannah Calls the spirits, they'll do whatever she asks!"

Celeste raised a cautious hand. "There is something you must understand about the spirits here at Havre des Gardiennes. They are not simply obedient to the High Priestess. They are controlled by her."

"Yeah, we noticed something wasn't quite right with them," Finn said, arms folded. "We thought they might even be Blind Summoners, the work of the Necromancers, like at Skye Príosún during the coup."

But Celeste shook her head. "No, but you're not far off. The spirits here have been in the High Priestess' control for many years." Here, Celeste threw a cautious look at Marguerite, and it was clear that she was choosing her words very carefully. "Finvarra was most concerned about the situation, and had hoped to address it with the leadership of the various clans before she passed away. The High Priestess has used the spirits to... maintain her fitness for her duties over the duration of her reign."

Based on everyone's expressions, we all understood this to mean Leeching. Catriona, however, frowned. "That doesn't make sense, though," she said. "One can only use spirits who are Crossing for... *that* purpose." She threw a cursory smile at Marguerite.

"It is my understanding that the High Priestess siphons the energy she needs and then closes the Gateway, so that the spirits must remain behind in their depleted state. Is that correct, Marguerite?" Celeste replied, tacking on the last question in a casual, curious voice, as though merely hoping to clarify the point.

Marguerite nodded. "In this way, the spirits can serve their High Priestess many times," she said <u>eagerly</u>. "It is a great honor, to be in her service. They sustain her so that she can carry out the great responsibility of overseeing the balance between the spirit and living worlds." She said the words like a mantra she had been taught, like a prayer.

All around the room, the rest of us were trying to mask our absolute horror at what we had just learned. To Leech from a spirit once, as it Crossed, was despicable enough; but to do so many times, taking more and more of the spirit into oneself while denying them their right to ever Cross and attain the peace that awaited them beyond the Aether? I was quite literally nauseous at the thought. Hannah's eyes, as she dropped them to the ground, were full of tears. And it was clear from Marguerite's youthful, if fragile appearance that she, too, had benefitted from the process many times, if only tangentially. I understood now, at least, why both women were so cold to the touch; they were sustained on such a large amount of spirit energy that they were barely human anymore.

"Was... was that why I was drawn within the walls of the castle when I approached?" Milo asked, his tone casual but his voice a bit shaky. "Is there a Casting on the place to draw spirits in so that the High Priestess doesn't run out of... supplies?"

Marguerite nodded, smiling pleasantly. "Simone's resources must never be in danger of running dry. She is too important to the spirit world."

Milo's form actually paled at her words, so deep was his horror; but he managed a small smile. "Excellent. Thanks for clearing that up."

Catriona was the first to recuperate from this new revelation. "And once the spirits have... uh... *served* their mistress... they no longer have free will, is that right? They are vessels to her will instead, which means that they obey her orders exclusively?"

"Well, they will also obey me, but not in defiance of Simone. At least, I do not think they will. I must admit, I have never given them an order that directly contradicts what my sister has demanded of them. Most of the orders I give them are on her say-so," Marguerite said, looking quite frightened at the very thought of disrupting the chain of command.

"But the spirits at the *príosún*," Catriona pressed, turning back to

Hannah, "they were little more than vessels for Necromancer commands, and you were still able to Call them."

"Yes, but not on my own. There were too many of them, and they were harder to reach, Habitating in Caomhnóir bodies. Lucida had to help me to... wait, where is Lucida?" Hannah asked, looking around at the sudden realization of Lucida's absence.

Catriona's face turned ashen. The answer barely escaped her tightly closed lips. "Dead. Necromancers."

Hannah gasped and threw her hand up over her mouth. "Oh... I had no idea. I... I'm so... oh my *God*..."

"The point," Catriona said, talking over her in a trembling voice, "is that she is not here to help you. You'll have to do it on your own."

Hannah dropped her hand, looking terrified. "I... I don't know if I can."

"We may not have a choice," I told her gently. "If we come across a spirit on our way to the Geatgrima, you're going to have to try."

"What about our Caomhnóir?" Celeste asked, looking at Marguerite. "Do you think there's any chance of you freeing them, like you did us?"

Marguerite shook her head. "There I cannot help you. They have been detained not in the dungeons, but in the Caomhnóir barracks. I cannot possibly enter those quarters without drawing suspicion onto myself."

Celeste's face fell. It was clear she was hoping to have the added protection of Seamus' Guardian skills. Hannah gave a sniff and I squeezed her hand. I knew that she was worried about Kiernan.

"Seamus and Kiernan can look out for themselves," I reminded her. "They'll be fine." I could not promise this, and so I knew the words rang hollow, but I had to say something to dull the spark of fear that had kindled in her eyes.

"If, by some miracle, we are able to reach the Geatgrima without being caught, how will we know what to do with the keys?" Annabelle asked. "And if we figure that out, if we somehow manage to get our hands on the counter-Casting, how will we know what we need to perform it?"

I shook my head. "There's no way to know the answer to these questions. We're going to have to improvise."

———

"This is starting to sound like a suicide mission," Catriona said bluntly.

"What choice do we have?" I asked. "Either we attempt to secure the counter-Casting, or we give up. We concede the Necromancers have won and we relinquish our control to them."

"Those aren't our only options," Finn said. "We could try to escape with the keys and alert the other clans. If we amass our collected armies at the gates of Havre des Gardiennes..."

"Then hundreds will die needlessly," I said. "Finn, we'll never get back in, let alone get anywhere near that Geatgrima, and you know it. We won't get another chance like this."

I knew he didn't want to admit it, but Finn couldn't argue with me, not this time. I looked around the room. Every face wore the same grim expression of determination; every head was nodding. I didn't even need to ask out loud. I knew we were all in, and fuck the consequences.

I turned back to Marguerite. "I guess that's settled then. Tell us what we need to do to reach the Geatgrima."

GIFT OF THE DARKNESS

T HE MOON WAS HIGH IN THE SKY. I glimpsed it when I dared take the tiniest of peeks out through the curtain from Marguerite's window. It had been hours since Marguerite had agreed to lead us out to the Geatgrima, and without a clock, the wait had been disorienting. Only by occasional checks at the window could we mark the passage of time, first by the position of the sun and, now, by the slow ascension of the moon.

We had agreed, grudgingly, that the best course of action was to wait until the middle of the night to make our way to the Geatgrima. It was agony to wait, but it made sense, strategically. In the first place, laying low would be the last thing anyone who was searching for us would expect; they would expect that we would try to get as far from the castle as we could as quickly as we could. This assumption seemed to be working in our favor. As the day wore on, we heard Caomhnóir running the halls, calling out orders and banging down doors. We saw groups of them fanning out over the grounds below, knowing damn well they were searching for us. And just as Marguerite had said, not a single one of the ghosts or Guardians scouring the castle for us even once disturbed the peace of her chambers. It was exactly as she said: no one could conceive of the idea that Marguerite de Chastenay, devoted shadow to her sister, would ever dream of rebellion. It was particularly satisfying to watch, even if it brought nothing but anxiety and doubt to Marguerite herself, whom we regularly reminded that she was rebelling for the good of her beloved sister, and for no other reason.

The most nerve-wracking period of the day was when Marguerite had to leave to attend to her sister as she usually did. No one asked what these duties might be—it was sufficient to know that she was required to be by her sister's side for hours at a time, and that she needed to meet that expectation or subject herself to scrutiny.

"She's ratting us out," Catriona had whispered after nearly four hours of dwelling in the gaping emptiness of Marguerite's absence.

"The Caomhnóir are going to break that door down at any moment and arrest us all."

Celeste shook her head. "I don't think so. The longer she observes her sister in the company of Necromancers, the more confident she will be that she's doing the right thing."

"We'd better hope so," Catriona replied. "But if you ask me, Marguerite is even more susceptible to suggestion than her sister. I wouldn't be surprised if the Necromancers had her converted by tea time."

"I guess it's a good thing no one *did* ask you, then, isn't it?" I snapped at her, just barely managing to keep my tone hushed. I had enough fear and doubt about our decision without Catriona descending upon it like a proverbial rain cloud. Part of me regretted being short with her, remembering what she'd just been through, but not enough to take it back. We'd made our choice, and now we all needed to commit to it, and I wasn't going to tolerate dissension in the ranks. Luckily, Catriona seemed to take my hint and kept her dark predictions to herself after that.

When Marguerite arrived at her room again well after nightfall, she looked pale and anxious. "They know you're gone. The Caomhnóir have searched the castle and are now concentrating on the grounds and fanning out into the surrounding mountains. I've never seen Simone so angry." She shuddered and gave a loud sniff. "She hasn't yet discovered that the keys are missing, however. It hasn't occurred to her that anyone could open the safe. Her concern at this point is that you will be alerting the other clans to the fact that Necromancers have infiltrated Havre des Gardiennes. She is desperate to track you all down before you are able to do so."

Ileana cackled softly to herself. Celeste gave her a warning look before replying to Marguerite. "And you are quite sure they have no suspicions as to your role in our escape?"

Marguerite shook her head. "Not one. Simone has... has barely spoken to me all day. She is deep in conference with the Necromancer."

"Have you been able to glean any more information about what the Necromancers might be planning?" Finn asked. His tone was gentle, but I could hear the intensity behind it.

Marguerite shrugged, looking tearful. "I have caught only snatches of their conversation as Simone has ordered me in and out.

But from what I have gathered, he is planning to concentrate his attack upon Fairhaven. That is the Gateway he wants to bring under Necromancer control. He said something about… about how Neil would have wanted it that way."

She gazed at me curiously, looking, perhaps, for an explanation, but I was too angry to reply. Just the idea of Neil Caddigan's havoc still being wreaked in this world, when he himself had left it, was enough to make my blood boil, and I wasn't the only one. The atmosphere all around the room had shifted tangibly at the mention of his name. There was not a single person there who didn't know exactly what chaos he had wrought, and who hadn't been personally affected by it.

"One thing did occur to me that will help us, I think," Marguerite said when it was clear I had no intentions of elaborating on the nightmare that was Neil Caddigan. "She asked me to order the ghosts in the servant's quarters to fan out and search the lower passages. We need to use one of those passages to reach the Geatgrima, so I made sure, when I gave them their orders, to steer them clear of the area."

Finn perked up at this. "That's excellent news. Well done, Marguerite."

"It does not guarantee us safe passage," Marguerite said cautiously, though she allowed herself a small smile. "But it does put one possibility of discovery to rest."

We agreed to set out at 2:00 AM. This, Marguerite said, was when the Caomhnóir would enact a shift change, meaning many passages would be briefly unpatrolled as reports were given and new Guardians were updated by the previous shift. With a little bit of luck, Marguerite said, we might be able to reach the courtyard in which the Geatgrima stood. Once we arrived though, all bets were off.

I knew I ought to try to get just an hour or two of sleep, but my body and brain refused to settle. Visions of Necromancer attacks, of charging Caomhnóir, of Charlie Wright's leering face, of Lucida lying lifeless on the forest floor, chased each other behind my eyelids until I gave up trying to keep them closed. Instead, I sat up with Hannah curled against my side dozing fitfully, Milo pressing his cooling, calming presence against her on the other side whenever her sleep seemed to dive down into nightmares. We looked at each other over the top of her curls.

"Does any of this make you wonder if the Necromancers are right?" I asked him suddenly, unaware that the question was going to come out of my mouth.

Milo frowned at me. "Have you lost your damn mind?"

"No, I'm serious. I mean, I always thought of the Necromancers as the bad guys, you know? It was all so black-and-white in my brain. They were the villains. We were the good guys. Now it all just seems so... grey."

"Life's always more complicated than good guys and bad guys," Milo pointed out.

"I know. It sucks."

"Yeah."

"It's just... they were right, weren't they? We shouldn't have been controlling the Gateways. All along, I had never doubted they were wrong until now."

"Okay, so the Durupinen fucked up," Milo said with a sigh. "They got greedy. But the original intention was good—all you've ever wanted to do was protect the Gateways—protect the spirits. And yeah, some lost that along the way, but you never have. Most of you never have. And now you're setting things right. The Necromancers have only ever wanted the Gateways for themselves."

"I guess. This is all just so messed up. I still don't know how we're going to get out of this. And I've dragged you all into it."

"You didn't drag us. We jumped in the backseat of this wild ride with a road trip playlist and a bag of snacks. We're here because we want to be, sweetness."

"I know, but... what if something..." My voice trailed away, and I looked helplessly down at Hannah.

"I won't let anything happen to her tonight," he whispered.

"I know," I said, taking a deep breath. "And neither will I."

"I know."

I smiled gratefully at him. "Whatever happens, Milo, I want you to know something."

A shiver passed over his face. "Yeah? What's that?"

"You'll always be the most annoying ghost I've ever met."

He grinned. "Well, if we're trading heartfelt sentiments, I've got one for you, too."

"Lay it on me, Spirit Guide."

"If all this Reckoning shit goes down and we're... like... un-Bound, or whatever... I will always find a way to let you know when you're being an emo fashion disaster."

I snorted so loudly that Hannah stirred in her sleep. "I'm counting on it," I told him.

"It must be nearly time," Celeste said, standing up from where she and Ileana had been talking quietly by the fireplace. "We'd best prepare to go."

Annabelle, looking drowsy, shook her head and rubbed her eyes as she jumped to her feet. Catriona, who had been unable to settle to anything but pacing, made her way across the room to stand beside Celeste. Finn, who had been checking the window every few minutes for the last hour, set his face in an expression of grim determination and strode over to the door, where he stood at near-attention. Marguerite rose from her bed, where she had been sitting and staring at the painting of her and her sister. Her complexion was pale with fear, but her lips were set in a thin line and she seemed resolved. She fished a locket on a fine golden chain out of her bodice and clicked the little door open, consulting the watch face that lay concealed within.

"Very well," she said. "I will gather what I can from the scene below, and we will make our way out to the Geatgrima."

She strode over to the window and pulled back the curtain just as I had done, to gaze out upon the many turrets, towers, bridges, courtyards, and gardens that comprised the view within the walls of Havre des Gardiennes. As we watched her, her eyes probed around anxiously and then fixed suddenly on a single point. Her body went stiff, her expression rigid. Her hand, upon the fold of silk curtain, tightened so that her knuckles went white.

I stood up, my heart in my throat. "Marguerite? What is it? What do you see?"

Marguerite did not reply. She gave no indication at all that she had heard me.

I flashed a panicked look at Finn, who stepped forward. "Marguerite? What's wrong?"

Marguerite remained motionless, unresponsive, bleached to a ghostly pallor in the strip of moonlight revealed through the curtain.

"What's happening?" Annabelle asked, her voice sharp.

Catriona was not waiting to be told. She walked straight up to Marguerite and stood right beside her, leaning in to examine her face. Then she raised a hand and waved it slowly back and forth in front of Marguerite's eyes. The woman remained frozen.

"She's gone into some kind of fit," Catriona said. "A trance, or... or something."

I hurried across the room to stand on Marguerite's other side. Catriona reached out as though to shake the woman by the shoulders, but I knocked her hand away. "Don't touch her," I ordered, and Catriona quickly dropped her hand to her side.

I turned, following the direction of Marguerite's gaze and my eyes fell upon a distant courtyard and there, just visible above the walls that enclosed it, was the unmistakable curve of a stone archway...

"This can't be happening," I whispered. "Oh my God. Not now."

"What is it?" Catriona hissed. "What's happened?"

But before I could answer, Marguerite's body became animated with a manic energy. Utterly oblivious to the more than half dozen people now staring at her in alarm, she turned on her heel and flew to the trunk at the base of her bed. She flung it open, rummaged around for a moment, and then pulled a magnificent fur-lined cloak from the trunk and draped it around her shoulders, fastening the gold clasp under her chin and tugging the hood up over her head. Then she slammed the trunk shut, snatched a small oil lamp from her bedside table, and hurried toward her door.

"Follow her! Follow her, everyone! Now!" I cried, crossing the room and pulling Hannah up from the chaise as I passed her.

"Why? What's happening?" she gasped.

"Wait, what? Are we leaving? Now?" Milo asked.

Celeste hesitated. "Jessica, we can't follow her if she's—"

"She's the last Sentinel!" I cried, no longer bothering to keep my voice down. "She's headed for the Geatgrima! This is it, we won't get another chance! Now, come *on!*"

Questions were flying at the back of my head, but I didn't stop to answer them as I pelted full speed out the door, following the trailing hem of Marguerite's cloak which was now whipping out of sight around the door frame.

By the grace of God, the corridor outside her room was deserted, for Marguerite was being neither cautious, nor observant. She looked neither right nor left before setting off with more purpose and confidence than she had ever shown while in possession of her faculties. She lifted the tapestry at the end of the hall and slipped through it, leaving the rest of us to fumble our way through as it swung closed again behind her.

We slipped down a maze of dark, narrow corridors, similar to the ones that we had taken from the dungeons. I allowed myself a temporary moment of relief—even though she was in the thrall of the Geatgrima now, at least Marguerite seemed to be keeping to obscure back passages to arrive at her destination. Perhaps the Geatgrima itself knew how crucial it was for its new Sentinel to reach her goal—perhaps it felt the inevitability of its own demise without her. The passages seemed to go on for miles—sloping downward, rising in spiraled staircases, connecting through portraits and bookcases and once, through a fireplace that spun in place to reveal a small office that led to yet another dank corridor. Marguerite seemed unaffected by the speed of our trip through the forgotten bowels of the castle. She plowed relentlessly on even as we stumbled and panted in her wake, unable to catch our breath as we tripped along in the gloomy half-darkness. Ileana was falling further and further behind, with Annabelle struggling to pull her along, but I knew that if we didn't reach the courtyard soon, we would be unable to keep pace.

Just then, Marguerite burst through a tapestry in front of us and we were all dazzled by the sudden brightness. We had arrived not in another secret servants' passage, but a wide octagonal room filled with exotic plants surrounded by floor to ceiling windows and skylights—a conservatory of sorts. Through the glass doors, I could see the Geatgrima looming up out of the star-strewn courtyard beyond. We'd made it.

But we were no longer alone. A half dozen spirits within the conservatory turned at the sound of our arrival and bore down upon us, blank expressions intent on our capture. A volley of shouts from our left alerted us that three Caomhnóir had also spotted us, and had begun a mad dash toward us from an adjoining greenhouse.

A whoosh of raw energy blew past me from behind, and all at once the spirits froze in midair, mere feet from us. I whipped around to see Hannah, eyes bright like stars, her hand outstretched, holding the spirits at bay with the sheer force of her gift. Whatever control

Simone had over them, Hannah's Calling had shattered it as easily as glass. Without speaking a word aloud, she flung her hand in the direction of the approaching Caomhnóir, sending the spirits like projectiles toward the men, who did not even have time to shout before they were knocked back off their feet and flung against the far wall by the spirits. They slid down to the ground where they lay in a crumpled heap, unmoving.

"Holy shit!" Milo cursed under his breath before breaking into a hysterical laugh. Having dispatched the approaching Caomhnóir, the spirits floated back toward Hannah and hung in midair, evidently awaiting her next command.

Hannah shook her head as though to clear it and stared over at me, her expression slightly frightened. "That was almost too easy. They... they have no will at all. No power of their own," she gasped.

"Jess! Come on! It's Marguerite!" Finn's voice called out, and I spun back around to see that Marguerite had not waited for the spirits to be subdued, but had run straight through the conservatory doors and out into the courtyard. I could see her blonde hair streaming out behind her like the tail of a comet as she raced to answer the Geatgrima's summons at last.

We all ran after her, the spirits trailing along behind Hannah like the obedient minions they now were. But we'd barely made it halfway across the courtyard when Marguerite reached the dais, threw back the hood of her cloak, and opened her arms in a triumphant gesture of welcome. Like a bolt of lightning, the power of the Gateway crackled from her fingertips, seeped from the tendrils of hair blowing around her face, bled across the dais from the tips of her toes, crawled and roiled and drifted from every part of her like a living thing toward the Geatgrima, which likewise seemed to be reaching for Marguerite, drawing her in to an ancient embrace.

As we all looked on in horror, several more Caomhnóir entered the courtyard from the far side. One of them, realizing that it was Marguerite upon the dais, gave a shout and ran forward.

"No! Don't! You mustn't touch her!" I shrieked, but I was too late. The man leapt up the steps of the dais and grabbed ahold of Marguerite's arm, clearly preparing to pull her back from the Geatgrima. Instead, he was catapulted into the air in a shower of sparks. His body slammed into a pillar and crumpled to the ground like a ragdoll.

The other Caomhnóir, at least, had learned from their colleague's mistake. They paced the perimeter of the dais warily, calling orders to each other, clearly at a loss for what to do.

"Fetch the High Priestess!" one of them shouted at last, and two of his fellows hightailed it in the direction of the main entrance.

The remaining Caomhnóir seemed to realize at the same moment that a group of escaped prisoners were also in the courtyard, and started for us, but Hannah sent the spirits pelting at them. The men gave cries of alarm and tried to fend the spirits off, but to no avail. Before they could so much as reach for their Casting bags, the spirits had soared directly into their bodies and taken them over like marionettes. At Hannah's command, the Caomhnóir threw their weapons and Casting bags aside, dropped to the ground, and lay motionless with their hands on the backs of their heads like hostages. Catriona and Finn hurried forward and collected the weaponry, arming themselves before tossing knives, Casting bags, and staves to the rest of us. I caught the knife Catriona sent my way and stared blankly down at it before handing it off to Ileana, who grinned at me and spun it deftly in her hand before tucking it into her belt. She would clearly be handier with the thing than I would ever be. I took an extra Casting bag with relief and tied it around my waist.

Milo shouted, "The keys, Jess! Get to the Geatgrima and see if you can—"

But before I could so much as reach for the keys around my neck, the courtyard flooded with people. Simone, a contingent of her Guardians, and several more spirits burst through a door on the far side. With her blonde hair streaming out behind her and her face alive with fury, Simone might have been a goddess of mythology, come to smite us all with nothing but the power of her gaze. I wasn't sure I'd ever been so simultaneously enthralled and terrified in all my life. But before she could speak even a word to us, Simone spotted her sister upon the dais and let out a choked cry of horror.

"Marguerite! No! What... what have you done to her?" Simone wailed, clutching at her hair, a Boticellian vision of despair leapt off a canvas to life.

"If you want to blame someone for what's happened to

Marguerite, blame yourself," I replied, surprised to find I could both find my voice and command it. "You could have stopped this, but you chose not to. She's the last of the Sentinels now, and there's nothing anyone can do to help her unless we restore the Gateways."

"You lie, Jessica Ballard!" Simone shrieked, pointing a violently trembling finger at me. Then she swung around and pointed the same finger at the nearest Caomhnóir, the one who had gone to fetch her. "You, there! Guardian! Remove my sister from the dais!"

The Caomhnóir turned around to look at his fallen comrade before bowing low to address Simone. "My sincerest apologies, High Priestess, but I cannot do as you ask."

Simone's face went utterly still. "What did you say to me?"

The Caomhnóir seemed to quake where he stood, but still, he did not move to comply with Simone's command. He swallowed hard and spoke again. "One of our Brotherhood has already tried to do as you request. He... he is there, High Priestess." He pointed to the corner of the courtyard where the Caomhnóir still lay unconscious, whether living or dead, it was impossible to tell.

"I... said... remove... her," Simone said, her voice a low and deadly hiss.

Clearly petrified to continue defying her, the young Caomhnóir shook his shoulders back and approached the dais. With much more hesitancy than his brother-in-arms, he set one foot upon the stone and reached slowly out to touch just the sleeve of Marguerite's robe. The effect was instantaneous. With a shriek, he was blasted backward, sent skittering away across the lawn, slammed into a wall and moved no more.

Simone let out a wail of frustration and rounded on the line of Caomhnóir, pointing at each of them in turn. "You! All of you! Rescue my sister! Remove her from the dais at once! I command you!"

But the Caomhnóir did not move. They had watched two of their comrades sacrifice themselves for nothing, and they were not willing to do the same.

"High Priestess, please. There must be another way to try to—" one of them began, but the rest of his plea was drowned in Simone's scream of rage. She turned to the nearest spirits, a pair of men who appeared to have once been gardeners. "You! Take over the Caomhnóir! Remove my sister from the dais at once."

Obediently, the spirits flew toward the Caomhnóir who braced himself for impact, but then, just as suddenly, they halted, motionless in the air, as though someone had hit the pause button. Simone stared around wildly and spotted Hannah, hand upraised, hair blowing around her face in the current of her power.

"What is the meaning of this?" she cried.

"If you're going to detain and lock up Durupinen so that you can betray the spirit world, you should probably make sure that one of them isn't the most powerful Caller in the world," I replied.

Simone's eyes went wide. She looked back at the spirits again. "Take over the Caomhnóir!" she screamed, looking quite mad in her frustration. "Do it! I command you!"

"They don't answer to you anymore!" Celeste said, stepping forward. "Your days of commanding them, of bleeding them dry, are over."

"Do you dare to question my authority?" Simone asked, an incredulous smile on her face.

"I dare question any Durupinen who puts her own selfish desires before the good of the spirits she has sworn to protect," Celeste replied. "And all those I stand with do the same."

"All those you stand with?" Simone said with a maniacal laugh. "What, this motley crew of misfits? This pathetic band of rebels you've cobbled together from the dregs of our world? You can't be serious."

Ileana stepped forward now. "This motley crew is not all you need to worry about, Simone." She threw back her head and gave a loud, shrieking caw, and at once, with a swish of glossy wings, her raven detached itself from the night and sailed down to land upon her shoulder. She pulled a tiny scroll from his leg and read it, a smile breaking over her features. "My winged friend informs me that the full might of the Traveler and Northern Clans approach your borders even now, and that they will shortly be joined by the combined forces of every clan who can reach the mountains by dawn. More resistance will be upon you every hour thereafter, as news of your treachery spreads to our sisterhood around the world."

My heart leapt. Was it really possible? I caught Finn's eye, and I saw him swell with pride. Beside him, Celeste showed no sign of surprise at the news that the Northern Clans were on their way. Could this have been what she and Ileana had been discussing together by the fireplace in Marguerite's room? I turned to Ileana and grinned at her, resolving to take back every snarky thing I ever said about that ridiculous messenger raven. If we got out of this alive, I would throw my cell phone through the fucking Gateway and communicate by nothing but birds for the rest of my life.

"Then we will smite them," Simone said, still laughing, still drunk with her own power. "My Caomhnóir are the most formidable fighting force in the Durupinen world. Let the rabble come and face their destruction. You there!" she shouted to the scarred Caomhnóir who had rescued us at the outpost. "Ring the alarm bell. Call the full might of my men here to me. I will give them their orders."

The Caomhnóir turned on his heel and jogged from the courtyard. Within a minute, a great echoing peal of bells resounded all around us, filling the mountains with cacophonous music. Before the echoes had a chance to die away, Charlie Wright, flanked by two dozen Necromancers, entered the courtyard. He approached Simone to stand beside her, greeting her with a respectful bow that was nonetheless full of irony.

"Well, well, what shenanigans have you gotten us into now, Jessica?" Charlie asked, his tone light but his teeth clenched. He took in the sight of Marguerite upon the dais, and I thought I saw a flash of panic in his eyes.

"For once in my life, I can't take credit for the shenanigans, Charlie," I replied. I felt more than saw Finn take a step toward Charlie, and I raised an arm to stop him. I flashed him a look that quite clearly said, "Back off. I've got this." Finn nodded and stepped back.

"You seem to have a talent for weaseling your way out of tight situations," Charlie said. "How is it you managed to escape the dungeons?"

"None of us would have, if Marguerite hadn't helped us," I said.

The angry flush in Simone's face drained away, leaving her complexion chalky. "Marguerite? You can't be serious."

"Oh, I am. She released all of us from our cells, and then she hid us in her own chambers until it was safe to leave. She planned to bring us here to the Geatgrima, to find the counter-Casting but... the Geatgrima had other plans."

"She wouldn't. She... she *couldn't*..." Simone gasped. She stared up at her sister as though she had never seen her before, as though a stranger now stood before her wearing her sister's visage.

"She could and she did," I replied. "But even then, she didn't believe she was defying you. She believed she was protecting you. You see, she didn't believe that you could ever be so misguided, so selfish, as to betray the Durupinen like this. I only hope she can't hear what we're saying now, because the truth would break her heart."

"Marguerite is a fool," Simone said, her voice breaking as tears gathered in her eyes. "So much power at her fingertips, and she never once reached for it. She should have come to me. I would have made her see reason."

"She was already seeing reason," I replied. "You're the one who's been blinded."

A low rumble of stomping feet alerted us all to the fact that the Caomhnóir were on the march and approaching the courtyard. They filed in from all directions, encircling the space five rows deep, weapons at the ready. I could feel our entire group tense and pull together protectively against a threat we knew we could never actually defend ourselves from. I heard Hannah's breath catch in her throat. I followed her gaze and saw that Kiernan and Seamus had been brought up as well, their hands bound behind their backs.

Simone's army came to a halt. She gazed around at them, a look of deep satisfaction on her face—a face that, for all its beauty, looked suddenly sinister. "So, Jessica Ballard. You've had your fleeting moment of victory. You somehow managed to turn my sister against me and make your way to this place. You've even managed to take control of a few of my spirit servants. I admit I would have thought it all impossible. But this is where the tables turn. Regardless of who waits beyond my walls, they will be defeated. The Sentinels have made their sacrifice—the Geatgrimas remain open, and we maintain our control of the Gateways. With the Necromancers' resources and the knowledge gained from their experiments, we will be able to take charge of the Gateways as never before in our long and storied history. What might have been an ending is now a new and glorious beginning. It is up to you, now, to decide what side of that history you are going to be on."

"And have you asked your Caomhnóir what they think of that

idea? Pledging their fealty to the Necromancers?" Finn called out, stepping forward. His face was suddenly shrewd.

"It is no concern of mine what they think of it," Simone said with a cold laugh. "It is not their place to offer me their opinions. They have pledged their loyalty to me, and they will lay down their lives to protect me, as is their sworn duty."

"You seem to have forgotten something, High Priestess," came a voice from the midst of the Caomhnóir ranks, and to my surprise, it was Kiernan who was speaking now.

"You dare to speak to me, a prisoner in my castle?" Simone asked, incredulous.

"I do," Kiernan said. "I dare speak to anyone who would misrepresent the central tenet of my Brotherhood."

"Misrepresent?" Simone repeated, sounding amused now. "In what way?"

Seamus stepped forward as well, adding his voice to the fray. "The Caomhnóir do not take their oath to protect any one Durupinen, no matter how powerful she may be. They take the oath to protect the Gateway, at all costs."

Simone rolled her eyes. "It comes to the same thing, Guardian. The Durupinen and the Gateway are one and the same. The Gateway they are sworn to protect runs within my veins."

"Not only in your veins," I cried out, for I saw a glimmer of hope at last.

Simone narrowed her eyes at me. "What?"

"The Gateway only exists within our blood because we put it there so many years ago," I said. "But now that the Reckoning is upon us, the Sentinels are using their Gateways to keep the Geatgrimas from collapsing. You can see it there, flowing freely outside of a Durupinen body for the first time in centuries."

I felt every eye in the place flick toward Marguerite, watching the glowing current of energy that now tied her and the Geatgrima together.

"Your sister shares your Gateway now, not just with you, but with the Geatgrima itself. This means that every Caomhnóir in this courtyard is now sworn to protect the Geatgrima as a vessel of the Gateway every bit as much as they are sworn to protect you as the same."

Simone's eyes flashed at me and I knew that she, too, had finally understood what I was trying to say.

I went on, "The Gateway needs protection now more than ever. It needs to be protected from the Necromancers, who would seek to control it. It needs to be protected from the Casting which has trapped it for too long within living bodies. And, I am sorry to say, it now needs protection from you."

Simone threw back her head and laughed. "Protection? From me? That's where you're wrong, you foolish girl. I am the Gateway."

"And the moment we began to believe that is the moment we lost our way," I said. Then, before anyone could stop me, I ran to the Geatgrima and stood upon the dais, so that everyone could see me. Several Caomhnóir started forward, but no one dared approach close enough to touch me, knowing what had happened to their comrades who had touched Marguerite.

"Listen, all of you, because everything I'm about to say is true, and I can prove it," I said, battling to keep the fear from my voice, trying to channel my sister, the way she commanded the Grand Council Room when she made her case to be on the Council. No one could doubt the sincerity and authority in her voice that day, and I couldn't afford for anyone to doubt mine now.

"Many centuries ago, the Durupinen had to protect the Gateways from the Necromancers. And so, we created a Casting that would strip them from their rightful place in the Geatgrimas, and put them in the safest place we could conceive of: our own bloodlines."

I waited patiently through the outbreak of murmuring that followed. "It is true. Your High Priestess will not deny it. The Necromancers here will not deny it. After all, it is one of the reasons they have fought against us for so long; because they have known all along that our gift is not our own."

All around the courtyard, eyes were turning upon the place where Simone and Charlie stood, their faces stony. The yearning was palpable in the air for Simone to say something—anything—that would dispute what I had spoken. She remained silent.

"The Casting was meant to be temporary. When we deemed it safe, the Gateways were to be returned to the Geatgrimas. Therefore, a counter-Casting was also created, and the moment it was to be performed was known as the Reckoning."

There was no murmuring now. The courtyard had gone suddenly, intently silent.

"But the Reckoning never came. We never returned the Gateways to their rightful place, even when we believed the Necromancers to be finished. Instead, we allowed the origins of our gift to remain buried, hoping, I suppose, that the moment would never come when we would have to face the truth and give it all up.

"But the Geatgrimas could not survive indefinitely, torn as they were from their true purpose. Now they are in imminent danger of collapse. Only the Sentinels keep them from destruction now, and unless we can perform the counter-Casting and restore the Gateways, the spirit world remains in grave danger of being cut off from the living world forever."

The scarred Caomhnóir stepped forward. "How is it you know this?" he asked. "Why should we believe you?"

"You don't have to take my word for it," I said, shrugging. "Ask yourself why your High Priestess doesn't shout me down. Ask yourself what her silence means."

Simone began to laugh, low and quietly at first, but soon it rose to a wild shriek. "The source of our gift and how it came to us does not matter. The Gateways are where they are meant to be, and we will continue to protect them as ever we have."

"But you haven't been protecting them. You've been abusing them," I said.

"Such lies," Simone said, waving my words away with a disgusted gesture.

"Lies, are they?" I asked, before turning to Hannah. "Hannah, Call the spirits of Havre des Gardiennes. All of them."

Her eyes widened. She looked absolutely horrified. "*All* of them? Are... are you sure?"

I gave her a reassuring nod. "Trust me."

Hannah stepped forward into the space between the Caomhnóir and the Geatgrima. She closed her eyes and, within seconds, a tidal wave of cold swept the courtyard. Spirits were flooding into the space from every direction: through windows, through walls, up from the very ground itself, stripped of their will and unable to resist the slightest beckoning of her Call.

A strangled cry made me turn. Simone was staggering, stumbling. Charlie Wright caught her as she clutched at her chest. A faint shimmering substance seemed to be drifting out of her, like smoke off a fire.

Hannah faltered at the sound, and the spirits all halted where they were. She turned to look at Simone, who was fighting to recover herself.

"What's happened? What are you doing to her?" Charlie shouted, pointing an accusatory finger at Hannah, who looked bewildered. But Celeste had understood something, and she stepped forward, standing beside Hannah in solidarity.

"She is giving you all the proof you need that the High Priestess has committed the most grievous of crimes. The spirits that Hannah has called to this place are mere shells—Leeched over and over again of their very essence by the High Priestess. Rather than letting them Cross, she has forced them to remain behind to be Leeched repeatedly and used as slaves to do her bidding."

It was clear from the expressions on the Caomhnóir faces around the clearing that they had been completely ignorant of why the spirits of Havre des Gardiennes were so obedient. If they had suspected it, they had kept such suspicions to themselves. They gazed up at the horde of expressionless ghosts with a kind of universal horror.

"When Hannah Calls the spirits, every part of them wants to obey, even the parts that Simone has stolen. You can see the very essence of them, being pulled from your High Priestess, who has sustained herself on them."

Simone's face was a mask of shock. Her hands went to her face, to her hair, to her chest. "You... you cannot Call them from me. Their essence is mine now! It... it is not possible."

"Oh, but it is," Celeste said, a triumphant ring in her voice. "You have so perverted the natural order, so decimated the rules, that they no longer apply."

"And if you order your men to attack us," Hannah added, her voice somehow distant in the midst of her Calling, "I will not hesitate to Call these spirits to our aid, and I promise you that every part of them within you will answer my Call."

Simone seemed unable to answer. The thought that one word from Hannah could leave her shriveled and deteriorated to her true form had left her too horrified to speak.

"You dare threaten the High Priestess of the International High

Council?" Charlie called out, still helping Simone to stand. "Her Guardians will never allow it."

"Don't you dare to presume what a Caomhnóir would or would not do, Necromancer," Finn growled. "You tried to enlist us once, to turn us to your will. The strong amongst us ensured that you failed. And the Caomhnóir of Havre des Gardiennes are the strongest you will find anywhere. You question their integrity at your own peril."

"And you question their loyalty at your own," Charlie shouted back. He looked quite mad, now. He was watching his great coup, his final grasp for power crumbling before his eyes. He released his grip on Simone, who staggered and fell to one knee, but he ignored her. "And even if you think you are right, to gamble your life on Simone's men, I assure you, it would be foolish indeed to gamble your life on mine. Seize the traitors! Defend the High Priestess!"

His cry rent the air and the masked men behind him sprang into action with lightning speed. All was chaos. The Caomhnóir, thrown off by the suddenness of the attack, scrambled to respond. They couldn't possibly know what side they were meant to be on, what or who they were fighting for—were they protecting us? Protecting the Geatgrima? Protecting Simone?

Hannah, however, knew exactly what she was fighting for. With a great summoning of her strength, she brought both hands high into the air and then thrust them apart, so that the spirits that hovered like a storm cloud over the courtyard broke off in every direction, Habitating, overpowering, disarming everyone they could reach. Under cover of the insanity, I looked all around the Geatgrima for some sign of what I was meant to do with the keys, and within seconds, I found it. Three rounded keyholes had been inlaid at the foot of the Geatgrima, right into the front of the top step of the dais. I gave a cry of relief and thrust my hand down the front of my sweater to retrieve the keys. I dropped to my knees just behind where Marguerite stood, still locked in connection with the Geatgrima. I separated the first key, the one I had gotten from Ileana, and inserted it into the first of the keyholes, and turned it with a loud, decisive click. The outermost of the concentric circles of stones that made up the dais began to rotate with the deafening sound of grating stone.

"NO!" The shout distracted me, causing me to raise my head. From his place beside Simone, who was now writhing on the ground, Charlie Wright had spotted me in the chaos, recognized what I was doing, and was sprinting toward me, a flash of a blade raised in his right hand.

Time itself seemed to grind into slow motion. I watched as a spirit flew past him, slamming into another masked Necromancer and blasting him off his feet. I saw from the corner of my eye that Hannah had spotted him, her eyes widening like windows into her greatest fear, and she reached out into the air for another spirit to fling in Charlie's path, to slow him down. From directly across the courtyard, Finn looked up from his own battle at almost exactly the same moment. I felt rather than heard him cry out my name, saw him break into a run, hurling bodies out of the way in his fight to reach me. I stared wildly around for a way to defend myself, finding only the Casting bag and the other two keys within my reach. Faintly, I thought I could hear both Milo and Hannah, calling out to me through the connection, desperate to warn me of the danger I had already seen coming and could not avoid.

Finn was too far. Charlie was too close. The spirit Hannah was fighting to pull from the fray would never reach me in time. And as he bore down upon me, I saw that triumphant gleam once again in Charlie Wright's eye, that surety that he was about to get exactly what he wanted, the revenge he had sought from the moment Neil Caddigan had gone sailing back through the Gateway.

His eyes went wide as mine closed, each of us expecting the same thing.

Neither of us expected Catriona.

With a cry like a wounded animal, she threw herself at him from over my left shoulder, sailing right over my head and colliding with him just as he raised his dagger toward me. A terrible flash of Lucida shot across my mind like a bolt of electricity and all I could think was "Oh God, no, not Cat, too." But with military precision, Catriona caught hold of the arm that held the dagger, forced it around and thrust it, with a guttural cry, right up between Charlie Wright's ribs and twisted it brutally. For one long moment, Charlie Wright stared right into Catriona's eyes with a look of mild surprise on his face. Then she let go of him and he dropped to his knees and keeled over onto his side, his eyes finding me as his face hit the grass. He opened his mouth as though to say something to me, and then the spark in his eyes went <u>dull</u>.

"That was for Lucida, you irredeemable bastard," Catriona muttered down at him. She looked up and caught my eye. "What are you waiting for, Jess!" she cried. "The keys!"

Her words jolted me back into the reality of everything else that was going on around me. Fumbling and cursing through my tears (though I didn't remember starting to cry) I pulled the second key free, thrust it into the second keyhole, and twisted it. A second ring of stone ground into motion, moving in opposition with the first. A spirit shot past me, tossing my hair in an icy blast of energy. A Caomhnóir dropped to the grass near my foot, groaning. My hand shaking madly, I forced the last key into the final keyhole and turned it hard.

A third concentric circle of stone began to turn, and within the center of the dais, the solid central circle of stone, the one upon which Marguerite and the Geatgrima itself stood, began to rise slowly from the ground. The sight of the Geatgrima lifting into the air brought the battle around us to a screeching halt. Distracted by the sudden movement of what they all believed to be an ancient and immovable relic, the Caomhnóir and Necromancers all around the courtyard froze. A moment's distraction was all it took for the spirits under Hannah's control to overtake the remaining fighters, pinning them to the ground or else disappearing within their bodies and forcing them to drop their weapons.

Finn arrived at my side, gasping for breath, but unhurt. "This is it, isn't it?" he asked. "The counter-Casting." He pointed at the face of the stone that had risen up from deep within the earth. There, carved into the rock, were the instructions and incantation to restore the Gateway to the Geatgrima.

Catriona was scanning the Gaelic. "This can't be right. It says it needs the blood of the creator of the original Casting in order to reverse it. The creators have been dead for centuries. How are we meant to—"

But I smiled, for I already understood. All the time I'd spent convinced that I was the absolute wrong person to be Agnes' messenger melted away as this last piece of the puzzle fell into place. "She is dead, yes. But her bloodline isn't." I looked up and met Catriona's eye. "Agnes was the Scribe who figured out how to perform the Casting. This is why she left the message for me, and not for anyone else. It had to be Clan Sassanaigh. The same blood that ran in her veins runs in mine."

By now, the fight around us had been subdued. All around the courtyard, Necromancers lay injured or dead, or else bound up and captured. A number of Caomhnóir casualties could also be seen, though how many of them had fought for Simone and how many for the Geatgrima itself, there was no way to know. The spirits which Hannah had called into service were gathering again above our heads, their task complete. I watched Hannah deep in concentration, limbs twitching, lips moving silently, exercising every ounce of control she had. On either side of her, Milo and Kiernan, who had somehow slipped his bonds, were poised, ready to defend her from any hint of an oncoming attack. Celeste, Ileana, and Annabelle had gathered behind her for protection, and Seamus had also fought his way out of captivity to join them, armed with weapons he had wrested from other Caomhnóir. I could have cried with relief at seeing all of them alive.

"Finn, give me your knife," I said, holding an impatient hand out for it.

Finn hesitated, "Jess, you can't possibly—"

"Finn, I'm not going to sacrifice myself on the altar, for God's sake! I'm just going to cut myself!" I snapped. "It's the only way, now hand it over!"

"All right, all right," Finn said grudgingly, pulling the knife from its hilt and passing it to me with the handle out. "But mind you don't touch Marguerite!"

He was right to warn me. Every eye in the courtyard was on me as I climbed up onto the central stone platform. There was dangerously little room for my feet to find purchase between Marguerite and the Geatgrima, and nowhere to grab hold; and the sheer power of the Gateway flowing between them whipped around us like a strong wind, blowing my hair around my face and buffeting me back and forth, keeping me constantly off balance. I repeated the Casting over and over under my breath; I would only have one chance to say it right.

I looked up at Marguerite, and in her rapt face, I saw Savvy, hundreds of miles away at Fairhaven. And it was of her and of Agnes that I thought as I raised the knife to my hand and dragged it across my palm, watching the blood and its stolen gift rise to the surface. And it was of my mother and Carrick that I thought of as I reached forward and pressed my hand to the Geatgrima, and watched the blood drip down the stones. And it was of the many spirits I'd guided through the Gateway over the years—Evan, Pierce, the Silent Child, and hundreds and hundreds of others—that I asked forgiveness from for what the Durupinen had done as I looked up at the Geatgrima and prepared to speak the words that would bring about the Reckoning. And just as I opened my mouth to begin, two voices, clear and strong broke into my head, encouraging me: my sister and my Spirit Guide.

"We're with you, Jess. Say them. Say the words."

And so I did.

> *"Ó fuil, mo chuid fola, scaoil saor,*
> *Ó feoil, mo chuid feola, athnuaigh,*
> *Ó laistigh na cosantóirí. díghlasáil na geataí*
> *Agus oscail go leathan greim an Aether,*
> *Chun pasáiste sábhailte abhaile a athbhunaigh."* [1]

The very blood in my veins seemed to bubble. I gasped, falling to my knees. I looked down at my hands to see the same shimmering tendrils of energy that connected Marguerite to the Gateway rising up from my skin. My lungs felt frozen, my body tingling, my blood crying out in pain as the gift that had resided there for all of my life drained away, being pulled like a soul toward the Aether, toward the Geatgrima. And it was like exquisitely painful music singing in my ears, a lullaby of loss and of longing, of sorrow and of hope. And I knew that, at this moment, all over the world, the Aether was singing its Gateways home at last.

And then the Geatgrima itself lit up like a beacon, newly flooded with power, and the concentrated beam of its true purpose shot into the sky over our heads. I threw my hands up over my face as the beam exploded in a blinding shower of sparks, sending comets of spirit energy shooting in every direction and illuminating the sky as bright as day before being swallowed once again by the inky blackness of the night.

A sudden rushing of icy wind filled my ears and I looked up

---

1. "From the blood of my blood, set free, from the flesh of my flesh, renew, from within the protectors, unlock the gates and throw wide the arms of the Aether's embrace to restore safe passage home."

in time to see the empty spirit hordes of Havre des Gardiennes swirling like a hurricane around the Geatgrima below, marking the eye of the storm. And then, with a great howling of a thousand trapped souls, the spirit cloud spun faster and faster, forming a vortex as the spirits were pulled inexorably toward the newly restored Gateway, which had flung its doors wide open at long last to welcome them. A great funnel formed, and the spirits whirled faster and faster until the very last of them vanished through the archway and out of the living world.

I sat up amidst the stunned silence they left in their absence. I looked down at my own hands, as though expecting them to look different, to somehow reflect the depth of the change that had taken place within me; but there they were, two ordinary hands, shaking and cold, but unchanged. How was it possible?

"Jess! Hannah! I'm here!"

The voice echoed not through the courtyard, but inside my head, and I let out a cry of joy and relief.

"Milo!"

I spun on my knees and found both Hannah and Milo barreling toward me, Hannah running, Milo soaring, both crying with happiness. Without the slightest regard for my safety, they both flung themselves at me in a hug that knocked me back against the stones and squeezed the breath from my lungs.

"Oh, thank God, thank *GOD*!" Hannah was sobbing into my neck.

Milo was laughing through his tears. "I can't believe you thought it was going to be that easy to get rid of me."

"Shut up!" she laughed, before bursting into tears again. Then she pulled away from me and said, eyes wide, "Do you feel that?"

"Feel what? I mean, aside from the two of you clobbering me?"

In answer, Hannah grabbed my wrist and intertwined her fingers with mine. A moment later, I understood. It wasn't what we felt, but what we could no longer feel: the strange rushing connection that flowed between us whenever we linked hands was gone.

Hannah's face twitched with grief, but I squeezed her hand and smiled at her. "Yes, I can feel it. For the first time, I know what it feels like to hold my sister's hand and feel only love."

She tried to smile, but it was all too overwhelming. I heard a groan behind us and turned to see Marguerite struggling to rise from the ground. I extricated myself from Hannah and Milo and crawled over to her, reaching out to take her hand.

Her wrinkled, gnarled, and blue-veined hand...

I gasped. The Marguerite who sat before me had aged fifty years in a matter of moments. Her long blonde hair had turned white, and her face, once so delicate and glowing, now sagged with wrinkled folds of skin that hung from her bones like oversized clothing.

She looked up at me, her expression one of deepest fear and bewilderment. "Jessica, I... where am I? What... what has happened to me?"

But before I could answer, a tortured scream rose from the grass behind us. We turned to see Simone staring down at her own hands with shock and horror upon her once flawless face, now as wrinkled as her sister's. "No! No, no, no!" she moaned over and over again, clutching at the sparse tufts of her hair and the shriveled hollows of her cheeks.

"When the spirits Crossed, all their stolen energy Crossed with them," I murmured. "We are seeing the High Priestess for who she truly is."

Marguerite stared at her sister, then at her own hands again, and then a strange joyful laugh bubbled up from somewhere inside her. "*Mon Dieu*," she exclaimed. "So, this is what freedom looks like." And she laughed again, tears gathering in her clouded eyes and rolling down the crags of her cheeks.

I helped Marguerite to her feet, and together, Hannah and I guided her down the steps of the dais and over to her sister, where she knelt down and wrapped her sister tenderly in her arms, whispering platitudes to her in French as she stroked her hair and rocked her like a small child who had learned, for the first time, what loss was.

"Will she be all right, do you think?" Hannah asked.

It was Celeste who replied as she swept across the lawn toward us. "She has her sister to take care of her, just as she always has, not that I'm sure she deserves it. Her Reckoning is only just beginning, however."

"Hannah! Are you all right?" Kiernan was running toward us, his expression wild with worry. Hannah succumbed to another round of tears as she abandoned ceremony and flung herself into his arms. Kiernan looked utterly shocked for a moment, and then, as though he could hardly believe he was allowed to do so, wrapped his arms around her shaking shoulders and embraced her, resting his chin gently on her curls.

Annabelle and Ileana came forward as well, both looking quite disheveled but relieved to find themselves both alive. Ileana's face was strangely vulnerable as she said, "I can feel it. It's gone."

Celeste nodded her head, and though her tone was resigned, her mouth trembled with suppressed emotion. "Yes. Yes, I felt it at once."

"But our job remains unchanged," I said. "We've got to protect them, just as we always have."

We all looked up at the Geatgrima, aglow with its newly restored power, and it was as though we were seeing it for the first time, our own gift made manifest. It was hard to describe exactly the feeling that rose in me, knowing that something great and ancient and ineffable had been restored, but it was something like peace.

"Come," Celeste said, tearing her eyes from the Geatgrima with a sigh. "We must gather the Caomhnóir and send word to our clans at the boundaries. There is much work to be done."

EPILOGUE

———————

"I CAN'T BELIEVE YOU ALL TOOK OFF on the adventure to end all bloody adventures and you just left me here staring at a bollocking lump of rock like an enormous great tit!" Savvy shouted, sending her tray of hospital ward food flying everywhere with one exasperated sweep of her hand.

"I'm sorry!" I laughed, ducking as a bowl of pudding whizzed over my head. "We didn't want to leave you, you know. But you didn't give us much choice, turning yourself into a harbinger of the Durupinen apocalypse."

We were all gathered around Savvy's bed in the hospital ward: me, Hannah, Milo, Finn, Annabelle, Frankie, and Phoebe. Mrs. Mistlemoore had long since flung up her hands in despair and resigned herself to the fact that rules like "visiting hours" and "quiet time" were going to be completely ignored. I only let myself feel guilty about it for about three-and-a-half seconds. It had been less than twenty-four hours since the Reckoning, after all, and it was our very first chance to see Savvy since she'd regained consciousness.

"Enough about our exploits, what about you?" Hannah said eagerly. "What was it like, being a Sentinel?"

Savvy gave a disgusted snort. "How was it? Bloody boring as fuck all, wasn't it? You'd think I'd have a hell of a story to tell you all, seeing as I was locked in a battle for my life with a portal to the spirit world, but I can't remember a thing! Last I recall, I was falling into bed after running my arse ragged in training all day, and the next thing I know, I'm lying on the ground out in the courtyard, stiff as a poker and freezing my arse off. I haven't been properly warm since. Two bloody weeks out there and not one of those tossers thought to throw a blanket over me!"

"Well, to be fair, one of them tried to touch you, and he's still lying over there, unconscious," Milo informed her, jerking his thumb over his shoulder at the only other occupied bed in the ward, "so don't be surprised if no one else risked it because they thought you might catch a chill."

Savvy shook her head with a sigh. "Blimey, I just can't believe it. So, what happens now, then?"

"The High Priestesses from all over the world are supposed to be meeting at Havre des Gardiennes today," Finn answered. "They've got to agree on a plan, moving forward. A new High Priestess will have to be elected, and a new strategy will have to be devised to protect the Gateways."

"Protect them from who, then?" Savvy asked, looking perplexed. "The Necromancers can't come back from this, surely."

But Finn shook his head. "I don't think the Durupinen leadership will ever be foolish enough to underestimate the Necromancers again. But as long as the Gateways exist, there will be those threatening to undermine them."

"I just can't believe it's gone," Frankie said quietly, voicing the sentiment that had filled the castle—and each of our minds—since the moment it happened.

"What do you suppose everyone will do?" Phoebe asked no one in particular.

Savvy managed to refrain from rolling her eyes. "What do you mean?"

"Well, my connection to the Gateway got damaged and I just—sort of—went home, didn't I?" Phoebe clarified. "Do you suppose everyone else will do the same?"

"I've been wondering about that myself," Frankie admitted. "I mean, is there any point to staying on as Apprentices, now that Gateways are gone?"

"They're not gone," Milo said. "They've just... moved."

"Yes, but seeing as they aren't our responsibility anymore, won't we all just go back to our lives as they were before?" Frankie asked.

"Some people will, I expect," Hannah said. "But for most Durupinen, there is no 'life as is was before.' Being a Durupinen is all they've ever known."

"And let's not forget that the Durupinen were a sisterhood long before they made the decision to internalize the Gateways," Finn said. "Along with the Caomhnóir, they've always been connected to the spirit world, always sworn to protect the Gateways. We'll just have to find a new way to do that now."

"Or an old way," I pointed out.

Finn smiled, "Indeed."

I looked down at my watch. "Shit, I've got to go if I'm going to catch Flavia and Annabelle," I said, jumping up from my seat. "I'll come right back, though. If Mrs. Mistlemoore brings you another tray of food, save me some chips, huh?"

"Not likely!" Savvy called after me loudly.

I found Annabelle and Flavia talking intently together down in the entrance hall beside a pile of suitcases that two Caomhnóir were in the process of carrying out to a waiting car.

"There you are," Annabelle said, smiling. "We were starting to think we would have to see ourselves off."

"Sorry, I was visiting Savvy and lost track of the time," I said. "You both all packed, then?"

"Yes," Flavia said, smiling nervously. "I still can't quite believe I'm going back."

Word had come the previous day that Flavia had been summoned back to the Traveler camp. The invitation came under the guise of giving testimony to the Traveler Council about her role in helping to bring about the Reckoning, but Flavia recognized it for what it really was: the extending of a hand, the opening of a door that had previously been closed to her. Ileana's warning sent from the Milkweed Teahouse had been enough to prevent another terrible attack on the camp. The Travelers had been ready for the Necromancers, reinforcing border Castings and enlisting the help of a Caomhnóir reserve from Fairhaven who agreed to help defend them. Having lost the element of surprise, the Necromancers found themselves on the defensive, and had been decimated before they could even set foot within the woods. After the devastation at Havre des Gardiennes, knowing the encampment was safe had been welcome news.

"Do you think you'll stay?" I asked her. "The Scribes at Fairhaven will be disappointed to lose you."

She shrugged her shoulders. "I don't know. I haven't gotten that far yet. I'm still struggling to accept the fact that I'm going to be allowed to set foot back in the camp again. Jeta is beside herself. She says she's planning a welcome home party for me. She also told me to invite 'the Northern Girl' along for the festivities."

———

323

"Tell her thanks, but some other time," I said, smiling. "Just as long as there's no Rifting involved," I added with a wink.

Flavia laughed. "Oh, no. I think I've had enough of Rifting to last me several lifetimes."

"And how about you?" I asked Annabelle. "Are you going to take them up on their offer of a place in the wagon train?"

Annabelle smiled. After her role in our adventure, it seemed the Travelers had come to view her as much more than a lowly outcast Dormant. A letter from the Boswell Clan, imploring her to come and stay, arrived along with Flavia's summons, both tied to the leg of a messenger raven. Though she was still away at Havre des Gardiennes, in conference with the other High Priestesses, I had no doubt that Ileana had had a hand in it.

"No," Annabelle said. "Zina will try to convince me, of course, but my life is back in the States, you know that. I've got my shop waiting for me, and the boys, of course. We all know their ghost hunting gig's nothing but a two-bit operation without me holding it all together." She rolled her eyes, but I knew she had nothing but affection for Oscar, Iggy, and the rest of Pierce's old team. They were her last and best link to him, after all. "But you'll see us all really soon, I expect."

I raised my eyebrows. "Oh, really?"

"Oh yeah," she said, seriously. "I've told them all about the Screaming Woods down in Pluckley. They've already booked their tickets for the investigation!"

"What?! Annabelle, you didn't!" I cried.

"Kidding, I'm kidding!" Annabelle said, raising her hands in surrender at the look of horror on my face. "Good lord, can't a girl joke about Elemental-infested forests anymore?"

I smiled appreciatively, but it faded quickly. The Elementals, I knew, were gone. Along with Finn, I had ventured into the Fairhaven woods the previous night, and attempted to summon the Fairhaven Elemental. It did not come. I wondered how Lira was taking it, and what in the world she would do with herself now. Despite what she had done to me to prevent my getting the second key, I had nothing but pity in my heart for her. The world as she knew it had altered forever, and she no longer knew her place in it. And she wasn't the only one.

Over the next couple of weeks, the new Durupinen world started to take the vague beginnings of a shape. An Airechtas was held at Fairhaven once again, and I would be lying if I said it had gone smoothly. There was much devastation and dissension amongst the clans as the hard truth sank in. Desperate to regain their former power, a collection of clans—Marion's amongst them—made a haphazard attempt to form a second Council, proposing to anyone who would listen that they would somehow restore the Gateways to Durupinen bloodlines again. They put forward motion after ill-advised motion—to take down the Geatgrimas, to attempt a reversal of the Reckoning, to have me thrown in Skye Príosún for "stealing their gifts." Their ravings, however, soon died away as they were met not with enthusiasm, but with the growing realization that our true purpose was emerging from the ashes. The Gateways, now standing once again exposed around the world, still needed to be protected. Spirits would still seek us out, asking for our help, our guidance, and our compassion. The very seeds of whom we had grown to be were sprouting anew, and we had to tend to them.

Only a few short months later, Savvy would be joined in her training on the lawns of Fairhaven by women from all across the Northern Clans who decided that they could best continue to protect the Gateways by learning to fight. The ranks of the Trackers would shortly be flooded with applicants, eager to enter under Catriona's leadership to rout out Necromancers and other threats to the secrecy and safety of Gateways. The Code of Conduct would effectively be thrown out the window as the roles of Durupinen and Caomhnóir began to blur around the edges. Kiernan would become the first Caomhnóir to be taken on officially as an Apprentice Scribe. And Celeste, thanks to her peerless leadership in steering the Durupinen into the future, found herself in serious contention for the position of High Priestess of the International High Council. Despite all the concerns to the contrary, life at Fairhaven and all around the Durupinen world went on with renewed purpose.

And of course, there were some things that didn't change at all.

"About bloody time you turned up," Fiona barked at me as I came skidding into the Gallery of High Priestesses only six weeks later. "What kind of time do you call this?"

I looked down at my watch, gasping for breath. "Uh... exactly thirty seconds after the time you asked me to be here."

"How do you expect me to properly shout at these gormless gits if I can't even see what they're doing wrong?" Fiona huffed, crossing her arms.

"These gormless gits" were two of the Novitiates who had been tasked with the rehanging of Agnes Isherwood's fully restored tapestry. I threw them both apologetic looks as they struggled to reattach the row of silver rings along the top of the tapestry to the waiting row of hooks, before replying, "It looks like they're doing a fine job to me."

Fiona snorted as though to suggest my idea of a 'fine job' was total bullshit. I decided it wasn't worth arguing the point. After all, she'd used her art world connections to get me an interview the following month for an internship at the Tate Modern, which was only the dream job of a lifetime for an art nerd. It wasn't worth incurring her wrath; I wouldn't put it past her to call the curator and cancel it.

"Is anyone else coming to see this unveiling?" Fiona asked once she realized I wasn't rising to her bait.

"They should be," I said, checking my watch again. "I told them to be here in about ten minutes." The truth was that I was both excited and relieved to see the tapestry back in its rightful place again, and not only because I'd spent so much time over the past few months doing the painstaking work of restoring it. There was a part of me that would feel uneasy until Agnes took her place back in the gallery. After all, the recent chaos had all begun the day I'd seen her staring down at me from Fiona's studio wall, and until Agnes was safely back where she belonged, I was half-convinced another loose thread or another hidden message would turn my world upside down again.

"Mind they're closing those rings properly!" Fiona snapped at me, pointing up to the top edge of the tapestry. "They've got to twist them tightly down against the grommets or the warp can snag. Here," she added, thrusting her hand out toward me. "I've had this made to hang beside it."

I took what she was holding out to me: an object wrapped in a paint-splattered handkerchief. I unwound the fabric and a shiny gold placard fell into my palm. I read the words engraved upon it.

Agnes Isherwood of the Clan Sassanaigh
Tapestry, circa 1045

Restored by Jessica Ballard, Assistant Curator, Fairhaven Hall

I looked up at Fiona, who was picking at some plaster under her fingernails and determinedly avoiding my gaze. "Assistant Curator?"

She shrugged. "Had to call you something. Couldn't rightly print 'Pain-in-the-Arse Lass Who Blunders Around My Studio Cocking Things Up,' now could I?"

"Well, you could have, but I'm not sure it would have fit," I said. I looked down at the words again, and felt a lump rising in my throat. "Thank you, Fiona."

Fiona snorted and opened her mouth, probably to tell me to shove my thanks where the sun didn't shine, but I didn't give her a chance. I closed the distance between us and folded her into a fierce hug. I heard her gasp in surprise, stiffen, and then, at last, relax enough to reach around and pat me sharply on the back.

"That will do to be going along with," she said gruffly after a few seconds, and I released her.

The Caomhnóir fastened the last of the hooks and stepped down off their ladders, waiting to be berated, no doubt. Instead, I thanked them and sent them on their way. They had just rounded the corner with their ladders, and I had just managed to affix the little plaque to the wall beside the tapestry, when Finn, Milo, Hannah, Savvy, and Kiernan appeared at the end of the hall. I gave a pointed look at Hannah and Kiernan's linked hands and then caught Hannah's eye. Hannah gave me a look that clearly told me to mind my own business. Milo then gave me a look that clearly said we would absolutely not be minding our own business under any circumstances.

"This everyone?" Fiona barked when she heard everyone's feet come to a stop.

I looked down at my watch again. "Well, I was really hoping Karen might make it back in time to—"

"Wait for us!" a voice called from the end of the hall, and I turned to see Karen rushing down the hall and, to my shock, Tia hurrying along behind her.

"Tia!" I cried, running halfway down the hall to meet them and practically tackling her in a hug. "What are you doing here?"

"I thought your best friend should be at this unveiling after all the hard work you've put in," Karen said, "so I gave her a lift on my way in from the city."

Tia laughed. "Karen called and asked if I wanted a ride out to Fairhaven to see what you'd been up to for the last few months." She looked over at the tapestry with a suspicious look. "But I assume that tapestry is barely the tip of the iceberg."

"You assume correctly," I said as Fiona cleared her throat pointedly. "I have a lot to tell you. But we'll get to all that. Come on, before Fiona gives herself an aneurysm."

"Right, then," Fiona said, and cleared her throat again to address the group as we all gathered around her. "Well, it's my duty to present the newly restored tapestry of Agnes Isherwood of the Clan Sassanaigh to her living descendants, with the compliments of the Office of the Curator."

Everyone stared up at the tapestry.

"So that's her, then, eh?" Savvy said at last to break the silence. "The troublemaker."

"It runs in the family," Karen said, casting her eyes at me and smirking.

"It's hard to believe that someone who lived so long ago could feel so present, isn't it?" Hannah said with a little shiver.

"You did a beautiful job on it," Karen said, leaning forward to examine the fibers. "Both of you."

"Jessica did most of the work," Fiona said stiffly. "I merely oversaw the process."

Finn reached over to squeeze my hand. "It looks magnificent. Truly. Well done, love."

"Thanks," I said, feeling a slight flush creep into my cheeks.

"It's uncanny," Tia said, leaning forward. "She really does look like you. All three of you."

"Durupinen genes are clearly dominant," Karen announced.

"Hey, you think they'll ever do one of these tapestries of the pair of you?" Savvy asked suddenly, waggling her eyebrows playfully at Hannah and me.

"Of us?" Hannah asked, laughing. "Definitely not."

"Oh, I don't know," Karen said, tapping her chin in mock thoughtfulness. "The long-awaited twins of the Prophecy? That might warrant a tapestry. Or at least a nice oil painting."

Milo soared around in front of the tapestry, assuming Agnes' regal pose. "Oh, come on. I can see it now! Jessica Ballard, clad in tragic black-on-black attire, a sketchbook in one hand and a large hot coffee in the other. It will be iconic, sweetness."

"But if I'm holding the coffee and the sketchbook, how will I flip you off?" I asked, batting my eyelashes at him.

Savvy roared with laughter, and slapped me on the back. "Come on, then. We're going to miss dinner. Tia, you can sit next to me, mate. Boy, have I got a hell of a story for you."

I lingered behind the others as they made their way back down the hallway, still gazing up at Agnes.

"Love? Are you all right?" Finn asked, tugging lightly at my hand.

"Yeah. I'm just wondering about Agnes."

"What about her?"

"She went to such great lengths to find me—to deliver those words to me. I just hope that, somehow, she knows that I did what she asked—that everything is as it should be again."

"I do not doubt for a moment that she knows," Finn said. "What was it she said to you? That the tapestries of your lives are intertwined?" He threaded our fingers together and gave my hand a squeeze. "She knows."

As I turned away from the tapestry, I imagined that I could feel Agnes' eyes on me as I walked away. Her legacy was set in stone now, hung upon a wall for posterity. In this new Durupinen world we had created, I was less sure than ever what my legacy would be. Everything was uncertain, rife with possibilities.

And that, I realized, was exactly what life was supposed to be.